SWIRL OF DEATH

Jalel Wordlaw

ISBN: 978-1-962624-87-9

Dedication

I dedicate this experience to all my readers who find entertainment and wisdom behind this cover.

Acknowledgment

I accredit the GoldenTouchPublications company for facilitating my writing journey and helping me develop my writing style, as well as guiding me through the revisions needed to make this book flow. I also would like to thank my mother for leading me to them and aiding in my ability to pay for their services as a final major gift before she passed away several months after.

Furthermore, I also would like to give a special shoutout to my fifth-grade elementary teacher, Mr. Everett Whittaker, for encouraging me to explore my creative potential at a very young age. He was the one to lead me into the thought of turning my raw imagination into refined written works.

I also must give a special thanks to my former classmates through middleschool and highschool, Izaih Young and William Hernandez. Both of these young men have supported my writing more than anyone else and were always some of the first to read the stories I wrote. They both inspired me to keep writing and make stories that were enjoyable for them to read. My young friend Izaih was the first person to read a large portion of this very story back when I was first writing it on paper back in highschool. And I'm thankful for his constant support of it.

Lastly I must thank all the other classmates, coworkers and all others who I've told about this project and have given me their praise or anticipation of its arrival. All of them have been a constant reminder to make this book sparkle and ensure it gets done right, as I have a direct view of a part of my audience. It has all helped reinstate the value of having people waiting for an experience that only I could give.

Table of Contents

Dedication

Acknowledgment

About the Author

Chapter 1: The Convergence   1

Chapter 2: Realization   11

Chapter 3: Another God Is Near   40

Chapter 4: No Man's Forest   67

Chapter 5: Our Nature Is Hard Work   106

Chapter 6: Sabbath Day   130

Chapter 7: The Start of The Quest, Battle of The Angels   138

Chapter 8: For Those You Hold Dear   167

Chapter 9: A King's Limit   190

Chapter 10: The Eighth God   226

Chapter 11: Ava Ramada   254

Chapter 12: Survive   282

Chapter 13: Spirit Animal   298

Chapter 14: Life and Death   310

Chapter 15: Rahricu's Troublesome Childhood   329

Chapter 16: Lights of Life   354

Chapter 17: As Perfect As A Human Can Get   380

Chapter 18: The Beauty of Death   390

About the Author

It takes passion and creative tenacity to execute the genre of fantasy fiction beautifully. Here is the myth, Jalel Wordlaw.

The story begins once upon a time in Desoto, Texas, where Jalel grew up with two older brothers and parents. His dad worked for a phone company, and his mother worked for Albertsons before she passed away. Jalel discovered his creative potential in fifth grade, where he was leagues ahead of his classmates when jotting down his bizarre imagination onto paper. Brainstorming ideas came naturally to him and in one of the most intriguing manners. He reminisces about writing a story that manifested entirely from events playing out in his mind and being praised for his unique composition and story-building ability in that young age. He eventually became known all over the school for his creativity and garnered praise from his peers. Quite the "protagonist" start to an about the author section.

He developed his writing style, which has now become his signature and trademark. Jalel takes his readers on a journey that is a mix of educational, dark, yet inspirational style engrossed with a pinch of humor to keep things light.

Jalel went through Cockrell Hill and Amber Terrace Elementary school and moved to West Middle School, eventually graduating from Desoto High School.

Chapter 1

The Convergence

The bright afternoon sun shines vividly on a windy day. The streets are littered with people, and the atmosphere is filled with their voices of conversation. The soothing breeze of the air whistles through the ears of the pedestrians as it blows through the trees, making a melodic sound with their leaves. Birds soar through the sky, catching the wind through their wings, and squirrels move through the swaying trees and grass, finding shelter for their nuts. Crowds of people pass by multiple buildings of all sorts, one being a small restaurant where a small group of four is seated at a table in the establishment while holding an interesting conversation.

"No! We cannot change anything now. My wedding's tomorrow! Everything's already set!" a beautiful woman in the group shouts. She has gorgeous brown hair and eyes complementing her pretty face. She has light brown skin that glistens softly with the touch of the afternoon sun. "Well, we're just saying scratch all that. We came up with something better," the guy across from the pretty woman says with a very calm but slightly raspy voice. The man has a gap in his teeth and a thin face. He sports a spikey hairstyle and has natural squints in his eyes. "And what's that Francis?" the pretty woman asks.

"We thought about taking things inside for your reception," Francis continues. "We're gonna surprise your fiancé with this huge party."

"Oh you know Jadeanu's not going to like that. I'll admit he has an adventurous side, but this isn't an adventure. It's our wedding reception. And the plan is to have things as easygoing and sentimental as he likes. Simple, fun, and meaningful. We don't need some huge party with dancing and drinking," the pretty lady says.

"Yeah, I guess you're right Tierla. We are talking about the guy who refuses to sleep with a woman before marrying her," Francis mentions. "Excuse me, Francis! But he's not the only one. In fact, you are the only one at this table who doesn't have enough self-control to reserve your precious body for someone who deserves it rather than giving it to strangers," the pretty lady known as Tierla sasses. "At least Scarlet has learned from her mistake."

"Yeah, and I agree with Tierla. There is no need to change anything. Not this late in the game. Especially not if the lady of the hour disagrees," the lady next to Tierla known as Scarlet says. Scarlet is a short young brown-skinned woman with braided long black hair and a friendly-looking face.

"That's why we met to talk about it in person," the last person in the group says. He is a slightly tall athletic guy. He has short light brown straight hair that extends just to his neck. He has brown eyes and light brown skin. He is a rather handsome young man with thick eyebrows.

"We don't want to do anything the bride would disagree with. After all, it is you and Jadeanu's wedding. We're not here to control anything. We just want to convince you of what we think is a good idea. If you still disagree, then we won't go against you. I'm asking you to listen to us and give your opinion."

"Fine then Luke. You may try to convince me. What's your plan?" Tierla asks.

"Francis and I were planning on renting out that big ballroom just West of here. You know what place I'm talking about, right Tierla?" Luke starts. "Yeah I know the place," she answers. "Yeah, we were planning on moving everything over there," Francis butts in. "We were going to add some more tables and put out more candy to make the environment friendlier for the kids that'll be there," Luke continues. "We were even planning to have some fireworks for the event."

"That's fine, but we already have everything set for outside the wedding building, near that beautiful lake. My fiancé and I were going to enjoy the simple and lovely outside. We had already set up several games to play over there, a photo booth, and ending everything near the lake during the sunset would be so romantic. It was designed to remind us of the first date we had back when we were still new."

"Nothing has to go to waste. We can keep the games and catered food. We just need to relocate it for the ballroom. And it can still be sentimental and romantic. I thought about bringing a few microphones and a few more speakers to have some karaoke. We know you like to sing and you're talented. I thought it would be very sentimental if you sang that one love song you seem to love so much. We were going to get Jadeanu to sing it with you. We all know you both like singing and are good at it, although Jadeanu rarely does it in front of people. It would be a great way to revive his adventurous side, and for you to draw it out with your beautiful voice would be perfect. I know he'd love it, and so would you."

"Jadeanu doesn't know about this right?" Tierla asks. "No," Luke answers. "It's supposed to be a big surprise. You know, to get him out of his comfort zone a little. We would use the hayride designed to get you two to the lake together and change the direction to the ballroom instead. It'll be a fun surprise for your fiancé. I know my little bro, and he would greatly appreciate it. You both deserve it, something more and something to get your hearts racing. That way you'll have a great reason to remember that day for the rest of your lives."

"Okay, and how much would all this cost, and who's paying for it?" "Leave that to us," Francis answers. "I, Luke, and the other guys will put our money and time in to ensure everything happens as it should." "Yeah, we'll handle everything. You won't even have to lift a finger," Luke reassures. "We'll put our hearts and souls into ensuring everything is in place for the event. We'll handle the decorations; we'll pay the expenses, we'll inform the caterers, DJ, and hayride driver to move to the ballroom. We'll transport all the other preparations to the ballroom. We'll rent out the ballroom tonight." "That's right! Leave it all to us!" Francis finishes.

"I left the wedding invitations in your hands, Francis, and it didn't go so well!" Tierla argues. "You chose to send out the invitations through email, which would have been fine if everyone had checked their email. But you didn't factor in that there were people who wouldn't or didn't use email! It's why our old friend Ricardio didn't get the invite and is forced to miss out on my big day! You didn't think things through. You don't think things through, Francis! So why would I leave something this important in your hands?!"

"Because I'll make sure everything goes smoothly," Luke resolves. "I'll make sure Francis does his part. I can't let you or my brother down. So I'll ensure we get things right within the short time frame." "Do you promise you'll get everything ready to go for tomorrow?" "Yes, I promise you Tierla, I'll get everything right."

"Okay, fine. Fine, fine, fine, fine. I permit you to arrange the ballroom. I trust you Luke. You've always been the guy to get things done and ensure things work out. Just like Olivia."

"My mom?" "Yeah. I see where you got your competence from. So if you say you can do it, I put my faith in you. I don't trust you though Francis. But if Luke is looking after you, I'll let it all slide. You just better make sure everything is perfect. I cannot let anything bad happen tomorrow. So you make sure everything is in order before one o'clock tomorrow. You still have to tend to my fiancé and ensure he's prepared for the event, **best man**. And you too, **groomsman**. You two make sure you get enough rest tonight okay?"

"Will do," Luke replies. "Oh this is going to be so fun!" Tierla states with barely contained excitement. "I can't wait to see Jadeanu at the altar! Thank you both for looking after him like this. I truly appreciate your willingness to go through all this trouble for us. And thank you for coming out here to talk to me and paying for us to eat." "No problem Tierla. You're about to become a part of the family officially," Luke responds. "Speaking of food, where is our waitress with our food," Scarlet announces. "We gotta hurry up and eat for our girl's night!"

Meanwhile, the very man of conversation, Jadeanu, walks outside his home and embraces the gentle sun shining on him. Jadeanu is a slightly short, handsome guy with a fit build. He gazes at the bright blue sky as the sun highlights his natural brown eyes and shaggy short brown hair that extends down to his neck.

"It truly is a beautiful day," he expresses. A gust of wind blows through the area causing Jadeanu's hair and clothes to blow in the same direction. Jadeanu then moves his face to the direction the wind had moved to. "Whoo! I just felt a strange chill down my spine. Ha, it's probably just pre-wedding jitters. I've got a long day ahead of me, so I'll just go for a jog to get my nerves in check. Then I'll go visit some family." Jadeanu then does a few stretches before darting off into the windy day.

Eventually, Jadeanu finishes his jog, gets into his shiny red Ford Mustang car, and drives out to see his parents and other relatives. They all spend their day with him, talking and enjoying each other's company, as do his bride Tierla and her bridesmaids until the day ends and the day of anticipation arrives.

His groomsmen wake up Jadeanu, and they start to get him ready for his big day. "Ya nervous?" Luke asks while helping Jadeanu get dressed. "Certainly. But I can't wait to see Tierla again," Jadeanu answers. "I'm ready to start this and finally marry her."

After Jadeanu is prepared to go, he and his groomsmen make their way to the wedding venue for the ceremony to begin. And after a lovely ceremony where Jadeanu and Tierla are officially Wedd, all their friends, family, and other guests make their way to the venue for the reception. Jadeanu and his bride get on a hayride with their respective groomsmen and bridesmaids to their next destination.

Jadeanu and his bride both ride happily while having a bit of conversation about the event. "Oh babe, let me tell you, I was so nervous about getting up on the altar in front of everyone today!" Tierla exclaims with a smile full of her white teeth. "I was all like, *'Oh my gosh! Don't trip over your dress in front of all these people! Do not trip!'* hahaha!" "Well then that makes two of us. I wasn't wearing a big dress though, so tripping wasn't on my mind," Jadeanu states. "But you know, all my fear left when my eyes met yours. I felt just so comfortable staring into the eyes of the woman of my dreams. Everything became just so clear to me then." "I love you Jadeanu." "I love you too, Tierla." Jadeanu then leans in and kisses Tierla, who gladly accepts.

"Okay, slow down with all this public display of affection. You'll make the single man, Luke, jealous," Francis jokes. "Awe come on. You know I'm not like that," Luke responds. "I'm happy my little bro is affectionate towards his wife." Jadeanu and Tierla giggle as they separate their faces from one another, and Jadeanu looks around and notices something off.

"Hey, this isn't the way to the lake. We're going the wrong way," he states. He surveys the area and then looks at his groomsmen, who all have devious smiles on their faces. "Wait, what's going on? Where are we going guys?" he catches on. No one says anything. Jadeanu then looks at his wife to see if she knew what was happening. She also has a mischievous smile spread on her face. "Where are we going Tierla?" he asks. She doesn't answer, only smiling harder at Jadeanu's confused face. "Really? No one's going to say anything. Fine, you keep your secret. I'll see what kind of nonsense you all planned soon enough."

Soon they all arrive at a huge building. They all excitedly exit their ride and stand in front of the entrance. "Tada!" Tierla says as she motions her body as if revealing the place. "It's a ballroom! The guys decided it would be better if we brought the reception here. Now let's get inside," Tierla takes Jadeanu's hand, and they both enter the building together.

Inside, the place was specially decorated and beautifully lit up. A large burgundy carpet was rolled out from the entrance to the end of a clear walkway, leading to a dance floor clear of people. Just past the dance floor was a set of tables covered in white cloth. The table in the middle had a beautiful layered cake, while the ones on the side had candy and other refreshments. Beside the carpet were round tables in rows covered in red cloth with chairs seated with guests pulled up. The tables had a bouquet of many flowers in a vase in the center, followed by candles in glass holders. There are also plates and silverware at each seat, empty and waiting to be filled with food. There was an area for music to the right of the ballroom where the DJ played music with considerably big speakers to fill the space with sound. The wedding buffet was to the left of the ballroom, followed by a bar. There were banners on each wall, saying words of endearment to the newlyweds, such as, *"Leave well wishes for the new MR and MRS"* and *"Soon to be MRS Stroyem!"* There was a station for wedding games, and balloons were everywhere.

"Wow, this place is beautiful!" Tierla says in awe. "You haven't been inside?" Jadeanu asks. "Nope. The guys just told me about it. But wow, they did it. They did all of this just yesterday. I truly am proud of those guys. They are something else."

Jadeanu and Tierla make their way across the entrance carpet and move onto the dance floor, where they start to dance together. Then soon, Tierla elegantly trails off, grabs a microphone held out for her, and begins to sing the lyrics to the love song the DJ is playing. Her voice is beautiful as she dedicates her passionate song to her husband. On cue, Luke gets Jadeanu's attention with another microphone to get him to join his wife's song. He dances over to grab the microphone and binds his wife in harmony as they both steal the show with their melodious voices while dancing to the song's rhythm.

After an outstanding performance, they both sit at the head table. Tierla's father gives a welcoming speech to the guests, and after, everyone goes to the buffet to get food on their plates. Jadeanu and Tierla go table to table and speak with their guests as Luke and Scarlet give heartfelt speeches to Jadeanu and Tierla. Then the floor is open for all the guests to have fun: dancing, wedding game playing, and gathering candy and drinks.

Tierla and Jadeanu continue dancing together. Though they dance slowly because Tierla is holding and nursing a drink. "You might want to slow down on the drinks Tierla. You don't want to get hammered at our wedding reception," Jadeanu warns. "It's fine! I won't get drunk," Tierla claims. "I don't want to spend a second in this lovely fantasy without being sober." Tierla then embraces Jadeanu with a hug while slowly moving her body to the beat of the music. "Oh you don't know how good it feels to call you my husband finally," Tierla says while leaning in for a kiss. "Now hold my drink. I've got to pee!"

Tierla hands Jadeanu her beverage before jogging off into the crowd. Jadeanu continues mingling with the groups until he makes it to his groomsmen and Luke. "Hey, I heard you all set this whole thing up. You did a great job," he appreciates. "Thanks, but we wanted to give you a wedding to remember," Luke admits. "Yeah, I'm glad you're enjoying yourself Jadeanu," Francis mentions. "Our hard work paid off." "You guys are the greatest, and I love you all,"

Jadeanu says as he hugs Luke and Francis while squeezing all the other groomsmen in. "Thank you all so much for doing this. I truly am grateful for all this. I hope we all stay friends for a long time." "As do I," Luke claims. "Alright, now I've got to talk to some of the other guests. Later guys," Jadeanu says as he gets back on the move around the crowd.

Then there is a sudden rumble on the ballroom floor. The dancing and music all stop with the sudden geographic change. "Is that an Earthquake? Now of all times?" Jadeanu wonders. The sound of thunder fills the ballroom with its mighty roar. "Thunder? There's no way there should be a storm today. It was supposed to be clear skies all day. That's why we planned to visit the lake."

Then without warning, horrified screams fill the air. Everyone looks to where the screams came from and sees the horror for themselves. People started to freeze up and then stiffly fell to the ground. When others attempted to investigate what was happening with those who fell, they discovered that they had just died without rhyme or reason. Many guests started dropping like flies, causing panic in those who had not yet met the same fate. Most of the living guests ran out of the building, fearing for their lives. It was as if the ballroom had become infected with a disease, and the first one out of the building would be the safest in the minds of the people.

"What the heck is going on?" Jadeanu fearfully says as he watches his friends and family drop dead before his eyes. "Oh no. I've got to find Tierla." Jadeanu rushes through the building in search of his beloved. "Tierla! Honey! Where are you?!" He continues his search until he finds her lying lifeless among the others. He puts her drink down on a random table and runs to her body in disbelief as he kneels to see if she is okay. "Tierla! Tierla! What the hell is going on here?! Tierla, please wake up! You were just dancing with me. There's just no way you could be…." Jadeanu sheds tears at the sight of his mysteriously deceased wife. He grabs her wrist and checks her now invisible pulse.

Luke runs over to his little brother in worry. "Jadeanu, come quick. There is something strange going on outside." "Stay away from me!" Jadeanu scowls with a peculiar, violent echo in his voice. His ordinarily brown eyes even glow a strange bright red. Luke jumps out of fear and concern. His eyes switch from brown to a glowing light blue. Jadeanu's eyes turn back to normal as fear consumes his heart. "Luke. What's wrong with your eyes?" "What was up with yours?" Luke responds. "We shouldn't worry about that now. Francis and some of the others are dead, but we can still meet up with the rest of our family and friends. They're outside. I-I'm sorry about Tierla, but you know there is no use in staying here with the dead. We can at least try to figure out what's going on by going outside." Jadeanu looks at Tierla with unease evident on his face but takes a deep breath, hugs her corpse, and then lets it go. Luke helps Jadeanu off his knees, and they both run outside the ballroom.

When they make it outside, they notice that the sky is purple, and the clouds are all pitch black. On the streets everywhere, people lay on the floor, completely lifeless. A car on the distant road speeds into a wall and explodes into a vast flame. The climate wind blows with a sinister chill. "What happened to our world?" Jadeanu questions.

Chapter 2:
Realization

Within the deep reaches of the purest of light lies the holy realm of Heaven. And within that Heaven, a mighty force can be found. This powerful entity could be broken down into a straightforward design; Life. A simple design, yet broad. Much bigger than many could comprehend. Yet it is not in the aspect, for he is a live spirit. He is beautiful and solid and has brown hair down past his neck, complementing his tan-looking white skin. His eyes glow a bright silver color, almost white, and white energy surrounds his body in the symbolism of his means. He wears white robes as he stands barefoot in his domain in Heaven.

His domain consists of pearly white stone decorating the floor, walls, and pillars used to construct the place. Life stands on a stone walkway leading to a blue and white throne. To the sides of the walkway sit a large garden full of beautiful flowers as far as the eye could see. There are clouds in the sky and waterfalls filling the space around the garden. Life's domain is truly a sight to behold.

Life reaches his hand toward some of the flowers in his garden, and abruptly, more blossoms begin to grow from nothing. As he moved through the garden, making more and more flowers, the colossal number of flowers in the place slightly gravitated and grew in his direction. At least many did. The ones that did not were deemed imperfect flowers by Life and were to be dealt with. Some were cut, others were left alone, and the rest, he made them grow ever more so that they may gravitate to him again.

Life rejoices with certain glee as he grooms his vast garden. Yet he does not perform this tedious task alone. Alas, he has many angels to aid him. They all wore white robes and traversed the garden with the elegant white feathered wings they used to fly. Life himself didn't have any feathered attachments. All of his angels had some type of animal feature, whether it was a tiger's arm, a lion's tail, the legs of a gazelle, or even standard human features.

Life's angels dance in unison and praise life's physical incarnation. There was true peace and happiness in the garden within Heaven. However, it has not always been this way. The Heavens have shifted and advanced to benefit a complex of powers among the celestial entities.

A few thousand years ago, the deity known as Death had crept his way into Life's garden with the will to bring an everlasting death to humanity. As sin would draw closer to the souls of man, Death would draw nearer and have his way with society. The wills will be decided through a duel. If Death were to defeat Life, the world's end would ravage the Earth. However, if Life wins, the end would be delayed.

As Life and Death skirmished in war, much of Life's garden was destroyed, and its effects went off to Earth. Much of the planet was destroyed by a massive tsunami. The weak, foolish, and sinful were vanquished, which were many. Yet, the genuine believers of the gods were saved. Though most were not true, only a single man was left alive. He was sinless, and his beliefs were true. Through his influential righteousness, his wife and the two genders of each animal on the planet were also spared. He would later repopulate the Earth and bring the world from sin.

Then, Life defeated Death with the help of his angels. They conquered and expelled Death further from the Garden of Life. Heaven was reconstructed and renewed. Life's angels stayed faithful to him and remained by his side to this day. They were all still alive as well. As they do not suffer actual wounds and cannot die unless a god kills them or a god's power consumes them.

Once the war of life and death was over, humanity raged on. As for the Heavens, they grew in size, and Life established a throne between his garden and the Heavens. That very throne is the connection between life itself and the spiritual side of it to an extent. Life also crafted a forcefield to protect the Heavens from another attack. Death was now far from Life, and humanity would thrive once again. Today, society has not once experienced another disaster like that again.

Over the centuries, people started to forget the gods and their teachings. People drifted away and invited sin and materialism once again. Corruption and lawlessness filled the Earth, allowing Death to draw near again. The forcefield of Heaven, which was strengthened by purity, weakened. Yet the barrier prolonged the sky long enough for Death to gain his prime and bring forth his 12 disciples and other angels. He breaks through the barrier and approaches the Garden of Life once again. Life halts his garden labor and pays his attention to Death.

"Do you have a special request, or is it time for the final judgment?" he asks with his powerful spiritual voice, which has an Australian accent. "This place is a lot bigger than I remember it," Death responds. "The more you give to the other life, the more they take for granted. Thus, I draw ever nearer. I came to give the mortals what they are entitled to; death." "Well, if it can't be helped…." With the rise of Life's hand, his 12 special angels, disciples, and other angels came to oppose Death again.

Death has a beautiful face with long curved eyebrows. He has perfect pale white skin and a stern look on his face. His eyes glow with a dark purple hue, and his straight black hair extends close to the center of his back. He stares at Life with a menacing glare.

Death has always been stronger than Life due to a potency complex. Life has granted himself a vast kingdom to reflect his essence. Death was not given much of an empire because he could not create it. With the order of all seven gods, he was granted more power instead of a kingdom to maintain balance. He has his domain in the Heavens, where he sits upon a throne of skulls. Life's Heavens have only gotten more prominent, so Death grows more potency.

"We shall fight there," Life suggests referring to an open spacious area before the garden. "I cannot allow your destruction to harm the Earth in the same way again." The two gods move to their respective sides of the battlefield and commence their war once again.

Five other gods are living in their respective kingdoms. They begin to understand that the time for the decision of Earth has come. The third god in the Heavens prepares his kingdom for the upcoming event. He is called Spirit. He controls the movements of life and death. He has a small domain. Thus, his power is weaker than Death's yet stronger than Life's.

These three gods rule the Heavens and control the flow of reality. They are known as the "Big Three." Spirit brings forth evil and grants wicked spirits eternal punishment. Life brings purity and grace and gives the pure hearts paradise. Death simply brings death and grants calculated judgment to the world. With these tasks, they work equally to keep the world balanced.

Life breathes life into the world, and life struggles to test its purity. Spirit gives that life an easy way through the struggle through sin. Eventually, that life dies with the essence brought by Death. Death gives the evil or ordinary spirits to Spirit, where they shall reap suffering for their harmful deeds. Death gives excellent spirits to Life where they shall be given prosperity and paradise. The cycle repeats until the world is broken beyond repair due to humankind's inevitable submission to evil. Then Death will destroy humanity.

The other four gods live in the spirit world on Earth, where the living may only rarely interact with but never see while alive. They each have their strength and own kingdom. Only one's power reaches that of the Big Three. They are Knowledge, Nature, Willpower, and Universe. Each represents a crucial part of humanity's triumph and power. "The prophecy has come to pass," the god known as Knowledge admits from the deep reaches of his kingdom within the transparencies of the Earth.

Meanwhile in Heaven, Life and Death clash fists. Their angels fight in the background, not daring to interfere with the gods. Death counters with a punch from his left hand. Life catches the attack. Death spawns a blade on the bottom of his feet and backflips, pointing the knife directly at Life. Life jumps back to avoid the deadly attack, even though gods don't suffer wounds.

Death flips in the air and kicks at Life's handsome face. Life blocks toward the attack with light energy covering his arm. Death's extensive force pushes Life into cartwheels. Life's hands light up with bright white light, and he shoots powerful balls of light at his opponent. Death effectively dodges the balls while returning fire with swords that shoot from his hands. Life gracefully evades, then waves his hand, causing a massive wave of blinding light to spring toward Death. Death jets to the side to avoid the attack. Once he returns to the task, he sees Life hovering above him, advancing through a swift dive.

Death barely manages to dodge Life's descension as Life slams his fist into the clean, white pavement. A large eruption of light consumes the area in a wide circumference. The angels nearby managed to escape in time so as not to be destroyed. Once the light clears up, Death speeds toward Life with a fierce kick with his bladed feet. Life blocks with an energy shield but is still sent back by Death's excessive force. Life begins to tumble, but he effortlessly catches himself with his hand, springing himself back to his feet with no damage.

Life readjusts and becomes tempered. The right side of his body glows orange, including his right eye. This conveys the two sides of Life, the beauty and the struggle. Life is a miracle and a torturous curse of which the god now embodies. Life jumps up and slams his fists into the ground. Two giant plant vines burst through the floor in pursuit of Life's target. The vine to Life's pure side is clean and elegant. The vine to his chaotic side is ugly, twisted, and thorny. Death easily avoids the vines with quick side swaying movements and flips. Life closes his gap to Death with blinding speed, grows a blade on his chaos foot, and performs a one-leg front flip kick, extending the knife directly at Death.

Meanwhile, many angels fall from the skies in combat. Being hurt and stunned but never injured or harmed. For this is a spiritual fight fit for none other. No one can interfere with any feud between the Big Three, not even the other gods. Life fails to land his blow, yet he summons a beautiful sword of white light and conjures a twisted-up spear of cacti. He uses them swiftly and elegantly while maintaining a brutal demeanor.

Death formulates a double scythe with a long blade on each end. They both clash multiple times to no avail. Death overpowers Life a few times, but Life is resilient enough not to get hit. Life dematerializes his rapier and creates a bow of celestial stone. He expands his number of cacti spears by two and slides all three on his bow. He shoots them all at the same time in the direction of Death. Death spins his double scythe and blocks all the incoming spears.

Then Life immediately puts both hands together and fires a mix of light and twilight at Death in a large radius. Death cannot create a similar blast, so he decides to block instead of firing back. The light beam proceeded past Death's defenses. Once the explosion clears, Death falls to a kneel from evident damage. Life recreates his signature sword and cacti spear to continue his assault. Death separates his double scythe into two more miniature scythes and defends with precision.

They clash weapons a few times, yet Death's power overcomes Life, allowing Death a tiny opening. Death pierces Life right through his heart. Life grunts and backs up, holding his chest. There was no blood, no wound, and Life was in no danger outside of pain. When a god is still within his kingdom, he cannot be placed in a state known as a stalemate.

A stalemate is when a god or angel is vitally injured. They are placed on temporary rest so their bodies can recover. Because Life is still within his kingdom, he cannot be stalemated due to the place's familiar energy keeping him stable. He's not out of the fight yet. Life confronts Death with his bare hands to increase his speed and efficiency. Death decides to do the same. They trade punches yet never land a hit on each other. Life, however, falters due to his still prevalent invisible injury. Death lands a punch to Life's stomach, another to his chest, and one more with all his force again. Life bolts away and lands on the stairs at the entrance of his kingdom's open gates.

Death then walks through the pathway forged from the garden. The path leads to Life's throne. As Death passes the flowers, they begin to shrivel and die. Death approaches the throne and prepares to sit down as a demonstration of his victory in battle; before he does away with all living creatures. "Wait! While you were away, I made the throne our spirit link! If you sit there, it will set off the balance of our system!" Life shouts. But it was too late. Death's behind had already landed in the chair. The throne immediately went from bluish-white to purple, the color of Death's aura. The dark energy from the throne moved to the flowers in the garden.

Even Spirit's kingdom was disturbed. The spirits from Hell flew out and released their negative energy into the flowers. Some spirits from Heaven also released their energy into the flowers. Many flowers died immediately, and some grew sickly. Some grew with purity and beauty, while others grew twisted and ugly.

"This is new," Death notices. "Death, you didn't end the world," Life foretold. "You combined life and death itself." "This isn't what

I came for, but it is intriguing. Let us see how this unfolds." "It appears something unwarranted has occurred. Go my angels. Do as thou wilt," Spirit authorizes for his angels. "Just don't abandon your angelic lawfulness."

"Sorry Life. This is my reign now. I like the idea of a force field; I'll be taking it," Death expels all of Life's angels to meet Life outside of his corrupted kingdom. He establishes the remains of Life's force field, which turns purple and stops Life from returning. "What are we to do now your grace?" one of Life's disciples asks. "Do what you want," Life replies as two substantial white wings bust out of his back. At the single flap of his wings, he takes off into the sky of Heaven. "Does that mean we can go to Earth physically?" another disciple asks the other. He shrugs.

On Earth, many people just suddenly dropped dead. The sky turned purple and the clouds black. Some people became weak due to a strange new plague. An epidemic ravages the Earth. Even angels were upon the humans, reestablishing their reality to non-believers. The entire world was suddenly thrown into turmoil that none could understand.

On Texas ground stood Jadeanu in awe and despair at the sudden change of the world. "Boys! Boys!" the sound of a woman interrupts Jadeanu's awestricken gaze at the new world. "Mom!?" Jadeanu and his brother Luke reveal. "Hey mom. I'm glad you're okay, but what about dad?" Jadeanu asks. Tears begin to swell in her eyes. "Your dad is...gone!" "Dad's dead?" Luke worries. "This is one heck of a night,"

"Do not worry children. This is a night of tragedy and opportunity," a random priest quotes from the roof of the church. "How did that weirdo get up there?" someone in the crowd of people outside of the ballroom says. "What's he going on about?" Luke wonders. "You're crazy, you old hag!" a middle-aged man rages.

'Who is this guy? There's just something that feels strange about him,' Jadeanu thinks to himself.

"Death is a tragedy, yet it is also a blessing. Do not falter at a loss and gauge the opportunity that may come forth. Remember your faith in the gods," the priest continues. "Yeah? And why would the gods allow this to happen? You're insane old man!" the middle-aged man rebuttals. "Hey isn't that Brother Joseph from church? I wonder why he's so cranky. Although I can understand how he must feel," Luke realizes, shifting his attention to him. *There is something seriously up with that priest. I just can't put my finger on it,'* Jadeanu hypothesizes. "Hey, where'd the priest go?" a woman yells.

Everyone looks up, and the priest is nowhere to be found. "None of that matters anyway. I'll kill whoever is responsible for all of this!" Jadeanu howls. His eyes turn red again, and he bolts inhumanly high into the sky. His rage inspires that of a few others. A few people in the crowd's eyes turn either blue or red. They commence an all-out brawl against each other.

Luke notices that everyone who has this change in their eyes has superhuman capabilities. One is enhanced strength. He uses his newfound power to protect his mother, who has not gained an unnatural glow in her eyes. He lifts a few massive boulders from the carnage and uses them to shield her. He then gazes at his brother Jadeanu, rampaging through the city, looking for "whoever is responsible." Luke takes the initiative and goes after him.

As he runs to the scene, his hands suddenly shoot out some kind of gaseous energy which rockets him forward, closer to his brother. "YEEHAW!! What is this stuff? Whatever it is, it's awesome!" He nears Jadeanu and aims his hand at him. He tries to fire some kind of energy, which unexpectedly comes out as a blue ball of gas. It connects and explodes on Jadeanu, knocking him out of rhythm but luckily not killing him.

"Jadeanu! Are you okay?" Luke worries. "I will get what I am owed. I will get my vengeance!" Jadeanu claims, but with more voices than his own coming from his mouth. He stands to his feet and lunges at his older brother with his fingers in a claw formation. Red essence reflects and flies off his erect fingers. Luke puts his hands up to block, suddenly creating a strange transparent energy shield. Jadeanu's attack strikes the barrier and cracks it severely, yet it sustains.

"Whoa! I get a shield too! Where exactly is all this power coming from?" Luke questions. He depletes his shield and shoots another ball of gas. Jadeanu is sent back a little from the resulting explosion. "Jadeanu! What are you doing? Stop attacking and listen. I've got a plan." "Vengeance!" Jadeanu replies, sounding like a possessed soul with multiple voices following. He front flips into the air, which he usually can't do, and puts all his body weight and force into a fist he uses to punch the ground. A red shockwave emits in his radius and crashes into Luke, knocking him off his balance.

Jadeanu rushes close to Luke, conjures up some red energy on his fist, and punches toward his stomach. Luke blocks with his arms as his mind thinks, *'No shield this time?'* Jadeanu's fist slams into Luke's arms. The power from the attack knocks Luke high into the air. Luke panics, considering how high he was launched. He is about four stories high when he starts falling to the ground. The wind takes him by his limbs, and fear grows in his eyes. "Oh...crap!" Luke screams. As he plummets to what seems like his death, he aims his hands to blunt his fall in a futile attempt to protect himself.

A bubble closes on Luke at the last second, saving him from the crash. The bubble immediately shatters like glass, and Luke's hands softly fall to the dirt. "Okay Jadeanu. I need you to come back to your senses. Even if that means I have to beat you up first," Luke resolves. He stands, puts both hands to his front, and rapidly shoots blue gas balls at his maniacal brother.

Jadeanu adapts and moves fast enough to dodge the balls. He moves toward Luke, using the red power of his hands to attack and destroy Luke's gas balls. Luke puts his hands together and shoots a gas beam at his pursuer. Jadeanu hadn't anticipated the sudden change in attack, so it connects and hits him away. Jadeanu falls to a kneel but soon recovers enough to stand up and pursue once more.

Luke casts a shield, Jadeanu punches it, and Luke dispels it and blasts Jadeanu again. They both initiate physical attacks—Jadeanu attacks with intense force, and Luke blocks and counters with a right uppercut. Luke's power is evidently inferior to Jadeanu's due to the lack of damage from the strike. They both put their arms together and push against each other's strength. Jadeanu overpowers Luke, pushing him down and backward. He then recoils and punches Luke in the face. Luke flies off into a nearby building. Jadeanu quickly approaches.

Luke emits a burst of gas to knock his brother back. He then rockets himself into the air and propels himself into a tackle. He pins his rampaging brother down and consistently blasts him with gas power. "Jadeanu, I know you're in there bro! Come back to your senses before I am forced to seriously hurt you! You'll never avenge Tierla in this state! What would she think if she saw you now? You're greater than this!" Luke reasons. Jadeanu's eyes return to normal, and his rage subsides as the damage he receives and his reflective thoughts calm him.

Luke gets off of him and helps him to his feet. "I'm sorry about that. I don't know what came over me," Jadeanu apologizes. "It's cool as long as you're back to yourself. Hey, if you want to find out what's going on, it would probably be our best bet to visit Ricardio. He might have an idea of what's up," Luke suggests. "It's been years since I've seen Ricardio. And he's a lot smarter than I am, plus he's more analytical. If anyone can piece together what's happening with the world, I'd put my bets on him. Of course, that's assuming the internet doesn't already know. I say we should meet up with him if he's alive."

Jadeanu and Luke return to their mother and drive her home in Luke's blue Chevrolet Sonic car as they change from the professional suits they were wearing into something more casual.

Jadeanu sports a red shirt and pants. Luke wears a light blue shirt and blue jeans. They both prepare for the journey and get back in Luke's car to move through the chaotic streets to Ricardio's home.

Luke sits in the driver's seat in the black interior of his car as he proceeds on the journey with his brother sitting next to him. The unnatural light blue glow in Luke's eyes stare into the lifeless road once filled with people. There are several wrecked cars around but with no passengers or filled with the bodies of those who have departed from this world. The death of silence is soon interrupted when Jadeanu looks at Luke.

"Hey Luke. Your eyes are still blue. What's up with that?" Jadeanu asks. "I'm not sure, but if it's a link to that strange power I had, I guess they should stay. Who knows what could happen." "Yeah, you're right about that… So many people just ended up dead. Out of Nowhere! Even my…" Jadeanu trembles with frustration staring at the ring sitting on his ring finger. "J-just what is happening here?" Luke cautiously takes a sympathetic look at Jadeanu. "I'm sorry about all this. We can only coast from what we have," Luke claims. Soon their car passes by many outraged people speaking their pieces with the only bits of explainable power they have. Their voices.

"This is the end! The gods have judged us and granted us divine retribution!" some of the older adults shout. "This probably does have something to do with the gods," Jadeanu establishes. "I have to admit that I haven't read the ancient text of our spiritual book, the Chako, but I definitely would have known about this through church or at least something. However, people randomly dropping dead can't be too much else. I'm quite desperate to believe anything right now. Anything that'll give a lead. I gotta know. I just gotta know what's going on."

"Maybe the Chako doesn't directly say it. After all, the decisions of the gods are outside of our comprehension, or so it says. What I'm trying to say is that something like this may be subtly mentioned in a way missable by most people. Maybe this is good for us. It's not like humans know right and wrong."

"You may be right, and that's precisely why I choose to obey the teachings of the essential seven. They provide an effective and healthy path toward existence as a human. To be honest, I just want to know what's happening and why I must say goodbye to my wife so early."

"Oh snap!" "What?" "I didn't fill my car up before we set off. I was in such a panic I didn't even notice how close we were to empty! I'm pulling over at the next gas station I see." "C'mon! Why didn't you realize that when we decided to choose your car? I still had about half a tank in mine!" "You could have thought about it at any time too you know. I had a lot on my mind as well. My bad though. I wasn't thinking."

Luke drives for a few more minutes before his car inevitably stops in the middle of the road. "Ugh, and we were almost there," Luke complains. "So, what now?" Jadeanu asks. "Look, the next gas station is just half a mile away. If we just push the-" "Push!? For half a mile?" "Yes. It shouldn't be hard with our new strength." "You might be right about that."

Luke and Jadeanu get out of the car and move to the back of it. "Alright, let's do this," Jadeanu quotes, and his eyes return red. He puts his hand on the trunk and nudges it. The car immediately moves accordingly. "This is easy. Hey, I've got an idea. Luke remember that propelling thing you did when I lost control, and we fought?" "Yeah?" "If you push on my back and propel from that position, we should be able to get there quickly." "Great idea Jadeanu."

Luke sets himself on Jadeanu's back with his own, and they lock arms. Jadeanu's hands are placed on the car, and Luke's diagonally extend toward the ground. "You ready?" Luke surveys. Jadeanu nods, even though Luke can't see it, and says, "Go on and start." Jadeanu begins running, pushing the car with ease. Luke blasts the ground, which accelerates their speed as planned. Jadeanu's shoes drag against the road, but his feet adapt by him adding red energy to them, causing sparks from the friction.

They reach the nearest gas station in a matter of seconds. Luke stops shooting, and Jadeanu slows the car to a stop. "Woo! That was fun! Who needs to drive when we can do this?" Jadeanu expresses. "You've got a point, but a functional car is still valuable," Luke reestablishes.

The parking lot of the place is empty, with no customers outside of themselves. Jadeanu and Luke walk into the gas station store. It's stocked with snacks, drinks, and gum but unlively and devoid of people. "There's nobody here," Luke points out. A TV above the service counter is the only thing making any noise. Jadeanu goes and looks over the counter and falls back in disgust. "What is it?" Luke wonders as he goes over the counter to see for himself. He spies a lone woman on the floor with no life left in her. She must have been the store clerk. "What the heck is going on here? Is everyone just doomed to die?!" Jadeanu worries. "Jadeanu! Come look at this," Luke motions toward the TV. The news of the very subject of interest was broadcast.

'It seems people are just dropping dead. The cause of such a tragedy is unknown. It doesn't seem to be some infection, nor does it come from global warming. People just randomly dropped dead. We have decided to call this phenomenon the Death Spiral because that's all it caused, and we know nothing else about it other than it's a spiral of death. There also seems to be a widespread plague that we refer to as the Death Disease. It is highly contagious, and everyone who has it seems to be slowly rotting away while still alive. It is likely they will die if nothing can be done about it. It is recommended that you stay away from anyone who has it. It is also unknown where it comes from. Another thing is that some people appear to be receiving some kind of supernatural powers. Just take a look at this footage we have amassed together.'

The TV then shifts to some people with ominous red glowing eyes wreaking havoc on their town, likely in a blind rage of frustration. *'It's not just happening in the United States. But it's everywhere! Nowhere is safe!'* the news reporter continues. "Well that's not a good sign," Jadeanu says. "That just means that this is a global threat. Humans couldn't have done this," Luke analyzes. "So we could just take the gas now, couldn't we? But I don't like to steal. Even if it's just lying here. There is still an owner to this establishment. The gas still belongs to someone," Jadeanu confesses. "Then we won't. I'm willing to put in the extra effort, if you will," Luke resolves.

"Not going to lie. Just because the world may be in a crisis, taking something like this won't sit well in my conscience. Especially knowing that there may be a chance that someone will still use or even need this place to make some kind of financial living. I may be overthinking, but I still like earning what I need rather than just taking it because it's convenient. We may just be able to find another gas station somewhere." The two brothers leave the gas station on foot because they can't bring themselves to steal, even from no visible victim. They are just too decent of people.

They approach Luke's car and kick off with it again. They continue down the road to Ricardio's place, watching for a place to get gas. Jadeanu eventually hears many enthusiastic voices, which occupy the path they must traverse. "Luke! Stop," he whispers as he comes to a halt. "You hear that?" "Yeah. It sounds like a riot. Maybe we should leave the car here and go check it out. See if we can make a path," Luke responds. He turns to his car and attempts to create a shield around it. The shield starts to form, but it never completes. "What are you doing?" "Trying to make sure my car stays safe." The shield still fails. "Dang it! Why isn't this working?" "Luke, let's just leave it. It'll probably be fine." "Alright fine. I'm trusting you on that."

Jadeanu and Luke turn the corner where the noise is coming from. A crowd of hundreds of people were surrounding something. Jadeanu approaches one of the guys and asks, "What's going on here?" "Yo bro, the guy in there is undefeatable! He's like...not even human bro! It's freaking AWESOME!!" Jadeanu cautiously turns to Luke and says, "Let's see what we can find." The boys push through the crowd and arrive at the front. There they see a 7'1 big, buff, brown-skinned man with long thick brown hair down to his rear. He gives off a significant, mysterious, but powerful presence and speaks with an accent from Trinidad.

There is another big buff 6'5 guy with glowing red eyes, symbolizing his excess power. He has both of his hands pushing against the force of the giant Trinidadian man's one hand, and he is losing. The red-eyed guy struggles intensely with veins bulging from his biceps, and his knees are bending as he descends inevitably to the ground. The Trinidadian is smirking while quickly pushing against the other man's force. "Ya see. Tere is no force you can have that can match me. Tere is no point in trying to equalize me. You need ta use your power for greater things, like helping people in need of ya strength." As he says this, the muscular challenger loses the rest of his strength and falls to the floor in defeat. "Wait! Let me be the one to bring him down," says someone from the crowd with red eyes.

"Since you think you're so great, I'll have to take you down a peg. That'll be through your definite defeat." "Ya talk big like you know all tings. I'll bring you back down to your place." "If that big guy couldn't overpower him, what makes you think you can?" another member of the crowd questions. "Because this bozo here is just a pathetic muscle head," he responds, picking the goliath of a defeated man up and tossing him back into the crowd with one hand.

"He had no concept of true strength, just like all of you. Now I will show you how to break someone down. Hey big guy! Let's play a little game. Let's close our eyes and take punches back and forth—no special powers. No tricks. Just a test of physical strength. I'll go first." "Whatever suits you." The Trinidadian man closes his eyes. "You fool!" The challenger then immediately disobeyed all the rules he had just set. He pulls out a knife, which sparks with charged red energy, accelerating his speed as he gets an optimal angle on the honest Trinidadian.

Jadeanu and Luke seem to be the only ones in the crowd that was even slightly bothered by this, wanting to step in yet hesitant to move. The excitement of a quenched bloodlust was enough to have everyone else in anticipation.

As the man approaches the nameless Trinidadian's throat, he notices that his target's face has never left his own parallel. Amazingly, the Trinidadian man knew what was happening without even opening his eyes. He quickly extends his fist and uppercuts his aggressor directly in the chin. The guy springs incredibly high above the ground by the surprising force of the Trinidadian man. The man soars over a skyscraper and falls behind it, landing on something hard. Whatever he landed on made a considerable noise, and it sounded an alarm. "My car!" Luke shouts.

The Trinidadian opens his captivating hazel eyes and scans the area. "Alright. Everyone clear the way!" another challenger demands. A section of the crowd disperses a bit, revealing an opening. The challenger is in a car with his head peering out the window. "If he can take this, you might as well all give up." The car he sits in is a very nice-looking red Ferrari capable of going at a tremendous speed.

The engine roars as he floors the gas pedal, accelerating at over 200 miles per hour at full speed. With all his might, he speeds and jumps out of the car at the last minute. The vehicle slams right into the Trinidadian, yet it immediately flies into the air, flipping violently. The car's hood splits in half, and the rest continues into a skyscraper and explodes. The Trini-man was perfectly fine, not a scratch on him. The stunt guy, however, was severely injured from jumping out of the moving vehicle onto pure concrete; it's a good thing he was strengthened by an altered density from his newfound powers. Otherwise, he'd surely be dead.

"Anyone else want to fight me?" the Trinidadian asks with genuine curiosity. Jadeanu's heart sinks in his chest as a paralyzing fear consumes him. He raises his hand and utters, "Sir, I'll...fight you." "Jadeanu! What are you doing?" Luke worries. "Don't worry. I'm not going to be like the others. I just want to see something."

"Jadeanu, I know it has been a hard day for you, but suicide won't make things better!" "That's not what I'm doing. Just wait and watch okay." Jadeanu takes off his wedding ring and hands it to Luke as he walks up to the Trinidadian man and kneels in respect. The Trini-man smiles sympathetically. "What is this guy doing? This is the street, not a church," a crowd member rages. Jadeanu gets up and prepares to fight. "Come on," the Trinidadian initiates.

Jadeanu runs up and kicks with red energy on his foot. The Trini-man blocks it effortlessly. Jadeanu jumps back and attacks again, and counters with another immediately after. The Trinidadian blocks both attacks. "Come on. I've got to hit him at least once." Jadeanu continues a ruthless assault to no avail. The Trinidadian guy's defenses were perfect. Suddenly, Jadeanu gasps in realization. An understanding of just who he's up against.

'I got it now. This power sure as heck isn't human. He must be..he... He's a god. He must be the god of Willpower!' Jadeanu analyzes. The Trini-man's facial expression changes to a more focused look as if he had read Jadeanu's mind. Jadeanu continues to attack, and the man continues to defend himself expertly.

'Yeah, no question. This power, this aura. The way he encourages the determination of others. It's gotta be him.'

The Trinidadian finds an opening and strikes Jadeanu in the chest. Jadeanu flies high into the air, losing all the breath in his lungs. He then prepares to crash into the ground, where the impact will kill or permanently injure him. As he hits the ground, the Trini-man nudges his finger ever so slightly, making all the potential energy leave Jadeanu's body, allowing him to land without damage.

He rises and moves off of his back onto one knee. Jadeanu spits out masses of his blood as his mind tries to alleviate his pain with a lulling dream. 'Augh. I-I can't feel my body. I-it's getting hard to breathe. But I can't die here. Not now. Not like this!' he thinks. "Serves him right. Nobody can go against this guy."

Those words ring through Jadeanu's ears, coming from a crowd member.

'I refuse to join you Tierla. Not yet. I've got to find out what's going on in this world. Luke is counting on me. So, so I've got to win this fight! Please forgive me.' Jadeanu begins to stand up. *'Without strength, I can't protect anything. That's why I'm not retreating. I need your power, Willpower!'* Jadeanu assumes a fighting stance. "Jadeanu, don't do this!" Luke yells.

"We'll stop here," the Trinidadian announces. "I've got something to show you. And for all others, tat building behind me is bout ta drop. You should evacuate duh area." The building that was hit by the car is now extensively coated in fire and preparing to topple at any time. Everyone freaks out and runs. "Jadeanu! Luke! You two come with me."

'He knows our names? That confirms it. He is something else.' Luke grabs his younger brother and aids him in walking away. The Trini-man stomps the ground, and the stunt guy, who can't move, rises into the air and lands in his arms. "He comes with us."

The three walk casually out of the area and pass by Luke's messed-up car. "Darn it, Jadeanu. I was counting on you when you said nothing would probably happen to the car," Luke jokes in a serious manner. He looks closely at the body lying motionless on top of his car. "Is that guy dead?" "Yes. I killed him with that uppercut I hit him with. A devious man like him roaming the streets won't do anyone much good. That's why I hit him with much more than I hit you with Jadeanu."

"Speaking of that, why did you save me when I fell, if I may ask?" "You are not to die by my hands. You're special. You are the only one who realized I was a god." "A god!? You mean you are one of the essential seven?" Luke asks. "Yeah I am. I am the god of Willpower. You may call me Will, but you cannot know my name. Names have power, and knowledge of that power causes vanity. It is a privilege that you humans lost long ago." "Thank you for your blessings Will," Jadeanu thanks him. "Thank you for being so good and prospective," Will humbles.

Not too far from where the two and the god are walking, a young teen boy peers around the corner. His blue-colored eyes gazing directly at Jadeanu. Will stops firmly in his tracks and doesn't even look at the kid when he says, "Are you just gonna sit there, or ya gonna say something." Luke looks around to see whomever Will is referring to and is entirely caught off guard by the teen, who responds by running up to the three.

"Hey, um… You guys all looked so cool out there, um. Can I ask your name?"

"Jadeanu."

"Okay, Jadeanu, sir. I have the power to heal wounds…."

"Really?" Luke wonders.

"Yeah, my name is Kinra by the way. Pleased to meet you."

"Luke." Luke greets him by shaking his hand. Kinra bows before the god of Willpower and greets, "It is an honor to make your acquaintance. Sir Willpower." "Thank you young one. But there is no need for formalities. Just call me Will." "Oh yeah. You can help him right?" Luke mentions as he lays Jadeanu down on his back.

"Yeah, it just works like this," Kinra claims as light green light fills his hands, and he rubs them on Jadeanu. "Where does it hurt?" "Everywhere." Jadeanu jokes though he is quite serious. "Mainly in my chest area though." Kinra touches Jadeanu's chest with the green light, lifting the pain from him. "That feels so much better," Jadeanu admits.

Kinra is a relatively short kid with a peaceful look of innocence radiating from his blue eyes. He has long black hair and a thin body coated in pale skin. "Wow kid. That's quite handy. Do you have someone waiting for you to return to, or can you come with us?"

"Can I?" "Sure, why not, as long as you don't have a place to be. We're out looking to understand what exactly is happening to the world. Speaking of which, Will, do you know what's going on with the world?"

"Life and death have merged. This results from what happens when you put both aspects together," Will responds. "It appears that about half of duh population has just dropped dead. Some others have been granted what you call the Death Disease—a condition where the essence of death is upon you but doesn't kill you instantly. The virus will spread outside your body until you inevitably die. You have undergone a spiritual metamorphosis for people lucky like you and Jadeanu.

When you die, your spirit goes off for judgment, but your soul is reincarnated into another life further down the line. The soul that is in your body has gone through a lot of bodies. The spirits that once belonged to them still have some attachment to them. When the spirits converged with life, your souls reacted with them, thus, giving you ya powers.

The spirits don't think the same as their previous self, and they once had a passion that the soul forgot. Now that passion has awakened. Though only the most potent force can manifest itself in you. The previous spirit's passion affects you. That passion manifested into powers to serve the purpose that the original spirit would have desired when they were still alive. Now your soul has transferred that power to you from their realm. Whether it's Heaven or Hell. Spirits in Hell represent their souls with red powers and red eyes. Spirits in Heaven represent their souls in blue." "So that's why-" Luke starts. "What!? Do you mean the main protagonist with my soul went to Hell? That sucks," Jadeanu finishes as he gets back up, now fully healed.

"Well you did flip out and lost control of your body in a vengeful pursuit," Luke points out. "Kinra. You heal him too okay," Will directs as he lays the stunt guy down and pops one of his broken bones back into place. "Yes sir," Kinra agrees. "So is there a way to end this convergence?" Luke asks. "There may be. You'll need help to get there though. I offer you the power to achieve just that. A power that already courses through you, but it needs to be heightened. You have strong passion, and you are worthy. You truly want to solve this; that is all you need to qualify you to gain what I have to give," Will explains as he walks with Jadeanu, Luke, and Kinra, leaving the healed stuntman to go home.

"Willpower drives you to venture forth and surpass your limitations. Your will to live kept you alive Jadeanu, and made you worthy. Yes, the fire within you and the generator of purpose. You understand more than your peers. You desire to end the Death Convergence, so your will creates a path. That is the divine force we have given to you humans. Power so vast, so destructive, yet so lively—the reason to exist and infinite power at your disposal. You two stay here. Jadeanu comes with me."

Will and Jadeanu separate from the others and enter an open field. "Now I am going to give you your gift." Will punches the ground, stands up, and motions his arms to open the cracks. Will and Jadeanu fall straight through the floor and down an incredibly long and dark tunnel through the Earth. Will stays perfectly calm and stationary, but Jadeanu's arms and skin are flailing uselessly as he decends. Tears run down his eyes, and sweat appears on him due to the intense heat of the inner Earth. Jadeanu nearly passes out but grasps hold of his inner will to enforce his consciousness. He summons red energy to his fingertips and shoves his fingers into the rocks around him to ease his way down just a little. Will glares at him with no emotion on his face.

They both fall into a cavern after a while. Will catches Jadeanu at the last second to prevent certain death. Jadeanu stands up and looks around at the beautiful scenery. Crystal clear waters and separate from that, lava coursing through in a swirling motion. In the middle of it all stands a stone structure resembling a shrine. The system has a small brown orb in its center. The globe has extreme energy surrounding it. Power so intense it felt almost godly.

"Sir? What is that?" Jadeanu gasps. "Your gift." Will reaches out with his hand, and the orb slowly flows to him like a magnet attracting another. "It is da Blessing of Willpower." "You mean the 7 Blessings exist? Physically? I was always informed of their universal power but thought it was just a metaphor." "They exist, I assure you." "I've read about them in the Chako. They're supposed to possess the power over the seven essentials of existence."

"They possess power **through** da seven essentials of existence. This is the power to command your will as it stands. You want ta fix everything. You will need da power of da Blessings ta do that. The downside is you can not touch the Blessings raw. The raw power of da Blessings will judge you and kill you if you are deemed unworthy ta wield them. You will need something spiritual and robust to hold the Blessings. Its aura alone will strengthen you, but it won't give you the power or wisdom you seek.

I suggest you cross over to Nevada. There is a rainforest there called Humboldt-Toiyabe. There, you will find Gibil, one of Nature's forge angels. With some of your assistance, you can help him create a weapon capable of harnessing the power of da Blessings. Until then, I will hold on ta this one for you. But first, I will have ta further test your dedication. Any questions on your mind before we proceed?"

"Yeah. Why was this Blessing hidden away? And what exactly do they mean to us humans?" "These Blessings have spiritual value. They are strengths given ta you but out of your reach due to a necessity for stability. They are like the great light, or as you'd call it, the sun. They affect you, yet there can be deadly consequences if you touch them. The Blessings were meant for humans and animals and all existing things. Kept just barely in reach with a consequence for the weak of spirit. But now, the world has weakened and grown chaotic. The same boundaries that protected them have been lifted, as have the margins of flesh and spirit."

"What does that mean?" "You're not the only one with access and will to possess these Blessings. With the ability to obtain power and the will to need it, other beings will be after them. Not all are worthy of handling them, but the ones that are, will be troublesome." "Okay, I think I get it. Now what is this test about?" "Let us go back to the surface first."

Will lifts his fingers, and a rock lifts under both guys' feet, pushing them back above ground. The ascension back up is fierce. The hot, damp wind smashes into Jadeanu's face, adding sweet and intense pressure to his body. A sensation much more damaging than his descension. He stands strong without a waver in his strength. Thus forth shows the power of the Blessing of Willpower's aura. Jadeanu and Will arrive at the surface shortly, planting their feet on the grass. Will observes the change in Jadeanu's spirit and how his progressive determination shows itself in his lively eyes.

"Now Jadeanu. I want you to fight me again. But this time, you will be strengthened by this," Will suggests holding his Blessing. "May I touch it?" Jadeanu asks. "Only to test yourself." Jadeanu hesitantly moves toward the orb of Willpower. He slowly wraps his fingers around it and clinches. The overwhelming power instantly engulfs his hand. "Aauugh!" Jadeanu cries out in pain as the light brown power moves through his veins. The energy then slows its way through Jadeanu's body. He releases the orb and holds his dominant hand (his right hand) with his other due to the burning sensation. The energy quickly evaporates from his arm, and the pain goes with it. Jadeanu's arm looks precisely as it always does. Perfectly fine, as if nothing happened.

Will picks up the Blessing. "You cannot handle this yet. But you are strong enough ta temporarily wield its power. If you were like the average man, you would have nearly died. Congratulations, but I will leave it here as we fight." Will creates a pillar of rock that launches from the ground to hold the Blessing. A brown aura consumes Will's body as he stands still, staring at Jadeanu, who switches to a martial arts combat stance.

"Begin!" Will yells, and Jadeanu immediately taps into his power to strengthen his legs as he darts full speed toward Will. He quickly switches the power to his hands and swings at his opponent.

'So I can only power up two parts of my body at a time. Okay.'

Will dodges the attack, causing Jadeanu to counter with a kick. Will moves his rather bulky body swiftly with a precise evasion.

Jadeanu quickly recovers and throws a sweep kick. Will jumps over it and descends with his fist aimed at Jadeanu. He slams his fist into the ground as Jadeanu rolls away. Jadeanu jumps to his feet and flurries with several attacks. All blocked perfectly by Will. Will attacks, but Jadeanu barely dodges it and counters. Will catches his fist and hits him directly in the nose. Jadeanu staggers from the blow as blood runs out of his nose and mouth. He nearly falls but stops his descension with his hands and picks himself up.

"Jadeanu!" Luke calls. "Hold on. I'm coming for you!"

"Let them be," Kinra reassures.

"Allow them to settle this like men, even if it turns out bad. I don't know why they're fighting, but I'm sure Will doesn't intend to kill Jadeanu. We'll just have to be patient. If he calls for us, we jump in."

'I can't go down. Not again. I have to win!' Jadeanu thinks.

'How can I help the world if I can't stand this? I won't let myself lose, no matter how hard I get hit. I'll just keep getting back up!'

Jadeanu attacks and Will dodges and counters, hitting Jadeanu square in his jaw. A greater stream of thick red liquid flows from Jadeanu's face. Jadeanu attacks a few more times but all to no avail, thanks to Will's efficient dodging. Will closes in with an uppercut. Jadeanu jumps back but not far enough. Will's knuckle slams into the bottom of Jadeanu's stomach. The knuckle pierces through his belly as it travels up his chest till it reaches his chin. The impact of the hit creates an invisible shockwave of energy traveling through the field, slightly blowing everything back, even blowing Kinra and Luke's hair. Jadeanu falls with no emotion in his still wide-open eyes.

Will picks him up, grasps the Blessing of Willpower, and waves it in his face. Jadeanu jolts up with violent energy. "So you see. You have duh Willpower, but you let it control you rather than controlling it," Willpower explains.

"I am a god, young one. I am eternal and unpunishable. You can never defeat me. Deep down inside, you already knew that. Yet you show promise. You have been strengthened by just the aura of the Blessing and me. Find an instrument capable of wielding the Blessing and return to me. Then it shall be yours."

"Thank you sir! I won't let you down," Jadeanu expresses. "I know you won't, but don't do it for me. Do it because you are obligated to yourself and the events that lead you to this path. You must make the decisions you know won't eat away at your conscience. Have no regrets on your path. That is how you unlock the key to your Willpower."

"Okay, I'll note that. And by the way Will, our car was destroyed when you hit that guy over that building. How exactly do you suppose we make it to Nevada and back, considering we're in Texas?"

"Ya have strong legs. A long healthy walk will build character and a greater appreciation for the journey ahead. Things will get dangerous, but danger and pain stimulate growth, which will be necessary for your adventure. Some things happen for a reason. It is a good practice to sometimes ride with those things."

Jadeanu nods and walks back over to Luke and Kinra. Luke hands Jadeanu back his wedding ring, which Jadeanu puts back on his finger.

"Kinra! Can you heal me?"

"Sure."

As Kinra puts his healing hands on Jadeanu, Luke begins to question. "What was all that about? Why did he beat you up again?"

"It was a test. We're going to Nevada. There is a rainforest there known as Humboldt-Toiyabe. Once inside, we'll find an angel named Gibil. He can craft a weapon capable of wielding that." Jadeanu points at the Blessing. "I touched that. It has immense power that we'll finally need to take revenge for this thing."

"What thing?" "The whole life/death convergence." "Oh yeah. Wait, how are we supposed to get to Nevada from here?"

"We can find a way. Someone's got to have a car, and if we're lucky, we might find a pilot and an airport or something. Either way, we just have to go with what we have. As of now, our best bet is to find Ricardio. He isn't far from here."

"Agreed. Come on Kinra. We're visiting an old friend of ours." Jadeanu stands up and gauges the vicinity. "Ricardio's home is in that direction. It won't be a far walk."

The three of them begin walking in the direction of Ricardio. The sounds of their footsteps crashing against the concrete road fill the air. Jadeanu passes by an alley and looks down the dark, sinister corridor. A middle-aged man is rummaging through some garbage bins. He stops and violently moves to look at Jadeanu with his neon-red eyes. Jadeanu gets startled and moves slightly further away from the alley. "Ugh. This Death Convergence is horrible," he whispers as they pass the passage.

"That would happen even without the convergence. But I still agree with you," Luke empathizes. "But I think it shows the inner you. You can't mask your desires anymore. The law doesn't govern us now either. We're completely free to do as we want. Now the question is where that freedom gets us."

Jadeanu, Luke, and Kinra walk past the last few houses in the area. Beyond that is a small fence dividing the city from a vast forest on a downward slope.

"There it is," Jadeanu points at a small house in the middle of the woods. "How about we make a shortcut?" Jadeanu suggests.

"You thinking what I'm thinking?" Luke reassures. "Of course I am! What we've always thought would be cool since we were kids," Jadeanu answers.

"After all, we are free, and we have these crazy powers. Why not do some crazy things? Kinra! Grab on to my back and don't let go."

Kinra does as he is commanded. "You ready?" Jadeanu asks.

Luke nods, and Jadeanu strengthens his legs with energy and jumps tremendously high toward the bulk of the forest. Immediately after, Luke blasts off in a more guided sense than his younger brother using his gaseous blue energy as fuel. He latches onto Jadeanu's leg and provides a more guided movement to him.

"Whoooo! Yeah! This is great!" Kinra shouts with a broad smile across his face as the intense wind from the descent slaps his and the other boys' faces.

"I know right!" Jadeanu agrees.

As they near the trees, Jadeanu takes the lead and extends his power-infused hand to grab a tree to weaken their fall. Hesitantly yet bravely, Jadeanu presses his fingers into a tree trunk. Wood and leaves break off and fly everywhere as they quickly fall. Towards the end of the descent, Jadeanu firmly grasps the tree and pushes off of it, thus breaking it in half with his superhuman strength.

Luke lands on his feet first, then comes Jadeanu and Kinra. Jadeanu lets Kinra down from his back, and they all collect themselves before continuing. Jadeanu looks at the fallen tree and then at his hand. "Wow, this is all so cool." Out of nowhere, a few wolves coated in grey fur run out to them due to sensing the disturbance of their habitat. The leader of the pack has red eyes, similar to Jadeanu's. He growls and lets out a sharp beam from his mouth.

Jadeanu narrowly dodges it, and the trees behind him that are hit all burst into flames. "The Death Convergence affects animals too?" Jadeanu complains. A startling blunt noise sounds from behind him, followed by a slightly rusty voice saying,

"Get on!"

The wolves immediately run away. Jadeanu looks to where the noise had come from and sees a bearded man with a gun. "Ricardio!"

Chapter 3:

Another God Is Near

Ricardio is an average-height man with a somewhat athletic and masculine figure. He has white skin, emerald green eyes, a short-boxed beard, and straight brown hair dangling near his shoulders.

Luke runs up to him and hugs him. He's glad to see him after a long time. It has been years.

"Long time no see Ricardio," Luke says, with a glimmer in his eyes and a big smile on his face.

"Sure has been. It's good to see...that you've gotten a lot taller. How's it been for you Luke?" Ricardio asks.

"A heck of an adventure but good, for me at least," Luke answers as he lets go of his friend. "Good to hear. Yo, Jadeanu, what's up with ya?"

"It's been rough, but hopefully things will improve."

"Heaven knows what you've just been through. Things aren't so great for me either. But they kept us alive and brought us together after all this time, so focus on what's good. Now are you gonna introduce me to your little friend?"

"This is Kinra. He's with us on an adventure, and we're gonna need your help too."

"Then let's go inside. It's much safer if we chat there instead of outside for the wolves to come back."

Ricardio leads everyone into his small home, which isn't far behind him. He opens the door, then closes it, and locks it once everyone is inside.

"I've had to deal with more wolves than usual today. Whatever's happened out there has made them a lot more violent. And it seems that they got some superpowers too," he says, looking at everyone in the room.

"Having one of those wolves could be quite handy for us," Kinra suggests.

"You don't want one of those," Ricardio assures.

"They want to kill everything in this forest. Trying to tame one of them is a suicide mission waiting to happen, especially with their new abilities. You three also were affected by this chaos fest considering your eye colors?"

"Yeah, that's why we're here," Luke responds.

"Remember that girl we kept teasing Jadeanu about for being so scared of talking to back in high school?" Luke asks Ricardio with a smirk on his face.

"Yeah," Ricardio looks at him, slightly confused.

"Her name was Tierla or something, right? You were head over heels in love, weren't you?" hearing those words only makes Jadeanu sad.

"Well, he managed to find his way into her heart. Their wedding was today, and as you can guess, it turned into a bloodbath. Tierla has passed away, and we want to get to the bottom of this situation and see if we can end it," Luke says.

"So you lost your wife too," Ricardio says, sympathizing.

"Too? You don't mean…." Jadeanu asks, confused.

"Yep. My beloved Annabelle is deceased as well."

Ricardio leads the others to his guest bedroom. There lies the motionless corpse of Ricardio's wife. Jadeanu stares with intensity in his eyes. Luke and Kinra's widen with sympathy. "We were just cooking dinner together, and she just fell. She no longer had a pulse, and I didn't know what to do or what to think. I was just so confused and angry. I later turned on my TV and figured it was happening everywhere without discrimination. I started to feel lucky that I survived, but I would rather it had been me instead of her. I just really want her back. Surely if something was able to kill her so quickly, there must be a way to get her back just as fast. I want nothing more than just that."

Ricardio becomes silent at this point, lowering his head, and staring at the floor mindlessly.

"I can understand that. Today has taken a heavy toll, believe me," Jadeanu suggests. "But listen. I know this may sound weird, but we are living in a conjoinment of life and death. There may be a way to reverse it if we can find who's responsible. We were hoping you would have any information about that."

"That means there's a chance I can get Annabelle back."

"Do you really think that's possible?" "Yeah. As I've said, if something could kill so easily, there should also be something to revive."

"That's great! I didn't even think of that! I've thought of stopping the spread of these horrors, but to be able to completely rewind its effects, that sounds too good to be true!" Jadeanu exclaims.

"I heard there was a lot of commotion up far north," Ricardio admits.

"People say they've found someone compelling and has power over life and death itself. People seem to think he's responsible for all this, but no one's been able to silence him yet. That's all I know about that whole thing."

"He may be a god," Luke whispers.

"Good. We have a start," Jadeanu says.

"Ricardio, we're on our way to Nevada. If we're going to stop something that powerful, we're going to need a weapon capable of harnessing great power.

We'll need help crafting such a weapon. Then we can move up north."

"You're in luck. I know a blacksmith that lives in Nevada. He lives in a forest there as well. But how are we gonna get there?"

"I was hoping you would have a car or something."

"Nope. Mine got destroyed by those cursed wolves."

"I guess we'll just have to walk. We can only depend on technology for some things. It's time for us to use our manpower," Jadeanu advises.

"But it's a little late, so I hope this can wait 'till tomorrow," Ricardio says.

"We've all been through a lot today. Some sleep is good for the mind. We'll need to rest up for this adventure. I don't have any unused beds, so I hope y'all are okay with sleeping on the couch or floor. I've got other blankets," Kinra takes the couch while Jadeanu and Luke sleep on the floor.

Morning comes around, and Ricardio is the first one to wake up. He leaves his squeaky, old wooden bed and quietly goes to the kitchen. He begins cooking something, and Jadeanu wakes up to the slight noise of pots moving around.

"Ahh. Something smells good," he says. Luke then wakes quietly, merely opening his eyes.

"I hope y'all eat deer steak and toast," Ricardio reveals his plans for breakfast. "I know y'all on healthy diets and stuff. I was just making what I had in my fridge."

"It's fine," Luke answers.

"Oh Luke. I didn't realize you were up," Jadeanu responds, slightly startled.

"I didn't think we'd wake up so early," Luke replies as he sits up.

"I always wake up this early, plus we should get on the road as quickly as possible," Ricardio adds.

"So once we eat, we head for Nevada?" Jadeanu questions.

"Yeah."

"Hate to be the one to say this, but how will we get to Nevada by foot? We have no idea where to go," Luke worries.

"We'll just have to try to find or ask for directions as frequently as possible," Ricardio answers. "Not the best idea, but it might be all we have," Jadeanu responds. Luke walks over to Kinra and shakes him until he wakes up.

"Wake up. We're leaving soon. Freshen up, then we'll eat," he commands.

So it is done. They freshen up and use tree bark to brush their teeth, seeing as they did not have any toothbrushes available. After that, they have breakfast and are set on their way. Ricardio grabs his trusty bow and arrow and quiver from a closet in his room.

"Um, okay, where to now?" Luke demands. Jadeanu shrugs. "Well my house is toward the northeast of Texas, so we should go West of my house. Our best bet is to find civilization over there." "Wait, you don't know where civilization is from here?" Jadeanu questions.

"Nope. I've rarely had a reason to leave here up until now."

"Well that's just great. That's why you couldn't come to my wedding?"

"Nope. I just had no idea you were getting married. And you know I'm a traditional man, so I don't use that social media stuff."

"Well none of that matters now. We just got to get out of here," Luke interrupts.

"You're right. Let's get moving," Ricardio mumbles. As the four of them move westward in the wilderness, Kinra's curiosity springs.

"So how long have you guys known each other?" he asks. "I met Ricardio when I was in 5th grade. I was ten at the time. He was a bit of a nerd back then, but he was also so resourceful that anyone who tried to bully him because of it was always at a loss. I wanted to learn a few things from him, and I didn't like that some people were so mean to him, so I helped divert the negative attention. We've been friends ever since," Luke answers.

"I met him soon after Luke. He introduced me to him. But I was only seven in the second grade at the time," Jadeanu replies.

"Even though they were much older than me, we all still bonded well."

"Yep, that was long ago. I'm 28 now. That means we've known each other for 18 years," Ricardio finishes. "We ended up being less involved with each other after high school. I was always a bit of a hermit, and I wanted an isolated life to focus on my craft as a mechanic."

Several minutes pass of just walking through the greenery of the forest, further talking about their past experiences.

"And when I returned, Francis was acting all high and mighty. Trying to belittle Ricardio," Luke mentions. "I'll never forget what Ricardio said to him. *I have several sharp items in my pocket, personal friends of mine on the way, and there's a chair right behind you, making it easy to throw you off balance. You don't want to do this.'* The look on Francis's face was priceless."

"But it didn't take long for Francis and Ricardio to become friends," Jadeanu states. "He just needed to know that Ricardio was not someone to take lightly."

"Hahaha. Yeah, that Francis sure was a troublemaker," Ricardio claims. "But he eventually-"

Suddenly a strange guy pops out of nowhere. He seems to be running for his life toward the boys. Sweat decorates his body, and he breathes heavily though persisting anyway. "Watch yourselves!" Ricardio calls out. Luke steps in front of the "ready to strike" Ricardio and yells, "Hey! Stop! What's wrong?"

The man stops reluctantly and puts his hands on his knees as sweat beads fall from his face. The man is a tall, lanky white guy with bushy brows and a slightly large nose. His eyes also don't glow with any mystical power.

"Is there civilization that way?" Ricardio asks.

"Yes, but you shouldn't go that way!" the man answers. "A demon or a foul spirit is lurking there! Anyone who looks at it ends up committing suicide. But you'll never know it's coming until it's too late; unless you feel its strange heat."

"That sounds oddly familiar," Luke claims.

"Then we just won't look at it, " Jadeanu says. "It's not as easy as you think. If you're headed to civilization, I suggest you go around the long way. But even that won't guarantee that you'll avoid it. Anyway, go kill yourselves if you want. I'm not going to end up like my previous deceased group." The man catches his breath and walks away.

"I should warn you that there are bloodthirsty wolves that way. They don't like people in their territory," Ricardio informs.

"Just wanted to return the courtesy of warning you as you warned us."

"Wolves? They aren't strengthened by the Death Spiral by any chance?" the man asks.

"The pack leader can cut down trees with as little as a growl."

The man swallows in nervous fear.

"It would suck for someone who isn't armed to run into them," Ricardio continues. "You could try to go around them and get lucky, but that doesn't guarantee you'll avoid them. Of course, you could come with us. We could help you get back home or to a place safer than here. In exchange, you'll just have to help us get past that demon or whatever it is. Think about it. You could get lost and killed by wolves trying to find your own way. Or you could be guarded and keep your eyes closed long enough to ensure you get back home. Your choice. You got away from the monster before. You can do it again."

"Fine, I'll go with you. But only because one death sounds more painful than the other," the man retorts.

"Great! What's your name?" Luke asks.

"Stougma Tergity."

"I'm Luke Stroyem."

"I'm Jadeanu Stroyem. We're brothers," says Jadeanu.

"And I'm Ricardio Riveras."

"Since we'll be traveling together, you should get familiar with our names," Luke concludes. "Yeah, whatever. Let's just please survive this," Stougma adds.

"So you've been running in a straight line all this time right?" Ricardio asks.

"Yeah I think so," Stougma answers.

"Then civilization is that way." Ricardio leads the others in the direction of seeming danger.

"Hey young one, you never introduced yourself," Stougma speaks to Kinra. "I'm Kinra Willfree." "You seem awfully young Kinra. Just how old are you?" "Thirteen." "Wow! So young. I hope you've lived a full life cause-" "Stougma! Just stop," Luke defends. "If only you knew what you were up against," Stougma continues. "Why are yall heading for town anyway? Surely it's safer to be in a place less occupied by people. At least that's what my old crew members thought."

"We're actually headed to Nevada...by foot. We'll need directions to ensure a quick and easy journey," Luke explains. "All the way to Nevada? Why? What could be worth risking your time, energy and life by going there?" "It's a bit complicated. But we're trying to find a way to stop or reverse this so-called Death Spiral," Jadeanu elaborates. "What we'll need to do that is in Nevada." "Good luck with that." All five adventurers continue walking through the bulk of the woods then suddenly, they feel an overwhelming presence, similar to the presence of Willpower. "That's it! That's the monster! Everyone close your eyes!" Stougma yells.

Everyone does as he says. "Come on and grab hands everyone. We're less likely to take a peek or get lost if we hold on to each other," Ricardio strategizes. "Just keep going straight." The so-called monster is a bright yellow light, so even with their eyes closed, they could tell where it was.

"Guys. It's whispering to me. It feels so wrong for me not to look at it," Kinra starts to panic. "I'm getting the whispers too. Try to block them out, even if it's hard to resist. You know what happens if we don't keep our wits about us," Ricardio adds. As the guys all move through the area in unison, all but Stougma seem to be struggling to not take a look at the thing.

As they pass by the light monster, Jadeanu receives a distinct whisper, gaining his full attention. His eyes remain sealed shut, but alas, his eyelids gradually weaken. "Maybe just a squint. What do I have to lose?" Jadeanu reasons as his eyelids open slightly, revealing only part of his eyes. The light immediately travels into his eyes. He remains squinting. "It...it's b-beautiful." "Jadeanu! Noo!" Luke shouts in the realization of what is occurring.

He separates his hand from being interlocked with Jadeanu's and uses it as a shield for his brother's eyes. Luke's eyes remain shut throughout the whole situation. Jadeanu swats the hand away from his eyes. "I see it now. You're not a demon or some sort of monster..... You're an angel," Jadeanu realizes as he shuts his eyes again and continues walking with the others.

They each only open their eyes when they feel concrete under their shoes and no longer feel the presence of the light creature's heat. "Yes! I made it out alive!" Stougma rejoices. "Jadeanu! You're alive! I guess that monster wasn't as dangerous as we thought," Luke relieves. "It wasn't a monster! It was an angel!" Jadeanu says with a tempered tone. "Okay, angel. Sorry," Luke apologizes.

"Yeah right! Like an angel would kill all my friends," Stougma disbelieves. Jadeanu's eyebrows arch. "I saw what it was with my own eyes! I'm the only one who did that without dying! I know what he is, and you will NOT disrespect him in my presence! Just because you're a coward doesn't mean you should judge things greater than you as foul! You understand!?" Stougma trembles in a newfound fear of Jadeanu. All the others give shocked expressions at what they hear.

"Jadeanu, what exactly did you see?" Luke asks. "I don't really know. It was so much information. All I felt was an overwhelming sense of beauty from it. But I'm sure of what it was," Jadeanu answers. "Well that doesn't matter now. You're alive, and that's what matters," says Ricardio. "Well we're in the city. Where is your home Stougma?" "Far up ahead. We should keep walking together till we get there. And even then, home isn't safe either, but I guess it's all I have. I just wish I knew that before my former allies got killed looking for a safe place." "The guilt must be horrible, but all I can say is that it's best to move forward. You'll find something else. Just don't let it get you down," Luke advises. "Let's go."

The five walk the streets watching the world plunge into chaos. People with powers rampaging and vandalizing property. Even severe cases of panicked theft. Jadeanu stops walking before reaching a substantial two-story church. "Huh. What's wrong?" Luke concerns. "Look," Jadeanu responds, pointing at the small balcony at the church's top. There is a man with red eyes holding another by the neck.

"You are a disgrace, not worthy of serving me anymore," the man holding the other says. "That's my boss, Mishu Herman. And that other guy is my coworker, Ren Torilase," Jadeanu reveals. "We all used to work in the same building before this Death Convergence. Now we're probably all out of a job." "You are a waste of space!" Mishu yells as Ren flies headfirst into the concrete in front of the others in Jadeanu's group.

"Hey Mr. Herman!" Jadeanu cries. "You shouldn't do that to your workers." "You all don't work for me anymore. At least, not the way you used to. I will take over this city and force all within it to bend to me. You were always one of my more efficient workers because of the way you think. But you hold yourself back with compassion. I know what kind of man you are, so I know you'll try and stop me. If you do, I'm afraid I will terminate you from my rule and your life," Mishu responds.

Jadeanu jumps straight to the balcony as Mishu walks mockingly inside the church through its double doors. The doors immediately and unnaturally close shut with extensive force. Jadeanu attempts to open them, but they won't budge. He kicks and punches the doors, but nothing happens. Somehow even his super strength isn't able to make a difference."Crap."

Luke rockets up to the balcony. "He forced the doors shut," Jadeanu says. "Jadeanu, he's just a distraction. He's not in our way.

You don't have to fight him." "I know, but he's horrible and has horrible intentions. You saw that. He needs to be punished, and now I can legally hurt him. Plus, we could use the practice to become more familiar with our powers. We can learn a few things for our mission while taking out a bully all in one. I say it's a win-win." "Well, if you're set on beating him up, let's do it," Luke supports him with a mischievous smile.

Jadeanu smiles as he backflips off the balcony, sticks the landing in a lunging position, and uses his power to accelerate directly into the front door of the church, thus busting it open. "Was that really necessary? You could have broken through the wall at the top," Luke responds as he rockets down from the balcony and walks into the seemingly vacant temple.

"What are you guys doing?" Ricardio demands. "We'll teach this Mishu guy a lesson real quick," Luke answers. Ren gets up and rushes over to Jadeanu. "You're gonna fight Mr. Herman?" he asks. "Yep!" Jadeanu replies. "Take me with you. I just tried to get my last check from him, and after that, I was gonna join him in taking over the city. You saw what happened with that though. I've got a family you know. I needed that paycheck to help support them, but now I'm just going to have to kill him and take it."

"You shouldn't kill him, even if that's what he deserves. But what you decide to do is up to you. May I ask what kind of powers you have?" "I can manipulate shadows...well, erm...it's kinda hard to explain." "Good enough for me. It's good to have another fighter on our team." "Stougma! You should stay behind," Luke advises. "Ricardio, Kinra. You two can stay or come. Up to you." "Well I'm not going to leave you behind," Ricardio insists. "Uh, yea." Kinra agrees. "Yeah, um. I'll just be out here," Stougma clarifies.

Jadeanu takes the lead and walks deeper into the church. The entrance is big and mostly empty. The floor is made of blue tiles, and the air is cold. Jadeanu surveys the place with his eyes and soon notices a man with a hat on, who's been chilling in a chair toward the back of the room, just in front of a door the whole time, without bringing attention to his existence.

"So you guys are here for Mr. Herman," the man says. "I'm sorry, but that can't happen." The man takes his hat off and tosses it into the room behind him through a large crack. He stands up with his hair all over his face and has very casual yet somewhat professional clothing. His body lights up orange, and his hair begins to stand up and sway around, revealing his reddish orange eyes. He pumps his fists forward and puts them together. His body's orange light pulses twice. "Pyro canon mark 2!" An orange blast of sheer energy fires from his fists.

Jadeanu moves out of the way of the blast, leaving it to slam directly into the others. The explosion consumes them all, erasing them from sight. Jadeanu takes an angle on the glowing man. He closes in as the glowing man stops firing, puts a hand in front of Jadeanu, and blasts him away with a much weaker and smaller burst.

Once the smoke clears from the last blast, Luke can be seen in the front of the group with a large shield with cracks in it. Luke relaxes his muscles, and the shield disappears. Just then, a whistle of wind passes through the room as the door behind the glowing man opens, spilling multiple sheets of paper into the room. The papers then magically gather and form into a whole person wearing ninjalike garments. The only skin present on him is the skin around his red eyes.

"Okay, so we've got Paper Ninja and Blast," Jadeanu jokes as he stands back up and runs for an offensive refund on who he calls Blast. Paper Ninja dashes in his way and kicks him in the face. Ren makes his shadow grab onto his own feet and skates forward, extending a spike made of tangible shadow ahead of himself. The guy nicknamed Blast, looks at him and pumps his fist forward, gripping his own shoulder with his other hand. His energy pulses as he says, "Mark 1."

A blast engulfs Ren and pushes him away. Ren falls to a kneel with steam radiating off of him. Luke shoots his gas energy balls at Blast, who reciprocates with equally powerful beams. Luke charges up a beam, and Blast prepares a Mark 2 cannon blast for the incoming attack. They fire their attacks around the same time. The two energies oppose one another with the beautiful sight of wrestling blue and orange energies fighting to progress themselves before exploding.

Jadeanu punches at Paper Ninja, who retreats into sheets of paper and moves behind Jadeanu with a counterattack. Jadeanu swings quickly behind in an attempt to land a hit on Paper Ninja, who returns to paper and moves again. Frustration fills Jadeanu, so he claws at the moving paper with enhanced power. He rips one of the sheets of paper, and Paper Ninja reforms with blood streaming from his arm. Jadeanu takes the opportunity to return a kick to Paper Ninja's face. Blood flies from his mouth as he is sent flying from the impact. He catches himself on his feet and then returns to paper form to move back in. Ricardio draws his bow with 3 arrows at a time and fires: piercing through three sheets of paper. Paper Ninja instantly reforms and there is an arrow in his arm, chest, and stomach with blood teeming out. "That's it! He's just paper when he's like that," Ricardio announces.

Luke, Ren, and Blast all initiate close combat. Ren jumps up with a shadow spike at his front. Blast quickly beams him away. Luke closes in, shooting balls of gas from point-blank range. Blast disengages the balls with counter beams of his own. He also dodges some and blocks Luke's inclosing hands. Blast finds an opening and beams Luke away.

Ren comes back in with more spikes but this time on his fists. He throws a punch; Blast evades it and fiercely sweeps Ren off his feet with a kick. Immediately, he presses both of his fists into Ren's stomach and blasts him diagonally into the church's roof. Blast directs his fists toward the ground and rockets into the air while spinning swiftly. He begins charging up his next Pyro cannon. Luke propels toward Blast as he utters, "Mark 2." He fires his beam as Luke creates a barrier around himself. The barrier cracks as it is pushed back toward the ground. Once the blast depletes, Luke continues rocketing while in his bubble toward Blast.

Paper Ninja's arms separate into papers and forcefully motion towards Jadeanu.

"You see. You're just paper," Jadeanu laughs in pity as he keeps slicing through the sheets with ease using only his supercharged fingers. Paper Ninja reforms. "Your powers are useful for being discreet and slipping away from situations but not very helpful in fighting. *I'm guessing your effective previous spirit must have been an introvert and liked being able to slip under the radar.'*

Jadeanu closes in with a side-flip kick. Paper Ninja returns to paper in an attempt to get away. He is shot with another arrow and returns to his human self.

"Goodnight!" Jadeanu quotes as he kicks Paper Ninja so hard that his head wrap flies off, revealing his short gray and black spiked hair. His red eyes ease into their native brown color as his eyelids close, and he drifts from consciousness.

Blast and Luke clash energies and burst away from each other.

"Okay, that's it. Boss Herman told me not to do this in the church, but I've got to defeat you. He'd be madder if you succeed," Blast says. He charges up once again and pulses three times.

"Mark 3. Pyro cannon full power." Blast fires an enormous explosion at Luke, who tries to rocket away.

Kinra, Ricardio, and all the others had already moved to where Jadeanu was, behind Blast and near the door guarding the church's interior. Luke deploys a bubble and takes the full power of the Blast. His bubble breaks quickly, and he flows with the current of energy. The explosion continues and breaks through the church wall and into the city. Luke's body lies on the scraped-up temple floor when the carnage clears. His body is covered in ash and burns with steam flying off of it. Kinra runs up to him and calls his name. "It's okay. My...s-shield k-kept me alive," Luke reassures with a soft raspy voice. Kinra immediately starts healing him.

Jadeanu's eyes gaze at the scene with emptiness. Blast starts charging up another beam. Jadeanu instantly rages and presses his feet into the ground to gain an extra boost as he starts running full speed at Blast. He leaves a deep footprint in the rocks under the tile floor. Blast turns toward Jadeanu and fires a Mark 1 beam. Jadeanu adds energy to his hand as he blocks the shockwave with it and advances.

"What!?" Blast exclaims as Jadeanu approaches and kicks him in the face. Blast spits out blood from the impact, yet he readjusts fast enough to attack again. He fires a normal blast. Jadeanu blocks and claws at Blast, ripping the flesh from his chest with his fingers.

"Jadeanu's going to kill him," Ricardio notices. "So what!?" Ren blurts out. "We don't kill people for no reason!" Kinra rages.

"No reason? He tried to kill us."

"True, but in the end his efforts are justified. We attacked them. We don't have to kill, so we won't, and that's that," Luke says, feeling much better yet still lying on the ground.

"He works for Boss Herman and kills whoever enters here. He's a horrible person and he needs to die," Ren persists. "You only say that because he beat you up," Kinra teases.

"Whatever brat."

Ren then summons spikes and runs after Blast, who is still overwhelmed by Jadeanu.

Jadeanu throws a punch at Blast, who then shoots a beam to accelerate the movement of his hand into an effective backhand to deflect Jadeanu's attack. Ren comes from behind and slices Blast's stomach from an angle. They both relaunch an attack. Suddenly Ren and Jadeanu are both hit by blue balls of gas, and they lose their attacking momentum and fall to the ground. Luke is now sitting up.

Kinra helps him stand all the way up. Jadeanu returns to his senses and stands up. He and Luke both walk up to Blast. "I've failed. If you're gonna kill me, you should go ahead and do it," he says. "Is that how he has you think of yourself? You should consider joining us instead," Jadeanu reasons.

"Hahaha. No. I've caused you too much trouble as it is. I don't deserve to join you all. Plus I'm not gonna go die fighting against the boss."

"Okay then, we'll just go up ahead."

Jadeanu takes his leave and begins walking through the inner church door. "What if he ambushes us?" Ren worries.

"Good thought. You can knock him out if you think he may be dangerous," Jadeanu responds. Ren creates a fist with his shadow and knocks Blast unconscious. "And yet we never got their names," Luke jests.

They enter the church interior, and there is only a circular staircase leading to the upper level of the place. Jadeanu leads everyone up the stairs quietly. There is no noise other than the squeaking of the old stairs. There's a huge door blocking the staircase from the top floor room. Jadeanu opens the door and enters a room with a bunch of benches in rows split into two columns. At the end of the room stands Mishu, staring straight at Jadeanu.

"You sure have caused a lot of trouble Jadeanu. You even made my subordinate destroy a part of my temple," Mishu says.

"I'll have to punish him for that. I don't kill him only because I'll need him." "You jerk! How could you be so narcissistic!" Jadeanu yells as he speeds forward toward Mishu.

Mishu slowly lifts up his hand, and Jadeanu halts in his tracks.

"You're one to talk about narcissism. I know you look down on weaklings like Ren," Mishu concludes as he tenses his hand, somehow making Jadeanu fly back toward his allies.

"Did you just call me weak!? I'll kill you!" Ren yells as he makes skates from his shadow and moves toward Mishu. He spawns shadow spikes on his fists and advances. He suddenly halts as well. "It's no use," Mishu calmly foretells. Ren instantly flies uncontrollably into the air and falls down onto the benches.

Luke starts firing gas balls at Mishu, and even the balls freeze in the air.

"What? He can even move my energy balls with his mind. But they're not even-" Luke gets cut off when one of his energy balls flies back to him. Mishu forces a ball to hit Luke, Ren, and then Kinra. Ricardio decides it's best for him to slowly back away from the fight as he wouldn't be much help. So that's what he does. Jadeanu grabs Luke by his arm, and they both charge Mishu together. Kinra joins them, and Ren approaches from the side. Mishu prepares himself.

Ren is sent slamming into the side of the church. Jadeanu flies up and hits the ceiling. Luke and Kinra hit the floor and continue to be crushed downward by Mishu's telekinetic force.

"You know the thing about narcissism. It's just a matter of realizing and practicing your obvious superiority over others," Mishu explains. He forces Luke and Kinra down even harder.

"Aaahh! He's crushing my insides!" Kinra howls. "It's all a matter of collective judgment based on your character. With the obvious facts here, it is clear that I am better than you. All of you."

Luke manages to muster enough strength to shoot an unsuspecting gas ball at Mishu, who dodges it but releases Luke and Kinra in the process.

Kinra takes multiple deep breaths.

"Maybe greater than us in power. But you sure as heck aren't better," Luke replies.

Ren stands up and prepares to charge again. Mishu lifts up multiple beaches and slams all of them on top of Ren. He mentally shatters a vast glass window above the balcony door behind himself. He shoots all the sharp shards at Luke and Kinra. Luke deploys his shield. The glass shatters on impact with Luke's shield. With the rest of the fragments, he fires them at Jadeanu.

"You know all about my narcissism, don't you Jadeanu?"

Jadeanu can't manage to dodge all the shards but guards his face with his powered-up hands. He takes multiple lacerations across the rest of his body. "That's why you're staying silent, isn't it," Mishu teases.

"Why do you think I was so quick to promote you when the opportunity arrived. I know how you look down on your peers for their inadequacies. You understood the true nature of power over others. The absolution of it shrouded over those unworthy."

Ren breaks through all the benches with an eruption of shadowy energy. Next, he attaches himself to his shadow on the ground as if they were sown together, and he silently creeps closer to Mishu. Glass continues attacking Jadeanu and Luke while Ren manages to get close to Mishu as he extends a shadow spike at him. Mishu calmly and casually places his hand out and pauses the spike's movement, then redirects the spike to face Ren.

The spike travels toward him as he attempts to resist it, but his powers are weaker than Mishu's, so the spike continues toward him slowly. Fear consumes Ren at the sight of his fate lying in front of him and how horribly his plan is backfiring.

Suddenly an explosion erupts on Mishu, sending him flying back into a wall. Ren regains control of his shadow, and Luke and Jadeanu stop getting pelted with glass. They all look behind them and notice Stougma standing there at the entry door with his eyes colored with a red glow. "Stougma!? You have powers?" Luke claims.

"You see, Mishu. Being narcissistic and thinking highly of yourself doesn't mean you should treat people weaker than you are badly. You just don't know when they may come through for you," Jadeanu states.

"There's nothing wrong with looking down on others, that's just a part of evaluation. We all do it. Some are better at it than others. It's about how you use the judgement instead of running from it. But it's still always better for everyone to treat each other with respect and empathy. That alone would have stopped you from getting your butt kicked." Mishu stands back up with blood on his forehead and a furious expression.

"You say that like you've won! You're gonna die just like the rest of you," Mishu rages as he immediately uses his powers.

He recycles the glass shards scattered around the place and surrounds Stougma with them. The shards all mysteriously combust on Stougma's command. "Oh, I see. Stougma's power is telepathic combustion? That's freakin cool," Luke analyzes. "Can this guy blow stuff up with his mind?" Ren contemplates.

'A mind vs. mind battle. Mishu can't control Stougma's mental attacks. It's perfect,' Luke thinks. Mishu halts Stougma's movement and lifts him in the air, crushing his neck with his telekinesis. Stougma causes one more explosion directly upon Mishu, launching him into the wall.

Smoke houses the area, and when it clears, Mishu is seen sitting, leaning against the wall with his face painted red with blood. Stougma falls on his feet and is once again able to breathe just fine. "Okay that's enough! If you do it again, he'll die!" Luke reasons.

"So what? If you don't kill him, I will!" Ren yells.

He adds spikes to his hands and speeds toward Mishu. He then stops suddenly and is launched to the back of the church. "I guess his powers still work," Jadeanu claims. "I hope you learned something about goodwill. Stop being such an oppressive jerk."

"Jadeanu, you're hurt," Kinra says. "It's fine. We'll get out of here first, then you can heal Ren. And after that, you can heal me."

Jadeanu and all the others leave the rundown church, passing by Blast, and Paper Ninja, who are still unconscious, and finally looking back at the giant hole in the building and the crevice leading out of it. That's where Kinra heals all the injured teammates.

"Hey Stougma. You had powers the whole time? How come they have only just now awakened," Jadeanu asks.

"I don't know. I was scared for you guys when I saw that huge beam spring out of there. Had I not decided to take a short walk because you guys were taking a while, I would have gotten caught in it too. After that, I was torn between going in to check on you and going against my better judgment. I did. I...I guess I'm glad I did though. You guys totally needed my help. I was... a bit scared of the thought of you all dying. I think my powers chose now to surface because of that fear, and the thoughts in my head wanted it to go away."

"So your secondhand fear is what gave you this power," Luke sums up. "That means he cares about us," Kinra blurts.

Stougma scowls. "I just didn't want to be alone."

"Ricardio, that means there's a chance you could have powers as well," Jadeanu hypothesizes. "I don't think so. If they come when you feel a certain way, then I doubt I have them," Ricardio responds.

"Well then, let's keep moving. We've still got a long way to go," Jadeanu initiates.

"Wait Jadeanu. Where are you guys going?" Ren asks.

"Oh, I forgot you just got here," Jadeanu responds. "We're going all the way out to Nevada. There's someone we need to see there." "Well I've got nothing better to do, so I guess I'll come with you."

"You sure?"

"Yeah I'm sure.

My girlfriend won't let me back in the house if I show up broke and can't provide for my stepson, especially after what happened with the world. Our relationship is on the rocks as it is. She was likely to break up with me for something else eventually. We're as good as over now." Ren's expression becomes increasingly frustrated, with a hint of despair in his eyes.

"I wanted to be there for my stepson. Be someone he could look up to. If I could have taken over a part of the city, maybe I could have protected him, but I guess I must leave that all behind me."

"Yeah. You might need to let them go. She doesn't sound like someone you should be near anymore. And may the gods show mercy toward the boy, but you've got to let go of the thought of being his stepdad. It wasn't meant to be, and the attachment is unhealthy for you."

"I know. But I really liked her, and they were all I had. Beggars can't be choosers."

"Well maybe you need to change what you beg for. We can find you a much better woman if you need it. No man should have to live under the oppression of a woman claiming to love him but only using him to satisfy her means. I bet she thinks she's helping you and making you into more of a man but has no clue about the horrors she extends to you. That's just no way anyone should live."

"Agreed. That's why I need to get as far away from this place as possible. So I'm with you." "Good! The more, the better," Luke exclaims.

The six guys continue walking for a few minutes, having a bit of conversation in the meantime before Jadeanu stops. "Your house is nearby, right Stougma?"

"Yeah. But how did you know?"

"I...I don't know."

"Okay, that's weird, but I've decided not to go back."

"Really?" Luke expresses his surprise.

"Yeah, why return when I've got nothing to return to. I won't find peace in this world, and I know that. You guys made me feel something I haven't felt in a long time. A feeling of liveliness that was able to awaken my powers! I would rather stay with you all through whatever you decide to do. I think it's much better and safer than anything else I could do."

"That's good. Your powers will definitely be useful in our group," Luke confesses.

Jadeanu takes the lead and continues ahead past Stougma's house. A few hours of walking pass as the boys notice the lights of the city area going out and electricity goes down entirely throughout the city. Stougma begins to feel exhausted from walking, as many would given all the time that has passed.

"Woo man! We're gonna be walking like this every day until we get to Nevada?" Stougma grieves.

"Probably," Jadeanu claims optimistically.

"Aww man."

"Don't worry, we might find another mode of transportation eventual...ly...."

Instantly, Jadeanu stops in his tracks.

He feels something, an overwhelming force. Yet a smile spreads across his face.

"This way. I feel something familiar. It feels like a bit of Will's energy but mixed with that angel from earlier?" "A-angel?" Ren stutters.

"Yeah, come on," Jadeanu starts jogging, and everyone follows behind him. He stops at the sight of a tall man with white skin and a strange orange gem on the center of his forehead. He has long straight brown hair down to his ribs and is carrying a sword in his right hand. He slowly turns to look at the approaching group.

All who were still jogging stopped suddenly, and their momentum made them all trip and fall.

"What in the… That power. I…I can feel it," Ricardio mentions.

"Greetings, Jadeanu, Luke, Ricardio, Ren, Kinra, and Stougma," the man greets with a bit of German in his accent. "I see that my angel has guided you to me."

"You are the god of Knowledge. That means that that angel of light was an angel of Knowledge. And this is what he had shown me?" Jadeanu concludes.

"So that means that thing **was** an angel," Stougma realizes.

Luke steps forward and kneels to the god of Knowledge.

"My angel gives those who look at him a deeper look into all that's on their mind. Giving knowledge about those things on a much more complex and deeper level. Usually, it is too much for some brains to handle, and the people tend to panic and slaughter themselves, hoping to unsee what was seen. You want to know where Humboldt-Toiyabe Forest is. He filled your brain with the exact direction you'd need to find it. As he did with other places. He knew that you would pass by me, so he granted you the passage to me as well," Knowledge answers.

"That explains how you knew where everything was without asking for directions," Luke mentions.

"You are wise for realizing the truth of my angel. I congratulate you Jadeanu."

"Thank you your grace." "I have come to warn you. You desire to attain all of our 7 Essential Blessings. You should know that my Blessing of Knowledge has already been taken unwarranted by a powerful and cruel angel named Ravah." Knowledge's forehead gem lights up and projects an image of a purple-skinned, rather handsome-looking, celestial being.

"Be aware of him. He is as dangerous as he is intelligent. For he is the right-hand Archangel of Spirit. He was created to tempt and torture evil souls; thus his ways are brutal. He is currently using the divine power of Knowledge to sway the world to do evil, for that is his nature. You want all the Blessings; you will have to fight against him. He is powerful; note that he attacks your spirit, not just your physical body. That means that, no matter how strong you are, his attacks will always reach you and potentially kill."

Knowledge's gem dims, and the projection fades away.

"So, um. With all due respect, sir, if you know that he's out there, then why don't you, um, stop him," Stougma suggests. Luke and Jadeanu look at him with questioning faces.

"You will all know in due time. He is not for me to destroy. He has purposes to serve," Knowledge tells them.

"Wait a second. If you're so great, then why would you let your angel kill so many innocent people!" Stougma complains, raising his voice in the process.

"Watch your tongue!" Knowledge demands as he puts his finger on Stougma's forehead. Stougma immediately loses all the tension in his body and goes completely limp. Knowledge touches his forehead again, and he returns to normal.

"I have given you all your knowledge. I can take it away."

Stougma falls to his knees in fear of Knowledge's power.

"Time makes the world run in a current of cycles. Things must happen for the future of things to come. I know all fates, yet I do not tamper with any because time is much too fragile for interference. You need not know why we do as we do, for you cannot understand the will of us. All you need is to open your mind to the possibilities on your own and find comfort in knowing that you have the liberty of possibility."

"Do I have a chance to actually be the one to end this?" Jadeanu asks.

"This convergence was started by the god Death. If you wish to end it, you will have to confront him. You will have to gain vast power and Knowledge, yet your fate is out of my hands. The power of the Blessings is finite, but the power of the gods is infinite. Despite that, if we welcome you to duel, your death is not our concern. If you follow your soul, you may gain what you are looking for and much more. All destiny is set, yet you have the power to decide how it will happen and sometimes even who will create the change. Proceed with open eyes and an open mind. You shall achieve favor and find a way for yourself," Knowledge advises.

Jadeanu bows.

"Thank you sir."

"One more thing," Knowledge continues. He puts his palm on Jadeanu's forehead, then retracts his hand.

"Now you have the path to my Blessing and, with it, to Ravah. Do not go to him without achieving your current goals."

"Will do. I am thankful for your guidance," Jadeanu responds as he leads his group back toward their original destination.

"Hey Stougma. Next time, please don't get an attitude with a god," Luke advises.

"Seriously, I thought you were dead," Jadeanu adds. "Yeah, sorry about that. I was just letting out my frustrations," Stougma apologizes.

In the city that Jadeanu and company had left some time ago, Mishu Herman still grieves his defeat. He speaks with a mysterious pale, athletic man with longish black hair extending just past his neck, red eyes, and a stretchy black suit that covers his neck down to his ankles.

"I heard you were an excellent hitman before the Death Spiral. You're even better now with your powers. I want you to kill a group of people for me," Mishu elaborates. "There's a man named Jadeanu. He's the leader of this group. He dared to go against me, shaking my reputation. Humiliating me! Well I'll have the last laugh. I want you to find them all and kill them."

"What's in it for me?" the assassin demands with a surprisingly deep voice. "Money isn't exactly significant anymore."

"Well, there are still places that require money, plus even in all this chaos, you still want to stay under the radar don't you? People finding out who you are could spell trouble. I can ensure that that won't happen. A service for a service," Mishu reasons.

"I'll fill your pockets with enough cash to match your weight, and I'll grant you your own private region in my city when it becomes mine. Not to mention that I know you enjoy the thrill of a challenging kill. There are at least five of them with interesting powers. You'll certainly get a kick out of killing all of them. You will also gain more experience with your new abilities and experiment with them. I see nothing but large gains for you."

"Done. I'll handle them, but you'll have to give me all the information you have on them. And a method of tracking them down."

Chapter 4:

No Man's Forest

The six guys journey forward through the nearby city. "Knowledge sure seemed more powerful than Willpower didn't he?" Jadeanu realizes.

"He definitely had a greater presence. But maybe it's because Will was holding back," Luke responds. "Hey Jadeanu, I get that you know the way to that forest, but can we please get a map?" Ricardio asks. "I'm just saying if something happens to you, I still want to find my way home."

"Alright fine. Ever since the Death Spiral, all smartphones have been out of commission, so there are no maps there. I suppose we could find a way to print one out though," Jadeanu suggests. "We're in a city, and despite our electricity shortage, someone's got to have a way to get a map." Jadeanu leads everyone into an electronics building.

Inside, there is an empty front desk with unorganized paperwork. There is a single computer in the front, on a desk, connected to a printer. Ricardio seizes the chance to try to print out a map. "As expected, the computer doesn't work. It must have been connected to the mainstream electricity, and people have stopped working on it." "We should go into the 'employees only' room. Maybe there's something we can use in there," Luke suggests. "There likely won't be anything in there, but there's no harm in trying," Ricardio states. Jadeanu opens a door at the end of the room labeled "employees only." "Aah!" A woman screams as she stands, startled.

"Oh, um, sorry. I didn't-" "It's okay. What do you guys need?" "Is there any form of electricity in here? We need to print out a map is all," Jadeanu asks. "No, sorry. I've been trying to find a way to get it back online. But there is a windmill farm somewhere nearby. The plant owners may be generous enough to let you use their electricity to do what you need. That's probably your best bet." "Okay thank you." "No problem."

Jadeanu and the others prepare to leave the store, and as Jadeanu walks through the building, he accidentally bumps into a stack of papers. The sheets fall and scatter across the floor. "Oh sorry," Jadeanu apologizes as he immediately acts to fix his mistake. "It's okay, I'll handle it. Go on. You all seem to have a lot of work ahead of you." the lady reasons.

Jadeanu and company all leave the place and go on their way to the nearby field of windmills. The sheets of paper that were on the ground, immediately rise simultaneously and form a man in stealth clothes. The woman is startled and reacts with no destination. Only pure fear in her eyes. The man's right arm forms a blade of paper. "You will tell me everything you know about where those guys are headed."

Meanwhile, Jadeanu and his group walk onto the vast field of short green grass and windmills slowly spinning with the slight breeze filling the area. "Look! There's the house," Luke points out. "Alright, let's see if there's someone inside," Jadeanu plans. They all rush to the front door of the only home in the field. Jadeanu knocks twice, but there is no answer. "Let's just go inside already," Stougma hurries and accidentally blows up the door. Luke and Jadeanu are appalled. "I'm so sorry if anyone owns this," Luke pleads. "Let's just get inside. It's okay; nobody alive probably owns this," Ricardio sympathizes. They all rush inside.

"Split up and search for a computer, or anyone that might be in here," Ricardio demands. "Okay-oh, never mind. Found it!" Luke sights a lone computer station not far from the front door. "Oh, that was easy. Let's see if it works," Jadeanu leads. Ricardio presses the power button on the computer, and it turns on. "It works!" he says as he immediately finds and prints out multiple pictures that map out the area.

"Why are you getting all of those maps?" Ren asks. "One broad long-distance map would be too vague. With a somewhat detailed map of every general area, it'll be easier to find our way," Ricardio explains. Jadeanu continues to take the lead as they all walk back onto the field after the successful map-attaining quest. "I'm glad we didn't have to worry about anyone in that house," Stougma says. "Yeah, that could have been much wor-" Ricardio stops talking and puts his maps into his bow quiver as he notices someone in the distance. "Watch out!" he yells as a tiny fireball travels toward the group.

The fireball is targeted at Stougma, yet he doesn't take it seriously due to the insignificant size of the attack. He barely dodges the ball, and on impact with the ground, the fireball explodes, filling a considerable radius for its size with flames. Realizing the error in his initial thought, Stougma immediately attempts to jump away. Once the fire and smoke clear up, Stougma is seen jumping out of the scene with steam emitting out of his right arm.

"AHH!" Stougma screams with extensive pain in his voice. He starts whimpering in pain from intense burns. Kinra immediately tries to heal him. Stougma's entire arm is scorched charcoal black with ash from his own singed skin all over it. "Oh crap. That's probably the owner of the house we just invaded," Ren concludes. The man is wearing dark fitness clothing and, in fact, has the identity of the hitman Mishu hired.

The assassin holds out his hand and fires another fireball. Luke steps forward and fires a gas ball at the pursuing fireball. On impact, the fireball perseveres through Luke's projectile and continues toward him. Fear enters Luke causing him to propel himself away instantly. The power of the fireball's collision with the ground accelerates his movement, knocking him a safe distance away.

Ren manipulates his own shadow and attacks with multiple extending spikes. The assassin fires another fireball at the shadow, and it goes directly through it as well. Ren adds skates to his feet from the remains of his shadow and moves out of the way of the pursuing fireball. "Okay then. How about this!?" Luke says as he charges up and fires his powerful gaseous beam at the assassin. The assassin fires yet another fireball at the beam. On collision, both attacks explode on each other and dissolve in the air. "What! But that attack is supposed to be…." Luke says, perplexed. "Guys, however you do it, get out of here!"

Luke starts rocketing away and makes a stop at Kinra. "No time to heal. We've gotta get out of this place!" "So we're not fighting?" "No. He just easily destroyed my most effective attack. We're clearly no match." Luke picks Kinra up and sets him on his back, then yells, "Everyone who has an ability that can accelerate your movement, grab the others on your back and go!"

"Who made him boss?" Ren complains as he picks Stougma up and on his back and engages his shadow skates. Jadeanu lets Ricardio climb on his back as he energizes his feet to run with accelerated velocity. "Just like old times," Jadeanu relates to Ricardio before he starts to run. They all move further away from the assassin. Jadeanu is the slowest out of them, whereas Luke and Ren are around the same pace. The assassin pursues.

"Something tells me that he isn't the owner of that house," Luke shares. "What makes you say that?" Ren asks. "He likely would have said something by now if he was. But instead, he just attacked us; and he's definitely pursuing with the intent to kill," Luke explains. Just then, another fireball comes into view. Luke slows down, allowing the others to pass him. He deploys his shield to take the blast.

He is immediately sent backward with an almost entirely cracked shield. He then expels his shield and speeds back up but just behind Jadeanu and Ricardio. "How is he keeping up with us?" Luke wonders. The assassin is just running but still keeping up with at least Jadeanu. "My guess is that he's some sort of trained professional. Like an assassin. Based on what I've seen, not even a normal superpowered guy can run that fast, and likely not for this long," Ricardio hypothesizes. "The way he moves and attacks without warning just screams assassin to me. Plus, the malice in his face, although hard to see from here, definitely gives off a deadly vibe to me."

The assassin's right-hand sparks up with pulsing yellow electricity as he throws skinny bolts of lightning into the air. The sky lights up over Luke and Jadeanu. Luke responds by casting a huge shield to cover himself, his brother, and their piggyback riders. Multiple thick lightning bolts strike the area. Ren looks back and snatches Jadeanu forward with his shadow. The lightning breaks through Luke's shield easily and collapses the area. Luke and Kinra are scraped by the intense lightning and tumble onto the ground with electricity and smoke flowing from their bodies.

"Oh snap! They're hurt! That means we're gonna have to fight right?!" Ren shouts as he comes to a halt and turns to the action. Jadeanu also stops and nods. Stougma drops to the floor, still holding his burnt arm. Ricardio climbs off of Jadeanu's back and readies his bow. "At least they managed to avoid the bulk of the lightning," Ricardio informs. "That's good," Jadeanu claims. "But Ricardio, you sure you want to stay and fight? Your body isn't strengthened by your spirit, so you'll be more vulnerable to damage." "Don't worry about me. Anyone who messes with you or Luke, messes with me. That's how it's always been, right? Well it ain't finna change here." "We're probably all gonna die," Jadeanu says with a sly smile.

The assassin slows down into a walk when he approaches the scene. He aims his hand at Luke and Kinra. He shoots a fireball, and Jadeanu jumps in the way, his arms filled with red energy. The fireball plunges into his arms and explodes. Jadeanu immediately flies off from the impact. His arms turn black in ash from the hit, and he tumbles into the ground, rolling uncontrollably on the Earth for several yards.

The assassin then holds out his hand and shoots a blueish-white sphere at Kinra and Luke. The sphere moves much slower than the fireballs did but still fast enough to be intimidating. Ren uses his shadow to snatch Luke away, but his shadow alone cannot move him and Kinra. The light ball hits Kinra directly before Ren can reuse his shadow to save him. The area then explodes with a giant ice ball trapping Kinra inside. The ball of ice is spikey all over, with two feet long spikes bulging outward in all directions. The ball then expands again into a 7-foot tall and wide iceberg with spikes protruding to about 4 feet in length.

Ricardio starts shooting his arrows at the assassin. The assassin easily dodges all the arrows and casts two lightning bolts to fall on Ricardio. Ricardio then jumps out of the way, avoiding the lightning. "Be careful," Jadeanu warns while coming back into the scene with energized legs and limped arms.

"Dang it. I never thought that I would need to learn this," Ren says. He starts moving his hands as if trying to make something happen, yet the effects still have yet to be visible. The assassin notices his shadow begin to move on its own. A spike extends from his shadow and comes up to attack, but before it can, it liquefies and falls back down. "Dang it!" Ren struggles. The assassin starts moving around out of caution regarding his rebelling shadow. The shadow still follows the assassin, but it becomes even harder for Ren to control.

The assassin closes in on Jadeanu with electricity in his hands. He taps Jadeanu's chest, and electricity forces Jadeanu onto the floor in buzzing pain. Ren catches when the assassin stops moving and puts all his effort into extending spikes from the assassin's shadow. The killer uses his lightning hands to destroy the spikes before they hit him. He then performs a front flip in Ren's direction. When the flip almost ends, he extends his hand and shoots a fireball at the ground behind him. The blast sends the assassin toward Ren with even more speed. He does another flip and shoots another fireball to blast himself forward.

Then when he reaches Ren, he grabs Ren's face and fills it with electricity. "Aahhh!" Ren screams. The assassin forces Ren's head into the grass. He then holds his free hand toward Ren's heart and shoots an ice sphere toward him. The assassin does a backflip away as soon as the compacted iceberg expands. The incoming spikes pierce right through Ren's chest and stomach.

Jadeanu rages and comes forth to fight again. The assassin runs up and palms Jadeanu's chest with electric hands. He then twists his palm, thus forcing more electricity into him. Jadeanu is pushed away by the power and tumbles across the grass again. Steam rises from his chest as his body twitches from the current.

A blue gas ball then peers into the assassin's view. He dodges it easily and gazes at his attacker. Luke is now standing up along with Ricardio as their last stand. "Okay. It looks like we can't win this. We have to consider running again. For those who can't move much, get with someone who can. If not, it sucks to be you. I'm sorry, but we're gonna have to leave you behind," Luke exclaims. He then grabs Kinra's iceberg and starts rocketing away while trying his best to shoot gaseous balls of energy at the assassin to buy time for the others to retreat.

With his shadow, Ren grabs his piercing iceberg and forces it off of himself. He immediately kneels, holding his chest and stomach.

He then adds skates to his feet, puts Stougma on his back, and follows Luke. Jadeanu opens his eyes and sees them leaving. He also notices Ricardio running toward him. With the last bit of willpower he can muster, he allows his more violent spirit to control his body foundation as he controls his movements. His fingers pierce into the ground as he pushes off of it and rises to his feet. His foot cracks the ground under him as he springs into a full sprint. He runs beyond human speed, grabs Ricardio, and puts him on his back. Ricardio holds on for dear life. The assassin pursues again.

"Glad you all made it! I was seriously worried about having to leave some of you behind!" Luke yells due to the high wind of their massive velocity. "No hard feelings right guys?" "Of course not! I know you well enough to know you only meant well. I would prefer some of us to get away than any other bad outcome," Jadeanu expresses. "Good! Hey Ren! I thought you were dead. What happened?" Luke shouts. "I would have, but I used my shadow to move away just in time to escape being skewered in the heart," Ren answers. "I'm just glad it didn't hit any vital spots. Or at least I hope it didn't."

Meanwhile, the assassin makes another lightning shower up ahead. "Everybody stop!" Luke yells as he follows his own advice. Everyone else follows suit.

The lightning strikes ahead of them then Luke and the others return to escape. The assassin is nearly keeping up but is still slower than all of the guys. "So we just have to keep him at bay till we escape?" Ricardio wonders. He reaches into his back pocket and pulls out a revolver. One arm holding onto Jadeanu and the other pointing the gun at the assassin. He starts firing to disorient the killer. "You had a gun the whole time?" Jadeanu asks with his voice influenced by the voice of his other spirit, trying his best to not sound too intimidating because of it. "Yeah. But I usually don't use guns. I'm better with a bow. Plus I don't bring extra ammo." "You've always been a more hands-on type of guy, but you're utterly hopeless when using other things." "Hehe. Yep."

Out of fear of being shot, the assassin casts ice to build up in front of him by shooting it from his hand. The ice expands into an iceberg to take the bullets instead. Ricardio starts to feel a bit relieved because he thinks he may have stopped the assassin from chasing them, yet he doesn't drop his guard.

Just then, the assassin is seen on top of the iceberg with a proper foot placement to do a front flip over it. He then starts shooting fireballs at the ground with each front flip he proceeds with to maintain his edge in the air while accelerating to catch up to Jadeanu and the others. "Ugh, guys, I'm out of ammo. And he's only catching up. We need something to stop him, or it's over!" As these words escape Ricardio's lips, the assassin engulfs in fire and smoke. He then falls to the ground. Everyone looks at Stougma, who has his head up and looks triumphantly at the assassin. "Nice one Stougma!" Ren says.

They all cross into a forest and continue peacefully into a suburban area. They eventually collapse onto the grass near a neighborhood. "Ahh, gosh. I cannot move anymore," Ren says, holding his bleeding torso. Luke tries to break the spikes off the iceberg that Kinra is still frozen inside. "Man this stuff is thick." Luke starts to charge up his energy. "Please don't hurt Kinra," he says to himself as he fires at the side of the iceberg. The beam breaks through a nice portion of the massive iceberg but still not what Luke expected. "This is gonna take a while. Hey Stougma, can you help me melt this thing?"

After several seconds of Luke and Stougma working on it, the iceberg is destroyed enough for Kinra to slide out. "Ah! What happened?" Kinra speaks as he shivers a bit. "Oh wow. You guys don't look so good. Let me heal you." He then moves to heal Luke. "Hey me first! I got hit first, so it's only fair," Stougma pouts. "Go on and heal him first. I'll be fine for now," Luke reasons. "Don't forget to heal yourself too. You also got hit by the electricity. But I'm sure your feelings are numb from the ice." "It's been too long. I'm hungry!" Stougma says. "Yeah, it's getting late. We should get some food and rest here," Luke plans. "But what if the assassin finds us?" Ricardio questions. "We should be far enough from him now. But we could find a more comfortable place in someone's abandoned home. But if we do that, we may risk another fight with someone else and a more confined area for the assassin to strike if he finds us," Luke answers. "Our best bet is to be free to run if he comes back." "Not sure if it'll be useful, but I've got money for food," Stougma says. "I'll go with you in case anything happens. The others still need to heal." Ricardio claims. The guys walk away into the civilization and after several minutes, come back with food. By that time, Kinra is done healing everyone. They all eat, talk, then drift off to sleep on the soft open grass.

They all begin to have vivid dreams. Dreams of their past, fantasies of the future. Filling their minds with the darkness and light of their current situations. Ravaging their hearts in fear, passion, and despair yet swarming them with a natural sense of ease. However, there is tension in preparation to disturb the peaceful atmosphere of rest.

Alas, in a nearby tree stands the assassin stealthily stalking his prey with his eyebrows arched in determined anger. He lights one hand with silent electricity and throws lightning into the air. As it prepares to fall upon all the sleeping travelers, a shadow in the night moves quickly to the middle of the lethargic men and says softly in a familiar voice, "Mark 3."

As soon as the lightning falls, the man fires a huge orange blast into the air. The thick lightning bolts clash with the energy blast and consume it. Soon the lightning will pierce right through the blast. With the collision, a loud thunderous roar sounds through the area, and soon the orange blast turns greenish and stops being overcome by the lightning. "Hey Blast!" Luke greets from next to him, firing his beam with Blast's power cannon. "That's not my name, but hey," Blast responds. Their combined attack and the assassin's lightning both explode into the atmosphere.

Blast fires a beam at the assassin. The assassin front flips off the tree branch he was on to avoid the blast. As he descends, he fires two consecutive fireballs. By this time, everyone is up and alert. Jadeanu and Ren jump out of one of the fire explosions. Luke deploys his shield and takes the hit of the other. His protection is thoroughly cracked then he deactivates it. Blast pulses twice and fires a Mark 2 cannon at the assassin. The assassin shoots a fireball at it, and they both explode once they collide.

"So Blast, what made you come help us?" Luke asks. "I thought about what you guys said. You all were so kind, even as enemies. When I heard that Boss Herman hired an assassin to kill you all, I just couldn't sit around and let that happen. I believe in equity," Blast explains. "So Mishu sent this guy after us?!" Jadeanu rages. In the midst of combat, a strange white-looking giant bird flies into the scene and then alters and forms the man, Paper Ninja. "Paper Ninja? So it was Mishu," says Luke.

Paper Ninja has clear rage in his eyes as he walks toward Blast. "What are you doing? We're supposed to be killing them, not helping them!" "I have reconsidered their offer. I have nothing to gain by being with Boss Herman anymore. It would be wise of you to join me." Blast rebuttals. "If you join them, you die with them." Paper Ninja's right arm forms into a paper sword. "This is nothing personal." Blast turns back to Jadeanu and the others and says, "What's our plan of attack?"

"We may be able to take on Paper Ninja, but the assassin…." Luke answers. "I know when I can't win. And Thrale has learned some new moves. The defeat he took earlier really had him motivated," Blast adds. "Thrale?" Luke questions. "That's the name of who you call Paper Ninja." "And what's your name Blast?" "It's Seinaru Reseku." "What?" "Just call me Blast for now. It's starting to grow on me."

"Okay then, Blast, our strategy is to run," Luke proudly claims. "Okay then let's go!" Blast then starts rocketing away. Luke follows, then Ren starts skating, and Jadeanu starts running. They all grab their respective piggyback riders from last time and continue.

"Oh no they don't," Thrale says as he returns to his bird shape and grabs the assassin's shoulders with his talons. His flying speed, added with the wind as his ally, causes him to catch up rather quickly. The assassin starts shooting a barrage of fireballs at the downward-inclined prey. "There's no way to escape with that paper ninja helping the assassin. We'll have to take him out first," Ricardio strategizes. "Stougma, can you concentrate on the bird and make him explode?" Ren advises. "But that would kill him, wouldn't it?" Luke worries as he looks Blast in the eyes. "So be it," Blast responds with a bit of coldness in his voice.

A fireball lands near Jadeanu, causing him to jump and tumble, releasing Ricardio off of his back. Just then, Kinra warns Luke of an approaching fireball, and Luke deploys his shield. His shield cracks with the explosion. After the smoke clears, another fireball slams into his weakened shield, breaking it and sending him and Kinra flying. Ren continues dodging with his shadow.

"I can't concentrate on anything other than not dying," Stougma panics. One of his explosions sets off one of the fireballs, yet the fireball still continues to the ground. Ren slows down and lets Stougma off of his back as the bird and assassin fly ahead of him. Thrale lands the assassin as he returns to his human form. The assassin immediately shoots lightning into the air.

"Crap!" Luke yells as he summons a huge shield to cover them all. The thick lightning bolts pierce right through the shield and strike the area. Everyone else could avoid the bulk of the lightning but was still hit by the weakened shock waves, except for Ren. He is struck directly by a bolt of lightning on the right side of his back. His eyes shift to a lifeless glare as he falls face-first onto the ground. Stougma looks concerned but then looks away out of fear that his concern would ignite an explosion on Ren.

Kinra runs, with a slight limp, at him and starts healing his wound. "This isn't good. The energy's already inside of him. There's nothing I can do," Kinra says. The assassin shoots a fireball at them. Luke grabs Kinra and Ren by the face respectively and throws both of them opposite of each other. He then quickly turns to the fireball and starts to deploy his shield toward his feet because the ball was aimed toward the ground. Luke's shield doesn't have enough time to expand to anything other than a smaller version of itself as it is hit by the fireball. The explosion breaks his shield immediately and hits his legs, blasting him feet away and tumbling into the dirt. His legs turn black with fire and steam coming off of them. He starts wailing in pain. "We're all totally going to die," Jadeanu jokes. "We got away before," Ricardio embraces. "Yeah, but this time we've got Paper Ninja to deal with," Jadeanu responds. "Way I see it; we have to take one of them out if we're going to escape." "If we could take out the assassin at all, we'll be fine."

Luke starts to twitch, thus conveying a desire to move yet stranded by his own injuries. *'Okay, I'm afraid. Let that fear turn to will. And let that will turn to power!'* Luke thinks, opens his eyes, and uses his hands to rocket into the air. He starts shooting his gas balls at the assassin, yet they come with a lot more force than usual. The assassin dodges all of the attacks and shoots a fireball at Luke. Luke barely dodges it.

Thrale folds his paper self into an origami bird and pierces Luke in the stomach with his paper beak. Luke falls back to the grass, nearly lifeless. Stougma takes the time to concentrate on the assassin and makes him explode with his mind. The assassin tumbles on the ground in smoke. He gets up with rage in his eyes. He turns to Stougma and starts running at full speed with an uncalculative movement to throw off Stougma's concentration. He adds lightning to his hand once he reaches Stougma. He palms forward with a twist of the wrist. Stougma barely dodges it, and a bolt of lightning flies straight forward.

The assassin gazes at the missed target with his raging eyes. Before Stougma gets a chance to concentrate on the assassin, he is swept by a precise kick. The assassin shoots an ice sphere at Stougma as he does a backflip away. Stougma barely dodges it with all its extending spikes. The assassin shoots a fireball at the now iceberg. Several of the spikes fly off the berg as the assassin jumps up and catches one while the other guys dodge the ones that jet toward them. The assassin starts swinging the spike he caught at Stougma like it's a spear, keeping him on the defensive.

He jabs at Stougma's feet, making him jump to avoid it. The assassin then chunks the spike at Stougma, who can't dodge because he's in the air. The assassin fires an ice sphere immediately following the spike. Stougma is forced to catch the spike between his two hands. The ice sphere then detonates into an iceberg, and its spikes push against the flying spike, thus forcing it into Stougma's intestines. He then falls to the ground in defeat.

Meanwhile, Thrale encounters his old friend Seinaru, also known as Blast. They both fight without powers at first. Trading attacks with respective blocks. Thrale then turns one of his legs into a bunch of sheets of paper, and the paper cuts up Blast's leg. The sheets of paper then shift to behind him, where they form a thin blade and pierce Blast directly in the calf. Blast kneels and fires a beam at Thrale, who reciprocates with a retreat into paper to avoid the beam. He then moves with the wind behind Blast. "They're trying to damage our quicker people, so we can't escape!" Kinra blurts out.

Jadeanu immediately closes in on the assassin and sweep-kicks him. The assassin catches himself with his hand and moves with the momentum back to his feet. He then, in return, sweeps Jadeanu off his feet and connects with a palm twist of lightning. Jadeanu flies off into the dirt. "The only way out of this is to take out the assassin. Paper Ninja likely won't follow us without help," Ricardio mentions from the sidelines. "What are you saying?" Jadeanu demands. "We have to outsmart our predator."

With Jadeanu out of commission for now, Kinra becomes the last stand for the assassin. Kinra runs and jumps to hit the assassin with as much force as he can muster. The assassin catches his fist and holds him out. The assassin then charges his other hand with electricity and palms Kinra, which eventually launches Kinra away.

"As you can see, he doesn't shoot his fireballs when you're too close to him," Ricardio analyzes. "He probably knows that even he can't take the force of his own attacks. He uses his taser hands when you get too close to avoid danger. He may use his ice attacks at close range because he can move quick enough, but if you take away his freedom of movement, he likely won't. His lightning is definitely his strongest attack. If we can get him to use his attacks against himself, we may be able to win."

"So how are we going to do that? We don't have powers like Mishu. We can't exactly force his attacks against him," Jadeanu grieves. "He's bound to use his lightning hands at close range, and at medium range, he'll either use that lightning or shoot ice," Ricardio continues. "If his hands are already buzzing, he's more likely to use his thunder. There is a small opening of time before the lightning comes down." "And with that opening, we can force him into his own lightning," Jadeanu finishes. "That's right."

"Just get him in front of me when he casts lightning," Luke says from on the floor, barely able to move. "But that would mean you won't be able to retreat in time. You could die too," Jadeanu announces.

"Maybe, but I'm as good as dead anyway without trying."

"But Luke..." "It's okay. I'll try something that won't make it come to death, but if it does, I'd be happy giving my life to save you all." "Okay then. Our strategy is to close in and back out rapidly, so he'll have to use his lightning hands, and if we are grouped, he'll likely use the overhead thunder," Ricardio plans. "Come on Kinra. We're gonna need you for this too." Jadeanu attacks first. Meanwhile, Blast and Thrale are fighting nearly evenly matched. Blast can't fire his pyro cannon at Thrale in paper form, and Thrale can't slice up Blast due to his precise evasion.

Jadeanu jumps up and attacks with a drop kick aimed at the assassin. The assassin grabs Jadeanu's leg in mid-air and then starts to aim an ice sphere at him. He stops and dodges an incoming arrow from Ricardio, who positioned himself behind Jadeanu. Kinra then closes in from under the assassin's sights. The assassin notices him and charges Jadeanu's still-held leg with electricity. He surges lightning on his own leg and lifts it above his head, and crashes it down full force toward Kinra. Kinra avoids most of the attack but still gets scraped by the electricity.

Jadeanu readjusts and throws a hook toward the assassin. The assassin releases Jadeanu's leg and evades backward into a backflip. "Everyone close in!" Ricardio commands, running toward the assassin. With the combined effort of Kinra and Jadeanu, they all manage to get the assassin right in front of Luke, who is waiting patiently on the floor for his chance.

The others all continue fighting until they find an opportunity to back up. When they do, the assassin shoots his lightning into the air. "This is it!" Ricardio highlights. Jadeanu grabs Ricardio, and super jumps out of the way. Kinra is unable to move quickly enough though. Luke shoots the assassin into the field of lightning. *It sucks that it must be this way,'* Luke thinks. Then he gasps in fear after the newfound sight he sees now that the assassin has been moved out of his way. He notices that Kinra is also going to get caught up in the lightning.

Suddenly, an orange blast hits Kinra in the back, which sends him flying. Luke sighs in relief. The assassin is now the only one in the wake of his own lightning. In fear, the assassin presses an ice sphere into himself as a final resort. He is then trapped in an iceberg as the lightning collapses the area. At that moment, Jadeanu looks at Blast, who shot Kinra, saving his life from the lightning. Blast breaks away from Thrale, who is scared into a state of shock. He then picks up Luke and Kinra then uses his legs to rocket away. Jadeanu grabs Stougma and Ren and follows Blast's lead. Ricardio reluctantly follows as well. Blast and Jadeanu aren't very fast though. Ricardio is even able to keep up.

They all pass by the neighborhood they are close to and go into the woods nearby. Blast suddenly falls to the ground. "Blast! Your leg!" Jadeanu points out Blast's bleeding calf. "You're one to talk about legs," Blast quotes pointing at Jadeanu's legs painted with bruises and burns. "What the...When did that happen?" he wonders as the pain of the injuries subtly creeps through his legs.

"You must have been hit by the lightning too," Ricardio predicts. "I must have been so worried that my adrenaline was pumping too much for me to even feel it." "Let me heal you guys," Kinra says while getting up from being dropped by Blast. "We can't stop here. The woods are dangerous, and the assassin might still be alive. We've gotta go," Jadeanu responds. "Well we can't just keep going. At the rate we're going, the assassin will still catch us, and we'll be vulnerable if he's alive," Ricardio reasons. "As things are now, Luke and Ren could be dead. We've got to at least do some healing."

Just then, a white furred wolf comes into the scene leading his pack. The alpha wolf has blue colored eyes, while the others in the pack all have red. "Things just keep getting worse, don't they?" Jadeanu worries. The alpha wolf sniffs the air around the troubled travelers. He then walks up to Blast. Ricardio reaches for his bow. "Don't... move," Blast commands. The wolf sniffs Blast and rubs his soft, furry face on him. The wolf then makes a call to the other wolves, and they start rushing over to lick and show affection to Blast. Ricardio stares, appalled. "Blast! They seem to really like you," Jadeanu expresses.

"My guess is that they somehow know about my history," Blast reveals. "I was born with a natural softness for animals. I'm just not so kind to people. Before I became a mercenary, I used to help out animals in their natural habitat as a hobby. That was a will passed down from my family. We're all named something that represents a light for nature. My name, Seinaru, means holy. I was designed to be the holy light of aid for animals in need. I'm not sure if these wolves can sense that about me, but I guess if you're kind to nature, it tends to pay off."

The alpha wolf takes a long look at Ricardio and walks toward the passage where he and his pack came from. He then looks back at Blast. "I think he wants us to follow him," Jadeanu proposes. A regular wolf with red eyes walks beneath Blast's legs and looks up at him. "No. I think they are offering us a ride," Blast responds. Blast lightly sits on the wolf, and with its enhanced strength from the effect of the Death Spiral, it holds him up with ease.

The other wolves also offer rides to the others. One wolf, in particular, wants the harmed Ren to ride it. Jadeanu gently puts Ren down on the back of the wolf, and the wolf's fur grows and wraps around him tight to hold him in place. The alpha wolf gestures for Luke to ride on his back. Blast releases Luke on the alpha's back, and the wolf's fur glows as Luke's wounds start to heal and his pain is lifted. "His fur has healing properties!" Luke exclaims. He ensures his burnt legs get the soothing sensation the most. Everyone else gets on a wolf's back, and they take off, all following their leader.

They ride through the suburbs with exceptional speed. "Woo! This is fun!" Blast suggests. Ricardio holds on tight in fear. Far away, back near the neighborhood, the assassin is still in one piece, trapped in a small iceberg. The lightning wore away all of the spikes and most of the ice. Thrale waits patiently for the assassin to thaw in the hot sun.

Meanwhile, Jadeanu's team travels non-stop for a while. They cross a bridge splitting a city area from another beautiful rainforest. "Are you sure we're going the right way?" Ricardio worries. "Yeah! We actually are! I don't know how they know, but we are." Jadeanu responds after taking the time to think. "Wha-" Jadeanu then looks over in the distance as if something caught his attention. Suddenly an extremely loud boom sounds in the area. Out of fear and worry, everyone looks where Jadeanu is already looking.

There is a huge explosion in the distance, big enough to collapse around an entire city like a nuclear bomb. But it was not of fire. Instead, it was a huge pulse of purple energy. "Whoa! What the heck was that?!" Stougma concerns. Everyone seems perplexed and amazed at the sight, but Jadeanu stares with absolute fear in his eyes. He keeps silent and then looks forward again.

In the distance where the explosion occurred, there stood three beings. There is a familiar tall being walking in the carnage of the explosive aftermath. This being is named Ravah. The very angel Knowledge warned Jadeanu about. One of the other beings, who is also an angel, opens his mouth to speak. "You really should learn how to control that energy of yours, Javean. You've been granted so much potential, yet it is wasted if you can't bend it to you."

The other angel by the name of Javean responds, "I'm sorry. I just sneezed because of all the pollution in the air. I underestimated how sensitive my nose would be in a flesh form. It's not like I tried to do it." "Vermunya is right Javean," Ravah intermissions. His voice is very firm, proud, and deep and has a slight angelic echo within it. "You just destroyed an entire city with that sneeze. Had I not moved quick enough, Vermunya and I could have been caught in that blast. Not like it would have killed us, but there are people you have killed. We are lucky your explosion was weak this time. You must control your inner energy; such chaotic behavior shall not stand with us. You are our weakest member, but you have the potential to be even stronger than I."

"Are you sure you can't turn it into another form or channel it into an energy attack?" Vermunya pities. "No, it's a bit complicated. It only responds to internal impulse," Javean explains. "You could have blown away our new bodies you know," Vermunya grieves.

"Not likely. Or at least not with a blast that weak," Ravah opposes. "Our bodies are created from flesh and blood to resemble that of the material world, but they are infused with our spiritual bodies and symbolize our divine yet physical involvement. In other words, these bodies of ours are superior to that of a human."

Ravah's physical body is tall, and he wears a purple crown guided across the side of his face to the top of his head, hiding his hairline. His hair is long and red, spikey yet silky. His clothing is also purple and royal looking, matching his crown. He has a spike on each of his elbows and has a royal waist apron that covers his backside like a long jacket end. It is stiff and sharp, literally and figuratively. He has tight violet pants with built-in boots with spikes on the front and back. He has long black angel wings on his back. His skin is purple, and his fingernails are long, sharp, and reddish pink and black. His nail design moves around like a colored stream. As if whatever is in them is alive. On his shoulder stands a small animal of a strange sort. It looks like a pink rhino-like monster with a sharp tail.

Vermunya's body is also tall, and, like Ravah, his skin is also purple, but he has a red crown across his sides and hairline, shielding his long blue hair. His clothes are dark blue with a red lining on certain parts of his suit. There is a small alignment across his chest, arms, and legs. The alignment is lined with a deep red that also moves slowly like a steady stream. He has dark blue bat wings emitting out of his back. He has a deep voice but not as spiritual sounding as Ravah's.

Javean is big and buff, unlike the other angels, despite being one himself. He is tall but not quite as tall as the others as well. He is shirtless with long black hair, longer than his comrades. He has big black angel wings on his bulky back. He wears barbaric royal pants covering his bison-like legs with an unnecessary loin cloth in the center. He wears boots with spikes on them as well. He's the only one without a very spiritual echo in his voice and a lack of a triumphant smile.

They all have these bodies to represent their renewal of purpose, but they all look like divine monsters. Another angel with white wings then flies to Ravah and his group. "What is it, Lilack?" Ravah asks. "There is a man with a small group who has favor with the gods. He also is after the Blessings as you are," Lilack responds. "So that means he'll be after this." Ravah digs into the pocket of his jacket-like waist apron and pulls out the Blessing of Knowledge with his bare hand.

"Yes," Lilack answers. "Tell me. What is his name?" Ravah demands. "Jadeanu." "Hm, Jadeanu huh? Good work Lilack." "You know, you're playing a dangerous game Ravah. Angels aren't supposed to touch the Blessings. They are for humans. That is a crime punishable by death! You know that," Lilack concerns. "I am aware. If the gods wanted me dead, I wouldn't be here right now. In the end, it'll be worth it, for I am going to need the Blessings if I am to be omnipotent." "It's your spirit on the line," Lilack says as he flies away. "So what are we to do with this Jadeanu?" Vermunya expresses. "We will wait for him. He'll come this way eventually," Ravah plans.

Back to Jadeanu and his company, all riding on wolves. They have been traveling nonstop for hours. It's a surprise that the carnivores haven't tired out yet. They enter into rocky terrain with occasional trees and rivers. A large boulder starts tumbling down a hill right toward Luke and the others. Luke holds out his hand, preparing to blast it, but before he can, it explodes into pieces that the wolves are able to avoid easily. Luke looks back, and Stougma has his body upright. They exchange smiles, then return their attention to the front. Another obstacle stands in their way. A mountainous pillar of rock stands blocking the way. The alpha wolf opens his mouth and shoots out a beam that easily pierces a huge hole in the center of the rock. Alpha wolf leads the pack into the hole and out.

They continue to travel until the rocks seem to become smaller under the wolves' feet. The rocks become smaller and smaller until there is only sand and, in front, a small indication of civilization. The wolves slow down when they reach concrete, and a small town settles on the sand. The wolves all halt and motion for their riders to get off them. Luke gets off his wolf and helps the still unconscious Ren off of his. Everyone gets off of their wolf as well. The alpha then gathers his pack, and they begin to walk their separate ways. "Thanks guys!" Luke appreciates. The wolves don't even look back.

"Where are we?" Ricardio asks. "I'm not sure. But we're really close to where we need to be. It's just a bit further from here," Jadeanu responds. "What matters is finding a place to rest and continue healing," Luke suggests. "Yeah. We've been up all night too. We need to rest," Jadeanu agrees. "If we're close to Humboldt-Toiyabe, then we can find my friend. He works as a blacksmith around here. But I don't know where we are," Ricardio complains. "We could have rested at his place." "Well let's ask around," Jadeanu plans.

They all enter a random restaurant which is one of the few buildings in the town. There is a single guy inside. He doesn't seem to work there. He's just there, likely to fill himself up with the remaining food there. "Hey, um, is there any place around here that's safe to rest?" Luke asks. "Well you are out in the middle of nowhere. There likely won't be much danger no matter where you are outside of the natural dangers of outside," the man answers with glee.

"Where exactly are we?" Ricardio asks. "I'm not really sure. I do know we are next to that huge forest over there." The man points out a huge area of trees close to the town. "That's Humboldt-Toiyabe right?!" Jadeanu questions. "Oh, you mean No Man's Forest." "Why is it called that?" "Because ever since the Death Spiral, people have gone into that forest, and no one ever comes out. It hasn't been a long time, but the place has already got a new reputation. How fast the world changes."

Jadeanu then turns to his group and says, "So, should we go to rest anyway?" "My friend lives there. Our best bet is to at least try looking for his house," Ricardio tells. "Whatever's in there, I'm sure all of us together can take it," Jadeanu pumps up. "Sure, that's some confidence considering that we just got our butts whooped," Stougma mentions. "Stougma. You're all better?" Luke confronts. "Yeah, Kinra was healing me while you guys were talking," Stougma reveals. "Anyways, we need to start asking the real questions, like how many people go into that forest at a time, to see if it'll even matter that we're in a group." "The max I've seen is a group of three," the guy answers. "It, of course, made no difference." "That said, we're still going in, aren't we?" Stougma asks. "Yep. And thank you," Luke says to the guy as he leads everyone out of the restaurant.

Ricardio pulls out a map and studies it. "Well, if Humboldt-Toiyabe is there, then we are here, and that means that that friend of mine is around here," Ricardio deciphers. "So is he just "that friend of yours" or does he have a name?" Jadeanu teases. "His name is Goldo. I was withholding his name so as not to confuse anyone." "Then we should keep moving until we find him, or at least his home."

The group of guys all walk until they get to the forest. It starts to get dark and cloudy outside even though it is about noon time. Soon it starts to rain. Ricardio's map gets soaked, so he gently puts it away. "We should stop here. I can't make out his location without my map," Ricardio quotes. Luke forms a huge shield to house everyone from the rain. "We rest here."

They all sit down under Luke's shield. "You don't know where he lives?" Blast asks. "Not exactly. I've been through here only one time. Then, I had a rental car. It's different by foot and without something telling you where to go," Ricardio responds. "Well great! We're in a dead people's forest, and we must stop here?" Stougma complains.

A grunt then escapes from Ren. "Where are we?" he whispers. "We're in Humboldt-Toiyabe or what's known as No Man's Forest," Jadeanu answers. "Ren! I'm glad you made it! I thought you were gonna die," Kinra expresses. "I thought I was too. I think I lucked out when the lightning only hit my right side. That means it missed my heart. The lightning was almost a complete direct hit, but I think

I fell before it completely engulfed me. I wouldn't be in this mess if I wasn't too weak to help myself. I'm just too weak. I need to get stronger. I need more power!"

"Don't beat yourself up! We all-," Kinra speaks but is cut off by Luke. "No, he's right. If I had been more powerful, none of us would have suffered so much either. I couldn't protect you all. And without power, you can't protect anything. I need power too." "It sucks to lose. We have a duty to attend to, and we can't even think of completing it if we're too weak," Jadeanu quotes. "Next time we meet someone formidable, I'll take care of them. I won't lose again." "Then from this day forward, we will become stronger, and we'll make it till the end of this," Luke inspires as he puts his hand out. Jadeanu and Ren put their hands on top of his. "This will be our promise. Our tri-tribute. None of us shall die prematurely until WE define our peace with it." They all nod.

After a while of sitting in the rain, Luke starts to get tired and begins to drop his shield. "Luke, you can drop it. I'll just hold my maps under me to keep 'em dry," Ricardio resolves. "No, I'll hold it. If I'm not strong enough to hold this, then I might as well accept death now." "Whoa, a bit intense there. But okay then, just don't push yourself too hard. You'll end up pushing and pushing, and before you know it, everyone will be pushed away. Then you'll forget that you've ever had anyone in the first place. Don't forget that you are not alone here. We'll help you if ever needed." "Yeah, I know. Thank you though."

Blast creates a fire to keep everyone warm from the moist breeze, and it adds to the camplike scenery. "So we're getting close to our destination huh?" Ren asks. "Geez, how long was I out?" "Not as long as you think. But yeah, now our real journey can begin," Jadeanu replies. "You said this place is called No Man's Forest right?" Ren questions. "Why is that?" "Because apparently people come here, and they don't come out." "Well great. Oh! And you never actually told me what exactly we are trying to accomplish by coming here."

"Oh yeah! So hear me out, there's an angel here by the name of Gibil, and he's going to help us craft a weapon strong enough to wield these powerful objects called Blessings. It's a bit weird, so I'll just have to show you." "Okay then. Makes me wonder. Maybe the angel knows or even is the reason that people disappear here." Luke butts in saying, "I doubt that's the case. Why would an angel have a reason to do that?" "I don't know about that," Jadeanu adds. "That Knowledge angel killed people, so I wouldn't be surprised if Gibil did the same. Angels aren't exactly the nicest people you can meet. They are warriors of Heaven."

Suddenly, the sound of leaves being crunched fills the ominous scene. The group stops what they are doing and looks into the distance, ready to fight. A very old man walks toward them, holding an umbrella with one hand and holding the other up in surrender. He doesn't have special-colored eyes, so he seems to be no threat.

"Oh, it's just an old man," Ren realizes, and everyone relieves from caution. "You know, you young people shouldn't be traveling in a forest like this in the rain. It could be dangerous, or you could catch a cold," the old man says. His voice is genuine and kind-hearted. He has long grey hair and a long, straight-down, flowing beard. "I have a cabin not far from here. It would be best if you came with me for some shelter. You all look tired; some rest will do you good."

Jadeanu turns to his group members. Stougma is the first to speak. "We shouldn't go. He's clearly trying to lead us into a trap. He's probably the reason people disappear." "I agree we should be wary of him, but I doubt he'll just attack us," Jadeanu inputs. "I think we should go with him," Luke suggests. "Even if it is a trap, there's only so much one old man who doesn't have powers can do. We need shelter. We don't have much strength left. Let's just consider it." Before anyone could disagree, Luke says, "Yeah, we'll go." "Good. Come with me."

The old man leads everyone through the forest, and they all stay under Luke's shield. "Ya know people disappear in this forest. You're much safer in a home. People who have a place of refuge don't have to worry about some outside force taking them." the old man says. "That means your friend could still be here," Luke mentions. "Yeah, possibly," Ricardio agrees. The old-looking wooden cabin the old man talked about peers into view quite quickly. The old man opens the creaky wooden door and holds the umbrella over Luke's head when he dispels his shield.

The old man lights a fire in his fireplace in front of his large, nearly empty living room. He has a wooden bench there covered with pillows, facing a small TV. He has a bookshelf full of books in the corner of the room opposite the corner where the TV is placed. "Make yourselves at home," he says. "What's your name sir?" Jadeanu asks. "It's Jinzen." Jinzen then walks into a nearby room and says, "I'm going to get some blankets for you all. You must be freezing from the cold."

Stougma seizes the current situation as an opportunity to check out the house for anything suspicious. "We should see how "safe" this place really is." "I'm against it. I get suspicion but don't go through this man's things," Jadeanu repels. "Yeah, don't ruin the guy's trust. Don't let your fear lead you to something you'll regret," Luke opposes. "I understand that you're decent people, but this may be life or death here," Ricardio agrees with Stougma. "I agree with Jadeanu and Luke here, but if you're going to investigate anyway, then the knowledge should come to all of us. I'll keep a lookout," Blast reassures. "You guys go ahead. Report any suspicious findings," Jadeanu plans.

Stougma leads the rest quietly around the cabin. They open a door in the living room and find a hidden flight of stairs. It leads up into pitch blackness. Blast uses his powers to generate a dim orange energy on his body to light up the area around him. Kinra then finds a light switch and flicks it on. Lights illuminate the staircase. Blast relieves his body's light, and everyone walks up the stairs.

Up the stairwell is a single door with a window to show what's inside. Stougma takes a peek through the window. Inside is a single structure holding a lamp. Not a lamp that lights up but a strange golden metal lamp that looks like a mug with an elephant trunk. It is luxurious, definitely not made cheaply, and has many glowing colors around it. "What is that?" Blast asks. "I'll tell you what it is," Jinzen's raspy old voice replies from behind them.

The boys all jump from fear as none of them had known that he was there. Jinzen smiles and answers. "That is my special lamp. An old family heirloom. Beautiful, isn't it?" he then pulls out a key and unlocks the door with it. Jinzen walks up and grabs the handle of the lamp. "It is said to be a symbol of spiritual freedom or binding. More of a swirl between the two. Some believe that it can trap souls, and the demon that traps them can infuse their body into the lamp and become an unstoppable force. A genie of unfathomable power. But I don't believe any of that. I just keep it around for good luck." Jinzen puts the lamp back where it was, closes the door, and locks it. "Now come. It's not nice to go through someone's things. Although I know your brains are likely filled with curiosity."

Jinzen leads everyone back downstairs to Jadeanu and Luke. They are holding the blankets that Jinzen promised to bring them. "Now I'm sure you all are hungry. I'll get you some food and hot coco." Jinzen walks into the kitchen. "Jadeanu we've got to get out of here," Stougma demands. "This guy's creepy, and he's got some weird lamp that he says can trap souls to turn someone into an all-powerful genie. He claims it's some kind of strange symbol of freedom and binding."

"Don't be rude about it. We really need to chill here for now. We'll escape when it's necessary," Luke suggests. "We'll stay cautious. There isn't anything he can do right now. If we stay respectful but not ignorant, we'll be fine," Jadeanu guides. "Now let's wait for food, then we'll get some sleep. After that, we'll make our escape." "If we don't get poisoned first, I suggest we trust Jinzen. It's our best bet for survival," Ricardio inputs. "Don't forget that that assassin could still be around too."

Jinzen soon walks back into the room, passing out full plates and mugs filled with steamy hot brown liquid to his guests. "So Jinzen, do you just live out here by yourself?" Jadeanu wonders. "Indeed I do," Jinzen replies. "I once had a friend who would come to visit me every day, but she was killed long ago. I was never a very sociable guy, and I haven't had company ever since. I thought it'd be better to just live out here alone." After several minutes of communion, as Jinzen further explains the wonders of his great and kind old female friend of his, everyone eventually falls asleep. Jinzen turns out the lights and walks away.

A few minutes pass by, and Stougma reawakens due to fear of being attacked in his sleep. He stands up and begins to scale out the cabin in suspicion. He is slightly startled by a rumble from close by. Luke then pops up and asks. "What are you doing?" "I can't sleep. I want to see if there is anything we need to worry about," Stougma whispers back. "Tell me if you find anything. I can't really sleep either." Luke lays back down. Stougma continues to scout the house.

Stougma creeps through a short dark hallway and into the master bedroom where Jinzen sleeps, but when he peers into the room, it's empty. Stougma moves cautiously to the room upstairs. He turns on the light switch and advances. He reaches the room with the lamp and peaks through the window. The luxurious magic lamp is gone too. Stougma's heart begins to race out of fear of the unknown. He hurriedly moves down the stairs trying to make as little noise as possible. *'Okay! I've got to take this guy out for good,'* Stougma thinks. *'He's clearly up to something. I just need a little bit of evidence to prove it.'* Stougma takes a deep breath and walks outside.

He creeps through the dark woods, unable to see much. The mission is to find Jinzen and confirm if the others are safe. He continues walking until he hears the distinctive sound of speaking. Stougma hides behind a tree and then takes a peek at where the voice is coming from. He beholds an unforgettable sight. He spies Jinzen talking to a spirit that looks like it is emerging from the magic lamp from earlier. Even more disturbing, Jinzen now has red eyes.

'Yup, it's confirmed. He's bad news.' In an awkward moment, Jinzen notices Stougma and looks in his direction. Stougma quickly hides back behind the tree in the hopes that Jinzen didn't actually see him. He looks down at his feet for a moment, then he looks forward. He immediately meets his eyes with Jinzen. An explosion quickly generates toward the old man from Stougma's fear. The explosion and Stougma both halt in place as Jinzen's hand is fully extended.

Stougma suddenly flies into the air. Jinzen then starts bending his wrinkled fingers slightly, which somehow causes Stougma's body to condense into itself. His body bends in unnatural ways and combines into itself. All of the bones in his body shatter as his body continues to brutally envelope itself. His body continues to horrifically dissolve until he is nothing more than a small sphere of flesh and meat.

Jinzen's hand, now almost completely balled, motions for Stougma's remains to fly into his fingertips. For that is the size of Stougma now. It all happened so fast that he never even had much time to scream. Jinzen picks up his lamp and adds Stougma's remains to an empty socket where the gems are usually stored. Stougma's orb turns orange as it is socketed. "Yes. One more soul and I will become an unstoppable force. Then I will finally be able to make this disgusting world collapse into flames," Jinzen narrates.

He then returns to the cabin with his eyes back to their native innocent amber color as if nothing has happened. Morning comes around, but it is still early and therefore dark outside. Jinzen moves around the cabin, and everyone else wakes up from the noise. "Where's Stougma?" Jadeanu immediately questions. "I think he went out. I do hope he didn't run into trouble," Jinzen responds in his innocent old voice. Luke looks sternly at Jadeanu and responds, "Stougma went out to investigate the place yesterday and never came back. The thing is, that you came back shortly after." Jadeanu then stands up with a vengeful look in his eyes. "Jinzen, what did you do to Stougma?" "I had hoped that it wouldn't have to come to this," Jinzen says as he walks toward the door of the cabin. "Admit it! You're the one that makes people disappear, aren't you?" Luke demands. "It doesn't even matter. I have what I need from you anyway." Jinzen replies as his eyes return to red, and he opens his door, jets out of it, and closes it.

Jadeanu and the others follow, but Jinzen seems to be gone. "How on earth was he able to hide his powers?" Kinra wonders. "I'm not sure, but I guess it would be possible," Ricardio theorizes. "You are all going to die! Just like this pathetic world!" Jinzen's voice echoes through the wind.

He then appears next to Ricardio and swings his hand with something in it. Ricardio's reflexes are quick enough to dodge the incoming attack. In Jinzen's hand is a knife. After missing the attack, he palms Ricardio, thus sending him flying into the air and tumbling to the ground. He tries to get up immediately but is restrained by the grass that moves on its own somehow and keeps him down. Ren uses his shadow to attack, making spikes extend. Jinzen performs a strong backflip, followed by many in mid-air. He sticks the landing perfectly, which is odd still considering his old age.

Blast frees Ricardio and makes an advance with Luke. They both start firing projectiles at Jinzen. He grabs a bush, and it turns into a shield of leaves. The shield is strong enough to take the attacks, then it turns into several leaf spears that pursue their attackers. Jadeanu jumps in to attack the spears with his energized hands. Jinzen's shadow then extends and stabs him in the ribs. "Augh! You youngins. Stupidly naive, fighting the inevitable as if it will change things," Jinzen shouts before jumping into some bushes.

"Good work Ren. You must have gotten a bit better at controlling other people's shadows," Luke congratulates. Everyone's shadow starts to move, and spikes extend from each of them toward their owners. Everyone moves in time to avoid the sudden attack. Ren looks confused though, saying, "That wasn't me." "Is there anything that he can't do?" Blast complains. "There's something strange going on here," Jadeanu analyzes.

Jinzen reappears out of an opening in the ground that wasn't there before. He throws his hands out toward Luke and Ren. Knives extend and travel toward both of them. Ren moves quick enough to dodge them, and Luke deploys a shield. Suddenly a small fist smacks Jinzen dead in the face. He backtracks from slight pain but withstanding very little damage. Jinzen looks at his attacker, who is Kinra.

He covers his mouth with the side of his fist, takes a deep breath, and blows with all his force. A searing orange flame proceeds toward Kinra with immense speed and force. Luke rockets forward and tackles Kinra out of the way. Jadeanu runs forward, does a front flip, and comes in with an obvious super punch. Jinzen forms another leaf shield that Jadeanu slams his fist into. It breaks very easily, and he lands on his feet but is distracted, stopping him from attacking Jinzen. "Last time, this shield was able to take attacks from Luke and Seinaru. But it just felt like paper when I hit it. Something odd is definitely up here."

Jinzen blows fire in Jadeanu's direction. Jadeanu moves quick enough to avoid the blaze entirely. "Hey Luke, come here," he motions. "What is it?" Luke asks. "Get him to attack this way. There's something I want to see." Luke obeys and fires at Jinzen. Jinzen blocks the attack with a knife and then points it at Luke. The blade extends at them both, and Luke creates a shield.

The knife pushes against his shield, causing sparks to fly. The shield holds up without much of a problem. "Luke! The knife is getting through!" Jadeanu panics. Luke fills with worry and looks at the collision. The knife cracks the shield at that very moment. "I knew it!" Jadeanu claims. The shield breaks as Jadeanu grabs his brother and jumps to the ground. "His powers aren't real, or rather they are only as dangerous as you think they are," Jadeanu concludes. "That doesn't make much sense, but it's the only lead we have, so I'll believe it, but will the others? And will they be quick enough for it to make a difference is the question," Luke states.

Ricardio runs up to the brothers with an idea. "Hey, we have no solid leads in this fight. That means we can't win as things are now. Maybe we should give him what he wants." "What?" "I mean that lamp of his. Something tells me that he's the demon he said can trap souls. He also mentioned that it's a double-edged sword. He wants to gain spiritual freedom by becoming a genie. He claimed that the 'demon' would become infused within the thing once they used it. Maybe we can trap him inside of the lamp somehow."

"Not sure what exactly you're talking about, but it does sound like our best course of action. Considering what we know about our enemy, defeating him might be out of the question, so…" Luke elaborates.

"Where is the lamp?" Jadeanu demands.

"It's upstairs," Ricardio answers.

Ren and Blast continue fighting off Jinzen while the three of them conversate. Jinzen notices them and spawns a spike trap underneath them. Luke carries Ricardio and bolts away. Jadeanu dodges, and with his momentum, he lunges toward Jinzen's cabin. He soars through the air and breaks through the wooden wall covering the upper levels of the shelter. He lands directly in the room with the lamp.

"There's definitely a malevolent aura coming from this thing." he claims as he grabs the lamp and jumps out back into the fray of the battle. Jinzen shoots a fireball as soon as Jadeanu lands. Jadeanu punches it with energy causing it to dispatch. "Okay, got it. Now what do we do?" Jadeanu asks. "I'm not sure. But that lamp likely has souls trapped within it. That's likely what happened to Stougma. We need him to try to release the bonds of the souls so we can try to trap him. We need to force him to use the lamp," Ricardio strategizes. "But if we fail, that would mean he would turn into…a…an all-powerful genie," Luke fears.

Jinzen goes into the bulk of the forest, and there are growls from within. Out comes a huge bear, and Jinzen comes out riding a red-eyed wolf. "But all we need to do is force him to believe that we can beat him, a bluff to entice him to use the lamp. Then while he's changing, we should be able to bind him in right?" Jadeanu plans. "I hope so. But if we don't do something, we'll all die anyway," Ricardio tells. "Our best bet is to tire him out. Despite his powers, he's considerably older than us, so he has much less stamina than us. Once he gets tired, he'll get desperate even if he has the upper hand. We just have to get him moving."

The bear comes toward Ren and attacks. Ren creates a shield with his shadow, but the bear's force goes through the shield and knocks Ren into the air. Thus his shadow falls back into just a faint image. He tumbles to the ground. "Everyone, focus your attacks on Jinzen!" Jadeanu announces. The bear walks up to Jadeanu and receives a back fist that sends the bear flying. The bear then runs back into the forest. Jadeanu then puts the lamp on the floor next to a bush. He tells Kinra to guard it so as not to get Kinra killed in the fray of battle. He then takes the lead and comes toward Jinzen and the wolf.

The wolf shoots a stream of fire from its mouth. "The fire isn't real. It's just what my mind perceives," Jadeanu calms. The fire gets smaller, but it continues toward him. Jadeanu dodges at the last minute. "Well I guess that attack was real." The wolf continues to blow fire, and Jinzen creates a huge gust of ominous wind then lightning appears on his hands. The wind blows everyone away from Jinzen. Jadeanu adds energy to both of his legs and holds his ground. "Why are you doing this Jinzen?" he demands. "If everyone is going to rip this world apart, then why not join the fun? And I've been wanting to help this world burst into flames far before now. With the power to do so, I will finally get the chance to make sure that it happens," Jinzen replies.

The wolf's fire accelerates because of the wind. Luke uses a shield to defend him and Blast as they push against the wind. Jadeanu and Ren are positioned away from the fire in their respective places. Jadeanu takes a step forward. "But why do you want to see the world's destruction?" he asks. "Because all of it is utterly revolting as is all life. Everything on this Earth is sinful and filthy. Bombings made to take innocent lives for selfish reasons. Mothers who don't love their children. A father who forces his ideals undetered on his only son! People who abuse the ones they say they love! I will take pleasure out of ending it all," Jinzen states. "Starting with you."

A flash of light emits in the clouds, and vast lightning comes down on Jinzen's attackers. Ren immediately fills with fear due to the trauma of getting struck last time. Luke looks up at the sky and moves his shield up to take the lightning. *It's not that dangerous,* Luke compromises. The lightning strikes his shield and disappears. "Whoa, it worked!" he celebrates. The wind had time to blow him and Blast out of the fire's range, saving them from being scorched. Blast fires a random beam during their backward movement.

Ricardio, who was standing on the sidelines, witnessed what had happened. Ren was to be struck by three whole lightning bolts at once due to his perceived fear of being struck. Blast had shot his beam at Ren to hit him away from the thunder. It was a calculated risk due to the lack of defense against the fire, but good thing that the wind was blowing. Jadeanu, being much closer to Jinzen than anyone else, was out of the lightning's range. Jinzen's wind stopped blowing due to the end of his attack. Jadeanu seizes the chance and runs full speed toward him. Jinzen quickly dismounts the wolf and runs behind some bushes. Jadeanu follows but is interrupted by the wolf.

The wolf tries to bite him. Consequently, he grabs the wolf by its neck with an energized arm. He then watches as Jinzen crawls almost pathetically into the bush and then disappears. He then reappears next to Blast, and they immediately initiate conflict. Jadeanu throws the wolf hard back into the bulk of the forest and joins in. *His moves must still work when someone still believes that he's really doing what he seems,'* Jadeanu guesses. "That makes it harder to win in a group."

Ren and Luke rejoin the fight. They all overwhelm Jinzen but fail to land any attacks on him. He begins to get exhausted from using his powers too much. Everyone does. Even Jadeanu loses his red eyes out of exhaustion. Yet they all have Jinzen surrounded. *'We're all on the ropes just as much as he is. But he still has the advantage with his powers. We just have to bluff him through it,'* Jadeanu hypothesizes. He turns to Kinra, yells, "EVERYBODY ATTACK," and motions for Kinra to throw him the lamp. Everyone then attacks.

Jinzen creates a shield of grass that takes everyone's attacks as Jadeanu catches the airborne lamp. He closes his eyes and reopens them. His eyebrows arch, and his eyes are now red again with the last bit of willpower he can muster. He looks at Luke, who is looking at him as well. Luke nods and stops attacking with his beams. Everyone else follows.

Jinzen brings down his shield and shoots fireballs at everyone. When a fireball comes toward Jadeanu, he adds energy to his arm and prepares to block the attack. He stares dead at it and whispers, "Come on." The fireball slams into his arm and knocks him back. He then throws the lamp toward Jinzen in an attempt to look like it was accidental. He falls to the ground, and the last bit of red in his eyes flees. The lamp falls by Jinzen's feet.

He notices it and picks it up. "Since you all are so concerned with your old friend, I'll have you know that he's alive. Just like all the others. But now you will watch him die what would seem like twice!" Jinzen quotes as he opens the lamp, throwing the top of it into the grass. A whirlwind emits from the top, and the same spirit that Stougma had seen Jinzen talking to comes forth. "Witness the power to destroy a world. I want the change now!" Jinzen shouts. The spirit then projects an image of Stougma getting turned into a ball of flesh and then socketed into the lamp as the orange ball.

Jinzen then turns into a spirit himself and levitates above the lamp. Jinzen becomes one with his desires, forcing his mind to see what event set him on his path. He thinks about a young woman with blonde hair and vibrant amber eyes, the very woman who he told the others stories about before they all went to bed in Jinzen's cabin.

"Why do you live out here in the middle of nowhere?" the woman asked. "Like I told you April, I despise people, the way that they think, and their filthy technology," young Jinzen answered. "I fear that if I run into too many people, I'd end up seriously hurting them in a blind rage." "You haven't hurt me. And from where I'm standing, you don't look like a guy angry enough at the world to hurt people." "I don't have a reason to hurt you. You seem nice." "Yeah, well, I've got to go. I'll see you soon!" "Soon? I don't usually have recurring visitors." "Well that won't do for me. I'll be back tomorrow!"

And from that day forward, April came to visit Jinzen in his forest every day, always arriving with a gift for him until they eventually became friends. "April! What happened to your leg?" Jinzen asked one day after seeing two small bloody marks on April's leg. "I got bit by a snake while making my way here to your house. Don't worry, though. I don't think it was poisonous." "You've got to be careful out there. The gods made animals very poorly. They are just selfish and violent brats." "Don't say that about animals. They are just trying their best to maintain what they have for the good of their own environment. Wouldn't you do the same in their shoes? I say all animals are wonderful creations despite the downsides."

Another day, April showed up at Jinzen's home with a slight bruise on her arm. "What happened to your arm?" Jinzen concerned. "There's this guy that I'm close to. When he's angry, sometimes he just can't control himself," April said cheerfully. "So he hit you?" "I know it sounds bad, but he's a good guy. He just needs a little help, that's all. You don't need to worry about me. Everything's fine. Instead, focus on this cherry pie I made just for you!"

Jinzen started to deeply respect April for her courage and optimism. He started to truly admire her, yet every day, she would show up at his house with more and more severe burns, bruises, and scratches. "April, why don't you stay here and live with me? A good woman like you should never have to endure someone's abuse. I can treat you the way you should be treated." "I'm sorry Jinzen, but I can't. You seem like a great guy. You're smart and handsome. But I can't live with you. The man who hits me is my fiancé, and I'm planning on moving to live with him. I'm also starting to fear that he's catching on to my visits here. It could make him jealous, and he'll take the frustration out on me, so I'll have to limit visiting you."

"Why do you still come here? You keep running into trouble with the wild animals, and you get beaten by your fiancé. This isn't good for you. You should make a solid decision about where you want to spend your time. Please stay with me and experience the life you deserve. You're the only person I have in this world. I don't like seeing you hurt." "I've made up my mind Jinzen. I appreciate your concern, but I want to walk through this. I want to please my fiancé, but I want to see you too. You both are good people who need a little push. So this is what I choose."

And with those words, Jinzen's admiration for April turned into stronger disdain for the way of the world and even toward April. He started to resent her foolishness, yet he kept his hatred masked in the hopes of winning her over. And with every bruise he saw on her, the more he started to resent her, but he was able to hide it with the kindness he had learned from her. Everything went south however, when April's husband found out about her constant visits to see Jinzen. On that day, Jinzen took a stroll to where he'd normally meet April, where he saw her beaten badly, lying with no life left in her body as the first person to have "mysteriously" disappeared in the very forest Jinzen lives in. On her body was a note saying, "You can have her now."

From then on, Jinzen desired nothing more than to see the world crumble. He thought that if the world was going to destroy itself anyway, he'd want to join in the chaos. He had lost everything with her death and wanted to make a statement in his forest, making others disappear as the world made April disappear. With the power he gained from the Death Spiral several decades later, he became able to do just that, but now with purpose. A purpose brought about through the sudden reaction of the magic lamp housing a once inactive evil spirit. It promised Jinzen the power to destroy the world as his world was destroyed. A promise to free Jinzen's bottled-up rage once covered in fear.

Jinzen aims to finish gaining at least most of the power he was promised, thanks to the number of souls he had taken. He triumphantly smiles as his body shifts to another image. But that image is then interrupted, and everything from the scene returns to normal in the blink of an eye. Ricardio had fastened the lamp's lid back onto the lamp, thus trapping the spirit form of Jinzen inside. Everyone breathes a breath of relief, and Jadeanu smiles before he relaxes and lays his head down.

Luke goes over to Ricardio and picks up the lamp. He looks at the orange orb and says, "If you are alive Stougma, then we'll get you back." "That's right if we can just find a god or an angel that can bring him and all the others who are stuck with him back…" Jadeanu hypothesizes. "Then it's settled. We bring the lamp with us," Ricardio commands. "I'll carry it with my arrows." Ricardio grabs the lamp and eases it into his quiver. "Are we sure that it's safe carrying that thing with us?" Ren concerns. "The lid is strong and sturdy, plus it locks. As long as we keep it on the thing, then we should be fine," Ricardio reassures. "We should all catch our breath before we move on," Jadeanu advises. "But at least we stopped the man responsible for the disappearances. A noble deed to consider."

Meanwhile, the angel Ravah and his followers explore the land. Ravah stops at a lake. This particular lake acts as a constant reminder of how filthy humans can be. The body of water is vastly polluted by human trash. Plastic, oil, paper, and many other forms of trash fill the water, turning it slightly green. Ravah sneers. "Humans can be so filthy sometimes. It's amazing how they think and act. Ever so contradictory. This world was given to them, and this is what they do? Disgusting."

Ravah throws up his hands, which creates a huge wormhole in the air coated with purple smoke. The wormhole sucks up all the trash and pollution in the water. The hole then closes and explodes. Ravah holds out his hands as in saying stand back nonverbally. He then does a high front flip and sticks the landing with his hands lightly touching the lake water. The whole lake creates a wave that continues forward, opposite where Ravah is standing. Once the lake is fully calmed, it returns to its beautiful blue color and glistens with the morning sun.

"Beautiful isn't it?" Ravah claims. "Lovely. Yet may I ask why you did that?" Vermunya asks. "We recently destroyed an entire city. At least it wasn't like that time Javean destroyed a portion of Heaven equal to the size of this planet. However, doing this is only fair to balance out our unfortunate deed," Ravah compromises.

Far away, Jadeanu and his acquaintances are fully rested and ready to continue on their mission. "My maps are dry now, or at least dry enough. We can find my friend now if you all are up to it," Ricardio says. "Okay good, 'cause I was getting sick of doing this."

Ren points to the ground. Everyone's shadow was connected to some sort of shadow web. "Wow, that's pretty cool. I see you've been training," Jadeanu realizes. "But yeah, let's go. We've got a lot ahead of us. Lead the way, Rico!"

Chapter 5:

Our Nature Is Hard Work

"This way," Ricardio gestures. "Just around these trees... Ahh, there it is." In front of the boys stands a big house made of red bricks. Ricardio knocks on the door hoping his friend is alive. After a few seconds, the door swings open, and a handsome, muscular man with white skin, brown eyes, and a thick short-boxed beard comes forth. A smile spreads across his face as the words, "Hey Ricardio," escape his lips. "Hey there Goldo," Ricardio responds. "I see you've got company. Why don't we come inside?" Goldo greets everyone as they enter his somewhat luxurious home.

There are many different types of weapons plastered on the walls. He also has a few dead animal antiques. Goldo closes the door and gestures that everyone sits down on his large brown couch. "So what brings you here Rico? You don't usually visit, especially with so many guests. Not to mention the situation we're all in." "Well, these two boys are the ones I've been telling you about." "So that's Luke and Jadeanu?" "Yep. My old childhood friends. They came all this way because they wanted some kind of powerful weapon. They plan on fighting some kind of god. You're a blacksmith, so I figured you could help," Ricardio explains.

"We might need you. There's a blacksmithing angel nearby. With you and him working together, it shouldn't be too hard to come up with something," Jadeanu adds. "This means I'll have to leave the safety of my home and go out into that crazy world. But fine, I'll help. I know you, and many people no longer ask for my services."

"I'm surprised he believes us about the angel. He didn't even ask," Kinra whispers to Luke. "Hey, may I ask about these animal antiques? Are you killing for sport?" Luke questions trying not to sound rude. "No no. All of these buddies were either for food or out of self-defense. No, here we all exist in harmony. We help each other around here. I could have let them dissolve into the ground, but I wanted to put their remains to use."

"Wait, do you believe us about the angel?" Kinra asks. "Well yeah. I felt something powerful enter these woods days ago. I know that the gods and angels exist, and I know about all the chaos outside the forest. I have no choice but to believe you. I'm just glad I'm not dead. I didn't get no powers either. So if we're gonna do this thing, I'll need help from all of you. This forest is big. I hope you all know where you're going." Goldo takes two swords from the wall. "I'm gonna need some protection."

Goldo leads everyone out of his home and into the dangers of the forest. "Now where to?" Jadeanu closes his eyes, then opens them and says, "There." He takes the lead, and everyone follows him. After a bit of walking, conversation springs up. "So, Luke, Jadeanu, what kind of weapon are you trying to make?" Goldo questions. "Well, there are seven of what I'm trying to put in the weapon. So maybe gauntlets? But then it won't be symmetrical…." Jadeanu brainstorms. "Hey you know after we're done with the weapon crafting, do you want to travel with us?" Ricardio asks Goldo. "Ya know I would do a lot for you, but this traveling stuff ain't for me. I'm here to help you forge, but that's all. I'm going back home after this," Goldo answers.

Suddenly the sound of fast-paced small footsteps came straight for the guys. A deer comes trotting their way at full speed. They all dodge it quickly enough. It appeared as if the deer was running from something. "Well that was weird. Let's all stay watchful in case we find what he was running from," Luke advises. A few more peaceful minutes pass and Ren asks, "How much further Jadeanu?" "It's still a bit far, but we're much closer," Jadeanu answers.

"Hey, by the way, have any of you guys run into an old man who lives out here?" Goldo questions. "He and I never met, but I've seen the guy a few times. I've seen him visit a lone gravestone of someone named April. Have you guys seen anything like that around here?" "We've met the old man, and apparently, he was good friends with that April woman back when he was young," Jadeanu mentions. "Turns out her death may have pushed the guy over an edge. It's a good thing you've never met him."

In the distance behind where the guys are walking, two men stand in the trees. One of them holds out his hand, and out comes a fireball. It travels through the air toward Luke's backside. He feels the heat behind him, then uses his feet to rocket away though he isn't fast enough. He only pushes a few inches before the fireball hits the ground and blasts him several feet. He tumbles severely on the ground in smoke. He grunts and says, "I'm fine." Everyone turns their attention behind them, where the attack came from. There stands the assassin and Thrale.

The assassin's eyebrows arch with intense rage as he shoots more rapid fireballs. Ren uses all his muscles to lift everyone's shadow up into a shield guarding each of them. The fireballs hit Blast's, Ricardio's, and Ren's shadows, thus causing them to explode, which deters the damage but not the impact, sending the three flyings.

The assassin adds electricity to both of his hands and mixes them both together into an extreme lightning current connecting the two. The assassin simultaneously puts both of his hands in the air. An entire storm of lightning begins to come down all at once. Luke looks concerned at Ricardio, who is now on the floor, completely defenseless. He then puts both of his hands together as he yells at the moment. "Hhhaaahh!" He lifts his hands into the air creating the densest shield Luke has ever created. "Whoa! That's one thick shield!" Ren exclaims. The lightning collides with the shield and pushes it down instantly. "Mark 3!" Blast yells as he fires an already charged-up Pyro cannon at the shield to support it.

About twenty lightning bolts are pushing against Luke's shield. Ren looks toward the assassin and Thrale, then throws his shadow at them as a blade. Thrale transforms into several sheets of paper and blows away. The assassin barely moves when dodging the attack. He returns the favor with an attack of his own. He shoots a fireball at Ren, who dives out of the way.

Just then, the shield above him cracks and breaks. The lightning goes through Blast's pyro cannon as well. The electricity shrinks substantially but still strikes the entire field. Luke is directly hit on his shoulder and is sent flying into the air from the immense energy. Blast gets struck directly in the face and bounces off the floor back into the air. Ren is hit on the back, which propels him into the air.

Everyone else is not directly hit, but the energy current still strikes all of them. They shake and stumble from the energy coursing through their bodies. Kinra lies on the ground, unable to move. Goldo is still standing, but he drops his swords. His hands have burn marks on them due to the metal of his swords conducting the electricity into his palms. Ricardio is barely fazed due to being mostly out of combat range. Ren struggles to stand. He then creates a cane out of his shadow to further lift him. "Guys you did it!" he blurts out while the blood drains from his forehead. "That lightning was a lot weaker than last time. Your shield and blast must have weakened it."

Luke stands back up, and his gaze immediately goes to the new member Goldo. "Sorry about all of this. We probably should have mentioned that these two have been traveling around trying to kill us." "What!? Oh well, I'll let it slide. For now, what matters is survivin'," Goldo responds. He reaches down to pick up his blades despite the pain in his palms.

"Is Seinaru okay?" Jadeanu, who has been standing the whole time, says concerned. Luke looks at Blast, who is still on the ground. Blast has his face covered by his palms. "Umm, I'm not sure," Luke replies. Just then, Blast throws his right hand in the air, signaling that he's okay. He then sits up, still holding his face with his other hand.

The assassin charges up another tesla jolt on both of his hands, ready to fire again. Before he could, Thrale comes from what seems like nowhere and shapes himself into a giant ninja star, and goes full speed towards Blast. The assassin discharges his hands. Luke starts shooting gas balls at Thrale, who moves precisely to dodge them.

Luke stumbles due to the damage to his body and discontinues his assault. Jadeanu steps up next with his feet grounded and his hands filled with energy, ready to stop Thrale in his tracks. Thrale curves around Jadeanu and strikes him in the shoulder as he passes. He continues straight for Blast, who is still just sitting there.

Blast quickly fires at him; he dodges it and continues his rotation to slice through Blast's flesh on his left arm, causing Blast to move it off his face showing a massive bloody scar all over his face. Thrale then shifts back to his human form, and with his spinning momentum, he kicks Blast square in his bleeding face. Blast's head is forced back as he grabs Thrale's leg with his left hand for leverage. With his right hand, he shoots a blast directly into Thrale, forcing him into the air. Thrale uses the momentum to perform a backflip and land on his feet, but as he does it, he is hit by another blast.

The assassin combines both of his hands to create a bigger fireball and shoots it at Ren. Ren uses his shadow to throw himself out of the way. The fireball hits the ground and creates an explosion double the size of his usual fireballs. "Wow, that thing was huge!" Ren exclaims. "I won't be able to keep dodging those things. Those shadow shields I made really drained me. It's only a matter of time before my body will be too tired to even use powers," Ren looks toward Goldo and says, "I'll try to hold him off. You should go focus on the other guy." Goldo obeys and moves toward Blast and Thrale. "Ren, Luke, Jadeanu! Come here," Ricardio commands.

Ren is fairly close to Ricardio, so he doesn't have to move very much. Luke stands up and jogs over there to them, and so does Jadeanu. "Alright, now we still have to take care of the assassin," Ricardio starts. "Depart!" Luke yells after looking in the assassin's direction. He grabs Ricardio and rockets off. Jadeanu and Ren quickly move away. An ice sphere hits near the ground when it explodes. It explodes to the full size of his normal ice spheres, then it erupts again, much bigger and with more spikes. "That thing's dangerous!" Jadeanu says in shock. "This must have been the product of two of those things put together," Ren hypothesizes.

They all come back together, taking refuge near the iceberg. "His attacks are still lethal against him," Ricardio resumes. "But if his own lightning won't work, what will?" Ren asks. Ricardio points at the iceberg and says, "This."

"That would mean someone's got to get their hands dirty," Jadeanu claims.

"Good. Now all we've got to do is get him out of the trees," Ricardio plans.

"I've got an idea," Luke tells him as he explains the plan to Ricardio and Jadeanu.

Lightning strikes the area, and Luke throws up his shield to defend himself, and with the shelter of the iceberg, the guys are safe. Then he motions for everyone to follow as he moves toward Blast and Thrale. Goldo is blocking Thrale's now paper sword hand while Blast sits and supports. Jadeanu closes in with energy on his hands and restrains Thrale's arm. The assassin's attacks stop now that all his targets are too close to his ally. He jumps down from the tree with lightning in his hands. He aims toward Kinra, who has just gotten up. He shoots a fireball at him. The plan could fail if someone makes themselves a target by trying to save him, making everyone a bit hesitant. Suddenly Kinra's shadow grabs and yanks him with the others. They all feel relieved and thank Ren with a nod.

The assassin walks closer with electricity still in his hands. "He's planning on prying us apart one by one," Luke reveals. "Then show him that that's a bad idea," Goldo says while giving Luke one of his blades. Confused, Luke looks at the approaching assassin and back at the sword. "Ohh, I see," Luke says as he places the weapon on Thrale's neck, holding it on both ends.

The assassin then stops approaching. Thrale doesn't do anything due to the fact that his arm is being thoroughly squished by Jadeanu. His other arm is a sword already opposing Goldo's, and Luke has a sword on his neck. If he moves, he will pay. The assassin, not truly caring about his comrade, shoots at Ricardio, who is the furthest from Thrale.

The assassin doesn't seem to care much if Thrale dies; he just doesn't want to lose an ally if he can help it. Jadeanu shoves Thrale toward the incoming fireball in an attempt to save Ricardio and jumps back. Everyone evades except for Blast. He pushes Thrale out of the way and tries to rocket away. He isn't fast enough, however and is caught by the Blast of the fireball when it hits the ground.

He bolts away but not in the way he wanted to. He spirals onto the ground with steam radiating from him. That's when a terrible sight is seen. Blast's left calf muscle and below are gone. His right leg is severely burnt, and his left knee and thigh are too. His whole body is scorched, but his legs are the worst. Luke is awe-struck. Jadeanu is shocked as well, but his expression is more internal. Thrale looks at his injured former comrade and then examines himself.

He looks at the assassin with sympathetic eyes. He runs to the assassin and says, "Look at him. This isn't what we are here to do. He was our ally."

The assassin ignores Thrale and shoots more fireballs at the others. "What are you even trying to gain out of this! There is nothing for you here! Don't you see Mishu is just using you! Just like he was using me with promises of a luxurious life to sway my judgment." Thrale continues and moves in the assassin's way, blocking his view of his targets. The assassin grips Thrale's face and moves him out of the way. "These are good people. I've tried to kill them, and so did Seinaru! But they saved us, both of us. I'm not letting you kill them!"

Thrale gets more aggressive and turns his leg into a blade, and stabs the assassin in the leg. The assassin scowls and shoots a fireball directly at Thrale. Thrale does what he always does when in danger. He turns into multiple sheets of paper and attempts to get away. But paper is highly flammable. The fireball hits one of the sheets and explodes on them all. The blast still slightly hit the assassin due to their close proximity. The assassin falls to the ground but isn't hurt much, so he gets right back up.

After the smoke clears, ashes and ripped pieces of paper fall to the ground, and Thrale is nowhere to be found. Blast experiences a severe state of astonishment at seeing that his former coworker is no more. Blast's eyes, which had originally gone back to brown, start to turn back red-orange. During Thrale's opposition, the guys all seized the chance and discussed their new plan for the assassin. Now they stand ready for the ongoing conflict.

The assassin runs towards the others at full speed. He shoots a fireball behind him at the ground, which sends him forward into the air. He puts both of his hands together and throws a greater ice sphere at the others. Everyone moves out of the way as it explodes. The assassin lands on one of the spikes and fires a fireball at the other guys. He then double-charges his hands with electricity, does a front flip, and slams his lightning into the ground. Almost everyone gets hit by the current causing them to tremble from the electicity. As the assassin stands back up, a hand grips the back of his head and quickly slams his face into a spike on one of his own ice boulders, thus killing him. Blast is the one responsible.

The last bit of red power drains from his eyes, and so does his anger as he stumbles to the ground out of a lack of use of his legs. "Kinra! Quick, heal him," Luke commands. Kinra starts to heal Blast's legs. "Your powers...they can heal wounds? Can they...heal someone from death?" Blast asks. "I'm not sure," Kinra responds. "Please go try to heal...Thrale." Kinra stops and stands up.

He then moves over to Thrale's grave of burnt papers. He puts his healing hands on them, and nothing happens. "It doesn't work. Now we should focus on the one who is still alive," Jadeanu expresses. Kinra resumes healing Blast. "Poor Paper Ninja. He was a decent guy, taken before his time," Luke empathizes while giving Goldo back his sword. "He may not even want to be back. Let's let him rest in peace," Jadeanu concludes.

Kinra heals Blast's missing leg into a stump. "Hey Kinra. You don't mind all this do you? Making you heal and watch these horrible conditions?" Jadeanu concerns. "No, I like helping people. Plus by now, I'm used to seeing all this horrible stuff. I always expected to see stuff like this anyway, considering that I always wanted to work as a nurse or something of the sort," Kinra responds.

"You know when all of this went down, both of my parents died all of a sudden. I didn't know what else to do, so I just wanted to help them if I could. That's what awoke my healing abilities, but I was useless. I never even tried to heal them. Instead, I used my enhanced strength to take them outside and leave their bodies on the ground so they could rest peacefully without smelling up the place. That's when I saw a bunch of people attacking that huge guy, Will. I couldn't do anything with my life, and I only had enough food to last a few weeks. I just helped by healing the people who got injured by Will, which was the kind of work I always wanted to do. Then I met you two. I wanted to help you, and I realized that you want to help people too, Luke. I knew that I could do exactly that if I followed you guys, and I'm appreciative that I've been able to. So, thank you." Kinra finishes healing Blast. "So Kinra, you have the ability to heal wounds?" Goldo emphasizes. "That's truly a gift. Do you mind? It's kind of hard to grip these with these burns on my hands." Kinra responds by quickly healing Goldo's wounds. "By the way kid. Thank you," Blast mentions. "You're welcome." "So I guess you can't regenerate lost limbs. But it's okay. I never expected that anyway."

Kinra heals everyone's damage, including his own, then the guys all continue their journey to Gibil, the angel of the forge. Blast is being carried by Ren due to his loss of a leg, therefore he can't walk. As they all make their way through the greenery, Goldo strikes up a conversation. "So, just wondering. There won't be no more attacks from now on, right? I'm not trying to get kidnapped next or somethin'. I might have to leave ya behind," he says jokingly. "No, I don't think anyone else will just attack us," Jadeanu reassures.

Not long after Jadeanu says that, the guys all take a few more steps, and Jadeanu blurts out, "We're here."

They all listen and hear the sound of metal clanking. They take a few steps and peak into where the sound is coming from. There is a slightly open area, surrounded by or rather covered by tall trees all around. There they see a man with vast white wings, blond hair, with blue eyes to complement. He wears a white robe. He holds a small blade down on an anvil and is looking directly at Jadeanu and the others. Their hearts drop in intimidation. "Have you come to make an order?" he asks politely. Jadeanu leads the others into Gibil's open field and says, "Yes if you're not busy."

"I'm not. As of now, I serve no purpose in making anything for my other brethren, so I am free. Now speak of what you wish to craft."

"I need a weapon capable of wielding all 7 Blessings of the Gods," Jadeanu answers. "So I see. Do you have a preference for what kind of weapon you wish to make?" Gibil asks. "I was thinking maybe a pair of gauntlets." "You shall be their wearer?" "Yes sir." "I see that your power is heavily weighted on your hands. A tactical advantage seeming that your hands may become unable to function with all the stress you put on them. An analyzed answer." Jadeanu has a gaze of surprise, unknowing how much damage his hands may have been taking. Having superpowers doesn't make one devoid of consequence.

Gibil stops what he is doing and drops his blade on the anvil. He then walks up to Jadeanu. An immense power now radiates off of Gibil. Jadeanu feels a little uneasy around the aura, but it isn't as strong as Knowledge's, so he and the others behind him stay standing. Goldo starts to topple down but is reinforced by Luke. "What are your names?" Gibil demands. "Except you, Goldo. I know you. You and I are blacksmiths in the same forest."

Being the first angel any of the guys have spoken to, Gibil sounds very sophisticated and has an angelic echo in his tone. "I'm Jadeanu. And this is my brother Luke. That's Ricardio, Kinra, Ren, and Seinaru. And you are Gibil, an angel of Nature." "Indeed. And I can feel that nature runs purely in all of you except you, Ricardio. You, my friend, have some nerve showing your face to an angel of Nature. However, I can see that you have a will with able-bodied nature enthusiasts, so I'll forgive your harmful past.

I shall help you all, for your bounds of the natural world are strong. As you have seen before, kindness in nature is to be repaid with another kindness when you need it the most. That is the will of nature. As long as your kindness is not so superficial as niceness for the purpose of getting something in return, then nature will eat you alive."

"Thanks Gibil, but may I ask you for one more thing?" Jadeanu questions. "Ask away." Jadeanu turns to Ricardio and tells him to give him the lamp. Ricardio places the genie lamp in Jadeanu's hand. "One of our traveling partners got, I'm guessing, his soul taken and placed in here. Is there a way you could bring him back?" "I'm afraid not. That is unnatural. I couldn't do anything to help you there. You would need Spirit or one of his angels to free his soul so Nature or Universe may reform his body."

"I see, but there is hope." "Yes, but do be careful. There is a strong presence in that lamp. If you ever remove that top, the spirit inside will burst out, finishing the transformation that has started. You won't be able to reseal him yourself. The contract will be complete, and your friend will die. Destroying the lamp would do nothing as well but ensure the genie can not be resealed. One last note, if the genie is released, he will have no recollection of what got him to that point. He will only know trickery and destruction." "So I see. Keep Stougma in here until we ensure he's safe," Jadeanu understands. "But we can save him, and that's worth trying something."

"Good then. Now before we get started, Seinaru, do you wish that I craft you a new leg?" Gibil concerns. "No thank you," Blast answers. "I lost this leg doing something for my old coworker. Sure it didn't stop him from dying in the end, but it's a nobility I can't take back, nor would I want to." Everyone else looks at Blast as if calling him an idiot nonverbally. "I've got to pay the consequence for my action. After all, a crafted leg would be unnatural." "That is the very foundation of nature. I'm proud of you," Gibil tells him.

"Now Goldo, you and I shall make the gauntlets. The rest of you will obey us and gather what we need. Let's get started!" Gibil gathers several plant species using his powers to make them animatedly move on their own and turns them all into a proper workstation. An anvil, a table, a structure for the assembly of gauntlets, and a few other things. Everyone starts moving. Ren looks Blast in the eye and says, "I am not carrying you again, considering that you chose to not carry yourself." Luke grabs Blast off Ren's shoulder and puts him down lightly. "Come on Ren, he's still our comrade," Luke empathizes.

Gibil slashes the air with his fingers and opens up a portal of some sort through the fabric of space, like unzipping the air's zipper.

He reaches his arms in there and then sticks his face inside. Soon he comes out with two large cement bricks. He closes the portal by doing the reverse of what he did to open it. "So those are the materials we're going to use for the gauntlets?" Goldo asks. "Yes. These blocks are made from celestial stone. The very stone that makes up the pillars in the Heavens," Gibil answers. "It's just the stone we need to create nearly unbreakable gauntlets."

"But if the stone is near unbreakable, then how are we going to form it?" Goldo wonders. "There are forces that can get through it. Pass me that blade there." Goldo grabs the blade that Gibil had when they first saw him. The blade weighs him down, making him almost drop it. For a blade only about a foot and a half long, it weighed a lot. Goldo could not pass the blade, so he held it outwards to Gibil with both hands. Gibil grips the sword with one hand and lifts it easily. "This is how." Gibil then grips the sword handle and cuts each brick into three big chunks of rock with hard swings of his sword.

"Now Jadeanu. Be a lamb and fetch us some firewood. You may bring Ricardio to verify if you'd like. Get a lot now. We'll be making a huge bonfire," Gibil commands. Jadeanu and Ricardio leave to gather the wood. "We are going to make a bonfire to melt the stone? Isn't that going to take days?" Goldo questions. "No. We'll have it done in a matter of minutes; you'll see. Now Luke. Would you be so kind as to fill this bucket up with water? There is a river and waterfall not far from here." Gibil hands Luke a cauldron-sized metal bucket. Luke takes it and asks, "Where's the direction of the waterfall?" "I'm sure you'll figure it out. Just listen for it," Gibil advises. "Umm, okay," Luke says in a state of confusion, but he carries the oversized bucket away.

"So what now?" Goldo demands. "We wait," Gibil responds. "That should keep them busy enough to come back around the same time. Are you all hungry? Now that we have a break, you might as well fill your bellies." Gibil then commands the arrival of bread, fruits, and vegetables from nothing. All the remaining people eat and commune. It was the afternoon, and the last time they ate was yesterday night, so they were undoubtedly hungry. They swallow up the food in silence, savoring the health of their meals.

Later, Jadeanu and Ricardio return holding huge piles of sticks. Jadeanu's pile is bigger than Ricardio's, though, thanks to his added strength to carry them. "You guys got food?" Jadeanu accuses. "I didn't even realize how hungry I was until I saw scrumptious delights. Um, so what do you want us to do with these?" Jadeanu asks. "Hold them out," Gibil tells him. They both follow his command. The sticks fly out of their hands and sparkle with green energy. They are all placed in a circle with the look of a giant campfire. "Now eat," Gibil commands.

"Seinaru, the nature of your power is fire. Come with me," Gibil announces. Blast tries to stand up on one foot. The moment he does, the grass under him grips his foot and moves him forward, next to Gibil, where he can stabilize on a tree stump. Gibil puts the celestial cement bricks into a large pot and sets it on the sticks. He then commands a red flame on his hands. Next, he sets the wood on fire. "We will melt the bricks, but we'll have to do it quickly. At this rate, the bricks will melt in a matter of hours. We're going to need to accelerate that."

Luke then comes into the scene, struggling to hold the huge pot of water he is carrying. He gently puts it down and says, "I want to help with that. I've got energy blasts too." "Your power is energy but not specifically heat. But if you wish to help, you can," Gibil proposes. "Come. After, you will eat." Luke trots over towards Gibil, who is still holding red fire in his hands. Gibil walks around the pot to the opposite side of Blast. Now I will hold this fire out; you throw your strongest beam through it and into the pot. Luke puts all his power into a single beam. It travels from his hands and into the fire in Gibil's hands. Once it hits Gibil's fire, his Blast turns into a blazing beam that strikes the bricks with fire. Luke stops after a few seconds and looks into the pot. The bricks are still perfectly normal.

"What? They haven't even started to melt," Luke complains. "I never said it would be easy," Gibil states. "Now join me up on that tree. It'll give us an angle on the pot and protect us from Seinaru's attack. Everyone else, stand back!" Gibil gracefully jumps on one of the branches of the tree right behind Luke. Luke rockets up there as well. "Wait, but won't Blast's attack destroy the tree we're on?" Luke concerns. "No. I've enchanted these trees with divine energy, just like that wood around the pot. It cannot burn, and it's tough enough to withstand your attacks. But it is able to keep a fire. As long as we stay up here, we'll be safe," Gibil elaborates. "Ready? Go!" Gibil announces.

Blast charges up and fires his Mark 3 Pyro cannon at the pot. Luke shoots his gas beam into Gibil's fire which directs into the pot. Luke is able to do this on a continuous basis, whereas Blast has to take breaks in between each pyro cannon. They both get tired, which is indicated by sweat, panting and then a short break. As the subtle idea of food crosses Luke's mind, his stomach fills the silence with growls, yet he ignores them. Luke and Blast both start back up again soon. Luke ends up having to take one more break over the course of the whole ordeal while Blast's eyes go back to brown out of exhaustion. His pyro cannons take more energy than Luke's attacks; therefore, he could not continue after a while. Gibil tells them both to stop as he flies down with Luke, telling him to go eat some of the food that was left for him.

Gibil enchants his hands with green energy and grabs the steaming pot right out of the fire. "You aren't being burned by that?" Luke concerns. Gibil waves his hand, and the fire left on the trees, caused by Blast's pyro cannons, and bonfire sticks, goes out. "I am the angel of the forge. I can't be hurt by my craft so easily," Gibil responds.

He pours the now lava into the gauntlet structure, thus making the lava take the form of two gauntlets. Gibil blows on the lava and then grabs two hammers. "Come, Jadeanu and Ren." They both obey. Gibil hands Jadeanu one of his mallets. "You have the most physical strength in your group. I need you to help me strengthen the density of your gauntlets. As for you Ren, you can create your own mallet, can you not?" "I'll try." Ren manipulates his shadow and creates a big hammer with a string of darkness, attaching the handle of the hammer to his now misshapen shadow. "Now I'll take the left gauntlet. You two take the right." Gibil directs. "Hammer it with all your force. Goldo, you may direct them."

Gibil grips his mallet with both hands and brings it down on the left gauntlet with all his force. Then he repeats. Jadeanu charges both of his hands with red energy and swings full power on the right gauntlet. Ren follows behind. Gibil stops first after two minutes. He then watches Jadeanu and Ren sweating while going at it, with Goldo instructing them on how to properly compact the newly forthcoming steel. Ren takes multiple breaks because he is still very tedious due to his fight with the assassin. Gibil cheers them both on to keep them going efficiently. "Gibil. Do you mind helping us now that you're done?" Jadeanu asks. "I could, but these are your gauntlets. This experience will be fulfilling once you see the product of your own creation," Gibil replies.

A few minutes pass, and Gibil tells them to stop. He then grabs both gauntlets, still encased with lava. He throws them both into the air and performs a hand motion. The gauntlets sparkle with yellow energy. He catches them both and submerges them under the water Luke had brought. He takes them out and places them on a counter that he had previously created. The gauntlets are now made of dense silver-colored shiny metal.

Gibil pulls out a small leaf from thin air. "Ricardio, you have good navigation skills. May you find six more leaves exactly like this one?" Gibil gives Ricardio the leaf and sets him on his way. Ricardio leaves for a few minutes, then comes back. "I have them," he says. "Good. Now Jadeanu, please hold this leaf still right here on the gauntlet." Gibil takes a leaf and demonstrates where to hold it. Jadeanu presses the leaf down with his finger. Gibil smiles slyly at him, causing Jadeanu to worry. Gibil grabs his sword and restates, "Make sure you hold the leaf still."

Gibil then moved so fast that all anyone could see was a blurry image. He then moves and passes Jadeanu three times, then stops right in front of him on the last. He then lifts his sword. "You may grab the leaf now." Jadeanu is frozen with fear but does as Gibil says. There is an outline of the leaf cut into the gauntlet. Gibil then pops the cut metal off and reveals a crevice. He places Jadeanu's leaf into the hole. "You see, I needed extreme speed with my force to cut into the dense metal," Gibil explains. "Now it must be done six more times."

They complete the process six more times in different spots on the gauntlets, placing a leaf in each. Gibil then extends many vines to flow into the gauntlets, creating designs into them. "Now it is done. Your weapons are ingrained with life. You may now put them on," Gibil permits. Jadeanu slides the gauntlets in respectively to his hands. "Whoa, I thought these would be hard to move in, but they aren't." "Yes, dense yet flexible. You shall be able to attack all you will, yet your hands will be ever protected," Gibil explains.

"The vines inside tighten to keep your hands from slipping out unless you want them to. You would just need to relax your hands. You may also charge them up with energy. They respond to you and therefore, can manifest your powers. And lastly, look at these two designs on the gauntlets." Jadeanu looks at two vine shapes, one respectively for each gauntlet. "The one on your left hand that has three carvings in it means Heaven. The one on your right with carvings means Earth. The four Blessings of Earth shall go there with Universe in the middle of your backhand. The Blessings of the Big Three gods of Heaven go to your left gauntlet," Gibil says.

Suddenly, there is a rumble in the woods. "What is that? It sounds like giant footsteps," Jadeanu tells. Blast stands up on the tree stump near him to see what's happening. "Don't be so alarmed. It's just another Ancient," Gibil announces. "An Ancient?" Jadeanu questions. "Yes. You see, when death and life converged, it made the Earth more responsive to the dead. You see, an Ancient is a being of pure spirit that exists in the abyss. Now they have been called back to Earth because of the spill of spirituality. These Ancients are old dead monsters never bound to a place, so they are able to continue on in the world of the living. They've been coming to this forest a lot lately. Strange considering that they're attracted to sin and just want to destroy anything they see."

A huge grey beast comes forth, toppling the trees in its way. "This one is rather small." "Small? That thing is bigger than my house," Jadeanu reasons. "That is very small compared to most of them, believe me," Gibil elaborates. "Now this may seem like bad timing, but even the bad things bring a purpose. You may find an opportunity in this. This is a good time for you to try out your new weapon Jadeanu! If you all can bring it down, I will finish it." "You're not going to help?" Luke concerns. "I already know I can beat this thing. Can you?" Gibil shifts the conversation.

The Ancient is an elephant-like beast with a spiky trunk, a spiked tail, and four sharp horns, respectively, on the sides of its face. The Ancient starts to attack. "Seinaru, we'll keep the Ancient away from you. You just give supporting fire. Luke, you should distract it and lead it away from Seinaru. Kinra, Ricardio, Goldo, you all stay back. One smash would kill you," Jadeanu directs. "And you think one smash won't kill you?" Goldo rebuttals. "He's right about you two, but I'm fighting." Goldo runs towards the Ancient and swings one of his swords swiftly at the Ancient's leg. Sparks fly out, and Goldo's blade stops on the surface of the leg. Goldo becomes confused and then scared.

"Oh yeah, and I should have mentioned that Ancients usually have very tough skin," Gibil adds. "They are hard to pierce through; your best bet is to use forceful attacks." Ren grabs Goldo with his own shadow and puts him near Kinra and Ricardio. "Sorry, but you'll have to let us handle him." "Ren! You ready to help me bring this guy down?" says Jadeanu. Ren nods. Jadeanu puts red energy into his new gauntlets. He jumps up and punches the Ancient on the nose. The behemoth takes a step back from the impact. The Ancient swings its sharp trunk at Jadeanu. Luke shoots multiple gas balls at the Ancient, thus shifting its attention toward him. "Scatter!" Blast yells. Jadeanu looks back and runs away. The others follow.

"Mark 3 pyro cannon!" Blast yells as he fires his Blast at the Ancient. The energy consumes it, but it is still alive and standing, though clearly injured. The beast moves towards Blast. Luke fires his blasts at it, thus diverting its attention back toward him. The Ancient swings its sharp tail at him. Luke creates a shield around himself, but it breaks on impact, sending Luke spiraling into the air. He is also scraped a little on his face by the blade of the tail.

Ren springs up and creates two shadow drills, one for each hand. He forces one drill into the Ancient's right eye and sends the other to attack the other eye on its own. The attack is a success, and the Ancient is blinded. It starts freaking out and attacking wildly while stomping its massive feet.

Jadeanu closes in from behind and throws his body at its right knee on its back legs. He uses energy on his gauntlets as he puts both hands together and, with his momentum, attacks with all his might. The Ancient loses balance and falls down. Its trunk proceeds directly onto the tree that Gibil is watching on. Gibil quickly but gracefully moves to another tree to continue observing.

Jadeanu looks at his hands, still encased by the gauntlets. *That normally would have hurt my fists. Even with the protective energy of my powers,* he thinks. The beast tries to get back up. Ren responds by turning his shadow into a giant fist and uppercutting the beast under the chin. He then turns Jadeanu and Luke's shadows into giant fists, which he uses to hit the Ancient on both sides of its face. Jadeanu then appears on top of the Ancient's face, indicating that he jumped there. He slams both of his fists onto the Ancient's forehead, forcing it back to the ground. The Ancient's trunk rises up and dashes straight toward Jadeanu. He notices and puts his hands up. He catches the blade as it continues forward, driving Jadeanu backward. Sparks fly from his gauntlets until the trunk stops. Jadeanu lets go of it and looks at his unscathed hands.

Soon giant plant roots spring from the ground, towering over the Ancient. Jadeanu jumps off of the beast and looks to see what's going on. The roots grapple the Ancient and bind it to the ground. Gibil then jumps off of his tree and approaches it. "Don't worry little one. Your nightmare shall end soon," he says as the Ancient goes from struggling to peaceful. Gibil spawns a rather big green and black sword out of thin air. He stops at the Ancient's head and brings his sword up. He gently slides it into the beast's brain. The Ancient then turns from a giant elephant monster into a bunch of red particles as it rises into the air and fades away.

"A monster spawned from the abyss, and to the abyss it returns," Gibil quotes. "You've all done well. And your experience is its own reward. I will no longer help you on your journey. The rest is up to you." Gibil then disappears into the forest. "Thank you Gibil!" Jadeanu shouts back. Gibil takes a look back and smiles despite the fact that he's too deep in the forest for the others to see him.

"Yo Jadeanu. That was pretty cool what you did before," Luke congratulates. "Hey wait, so he had a blade that could pierce through that thing's skin the whole time?" Ren grieves. "It would only make sense. He does craft legendary weapons," Jadeanu acknowledges. "Hey, let's all talk about what's really important," Ricardio interrupts. "Now that you've got your gauntlets, where do we go now? And Goldo's got to go home."

"Oh yeah, right. It's been a pleasure working with you Goldo. You sure you don't want to come with us?" Jadeanu mentions. "Yep," Goldo answers. "If these battles are what I have to look forward to, count me out. I've done what was asked of me. Now I just need to set my way home." "Here. Take these maps. They'll help you find your way, and I don't need them anymore," Ricardio expresses. "Thank you. Now you all be careful out there."

Goldo takes his leave, and now Jadeanu and company must start their journey. "Now Ricardio. You said up north there was a powerful being, right?" Jadeanu recalls. "Yeah. So is that where we're going?" "I guess so. How far north is it?" "I don't know. It's just somewhere." "Well we've got a start. I kinda now wish we held on to one of those maps. I'm pretty sure we're lost."

"Well Goldo shouldn't be far, and Gibil might be able to help," Ricardio recommends. "Gibil has done so much already, but we could ask Goldo. Or maybe…" "Could that be a..?" Luke adds. "No mistaking it. There is a Blessing here," Jadeanu concludes. "Come on, this way." Jadeanu leads everyone through the vast forest feeling the strange spiritual energy getting stronger. As they get closer, more animals become present in the area, from deer to foxes and even monkeys, all minding their own situations. There are also several bushes of all kinds with colorful fruit and, beyond them, an unexpected sight.

There is a strange plant with a huge orange flower in full bloom. In the center of the flower, there is a light green orb radiating an embracing calm but violent energy. However, there is one more thing. There is a man with long black hair and light green eyes walking in the field. "Are you the god of Nature?" Jadeanu asks. "And you are Jadeanu Stroyem. The very man who wishes to put an end to this Death Spiral," the man replies.

"That is the Blessing of Nature right?" "You have come to me in search of this object, and yes, it is indeed the Blessing of Nature, yet you focus so much on your quest that you forget to greet your father," Nature states. Everyone except for Jadeanu and Luke looks around and mumbles in confusion. "You mean you," Jadeanu assures. "My apologies. Hello Nature." "And hello to you, Jadeanu." "You have a

Blessing here. Are you guarding it?" "No. I was preparing it for you. I brought it here all the way from its home. Deep in the soil of another forest. Now say thank you." "Thank you sir." "You're welcome my child. Now take it. It is yours now."

Jadeanu grasps the Blessing of Nature in his coated hand and places it on the middle socket of his right gauntlet. "Your journey will be dangerous, and with this power you now wield, things will become much more chaotic. Make sure you do not get consumed by the harsh reality you now live in. I advise you to find something or someone to love. Love deeply and never let that thing go. For if you grieve, things will only darken."

"Thank you, but may I ask, why do you help us?" "Because the strings of time have circled a dark point for all that is natural. It poisons my children and harms my will. Yet you are one of the few that can see beyond yourself. You wish to restore that which was. You have my guidance. For I am Nature, and I live in all of you, yet you have come back to me in remembrance. Many young souls lost in their newfound strength and enhanced reflexes, all crafted by us, the gods. Never forget where you came from. I love you Jadeanu."

"I love you too Nature." "I know. But it is great to hear. Appreciation is truly a blessing for any to hear from their creation." "So where do we go now? We need to collect the rest of the Blessings, but how will I know where to find them?" "Follow your heart. For my Blessing will bring out the Nature within all of you. You shall have a higher resonance with the energies around you. Make sure you do what you feel is right. Other than that, I will not help you. This journey is yours."

"Oh, and Nature. Our friend was trapped in a magical lamp. I was wondering if you could help us get his body back." "I won't just help you with that. You must prove it to be worth it with your dedication to your journey. You must find Spirit or one of his angels, and then you may come back to me. I have my own work that I need to deal with." Nature holds his hand out.

"You see, deep within the tranquility of the natural world, there are things out to destroy it." Nature lifts both his hands up, and many bottles and paper of all types, glass, plastic, tissues, and food packages all rise into the air as if tossed up by the plants around. "This is the product of human activity," Nature mentions. "It destroys your food sources and kills your animals. I have given this world to you humans, yet you all disrespect it so."

Now there sits a giant cloud of trash above. Nature uproots several trees with the distant flicks of his wrist. He then makes them all fly into the sky and surround the cloud of pollution. With the clap of Nature's hands, the wood from the trees splits and expands, consuming the cloud of garbage. As Nature clenches his fist, the wood collapses on the waste reminding Jadeanu of what Jinzen showed the guys about the fate of Stougma. The wood swallows the junk and vanishes.

"This world is for you to have but do take care of it. These animals were made for you to eat and have for other use, yet they must be respected. For you are one with them. All of you humans represent so much in the natural world. You insult each other with animal antics, yet all humans have the look and behavior of some kind of animal. For all of your faces are a cycle of a being before you and will become the face of someone after you as well. Seek enlightenment and align your spirit to overcome humanity and gravitate back to us.

There are seven chakras within the alignment of your spirit and body, seven Blessings, and seven gods. One for another. Strengthen them and gather power and wisdom. You'll need it. And take these, Luke." Nature holds out his hand, and three bubbles form from nothing like being blown from his hand. Nature gives them to Luke, who grabs them, half expecting them to pop, yet they don't. "These here will wash you and your clothes whenever necessary. One will wash all those around you. Cleanliness is still very important. As of now, you are all filthy. Let me show you how it works." Nature forms a huge thorn in his hand and pierces through one of the bubbles.

Immediately, an unnaturally immense amount of water comes out of the bubble and wraps around everyone except for Nature. Soon, the water vanishes in thin air, and everyone and their clothes are squeaky clean. Luke grips the bubbles and places them cautiously in his pockets, one per bubble. "Do not worry. Those bubbles are very tough and won't pop easily. They need something really sharp and forceful to pop them. You won't have to worry about them breaking.

Heed that tomorrow is the Sabbath. I forbid that you work then unless absolutely necessary. The Death Spiral occurred on Tuesday. It is now what you call Friday. It has been three days since it started. You will need to rest for your journey. Take advantage of the Sabbath. For every seventh day is sacred and useful to you. Now go. You have your work to do." "Nature, you know the way out of here-" "You want me to send you North out of here. Hahaha. You'll find your way around eventually." "Thank you Nature." "You are always welcome."

Jadeanu and the others all leave Nature's field. "Jadeanu!" They hear from behind; Jadeanu turns around. "Catch!" Nature yells as he throws something pretty big in size. Jadeanu barely catches it. It is a considerably large light green and silver sword. The blade is about more than half of Jadeanu's body. Standing on its tip, it is up to Jadeanu's chest. The blade is thick and has a sparkling leaf on the bottom of the blade, trapped in a dedorative circle near the handle of the sword. The sword is rather heavy but light enough for Jadeanu to barely lift it with one hand.

"I crafted that for your journey," Nature says. "You can power it up with that energy of yours. Think of it as an extension of your arm. You will no longer just fight humans. You need a weapon capable of harming spirits as well. You'll have to fight angels. My last gift to you." "Thank you again," Jadeanu replies. Jadeanu takes his new gift and leads the group onward through the bulk of the forest.

Chapter 6:

Sabbath Day

Jadeanu ventures through the forest with a vast smile on his face, glad to have the gifts from the greater spirits watching over him. His own spirit is filled with genuine gratitude for the fortune his journey has provided thus far. He leads his companions through the great forest of Humboldt-Toiyabe as the sun falls, not at all sure where to go. "Hey Jadeanu," Luke calls. "Let me use that sword." "And what are you going to do with it? You're still carrying Seinaru. But if you want to try it out, sure, I'll let you-"

"Dude, I'm joking. It was made for you. You should wield it." "But how come you get all this stuff? I want a cool sword," Ren complains in a joking manner. "Can't you make one with your shadow?" Jadeanu rebuttals. "Good point." "Hey, don't mean to be the party pooper, but it's getting late," Ricardio claims. "We should rest. The Sabbath the Nature god spoke about is coming." "Yeah, we should," Jadeanu agrees. "Seinaru do you mind…." "Yeah, I've got it. Just put me down Luke," Blast compromises.

Luke pulls him off of his shoulder and sets him on the ground gently. Ren uses the darkness around to grab a few sticks and puts them into a pile where Blast can heat them up into a campfire. "I'm glad we all get along," Jadeanu expresses. "If we rest here, will we be safe from the wild animals around?" Ricardio concerns. "If something happens, I should be able to hear it before it gets dangerous. I was trained for that," Blast explains.

A few moments pass, and the sounds of crickets and owls fill the air. "Hey Jadeanu," Ricardio says. "If the god of Spirituality can help Stougma get his soul back, do you think he can restore my Annabelle's soul and your Tierla's soul?" "I believe he can, but will he is the question. And what about the god of Life? But as Knowledge had mentioned, time is fragile. What happens happens. All we can do is hope," Jadeanu adds. "I really do miss her," Ricardio reminisces. "I know."

Jadeanu gazes at his right gauntlet, still holding the Blessing of Nature in it. He takes his left gauntlet off and places his naked hand on the Nature Blessing. The light green energy spreads through his veins. He just stares at his hand. Suddenly, the energy spreads uncontrolled through his arm, and he starts screaming, yet he holds on to the Blessing. Luke rushes to his rescue and forcefully takes Jadeanu's hand off. Jadeanu's body stabilizes.

"Dude were you trying to kill yourself? What was that about?" "I'm still weak! I am unworthy!" Jadeanu grieves. "These Blessings judge worth, and I'm unworthy to wield them. That's why I need these gauntlets in the first place!" "You'll get there bro. And we've got your back. Just try to think about what you've learned from the gods if you're so worried," Luke reassures.

"Yeah, well, Will said that I was special...different from others. He said because of my inner passion, I was worthy. Knowledge told me to follow my soul and guide my destiny. Nature mentioned that there are seven chakras in the center of my body. Seven of those, just like there are seven Blessings. Of course! Each chakra is a correspondent of one of the Blessings. That's what Nature was saying. If I guide my soul as a vessel for a well-rounded spirit, I will gain mastery over the Blessings. But then, how do I awaken my chakras?"

"I'm not sure, but I'm sure you'll figure it out eventually. Let's get some rest for now. It'll calm your thoughts," Luke suggests. "Yeah, good idea." All the others gather around the fire using tree leaves to cover themselves as much as possible from the cold midnight breeze.

The darkness of night moves on peacefully, and everyone sleeps well as a serene peace fills the moonlit wilderness. The sun later comes up, signaling the start of the Sabbath day. Everyone wakes up on their own time. "Wow, it's beautiful out here," Jadeanu suggests gazing at the calm morning forest. "It is, isn't it?" Blast agrees. "A day to take a break from our venture. The whole forest is ours." "Hey I'm hungry. Does getting something to eat count as work?" Kinra expresses. "I don't think so. He did say we could work if absolutely necessary," Jadeanu claims. "Well can we trust the berry bushes?" Luke questions. "No! Do not eat random berries! Trust me," Ricardio demands. "Our best bet is to go hunting. That's my specialty anyway. There should be some deer around." "Alright then. We're following you," Jadeanu commands. Ricardio starts the hunt.

He draws his bow and starts trotting. He soon spots some footprints in the dirt. "Look there. Those are...mountain...lion tracks? Let's turn back. We are NOT looking for one of those." Ricardio redirects everyone elsewhere. "Aha! Antelope tracks. We're getting warmer." Suddenly, Jadeanu, Luke, Ren, and Kinra stop. This causes Ricardio to also stop. "What's wrong?" he asks. "Do you feel that?" Luke demands. "Is that Will?!" Jadeanu wonders. "It is! That's Willpower!" Kinra confirms. Jadeanu runs in the direction of the energy he senses. "So just forget about the food huh?" Ricardio complains.

Jadeanu stops at an open field of grass. There lies the god of Willpower on top of a big rock. He rolls over toward Jadeanu and says, "Hey Jadeanu, I see you've met more friends along your journey." "Hey Will. It's good to see you again," Jadeanu greets. "You've come to me through the aura I've sent to you. I told you I'd hold on to this...." Willpower pulls out the Blessing of Willpower.

"...until you've got a weapon capable of harnessing the power of it. You have that now, so I've come to give you what is yours." Will gives the brown orb to Jadeanu, who takes it and sockets it onto the left opening on his right gauntlet.

"Thank you Will." "Just fulfilling my commitment." "Hey Will. What happened to your accent?" Jadeanu questions. "We gods are not subject to one region such as you humans. I desired not to use it; nothing more, nothing less. But that is not important. You all have not eaten, and breakfast is important for health." Will then stands up and takes a strong stance. He then throws his hands in the air in specific directions of the forest. Soon, fruits and vegetables of various types come forth, riding on top of discs of rock. They ordered themselves on the huge rock Will was lying on.

Then an alive antelope flies from the inner forest into Will's hand. He looks at Ricardio and says, "This is what you were looking for." He gently puts the antelope down. "I'll let you kill this one." Will sets the antelope free. Ricardio starts to reach for his bow but doesn't finish out of sympathy. "I see," Will announces. "But if you have the will to eat, you needn't be ashamed to kill." Will then flicks a rock from the Earth toward the running antelope. The rock slams into the deer's face and breaks its neck.

Will's eyebrows arch in rage, and an orange blaze covers his body. He spreads the fire to the grass, and it becomes huge but controlled. He telepathically lifts the antelope and lifts up a sharp stone. He uses the stone to cut the head off then he brings it forth into the fire. He telepathically rotates it around the fire. Will takes in a deep breath of the pleasant cooking aroma.

He then summons many diced-up fruits, vegetables, and specific rocks from all around and throws them all over the antelope. He then throws five rocks into the roasted deer and splits it into five meat portions split onto five respective plates, giving everyone their preferred part of the deer and desired portion size. The fire is then extinguished, and the grass it sat on is unscorched.

Everyone gets a respective plate except for Luke. "You will not for meat. Explain this," Will demands. "Under normal circumstances, I would get some. But seeing the deer die like that just makes it horrible," Luke answers. "Well that's nature for you," Blast admits while being seated by Luke. "Nature said it himself. Nature is violent. This is what animals have to go through to get the meat you love so much. You might as well accept it." "If you will not eat, then I shall take your offering." Will completely burns the rest of the deer and inhales the smoke from it. The other guys all begin to eat.

Will suggests that no one should talk as they eat. So they each eat in silence. After everyone has had their fill, Will signals for everyone to come with him. They all follow his lead. He forces the pavement they stand on up a mountain. Now on the peak of a mountain, everyone gazes at the beauty of Humboldt-Toiyabe Forest. They bear witness to all the trees, waterfalls, valleys, and lovely ecosystems that so many animals call their home.

"Look around. The forest is truly a beauty. A beauty made for you," Will declares. "You wish to move North. Look over there. That is where you need to go. You can see the entire land from up here. Take in the essence of the world around you. This world is yours to explore. You have the power to strengthen it, and you have the power to destroy it. So much power. Do not let it fall into the wrong hands. For you each have much more power than you know. I hope you have taken in enough of the environment because I have more to show you. First, choose where you want to go while still on your path."

Jadeanu starts, "Can we go…." "To the waterfall!" everyone joins in. Will forces the mountaintop to flip, thus throwing everyone towards the northern waterfall. They all fly through the air for several seconds. "If I were you, I'd take off the clothes I prefer dry," Will announces. They all obey, taking off everything except their underwear. Will remains fully clothed. Soon, they all slam into a water current, and their clothes are placed on a dry rock with Will's powers. "Hey Will. Swimming isn't working right?" Jadeanu asks with hair all in his eyes. He still has his gauntlets on out of the caution of losing them. "The Sabbath is a day for relaxing, worship, and lastly, fun!" Will replies.

Jadeanu smiles and dives underwater. The water starts to swirl up, and a jet of water catapults from below Luke, propelling him into the air. Jadeanu then surfaces below where Luke was with both hands up. The Blessing of Nature is now lighting up green, then it subsides. "So these Blessings are able to do that kind of stuff?" Jadeanu says to himself.

Ren uses his shadow to create a giant hand to splash Jadeanu back underwater. Blast fires a beam on the water's surface, causing a slight wave to engulf Ren. Luke emerges from on top of the waterfall while everyone else is distracted. He creates a bubble around himself, trapping in much of the water. He then jumps off the cliff and deactivates his bubble when above everyone, thus letting water drop on everyone. He then rockets himself face-first into the water.

"Seriously, you guys are too old for all this childish splashing," Ricardio grouches. "Give your bodies time to digest like me, Kinra, and Wil-" Just then, Will makes a giant rock slam into the pond, causing a huge wave to scoop everyone up. Ricardio, now wholly soaked, gets out of the water. "I'm gonna take a nap." He then lies on the grass, still nearly naked, and looks up at the sky.

"Let us not exert ourselves. We may have fun, but we must relax and never tire," Willpower directs. "So how about this instead." Will then turns the waterfall into a waterslide with his rock manipulation, yet smooth enough to go down unharmed. Will lifts a rock from underwater to raise everyone on top of the waterfall. Kinra is the first to slide down. Last is Will, who does a perfect dive into the pond. He then gets out and chills on a rock. Everyone else continues relaxing in the water.

Soon, Jadeanu looks toward Ricardio and then looks at Will. They both are sipping a fruit shake out of a straw. "Hey! Where did you get those from?" "Aye, the man willed for it, so he got it," Will responds. "Well then, may I have one as well?" "You have my Blessing. You can make it yourself. But don't make a mistake; although a mistake may not be harmful now, as things become more difficult, you may not be able to undo what you've done. In other words, these Blessings are not toys, nor are they easy to use. One mistake could cost you or your friends their life. Now concentrate and deeply will for what you want while engaging my Blessing."

Jadeanu clenches his right fist and concentrates. The Willpower Blessing lights up, and the veins on his right arm light up brown, the same color as the Blessing. A tall glass of strawberry smoothie appears in his hand and the glowing stops. Soon everyone asks for one, leaving Jadeanu with the mental training to master that technique. Later, everyone enjoys the quality of relaxing, both inside and outside of the water. They all enjoy some quality conversation and board games.

"You know the Sabbath is not to restrict you. It and all laws were made for you. Just like the Blessings," Will tells. "Made just for you, for your well-being. All the power is through discipline and control. Don't let the desire to be righteous stress you. You are not a slave to the law, it is a template for you to live a good and healthy life. You may disobey the laws when necessary. Just see for yourself." Will boosts himself and everyone else above the trees using a large rock surface. "But take a look."

Within the forest, a giant gray scorpion is fighting a man with wings. "Hey, isn't that Gibil?" Jadeanu realizes. "And that Ancient is much bigger than the one before." "Ah. But you see the serenity of the world. The only ones who disobey the day of rest are you humans. The gods, the angels, and even the animals rest on this day. For every seventh day is holy. Remember that.

Yet as you can see, Gibil fights the Ancient. Not out of labor but out of a need to protect his environment. Now close your eyes and feel the Earth." Will commands as he allows everyone to descend.

Jadeanu closes his eyes and then opens them immediately. "Your heart skipped a beat. You felt it?" Will mentions. "Yeah...Ravah is up North of the forest. The angel we were told to watch out for." "You will have to deal with him. He knows who you are and you have what he came for. But he is at rest. You could attack him now, but it would be of disobedience. Tomorrow he will be returning from rest. You may have the advantage then if you are early enough. And lastly, as a lead for your quest. We've told you to follow your heart for guidance. We've told you to follow your soul for direction. But to find the Blessings, you'll have to follow your mind. Where you deeply think a Blessing exists, it exists there. Let your intelligence be your leader." Will then walks away, leaving the others in the now darkness of the forest.

Chapter 7:

The Start of The Quest, Battle of The Angels

Jadeanu and his company decide to make a campsite and sleep again. The night passes peacefully, and the start of a new day ensues. It is early, and everyone wakes up, yawning from the excellent nap. "Wow, that buff guy was right. That resting day did wonders for my sore muscles," Blast acknowledges. "Buff guy? You do realize that was the god of Willpower?" Jadeanu adds. "Wait, really? That makes much more sense."

"Nevermind that. I'm hungry. And we have to fight Ravah soon. Fighting on an empty stomach is not good," Ricardio announces. "Well then, go hunting. I've got something else in mind," Jadeanu suggests. "The sun hasn't even come up all the way yet. We've got time." Jadeanu grabs his sword, stands up, and starts swinging it with both hands.

"You're training?" Luke questions. "Yeah, I've got to learn how to handle this thing eventually. Which reminds me…." Jadeanu puts his sword into the ground and looks at Luke. "I've still got a score to settle with you. Remember when we first got our powers, and you kicked the crap out of me?" Jadeanu charges his fists with red energy. "Alright then," Luke responds with a slight smile on his face. "Let's go."

Jadeanu runs toward Luke, who shoots multiple gas balls at him. Jadeanu dodges them all and throws a punch toward Luke. His gauntlet-covered hand slams into a shield, thus cracking it slightly. Luke deletes his shield and throws a gas ball from point-blank range directly into Jadeanu's stomach. The blast throws Jadeanu several feet. "Hey, don't use those Blessings. This will be just between us," Luke concerns. Jadeanu cracks a smile and runs full speed toward Luke. Luke deploys a shield that is still slightly cracked but mostly healed. Jadeanu punches it, then hits it repeatedly until it is severely cracked.

He then moves back, drains the energy from his arms, and moves it to his legs. He digs his feet into the ground, then lunges forward at an incredible speed. He quickly moves the energy back to his arms and punches through Luke's shield. Luke dodges and places his hand on Jadeanu's chest. He then fires a beam, launching Jadeanu into the air.

Immediately, Luke puts his hands together and fires a stronger gas blast. Jadeanu blocks with both of his hands. As he descends, he separates his hands with force, creating a red shockwave of energy that destroys Luke's attack. Jadeanu quickly closes in with a punch. Luke avoids it, noticing that a small shockwave comes out of that attack as well. Resembling that of a shotgun spray. Luke accidentally manages to create two bubble shields, one around each of his fists, with his desire to use his powers more offensively. He looks at his fists with surprise but then counters with a shielded punch to Jadeanu's chest.

"Hey they weren't able to do that stuff before," Kinra points out. "They weren't on even terms before either. They've gotten stronger," Blast realizes. Jadeanu's gauntlet clashes with one of Luke's bubbled fists. The bubble starts to crack. The same situation happens between Jadeanu's other fist to Luke's other bubble. Luke then launches his leg, using his gaseous energy as a propellant toward Jadeanu, who jumps back to dodge it.

Luke creates a shield and tosses it like a frisbee toward his brother. Jadeanu punches the shield, and his added shockwave destroys it. He quickly bolts to Luke and socks him in the face, drawing blood from his mouth. "Oh, sorry," Jadeanu worries. "It's fine," Luke reassures before sweeping Jadeanu off his feet with a kick and blasting him. Jadeanu blocks it with a burst of energy.

"Hey! We get that you two are pretty even, but I want to join in and see where I stand now," Ren announces. "Alright then, come on!" Jadeanu allows. Jadeanu's face gains a worrisome smile on it. Luke shoots a blast at both him and their new challenger. Ren uses his shadow to shield himself then he uses Luke's shadow to trip its caster.

Jadeanu uses his power to go through and close in on Luke, who forms a giant shield to protect himself while on the ground. Jadeanu punches the shield a few times, causing it to crack. Luke throws the shield up forward with Jadeanu now mounted on it. Jadeanu shifts his energy to his legs and leaps off the shield, shattering it with a shockwave. He lands near Ren and performs an overhead axe kick. Ren snatches himself out of the way with his own shadow. Jadeanu's foot lands on the solid ground causing a massive burst of red energy.

Jadeanu has a broad smile of mysterious origin spread on his face. "Hey, is it just me, or is Jadeanu more vicious than usual?" Blast asks. "Yeah I wonder what's making him so antsy," Kinra responds. "All this fighting so early in the morning. Could it be one of those Blessings?" "Maybe. But those Blessings only bring out what was already inside of you. So that would mean...."

Luke tosses his hands up in surrender and says, "Okay I'll leave you two at it. I think it's obvious that we're all even." "Well then if it's just us, then I want you to use your sword," Ren claims. Jadeanu doesn't hesitate to grab his big blade and advance toward Ren, still with a vicious smile. Ren forms a blade from his shadow. Jadeanu swings his blade downward toward Ren, who grips his shadow blade with both hands and blocks. Sparks fly, and the tension between the swords is exhausting to the involved fighters. Their blades separate and clash again.

They struggle a few more times, then collide once more. Jadeanu notices the shadow string attaching Ren's sword to his thinned shadow. Jadeanu quickly withdraws his weapon and slices at the string. The string bends but resists Jadeanu's cut like a chain. Jadeanu extends his energy to his blade until it glows red. He then quickly retracts his sword and swings it again. This time, the sword cuts clean through the shadowy string, forcing Ren's shadow to liquefy and return back to the harmlessness of Ren's plain shadow. Ren is now defenseless.

Jadeanu brings his sword down, ready to stop it short so as not to kill his comrade, just to convey a sense of defeat. Ren crafts a shield using Jadeanu's shadow. He quickly turns the shadow into a sword which he uses to block another of Jadeanu's slashes. He aims the sword's tip at Jadeanu's face and extends the spike. Jadeanu narrowly dodges the attack and is scraped on the cheek. Jadeanu uses his free left hand to palm Ren on the chest and extends a shockwave, launching Ren into a tree. Ren's back smacks the tree hard before he falls. He places his hands on the ground and struggles to lift himself up.

"Okay, well how about this!" Ren opens his body up by placing his hands out to the sides. He then goes for a full-force clap. Immediately, all of the nearby shadows cast by the low-hanging sun all rush toward Jadeanu, surrounding him on all sides. They all turn into spikes, ready to skewer Jadeanu. He guards with his sword, but it wouldn't be enough to escape an all-around deadly spike trap.

Luke jumps in the way and generates a bubble around himself and Jadeanu to protect his younger brother. The spikes all compound on the bubble shield. It cracks severely, and some of the spikes get through, slightly stabbing Luke. Jadeanu somehow catches one spike and blocks a few others all in the sudden instance. Ren's eyes return to his natural dark blue color, and he falls to the ground. That attack completely drained all of Ren's energy. The shadows return to their natural position and Luke's shield breaks.

"Oh thank you so much Luke," Jadeanu appreciates. "You're my little brother; of course I'm gonna protect you whenever I can." "So I see. Both you and Ren are nearly defenseless when your power breaks. It takes time for you to recreate, rather, control your power again," Jadeanu hypothesizes. "I guess so," Luke responds. "Hey, do you guys want me to heal you?" Kinra suggests. "No. These marks will only make us stronger. You shouldn't always undo the pains of hard labor. Those pains are motivators for strength." "Learning from me huh?" Blast presents. "Well, if you guys really want to see how powerful you've become, I've got something for you. How about you try to defend against my Mark 3 Pyro cannon?" "Sure, let's do it."

Jadeanu and Luke stand in front of Blast and prepare for the challenge. Jadeanu puts his sword down and channels red energy onto his gauntlets as he takes a defensive stance. Luke positions himself behind him and creates a huge shield, big enough to completely guard something the size of the Ancient they all fought earlier.

Blast charges up and releases his full power blast toward Luke and Jadeanu. The blast pushes against Luke's shield, and it starts to crack. It cracks more and more until it inevitably breaks, and the giant blast engulfs both Luke and Jadeanu. Jadeanu's energy block resists the blast, but it still goes through.

After it clears, Jadeanu and Luke are still standing with steam radiating off them. Jadeanu's arms are dangling to his sides, and his face is aimed at the sky. Luke is stuck looking at the ground, likely from shocking pain. "Man that really stung," Jadeanu acknowledges. "Yeah it sure did, but it hurt a lot less than it did before. I guess we did get stronger," Luke analyzes. "Now Kinra. These wounds, you can heal," Jadeanu allows.

Jadeanu and Luke heal up and then promptly show their appreciation for the one who healed them. By this time, Ren is rested enough to fight again. Ricardio had brought back and cooked a deer for everyone to enjoy. After the meal, everyone sets their way North with Luke carrying Blast again. There isn't much more to go until they are out of Humboldt-Toiyabe. Soon they see the light of a new land just beyond the trees.

As they approach, Jadeanu's heart skips a beat. "Wait!" "What's wrong?" Luke wonders. "Ravah. He's nearby. I can sense it." "Alright, so what are we gonna do?" "Well if Ravah is nearby, then the Blessing of Knowledge is close too. It's early, so Ravah likely won't be active yet, meaning we may not have to face him. We would need to steal the Blessing without confrontation. Not to mention, we might have to worry about others that may spot us. I don't know if it's true, but I feel as if Ravah isn't alone."

"And why is that?" Ren demands. "Remember when we saw that huge explosion while we were riding wolves? Oh right, you were unconscious. Well anyway, I knew Ravah was over there, but he wasn't close to whoever started it. He vanished and then came back perfectly timed to avoid the explosion. I could tell because I knew where the Blessing of Knowledge was at the time. That tells me there must have been another angel. And fighting one angel sounds t-troublesome b-but fighting two sounds i-imp-impossible." "Why are you shaking Jadeanu?" Luke concerns. "Because I'm the only one of you who has fought a god and encountered an angel. I know how powerful they can be. I'll admit it, I'm a little scared of what we're about to do." "A little? You're freakin spooked," Blast comments.

"But nonetheless, if there's two of them, then it would be best to get rid of one; or just avoid them both altogether," Ricardio strategizes. "To do that, our best bet is to use some kind of diversion," Luke plans. "We'll need someone to take their attention." "Will said that Ravah knows about us and is likely looking for us. So if one of us subliminally tells who we are, they'll want to investigate to find the rest of us. That person will act as the diversion."

"It only takes one to investigate, so we'll have to move while one is out." "We'll have to hurry and get the Blessing, but the problem is, will Ravah leave it behind?" "If not, then we may have to fight him anyway. I guess we'll scavenge the area before we strike." "And if we find it, we take it and free our decoy in captivity. Then Jadeanu will use the Blessings to help us escape," Luke finishes.

"The plan started out great, but the Blessings aren't exactly easy to use," Jadeanu adds. "We have a way in, but our way back out will be troublesome." "Well if you get the Blessing of Knowledge, you might be able to use it to learn how to use the others," Luke brainstorms. "Well that's one big might! But I've seen the power of Knowledge and his angels; we might just be able to. It's all we have. That means everyone will be counting on me. I'm fine with that. Now we just need someone to be the decoy."

Everyone starts to cringe at the thought. Then Blast yells, "I'll do it." Everyone looks at Blast in surprise. "Blast, are you sure? You're crippled!" Luke concerns. "All the more reason to do it," Blast agrees. "So far I've been a burden on your group. You all have had to carry me around, and before that, I tried to kill you. Sure, I saved your lives, but as far as I'm concerned, I still haven't truly paid back my debt. At least let me do this." "Fine. But consider Ravah an angel of torment. He will torture you ruthlessly for information until we save you," Jadeanu establishes. "I'm a trained mercenary. I can take whatever they do to me," Blast claims.

"Alright then, we have what we need. Remember everyone, if we fail, there is a good chance that all of us will die. Make sure you're prepared for that." "Not like we've got anything else to do. We've come this far. Let's see it through," Ren compromises. Everyone else seems to be in agreement.

"Wait! I just thought of something." Ricardio interrupts. "Knowledge said that Ravah is one of Spirit's angels. Maybe he's nice and would help us get Stougma back! And at that, he may be able to bring our wives back with his soul manipulation powers or something." "Well I wouldn't bet on it; but Seinaru, maybe you can mention it when you get caught and see where things go from there," Jadeanu strategizes. "Sure why not," Blast compromises. "Okay then let's go."

Jadeanu leads his allies up to the end of the forest, and they are finally out. They stop at some bushes and hide behind them. They gaze at the new land. It is a village. A broken-down village full of huts and tents. One could tell that the place was heavily impacted by the Death Spiral. Out of one of the huge tents comes a male with purple skin and long red hair down to his thighs. He has black feathered wings and is quite handsome.

"Is that Ravah?" Ren whispers. "Shhh," Jadeanu hushes him and then nods. Ravah walks out of the tent and calls back to someone else who must still be inside. He says, "I've got work to return to now that I am well rested. You guard the tent; we cannot have anyone getting into what we possess. I'll be back shortly." Ravah then creates some kind of purple portal with the wave of his hand and steps into it. The portal then vanishes.

Jadeanu and his allies take the time to look into the tent from a distance in an attempt to see where the Knowledge Blessing is. "There it is!" Jadeanu spots it. The orange orb is placed on a miniature podium to the room's left, and right of Jadeanu's position. "It should be easy enough to get." As Jadeanu says this, Vermunya comes into view, standing as a guard for the tent. "I knew there was another one," Jadeanu triumphs.

Then Javean comes out of the tent. Jadeanu's heart drops. "The-there was another one?" "It's okay. They may not be the only two, but we have a chance. Blast! Can you stand?!" Ricardio takes control. "Yeah." Blast then stands up on his one leg, struggling severely. Then he rockets off around the forest first and then to the tent to not show the two angels where his allies are.

Blast approaches Javean and Vermunya and stops rocketing. His body is unable to stabilize, so he falls forward. He then fires blasts forward at the ground to readjust to standing. "Hey are you two angels under the god of Spirit?" Blast asks. "Why do you ask?" Vermunya demands. "Because I have a friend that got his soul stuck in a lamp. I was told that you could free his soul." "But Vermunya, isn't that what happened to that one kid traveling with that Jadeanu guy?" Javean interrupts. "I see. Well then getting that guy's soul back should be the least of your worries," Vermunya adds. He and Javean grab Blast by the arms. "There is something I need of you. Please cooperate with our demands."

They both then take Blast inside the tent. "Now!" Jadeanu signals. Everyone moves quickly but cautiously toward the tent. They check inside to see if Vermunya and Javean can see them, but they are gone behind a wall built into the tent. It must have been a circus tent, and the back was where the owners kept the animals in cages. Jadeanu's crew carefully sneaks into the tent.

Meanwhile, in the back. "Where are you taking me?! What is all this?" Blast pretends. "Why do you care about the fact that I know Jadeanu?" "You possess the key to our mission. We will get it through you," Vermunya responds. They both place Blast on a seat, and the chair automatically restrains him to it. "Now tell me, where is the boy?" Vermunya asks.

Blast says nothing. Vermunya pries Blast's mouth open, grabs his tongue, splits it in half relentlessly and rips it entirely out, and tosses it on the floor. Javean shoves something into Blast's throat, stopping him from screaming through the cutting of his voice box. "We don't exactly need you to speak to do what we need," Vermunya expresses. Blast's mouth is full of blood now as he experiences great pain that he can no longer express through shrieking, no matter how much he tries.

"Now Javean. You're new to this, so I'll let you do the torturing." "So what should I do first?" "Break his arms." Javean grabs Blast's left arm and breaks it by bending it severely at the elbow. Blast's face makes an expression of grunting in silent pain.

"Tsk, Javean. When you break an arm, you break it like this!" Vermunya grips Blast's broken arm at the forearm and snaps the bone in two. He twists the arm at the wrist, thus breaking it and finally pushing it forward, snapping the shoulder as well. Instead of letting go, he continues pushing with his super strength until something comes through his now bloody shoulder. The object that pierced through his shoulder gleams in a dimmed white. It is his bone. Blast rocks in the chair hysterically in pain. Now he has only worry in his eyes.

Back to Jadeanu and his friends. They search through the place in hopes of finding something capable of freeing Stougma or helping in their journey. There is nothing but old circus materials. Jadeanu approaches the Blessing. *It just might work!* Jadeanu thinks.

While this occurs, in the back Vermunya pries Blast's fingernail clean off, causing blood to flow freely. Blast screams inaudibly. Vermunya then forces the tip of the nail into the top crease of his finger and moves it back and forth vigorously until the top of the finger is somehow severed from the rest of it using some kind of unknown force. "Now we must get this done quickly; we don't have much time," Vermunya expresses. Tears stream down from Blast's eyes as his mind drifts off to an understanding that he may have to live disfigured for the rest of his life if he lives at all.

Jadeanu grabs the orange orb and feels it in his gauntlet. "What the? I just don't...." "What's wrong, Jadeanu?" Luke asks. "I don't feel any power from it. But there's no way. It's...a fake? Then where's the real one?" Jadeanu's heart stops for a second. "Oh, there it is." Jadeanu starts shaking, then he hears a strange voice say, "Did you really think that we would just let such a valuable relic stay out in the open?"

Jadeanu hesitates to turn around to see who is speaking. He then sees Ravah flapping his wings as he descends from a portal several feet above the ground. Ravah digs into his right cloak pocket and pulls out the real Blessing of Knowledge. "This is the real Blessing of Knowledge. The one you hold is a fabrication crafted by me. I was able to mimic the Blessing's aura but not its power. Quite a simple trick I must say." Jadeanu charges power into his hand and crushes the fake Blessing.

"I have all the knowledge this world has to offer, and yet you think I wouldn't use it to look into a possible future. I knew what you were scheming, and I've come up with a counter plan for you. And you Ricardio, I know how much you want to see your precious loved one once again; but I'm here to tell you that it won't happen by any of us. Once someone dies, they stay dead. It is forbidden to undo the cycle. But your partner Stougma is not dead, so he can be brought back. And I've got the soul manipulation powers to do it. Vermunya and Javean do not, but I do, yet I do not will to help you. That being said, you can bring him out now."

Javean then comes out from behind the tent wall, pushing Blast out on the chair, followed by Vermunya. Everyone cringes at the sight. Blast's left arm is completely destroyed by what Vermunya did earlier. His eyes are gone, and the sockets are covered in the thick red liquid that symbolizes death. One of the angels had gripped his eyeballs and crushed them. Blast's face is skinless, and his mouth has no lips or tongue. All of his fingertips are gone. He has spears through his limbs. His shins, calves, knees, thighs, hands, forearms, biceps, and shoulders are impaled. In the center of his chest, there is a sword in his heart, guarded by many spears around it, skewing Blast's entire torso and chest before the sword had gone through him. Blast is undoubtedly dead and in such a horrendous way.

Jadeanu's companions all are mortified, and Kinra gags. "You are all monsters!" Luke rages. "Perhaps we are," Ravah agrees. "But what defines monstrosity? And are humans really the opposite of it?" "For the record, if I really wanted to find you, I would have just tricked Seinaru into leading me to you. No need for violence all the time," Vermunya adds. "So thanks for the free kill." "And now that I know what you all look like and have a direct sense of your specific energy signatures, with the Knowledge Blessing, I can always find you all whenever I desire," Ravah admits. "But now I've got work to do elsewhere. I'll let you two have your fun with them." Ravah turns his back and creates a portal.

Now Jadeanu can see the miniature monster on Ravah's back, hanging onto his shoulder. The creature must be Ravah's pet. Jadeanu sees Ravah turning his back as an opportunity to strike him. Jadeanu fears Ravah, so he decides to take care of that problem as quickly as possible. He charges energy into his sword and swings it. There is the sound of metal clanging then Jadeanu staggers back. Ravah's cloak had moved and shifted into sharpened blades, blocking Jadeanu's attack. Ravah doesn't even stop. He just smugly walks through his portal and vanishes.

"Well now we get to play with all of you," Javean announces. Jadeanu looks at everyone and whispers, "Run." He and his allies all break for the exit of the tent. "How typical," Vermunya says calmly. Javean flicks his wrist, and metal shields emerge from the ground blocking the exit. "Now Javean. Do note that these are still enemies. Have fun with them but do kill them."

"Even the young one?" Javean gestures at Kinra. "Maybe we won't need to, but if you must, kill him too," Vermunya answers. "For all of you, don't even think about escaping. It will do you no good. I am Vermunya, one of Spirit's high disciples." "And I am Javean, the newbie of Spirit's disciples." "High disciples? That means you're both archangels? Why exactly are you doing this?" Jadeanu wonders. "That doesn't matter because this is where you all die," Vermunya replies. "Okay then!"

Jadeanu leads everyone to charge the two angels. As they start running, Javean punches the air in front of him. An immense gust of wind exits the force of the attack and blows Jadeanu and company backward. The wind is short-lived, and Jadeanu resumes running. Javean repeats, forcing Jadeanu back. "Haha! I'm so much stronger than the humans that my mere attacks create so much wind that they can't even approach us!" Javean gloats.

"Don't get too carried away. We are supposed to kill them and take the two Blessings Jadeanu has. We must ensure that we complete that task. For Ravah's glory," Vermunya humbles while moving Blast's body out of the battle area. "Dang it! This isn't how this was supposed to go at all!" Jadeanu pities. "How on earth are we supposed to beat two archangels?"

"Get your act together!" Ricardio commands. "Your fear will only get us killed! We didn't ask for this fight, but we got it! And now we have to win it, or we all die! Where there is a will, there is a way. You would know that best! Now stand up straight and be a man!" "You're right. One vital swing with this, and we'll win." Jadeanu looks at his sword. "We don't actually have to beat them," Jadeanu adds energy to his legs and runs forward.

Javean creates another wind current with a punch. Jadeanu holds his ground. The wind is still too strong and pushes him back, to which he responds by putting his sword into the wooden floor to brake. Both of the Blessings on Jadeanu's hand start to glow. Jadeanu takes a step forward and smiles at Javean. "Okay bring it on!" he says. The moment the wind stops, he charges forward at full speed. But not towards Javean but toward the non-engaged Vermunya. He brings his sword forward, ready to swing.

He swings. Vermunya calmly dodges the attack and knocks on Jadeanu's head with his back knuckle. Blood springs out of Jadeanu's nose as he tumbles into the ground furiously. Jadeanu's Blessings stop glowing.

"Be warned Javean. This blade of his is capable of killing us, I can tell," Vermunya warns. "I don't know where a human could get one of those, but do be wary." "Noted, but we still shouldn't have much of a problem," Javean replies. "You sure about that?!" Jadeanu says as he gets back up with blood leaving his nostrils and a bruise on his head where Vermunya hit him.

"You humans are a lot tougher than I expected," Vermunya admits with shock at Jadeanu's quick recovery. "Luke, Kinra! We'll attack Javean. Ren, you'll attack Vermunya. Ricardio, you support him. If you can't beat him, just hold out as long as you can." "Wait, which one is Vermunya again?" Ren questions. Jadeanu and Luke move toward Javean. "Oh okay. So you must be Vermunya." Ren moves to attack Vermunya.

Jadeanu attacks with his sword. He slices into Javean's shoulder as Javean makes no effort to dodge. The sword slices clean into him but stops soon after impact. The moment the blade enters the bloodstream, it completely pauses. Javean motions his body down and gestures as if holding his stomach from a sudden ache from within. His body glows purple, then he leans back, unraveling his arms, and a purple explosive wave stems from his body, blowing Jadeanu back.

Steam rises from Jadeanu's body, and blood streams from his forehead. Luke shoots a beam at Javean, and the same thing happens, destroying the attack. "Hahahahahahahaha! You can't hurt me!" The small cut on Javean's shoulder seals up as if nothing had happened. "Okay how about this!" Jadeanu adds energy to his foot and stomps with all his might and then adds energy to his sword as he forces his body weight forward and swings his sword again with both hands.

The sword slams into Javean's guts and once again stops once it slightly enters his body. Javean explodes again, sending Jadeanu backward again. Blood gushes from his mouth. *What? I could have sworn I put all of my body weight into that and it still couldn't cut deep into him. Does that mean we really can't win?* The gash on Javean's body heals instantly. It is as if his body has a natural Kinra to heal his wounds.

Meanwhile, Ren summons a shadow sword and attacks the non-hostile Vermunya. Vermunya blocks the attack with his arm. "What!?"

Ren looks closer and notices that the red lining on Vermunya's clothes hardened, blocking the attack. Ren withdraws his sword and attacks again. This time, Vermunya makes the red liquid form a blade and blocks Ren's sword.

A piece of the red blade liquefies and expands and skewers Ren's arm. Vermunya calls the liquid back onto his clothes. Ren stares at his unexpected wound. The blood from it then moves out of his arm and turns back, then sharpens to skewer his arm again. Then Vermunya combines both of the blood streams from the wounds and stabs through Ren's ribs.

"So his power is blood manipulation," Ricardio analyzes as he shoots arrows at Vermunya. The tips of the arrows crack and shatter on impact with Vermunya's skin. "And regular weapons really don't work on angels."

"Um, guys. Ren is really taking a beating," Luke worries. "Then go help him. He could use your shield more than I could right now," Jadeanu resolves. Luke moves over toward Vermunya and adds miniature shields to his fists. He creates another shield and launches it at Vermunya. Vermunya turns to the shield and uses the blood on his suit to grab and crush it. Luke then closes in from the other side. He punches Vermunya in the face with the added momentum of his gaseous rocketing. The attack does minor but evident damage.

Vermunya smiles and lets the blood from his suit extend and sharpen towards Luke, who tries to deploy a shield but can't because it is already broken and hasn't had enough time to regenerate. Ren snatches him back as he rockets away.

Vermunya opens up his chest, and the blood from there molds into multiple whips and starts lashing the area. Ren creates shadow whips to combat Vermunya's. The blood whips easily beat and destroy Ren's. One whip smacks Ren on the arm, taking the skin off of that part. Ren holds on to the mark and breathes in heavily as he stops himself from screaming. "Is this how he skinned Blast's face? Man that's rough," Ren mumbles.

Jadeanu runs at Javean with his blade in his hands. Javean flicks the air, and a blade appears out of thin air aimed at Jadeanu's sword. Javean's sword moves immediately and knocks Jadeanu's weapon clean out of his hands. Javean waves his hand, and three sharp weapons appear above Jadeanu. As Javean moves his hand down, the weapons come down toward Jadeanu, who moves in time, avoids the attack, and goes for his sword. He grabs it and comes back.

Javean summons a dense sword and prepares. As Jadeanu comes with his sword, Javean swings his at Jadeanu's. Jadeanu holds on to his sword and is immediately sent back. He tumbles and keeps hitting the ground repeatedly as he slides and moves uncontrollably for at least fifty feet. Javean clearly overpowered Jadeanu. Jadeanu struggles to get up and then continues toward Javean. "That's some determination. Or maybe it's that Willpower Blessing keeping him going," Ricardio mentions from his safer distance.

A blue gaseous beam hits Javean as Jadeanu approaches. Javean bows down. His body is preparing to erupt energy. Kinra comes and hits Javean in the ribs with all of his might, which resets Javean's explosion. "Jadeanu now!" he yells. Jadeanu slams his blade down on Javean's forehead. The blade doesn't even pierce through his body. The purple energy guards him like armor. The attack only resets the energy.

Then he explodes. The explosion is much bigger than all of the others were. Kinra is sent back and bounces off of the wooden floor, causing it to break on his behind. Jadeanu is sent back, and due to his momentum, he is sent into a backflip. He lands at a kneel and looks at Javean, who is smiling triumphantly. "He looks like he enjoys his own self-detonations. So we really can't hurt this guy. We really have bit off more than we can chew," Jadeanu admits. "No, I can't think like that! We just need to find a way."

"Hey we may not be able to hurt Javean, but I've got an idea," Ricardio strategizes. "Hey Jadeanu. You think you can take another one of those shockwaves?" "To be honest, no." "Well I can shield him," Luke solves. "Good then. Everyone just wait for my instruction,"

Ricardio advises. Vermunya throws his blood at Ren, who can't use his own shadow because it still needs to reset from being destroyed by Vermunya's whips. He just runs.

Luke throws out a shield to protect him. The blood forms a sharp crescent and goes straight through Luke's shield, but luckily, Ren is away from the attack. Vermunya turns the blood into multiple drops and extends them as skewers. Ren is now close enough to Luke to use his shadow to grab himself out of the way. Vermunya pursues, which is when Ricardio yells, "Everybody attack Javean!" Everyone follows his command without hesitation.

Luke adds a shield around Jadeanu and shoots a beam at Javean. Jadeanu strikes him from around the shield but still stays behind it. Kinra attacks with all of his body weight. Ren even uses everyone's shadow except for his own to attack. Javean goes into his explosive state, and his eyes glow white as he emits an explosion big enough to nearly fill the entire tent.

Luke's shield immediately breaks, and everyone is engulfed by the radius. Vermunya is also hit by the blast. He is sent back into the tent wall and falls on his butt. Ricardio is even hit by the edge of the eruption. He is sent through the fabric of the tent. He lands in the grass outside. He has blood all over his face and body, but he is still alive, just barely. The burst reduces many of the items scattered around the floor into nothing. Everyone else is spread around the floor in aching pain. Kinra tries with all his might to crawl very slowly while healing himself, towards Ricardio. Jadeanu himself has blood all over his face and rips in his clothes.

"Oh sorry Vermunya," Javean apologizes. "It is fine. I am not badly hurt," Vermunya replies. "Yet it was such an idiotic calculation for the humans. Did they think that would hurt me enough to give them a chance?" Jadeanu has his eyes closed as he clenches his blade. He thinks back, and the beautiful face of his former wife, Tierla, flashes into his mind. *"I miss you Tierla,"* he says in his mind. *"But*

I know I'm not getting you back. So I'm going to protect the ones I don't want to die." The image in Jadeanu's mind shifts to a picture of his current allies. Tierla symbolically moves behind him. "I love you Tierla. I love all of you, and we are going to make it through this!"

The Blessing of Nature starts glowing, and Jadeanu lifts his eyelids. His eyes glow light green, and all of his wounds slowly heal as his torn clothes seal up as well. Then Kinra, Ren, Luke, and Ricardio's wounds and clothes start to heal too. "What?" Kinra notices. The Blessing of Nature stops glowing, and the Willpower Blessing starts. Jadeanu stomps his left foot and runs at Javean at full speed. Javean holds out his blade and releases it, thus making it fly forward.

Jadeanu holds out his hand and blocks the incoming projectile with his gauntlet-covered palm. The force from the attack sends Jadeanu right back where he started, but he lands on his butt. He gets back up and sprints again. Javean spawns seven swords around his body and sends them at Jadeanu one by one. Jadeanu dodges them all, jumping and evading while still running forward. Javean forms a cannon out of midair and fires cannonballs at Jadeanu. He barely dodges them and finally gets close to Javean.

He jumps, and his foot lands on Javean's shoulder. He kicks off Javean and brings his sword up as he approaches Vermunya from the air. Vermunya notices him and opens up his chest, and a storm of blood nails comes out for Jadeanu to land on. Panicked, Jadeanu flings a rock from the condensed ground underneath the tent's floor using the Willpower Blessing. He kicks off the rock and lands back on the wooden floor. Vermunya calls back his blood. "Javean. They have become a threat now. Commence operation double cutlass," Vermunya orders.

Javean hops directly behind Vermunya. They both gesture their arms around as a martial arts monk does in movies, to symbolize that they are moving so swiftly but calmly that their arms create afterimages. Then Javean completely disappears behind Vermunya.

Vermunya throws out his right arm at Jadeanu, thus making blood spring out as multiple spears. At the same time, on Vermunya's left, a few swords appear and thrust toward Ren and Luke. Jadeanu dodges the blood, but Luke is scraped by one of the blades as he does not see them coming until it is too late.

Vermunya moves Luke's blood and further stabs through his ribs. At the same time, swords and spears come from the other side and strike through Kinra's ribs. Jadeanu looks at the damage and angrily charges toward Vermunya. Vermunya closes in with exceptional speed and pushes against Jadeanu's blade with a blade of blood, reversing his momentum. At the exact same time, Javean closes in on Ren, pushing his sword into Ren's own left shoulder. Blood splashes everywhere.

"Notice that this is my main weapon," Javean says in regard to his thick silver broadsword. "All of the others were formed, and I collected them. But this sword is my designated one." Ren attacks Javean with a shadow spike to stop the sword from cutting all the way through his body. Javean explodes, knocking Ren away. Javean's big sword has two circular carvings toward the blade's handle. One of the circles is now filled with a purple aura, while the other is empty.

Luke comes to attack Javean. Both Vermunya and Javean attack in unison. They both swing their weapons with their right hands in a horizontal direction. Jadeanu and Luke jump back to avoid damage. Javean and Vermunya swing their weapons from left to right diagonally. Once again, Jadeanu and Luke jump back. Then quickly, Vermunya and Javean both switch to attack with multiple weapons telepathically. Vermunya's of blood and Javean of sharp utensils of course. They attack from the right, then from above, and then the weapons move up and thrust forward as if concluding a combo attack.

For Jadeanu, the blood from Vermunya attacks Jadeanu's left side. He slices through the path of the blood, and his sword goes through it in liquid form. The front of the path hardens and slices into

Jadeanu's flesh. He instinctively jumps back to avoid the overhead blood but is stabbed in the guts by the quick forward pierce.

For Luke, he evades an attack from multiple swords to his left. He tries to move back but is still severely lacerated in the legs from the overhead swords. He tries to rocket backward as the weapons protrude forward at him. He manages to dodge the assault and stands on his hurting legs. He grunts from pain. Vermunya and Javean open up their chests, and weapons protrude from their chests in an upward motion. Jadeanu and Luke sidestep the attacks. Vermunya and Javean swing their main weapon down into the ground, bringing both Jadeanu and Luke to look down, respectively, as they dodge the attack.

Vermunya grabs Jadeanu's chin while Javean grabs Luke's. Vermunya lifts Jadeanu effortlessly with his great strength. He slams Jadeanu down on his back and commands the blood from his arm lining to lift up and sharpen, descending towards Jadeanu's neck. Javean lifts Luke up. "This blade of mine allows me to use just a tiny bit of the power inside of me. I'll show you what it feels like!" he says as he slams Luke down on his back and surges energy to flow directly upon him like a miniature bomb of purple energy going off. The energy engraving on Javean's sword now becomes empty.

The blood spikes move down toward Jadeanu's throat, and he accidentally bends up a rock underneath him to force his body into a backflip which dodges the blood. "Whew! The Willpower Blessing protected me." As Jadeanu lands on his feet, Javean rushes toward Vermunya and receives a leg up from Vermunya into the air. Javean creates a wall of swords and sends them all down toward everyone except Vermunya. Everyone does what they can to dodge the shower of swords. Everyone ends up getting stabbed a few times. Luke takes a stab wound to his left calf muscle. Jadeanu takes two sword stabs to the outermost sides of his back. Ren is stabbed in his right shoulder. Kinra is stabbed in the stomach. Javean moves back toward Luke, and Vermunya moves back toward Jadeanu.

Vermunya uses his blood and all of the blood drawn out of Jadeanu from the stabbings. He surrounds Jadeanu on all sides with the blood ready to stab. "Dang it! I can't heal. So using the healing from the Nature Blessing was a one-time thing," Jadeanu realizes as he takes the two swords trapped in his back out.

He ducks down and places his sword on the ground behind him. He leans onto the sword and guards his face with one of his gauntlets and guards his chest with the other one. The blood collapses on him. Jadeanu is pierced multiple times. His vital organs are guarded however. Vermunya brings out more of Jadeanu's blood and prepares to do it again. Jadeanu lifts up a rock from underneath Vermunya. The rock uppercuts him directly in the chin, causing him to lose control of the blood and drop it.

Javean forms a hammer and swings it upward at Luke, who forms a shield. The hammer goes right through the shield and hits Luke on the chin forcing him high off his feet. Javean spawns a few swords and throws them at Luke, thus slicing and piercing through him. Then he forms a cloud of swords to completely surround Luke on all sides.

"Holy crap! That's a lot of swords. That's got to be about 100," Ren guesses as he takes the sword out of his shoulder. "I've got to do something." As the swords prepare to shred Luke all at once. Ren stabs Javean with his own shadow. Javean explodes again, thus diverting his energy and making the swords disappear. Luke safely lands hard on the ground. The fall still visibly hurt Luke, as seen by the wrinkling of his face. Ren breathes a breath of relief.

Due to a failure in their plan, Vermunya and Javean try to regroup. Javean dashes in Vermunya's direction. *I've got to throw off their momentum,'* Jadeanu thinks as he chunks his sword at the front of Javean's path. The sword's blade hits Javean and forces him to stop and explode. Vermunya is concerned with Javean's interruption and watches him to see if anything happens. Jadeanu keeps running and punches Vermunya in the face with energy on his fists. Vermunya suffers very little damage and adjusts to look at his attacker.

Immediately, he is hit again and again. Then Jadeanu punches Vermunya with both hands in the gut, causing a shock wave that is almost enough to make Vermunya stagger backward. Vermunya lets all of his blood extend as needles around his body. Seeing the attack coming, Jadeanu jumps back and goes for his sword near Javean.

Luke starts firing multiple gas balls both toward Javean to stop him from attacking Jadeanu, and at Vermunya to keep him in defense. He shoots a beam toward both of them. Vermunya uses blood to block his incoming attacks. Javean just keeps exploding. Jadeanu finds a gap between the bursts and grabs his sword, and runs. "Jadeanu! I've got an idea! Come here!" Ricardio yells out, now standing in the tent from his healed injuries.

Jadeanu jets to Ricardio. Ren sees Luke's diversion as an opportunity to damage Vermunya. He uses Vermunya's shadow to stab and pierce him in the stomach. He then closes in and attacks with his own shadow. Javean moves in front of Vermunya and creates multiple blades around him to act as shields. He then throws his arms out to take the attacks instead. He eventually explodes, knocking Ren back and blowing Vermunya away but not damaging him due to the protective swords around him.

"Okay Jadeanu," Ricardio starts. "Those blessings of yours are made of energy right?" "Yeah." "And so are your powers. If you can find a way to join them, you can create enough power to defeat the two angels. Maybe using those strong bursts of energy that come out of your fists. You think you can do that?" "Maybe, but it won't be so easy. Controlling these things is a lot harder than it looks. But I'll have to try," Jadeanu replies. Then he starts to concentrate and flow his mind with the energy of the Blessings. "Can you guys hurry up over there!?" Luke yells as he continues throwing energy at Javean. Vermunya is still injured, but he is healing; leaving only a small opening of time for the guys until he rejoins the fight at full strength.

The Blessings on Jadeanu's gauntlets start to glow. He meditates deeply with them, and his blade starts to glow brown and green. He opens his eyes and throws his whole body forward, swinging his blade in a downward motion toward Vermunya. A crescent of brown and green energy flies from his sword. Vermunya sees the attack and hastily flies out of the way. The energy goes right through the tent, still keeping it intact though. The Blessings stop glowing, and Jadeanu falls forward, catching himself with his sword.

"It worked, but I missed," Jadeanu pities. "But you can do it though. And Vermunya clearly saw it as a threat," Ricardio strategizes. "All we got to do is get them to where they can't evade. That should be easy with Javean, but what about Vermunya." "Sure Javean may be immobile while he explodes, but can we actually pierce through his energy?" "It may be the only thing that can hurt him. We've got to at least try. You think you can do it again?" "I have to."

Jadeanu begins his concentration. The Blessings glow once again. Luke is hit with a metal shield from Javean. He flies back with blood spilling out from his face as blood is now covering it. Kinra hits Javean and is exploded away. Blood on his face as he collapses to the ground. Ren uses Javean's shadow to attack. Javean dodges the attack and sends a few swords into Ren's body.

"Oh crap! One more explosion and Kinra and Ren could die," Jadeanu concerns. "It's a gamble, but you can heal their wounds before they die can't you?" Ricardio asks. "No, it doesn't work that way. Unfortunately." "Well then, make sure you just don't fail." "I won't." "You ready?" Jadeanu nods. "Everybody attack Javean now!" Ricardio yells.

Jadeanu gets closer to Javean. Luke shoots a gas energy ball at Javean. He starts his exploding process. Ren attacks him with his shadow and resets the explosion. Javean looks up and sees Jadeanu throwing the slash of Blessing energy at him. Javean has a look of panic on his face as he hopes his explosion will set off quick enough for him to get away. Then Kinra hits Javean, thus resetting the explosion yet again. Ren and Kinra then jump away as best as they can as the crescent slash collides with Javean. The slash continues through the back of the tent, and there is no resulting purple explosion coming from Javean's body. The attack worked. "Javean!" Vermunya yells.

Where Javean was previously standing, there is a shirtless man with white wings and white pants kneeling, surrounded by purpleish red blood. He has long, wrinkled brown hair covering his face as he just stares at the ground in defeat. "We got him! But he's not dead?" Jadeanu questions. "Ah, so you don't know," Vermunya adds. "Well then, I have no reason to hold back. I cannot fail Ravah." Vermunya grabs his left wrist with his right hand and yanks with all of his force. He then uses his blood to saw the arm off. There is now a stub of blood and a bloody pale white forearm extending from it. The arm wiggles a little before going limp. "So their bodies are fake?" Ren wonders.

Vermunya then sucks up all the blood from his lost arm and covers his real arm with a huge arm of blood. "I feel some kind of strange signature from the Willpower Blessing. Like it's trying to talk to me. It tells me that there is a way to banish Javean back to Heaven, but I'm not sure for how long," Jadeanu says while watching the lone glowing Willpower Blessing. "It'll take time, and Javean doesn't seem to be able to attack, so it's worth a shot to ensure that he can't get back up." "So we'll have to protect you," Ricardio says. "We won't be able to do that too much longer, but sure," Luke says.

Vermunya interrupts by grabbing Jadeanu with his huge extended blood hand. He slams Jadeanu onto the ground and hardens the blood, binding Jadeanu to the ground. Jadeanu uses the Blessing of Willpower to break through. The hardened blood around him then liquefies and extends toward him.

He quickly places his sword down, leans on it, and guards. Kinra tackles Vermunya, but he still forces all of the blood to extend toward

Jadeanu. Ren circles Jadeanu's shadow around him as a shield, and Luke forms a barrier around that barrier. Some of the blood still manages to get through and stabs Jadeanu. *'How am I so resistant to this pain?'* he thinks.

Vermunya stands back up and sucks all of his blood back into his arm. The Blessing of Nature is now glowing. "Okay, I'm starting," Jadeanu announces. Vermunya picks Kinra up by his face and sends his blood to him in sharp increments. Luke shoots gas balls at Vermunya's feet. He falls to the ground while still holding Kinra. Luke closes in and kicks Vermunya in the face. He lets go of Kinra. "The Blessing of Nature tells me that if I put enough power into a vital attack, I can actually kill the angels, "Jadeanu says. "But I'm not going to. I just don't feel right about it. "

Vermunya turns his blood arm into a scythe blade and swings it at Luke. Luke jumps back. Vermunya slams it into the ground, liquefies it into a puddle, and then brings spikes up into Luke's legs. Luke staggers but holds his ground. Jadenu then yells "Done" as he points the Blessing toward Javean, and Javean's body glows green like the Nature Blessing. Then his body turns into a small light and flies up through one of the holes in the top of the tent. "Javean! You have found out how to banish him. The cunning of your human minds!" Vermunya expresses. "But how long will he be gone?" Jadeanu asks. "Long enough to tell Ravah that he has lost an ally for his will." "That's long enough for me."

Vermunya sharpens his blood into a blade. "You know all angels have a designated weapon of their own, but unlike Ravah and Javean, I don't carry mine around. Blood is my power, no need for a simple sword." Vermunya then cuts his own chest down to his stomach to draw out more blood. "Hey Jadeanu, all we need is to get a single powerful attack," Ricardio strategizes. "The more we damage him, the more dangerous he becomes. We need one decisive hit, okay?" Jadeanu nods. He starts concentrating again.

Vermunya makes all of his blood from multiple tendrils sharpened at the tips. Vermunya attacks Luke with a few of them. Luke rockets up while firing beams at Vermunya. Ren attacks from Vermunya's left, nearly overwhelming his attention. Vermunya creates a bubble of spikes around his body, extending them in every direction. Ren manages to escape in time, and Luke is safe in the air.

Vermunya withdraws his bubble quickly, knowing what Jadeanu is trying to do and ensuring he doesn't stay in one place for too long. Luke then attacks from close by to Vermunya's right. Ren returns to the left with shadow spikes and swords extended. He even supports Luke with some shadow spikes. It happened so fast that Vermunya was able to use his blood to protect himself but not counterattack. But once he tries, Kinra thrusts his full body into a two-handed punch to Vermunya's stomach. Then suddenly, Vermunya's eyes widen with surprise as a light green and brown crescent is sent flying directly behind him. Luke starts blasting away, and Ren snatches himself away. Kinra jumps back and runs backward while watching the scene from up close.

The crescent goes through Vermunya's back and continues through the front of the tent, destroying its foundation and ripping it down. An explosion of blood erupts from where Vermunya is standing. Then all of the blood extends into hundreds of long sharp spikes spanning a relatively large area. It must have been Vermunya's last effort of attack. Luke manages to get away. Ren is scraped all over his limbs, but okay. "Are you alright Ren?" Jadeanu worries while walking to the scene. "I'm fine. But what about Kinra? He was here with us!" Ren, Luke, and Jadeanu move around the spike trap in panic. "No, no, no. Kinra." Luke saddens, with strong despair in his eyes. Everyone's face gets a fit of sadness once they see what happened.

Kinra's body is stuck to the blood spikes from head to toe. Every inch of his body is skewered. There is no way he could have survived. The blood soon liquefies and falls to the ground. And so does what's left of his body. "Kinra. He was only 13 years old, and now he's dead.

I was supposed to protect his youth! Why couldn't it be me instead?" Luke grieves with water surfacing in his eyes. "We've lost our healer," Ren realizes. "All damage from now on will be permanent." "Hahahahahahaha," Vermunya laughs while having now pale white skin, white wings, and robes. He is now in a kneeling position.

"Jadeanu. Kill him. You said you could right?" Ren commands. "No. I'm not going to kill him," Jadeanu replies. "But he killed Kinra and Blast! There's no point in just-" "WE'RE NOT KILLING HIM! We broke into his home trying to steal. We gambled, and we lost; that's it." Jadeanu concentrates on banishing Vermunya with the Willpower Blessing.

"If you struggled with Javean and me, then prepare for trouble. When Ravah hears about this, he'll kill you," Vermunya starts. "Javean and I were strong, but with Ravah, the full power of an angel will come down on you. You won't stand a chance. Not only is Ravah a top-ranked angel, but he's one of the strongest angels there is." Vermunya's body starts to glow and then is transported elsewhere.

"Guys, um. I'm pretty sure I'm gonna bleed out," Ren calls out. "You think that's bad," Ricardio starts. "Imagine getting burned up to the flesh, not even being able to move." "When did that happen?" "When Javean did that huge explosion. I got caught up in it. It badly burned me until I was mysteriously healed. But even after that, I was so distraught that it took a while before I could understand what happened and move."

"Speaking of that, hey Jadeanu, let me use the Blessings. I want to see if there is anything that I can do with them to help us heal," Luke expresses. "I know the Nature Blessing can do it, but you don't seem to know how to make it work." "Uh, sure." Jadeanu then takes his right gauntlet off and gives it to Luke. Luke puts it on. The Nature Blessing starts glowing, and Ren's wounds start closing. "What in the?" Luke concerns. "What's wrong Luke? Isn't it working?" Jadeanu worries. "I'm not doing that. The Blessing is acting on its own."

"Well I told you they weren't easy to use. They work very strangely."
"Well then."

Luke continues accidentally healing everyone with the strange power of the Nature Blessing. "Okay, this is weird." After the wound sealing, Luke quickly takes off the gauntlet and gives it back to his brother. "Wait, what was that?" he demands. "What do you mean?" Jadeanu asks. "The Willpower Blessing just told me something. Rather, it made me feel something." "What is it?"

"When you used it, it must have heightened our will to survive, but it also weakened Javean and Vermunya's." "That's why they allowed us to hit them so much. That would explain why we were able to make it through this. We relied on the shift of will for defense. But if only I was a better protector. If only I was stronger. Kinra wouldn't have had to die. All of that strength just led us to the mercy of the Blessings. But how did you do that Jadeanu?"

"I don't know. I didn't even think I could lower someone else's will like that," Jadeanu answers. "But that doesn't even matter right now. We've failed our mission. So we've got two options. We can either track Ravah or keep going northeast to find whatever's going on over there." "I think we should go northeast, and when we run into Ravah, we fight him and take our revenge, then take the Knowledge Blessing," Ren suggests.

Meanwhile, far away, Ravah is speaking to a young man. "Do you believe that the gods want you to be docile with your powers?" Ravah speaks. "For it is sinful to not use your gifts. With that, you should use it to gain the justice you need. You shouldn't be restricted to accepting what comes to you. Choose your liberation." The man nods and walks away.

A white light rushes toward Ravah from the sky suddenly and stops in front of him. The light appears to be a bright white glowing being with long white wings. He is like an angel of light. "Ravah, surely you know that your underlings have failed. I watched it happen," the angel speaks. "I am aware. But why is it that you've come to tell me?" Ravah asks. "Because I know why they failed. And I can get rid of the one threat for you. If you desire." "When it comes to mischief, I trust you the most. You have my permission, Lightwalker." "Good choice Ravah," The angel says. "This will be fascinating to see through." The angel known as Lightwalker leaves.

Chapter 8:

For Those You Hold Dear

Jadeanu and his remaining companions all walk out of the broken tent where they survived the encounter with two archangels and out to the gloomy purple sky, saddened by their loss. Luke takes one more look back at the scene of drooping curtains on a messed up wooden floor, covered in blood, and then continues walking.

"So does anyone actually know where we need to go?" Ricardio asks.

"Nope. I just know that if this is north, then we need to keep going through here and to the east," Jadeanu hypothesizes. "Surely someone's got to make mention of what's going on there."

"We'd best hope."

They continue walking through the messed-up village, looking around and gauging the environment. Empty huts and homes, barely recognizable disheveled structures, and only the sound of their footsteps fill the cold air now. Then suddenly, that silence is cut off by hysterical laughter. *"Hahahahaha."*

They all look and see a man standing on his own with red glowing eyes. "I've found you. Hahaha," the man says. He is the very man that Ravah was recently talking to. "I was looking for the ones makin' all that noise. It must have been all of you."

The man sounds either drunk or just insane.

"You all know why this place is abandoned and empty? It's because of all the destructive maniacs, those giant things, and the people with wings. Yep, they ripped this place apart. Those huge things keep goin' through here for some reason. Only me and a few others are left. I would have given up hope, but the 'Enlightened One' visited me. And now I realize that everything's going to be okay."

"What does he mean by that? And who is the 'Enlightened One'?" Luke mumbles to his group.

"Don't listen to him. He's clearly crazy. We need to move past him and keep going," Ren whispers.

"Do you know about some powerful guy somewhere Northeast of here?" Jadeanu asks the man. "So, you're planning on leaving this place. I'm afraid I can't let that happen."

The man then forms a gun symbol with his right hand and fake fires at Luke while saying, "Bang." A small red ball travels out of his fingers at an exceptional speed. Luke grunts and holds onto his chest. He looks at his hand, that now has blood on it, and says, "What in the?"

'His power is gun hands?' Ricardio wonders.

"My power is to shoot these red bullets out of my fingertips," the man explains. "I found that out when I was with my best friend. We were just chillin, trying to explore what kind of power I would have, and as a joke, I made my fingers like this and shot at his head. He died instantly. The last person I had in my life, I'm the one that killed him. Isn't that something? I didn't want him to die, but you know these things happen. Thanks to the Enlightened One, I realize I'm free. Free to share my experience with others. Maybe I should name the Enlightened One 'Lucifer.' Yes, it's perfect. He will be known as

Lucifer the Light-Bringer. For he has brought light into my life of darkness. And now I will share that light with you."

The man aims both of his hands in gun formation and shoots rapid fire. Luke is now prepared and makes a huge shield to defend everyone against the incoming fire. The red energy bullets bounce clean off of the shield.

"This big shield takes a lot of energy, but if I drop it, we'll all get demolished. We need to take cover," Luke gestures toward a partially destroyed two-story house. He leaves, and everyone runs, still behind the shield, to the house. Luke depletes his shield and takes cover behind one of the house walls. Everyone else follows, with Jadeanu handing the others his sword and then deciding to go up to the second floor.

The guy continues shooting the building, which takes a small chunk of the bricks with each shot. Luke shoots a few gas balls at him, still behind the brick structure. The man jumps out of the way. Ren manipulates the guy's shadow and stabs him in the legs. But the guy stands up again and shoots his shadow, thus stopping it. "You see? You all have these colorful powers, and all I'm left with are guns, something you can buy at a store!" he announces.

"But you see, I'm the one with true power. All the others had all these great and strong powers. Heck, I've even seen others with simple powers, but they were much stronger than mine."

He puts his hands together into one slightly larger literal handgun and fires at the building. A much bigger bullet comes out and slams into the side of the house, knocking off a considerable chunk of brick. "Guys, I'm getting kind of tired," Luke pants. "But we're just now starting," Ren calls out. "Yeah but it was only minutes ago that we were fighting Javean and Vermunya."

"All these newly powerful people. All of this potential," the guy continues, "But most of them got that Death Disease, and all died before they could enjoy that new power. But isn't it ironic? How a weakling like me is still alive. I have this 'weak' power. And it doesn't get much better than this. But I'm alive, and everyone else is dead. And I'll make sure it stays that way." Jadeanu then jumps from the second floor of the house with both of his gauntlets full of red energy.

The man aims his gun at him, to which Luke responds by throwing a shield at Jadeanu. Jadeanu grabs the shield and rides down with it blocking all the bullets. Once he approaches the man, he throws down his shield and punches the guy in the face. The extra momentum from the long jump and the red energy slam into the man causing him to fall straight to the ground, tumbling ruthlessly. He lands head-first on the concrete, with blood sprouting all around.

"You didn't kill him did you?" Luke shouts while holding Jadeanu's sword that he left with them. All the guys come out in the open.

"The only problem here…" the man says, "is that you didn't kill me!"

He then makes a gun symbol and points it at Jadeanu's head. He fires. Jadeanu moves just in time with inhuman reflexes. He dodges the bullet and grabs the guy's hand.

He grabs his pointer finger and bends it backward at one of the joints, thus breaking the finger. "Aaahh!" the guy howls.

Jadeanu grabs his other hand and snaps the pointer finger bone. "Now you can no longer use your power to harm anyone again," Jadeanu claims. "You are no longer a threat. I have no reason to kill you. Maybe if you had an ally to gain here instead of chasing them away, you could have had a medic to heal you."

Luke hands Jadeanu back his sword. "If you want strength, you should find a reason to have it and pursue it. Now I've got a few questions for you. For starters, who is this 'Enlightened One' you speak of?"

"I don't know him, but all I know is that he has purple skin, and he's like some sort of god," the man responds. "So that's what Ravah has been doing with the Knowledge Blessing. He's been feeding people's heads with information," Jadeanu realizes. "Um, Jadeanu. That doesn't sound so bad," Ren establishes. "I know, but it still doesn't sit right with me."

Jadeanu shifts his attention back to the guy. "Now answer me. Do you know anything about a being somewhere Northeast with unmatchable power and the ability to manipulate life and death?"

"I, I do know o-of a powerful man if you just keep going where you're already going. He's very unmatchable, but I don't know about control over life and death, but surely you'll see for yourself."

"Thank you sir," Jadeanu appreciates and leads everyone to walk away. The man starts sobbing quietly. He's clearly a broken man.

Jadeanu and his crew continue walking through the village. "Look over there," Luke points out. There's a young woman taking her kid outside. Probably to get some food or exercise. The woman's eyes are normal, but the boy has red eyes. But they both have black markings on their bodies. If you look closely, you can even see the bone where meat once was. It was a sign of Death Disease. They both had it, and it was constantly spreading until they both inevitably died. "Those poor people," Luke sympathizes.

"Yeah. It's sad. But it's our world now. And we need to stop it," Jadeanu says.

They all continue walking.

"So let me get this straight," Ren begins. "We're looking for all of these Blessings so that you can gain enough power to beat a god. And by doing so, you might be able to stop the Death Spiral. You're a noble man. But if Ravah wants all the Blessings too, then what do you propose he's after?"

"I don't know but I want to know what you're after. And what about you Luke? Why exactly did you choose to stay with us despite all that we have gone through?"

"I'm here because I've got to look after you bro. I want to see you at peace. And bring the world back to peace. I don't want to see these people die just as much as you don't," Luke says.

"And well, I never really thought about it," Ren confesses. "But if I had to guess, I would say it's since you helped me find a nice place to be here. I guess I feel obligated to help. I also like seeing some of these people getting what they have coming to them. Plus this power is exhilarating to use."

"And that, we can agree on," Jadeanu says.

He stops at a big building that stands tall in his path. "Is this...a temple?"

"Yes it is," an old man says, struggling to walk with his cane yet proceeding toward the group.

"Hey young man. You seem rather strong. Could you help me get to the nearby city? I've been walking in this dangerous place for a long time," he gestures toward Ren. "Should we help him? He doesn't have strange colored eyes, so he probably doesn't have powers," Luke suggests.

"Yeah, but you remember Jinzen," Ren reminds him, wary of the old man.

The man continues staggering forward. "Get behind me Ren," Jadeanu steps forward. Once the old man gets close, Jadeanu brings his fist forward, and brown and light green light emits, hitting the old man backward. He tumbles on the ground with steam coming off of him. Everyone looks at Jadeanu in shock. Has he finally gone mad from all he's seen? White wings suddenly burst out of the old man's back. His wardrobe and appearance start to change. He then looks up. He now resembles a young man with no facial hair, pale skin, purple eyes and an all-black suit.

"Jadeanu, how did you know–" Luke starts.

"More importantly," Ren interrupts, "When did you learn how to use the Blessings like that?"

Jadeanu doesn't answer.

"Good move boy. I'm impressed Jadeanu," the angel says.

"I know you're an angel, but who do you serve?" Jadeanu asks. The angel flaps his wings and then answers, "I am an angel of Death. Smart to not let me touch you. I, as one of Death's angels, carry the Death Disease. A plague capable of rotting a person from the outside in. Very contagious."

Jadeanu feels the power from the angel and falls to his knees. So does everyone else.

'This power. It's drastically stronger than Will's and Knowledge's aura,' Jadeanu thinks.

'But gods are supposed to be much stronger than the angels. And if that's the case, that would mean that Will was holding back much more than I thought, and I still couldn't beat him.' Jadeanu's heart sinks in piercing fear.

"I'm afraid I must take Ren's life," the angel continues. "As an angel of Death during the end times, I am tasked with taking the lives of sinners and those deserving." The angel draws his sword from his suit.

"So what?! We beat Javean and Vermunya. What makes you think you can beat us?" Ren brags.

"Yes, I am aware of your feat. Quite impressive. But you'll find me a bit harder to beat than them, considering that I always keep my sword close," the angel replies.

Everyone slowly stands right back up. "I will not kill you others but do beware of my Death Disease. Contact with me or my power will pass it to you. Then you have two days to make amends before you rot to death. A very dreaded and painful way to go." "But why do you wish to kill Ren? Sure I don't know his past, but I do know that he's with us," Jadeanu claims. "We aim to do something noble and justified by the gods. Ren is a part of that. With all due respect, why would you want to take from that?"

"Despite noble intentions, the sins in one's soul have already been judged," the angel says. "My task is to destroy that. Ren, a man who betrays and blends into the shadows, waiting to strike with an unnecessary vengeance. It's nothing personal, only consequence."

The angel swings his sword down, causing a dark sinister energy to come forward toward Ren. Jadeanu jumps in the way and blocks the attack with his sword. The excess power pushes Jadeanu into Ren and they both fly backwards. Ren's back crashes through the temple door and he and Jadeanu fly straight into the temple with a loud crash.

Luke and Ricardio look at each other in surprise and then they rush into the temple afterward. They notice that the place is vacant of people. Ren and Jadeanu are at the back of the empty temple. There is a large dent in the wall behind them. Ren's back must have made the dent.

"You guys didn't get any of that stuff on you, did you?" Luke asks.

"No. This sword is awesome! I'm sure I would have died a few times if it weren't for this," Jadeanu answers. The angel flies into the temple and Jadeanu helps Ren to his feet.

"Well would you look at that?" the angel begins. "Here I am at the only exit and entrance of the place. And all of you are at the opposite of it. Tell you what, I'll make you a deal. Since you all seem so determined to save Ren, and I don't want to have to kill the rest of you, if you can get Ren through this exit alive, I'll let him live, and I won't pursue him anymore. I can't say the same for any other Death Angel though. But if you can't, well, you know what happens. Do we have a deal?" Jadeanu nods and never lets his eyes from the angel.

"Ren, prepare to be treated like property," he says. "Now I want you to skate full speed toward the exit and let us do all the defending. Now go."

Ren immediately creates skates from his shadow and proceeds to the exit.

"You just stay back Ricardio," Jadeanu advises while adding red energy to his legs and coming after Ren. "Yeah I know," Ricardio says. Luke also rockets ahead. The angel dashes ahead with his sword in a stabbing position. Jadeanu advances in front of Ren but is a little off to the side. Once the angel comes close, Jadeanu swings his blade upwards, hoping to disrupt the angel's blade but once his sword hits the angel's, it bounces back down due to the unwavering stillness of the angel's strength. The sword continues toward Ren's heart.

Strategically, Jadeanu uses his downward momentum to slam his body into the angel's legs. The angel trips causing Ren to advance past him. The angel doesn't fall all the way down; however he catches himself and swings his sword at Ren's calves. Jadeanu places his sword into the ground in the angel's sword's path, blocking the attack and providing a foundation for Jadeanu to stand up on.

The angel flies up and swings his sword down, causing an energy shockwave to move toward Ren. Jadeanu is unable to move in quick enough to defend against it. It travels straight to Ren. But then Ren is hit with a blue beam and is launched forward, away from the angel's attack, but now Ren is on the floor no longer skating. The angel throws another shockwave toward him. Ren uses his shadow to lift himself up.

Jadeanu closes in on Ren and grips him on the shoulder and throws him away from the attack. Ren stumbles for balance but manages and continues reluctantly skating toward the exit. Jadeanu, on the other hand, is left to block the shockwave. He blocks it with his sword and is sent back but catches himself with his power and aid from the fortification of the Willpower Blessing. He lands nearly sitting but the excess power from the shockwave almost touches him.

Luke looks at the situation with fear, but then bravery takes over.

"I'm sick of all this. Having to be defenseless while watching the people I care about nearly get killed! I have to be better! I will protect you!" Luke rages and suddenly, a shield self-constructs on the fronts of Luke and Jadeanu and on Ren's back. The shield is big enough to protect their whole body yet thin enough to fight past.

"What is this?" Luke wonders. The angel throws another shockwave at Ren. Luke quickly shoots a gas ball at Ren's back shield which accelerates his speed past the deadly energy attack.

"Good idea," Jadeanu says as he adds energy to his left leg and springs forward. He brings red energy to his two arms, taking it from his leg. He hits Ren's shield with all of his force. The shield breaks and Ren is launched out of the entrance of the temple.

"Ahhhh!" Ren rubs his back. The Death Angel flies down gently and lands on his feet.

"Congratulations. As promised, Ren Torilase's life will be spared." Everyone breathes with relief. "Now everyone, please join me outside," the angel speaks as he moves outside. Ren panics and quickly moves away from the angel. "Do not worry Ren. Although I understand distrust, rest assured I aim not to harm you."

Ricardio, Luke and Jadeanu walk outside. "Stand back," the angel commands. Everyone follows and gets behind the angel as he is facing the temple now. He raises up his sword and swings it fast and hard. The mere wind from the attack completely eviscerates the temple and proceeds to pave a long path behind it.

"Jeez," Luke snarls. "You think he was holding back when he fought us?" Ren whispers.

"If you follow this path, you'll end up near a huge city. You'll need to pass through there to get where you are trying to go," the angel says. "Be warned that there are many powered animals through here. Just because I didn't kill you doesn't mean they won't."

"Uh, thank you," Jadeanu appreciates the warning. "My pleasure. Also let me inform you that you saved the man you met earlier. By breaking his fingers, you have given him a chance to make amends. Thank you. And now my work here is done," the angel spreads his wings and flies away.

"Well that was kind of him," Jadeanu claims. "Alright guys, let's go." They all continue their pilgrimage through the new path. "So what's up with today?" Ren questions. "What do you mean by that?" Jadeanu asks. "Well it's only daytime, and already we lost two of our comrades and we fought a crazy guy with gun hands. And lastly, we had to deal with a Death Angel trying to kill me. Is the universe trying to kill us all today? And to think just yesterday we were all chilling."

"Yeah that's all true but think of all the power we've gained. Maybe this is all to make us stronger," Jadeanu lightens.

"Yeah but maybe we should–" Luke is interrupted by a loud roar.

The four men look in the direction of the noise. They see a large bear with red eyes. The bear roars again, except this time, a reddish-purple energy beam emits from his mouth. Ren, Luke, and Ricardio dodge to the bear's left, and Jadeanu moves to the right. The beam crashes into the dirt path, lighting it with very temporary fire.

"Hey, you know it's not nice to interrupt someone in conversation," Jadeanu says as he jumps up with energy in his fists. The bear smacks Jadeanu down and throws a blast at him when he hits the floor, temporarily lighting him with bright orange flames.

"Just because you have this power doesn't mean that you're just that much stronger than everything else," Luke lectures. The bear then lunges at Jadeanu's leg. He adds energy to his leg to protect it. The bear bites down on his leg with incredible strength. Jadeanu grunts and starts to whimper from pain.

The bear then pulls out his claws, ready to rip Jadeanu to shreds. Luke shoots the bear with gas energy balls, but it doesn't stop it. Then suddenly, the bear's eyes shift to a cold black glare, and it stops attacking. Ren makes a motion, and a large shadow spike descends from a giant hole in the bear's chest and reforms into Jadeanu's shadow.

Jadeanu lifts the dead animal off of him and tosses it to the side. "I'm sorry it had to be like that," Ren sympathizes.

'That's not like Ren to say,' Jadeanu analyzes.

"Well the angel wasn't kidding about the animals here," Luke mentions.

"Yeah well I would say that it's good for hunting, but we can't eat the likely aggressive animals," Ricardio inputs. "And I can't really kill any of these superpowered things either."

"It's kind of sad," Luke says. "We have to kill these poor animals just because they have these new abilities messing with their minds."

"Yeah but it's all we can do for now. Maybe next time we should try to just chunk the thing back into the wilderness," Jadeanu suggests, "But for now, let's just keep moving and stay cautious."

They continue forward for a while.

"Man. How long is this path?" Luke questions. "I'm more concerned about how that angel made this long trail with just an attack," Ren says. Ricardio looks around and then looks up. He gazes upon a bird with light blue eyes soaring freely through the sky.

"Yeah this place is storming with wildlife," he notices.

"Hey guys wait," Jadeanu pauses. "Something really strong is coming. I can feel it," Luke responds. "What the heck is that thing?" Ren asks.

A big white light comes into view. The light moves quickly and pauses in Jadeanu and the company's path. The light then spreads his wings and reveals himself to be the angel known as Lightwalker.

Jadeanu, Ren and Luke all fall down to a knee from Lightwalker's power. Ricardio hits the floor, unable to stop himself.

"Everyone, stand up!" Jadeanu commands. He tries to get up himself, but is very unsuccessful.

"I don't think I can with this guy!" Ren comments. "Yes you can! All you have to do is will it so," Jadeanu quotes and the Willpower Blessing starts to glow.

Jadeanu then slowly stands to his feet. Ren follows and then Luke. Ricardio struggles the most, but eventually, he gets up as well.

'Is he an angel? If so, why does it look like he's made of light?' Jadeanu reflects.

"Who are you?"

"I am the Angel of Opportunity. For that is what I have to bring to you," Lightwalker replies with his powerful angelic voice.

"What kind of opportunity?" Jadeanu asks.

"I sense grief in the hearts of two of you. Or at least a personal grief once bound by the will of two lovers. A soul's promise," Lightwalker expresses.

"I offer to end that grief for one of you, but I'm aware the other would not have it. Too obligated."

"What are you proposing?" Jadeanu demands.

"I propose your wives. Tierla Stroyem for you and Annabelle Riveras for Ricardio. I am an Angel of Life. The ability to revive is within my grasp."

"But Ravah told us that resurrection is forbidden. How can we trust you?" Jadeanu questions him.

"This deal is not exactly for you but for your friend Ricardio. But if you do not believe me…"

Lightwalker waves his hand and a mortar of light lunges from the sky to right beside him. There is a woman standing inside of a transparent crystal with her eyes closed. The woman's face is undoubtedly the face of Ricardio's deceased wife. Ricardio looks at her with a mix of disbelief and hope.

"This can't be…" he mumbles. "Her body was still whole. All I needed was to alter and reverse the effects of her death. And she can live once again," Lightwalker says to them. "And she is the same as when you left her."

Annabelle opens her eyes. It's truly a miracle. The crystal around her shatters, and she looks at Ricardio, who is now in tears.

"R-Ricardio?" she speaks. Ricardio looks at the wedding ring that's been on his finger through this journey and looks at the one on Annabelle's finger.

Lightwalker looks at Annabelle and says, "Go to him." She runs and gives Ricardio a hug so serene it calms Ricardio's entire hunger for journey. He gives Annabelle a big kiss, one he well deserved after all he's survived.

He quickly retracts his lips.

"What's wrong?" she asks.

"I…I just don't understand," he responds. "Despite your doubts, I assure you she's the real thing," Lightwalker establishes.

"Now, here is what I want for you to do. In return for bringing back your beloved, all I desire is that you spend the rest of your energy with her in your sanctuary. She may have a few aged marks on her from decay, but I promise you she'll heal it off. Now enjoy her and cherish her. But you must leave here. You must leave your mission here with Jadeanu and return home. It is all I ask. If you do not, she must return to her coffin. It's your choice. Think it over. You mustn't regret your choice."

"I'm sorry guys, but I must choose Anna," Ricardio replies to his group.

"What!? After all we've been through. You're just gonna leave us like that?" Ren complains.

"It's okay," Jadeanu empathizes. "This is what he always wanted. This is where his loyalty lies. You just need to focus on your own."

"I get it. But are you sure Ricardio?" Luke expresses. "This is no small choice."

"My mind's all made up. It has been before we ever even started on this adventure," Ricardio exclaims. "Good luck on your journey here."

Ricardio pulls out the genie lamp from his bow quiver and gives it to Jadeanu.

"I won't be there to see it, but you have to be the ones to free Stougma on your own. This is hard to say, but...bye guys," Ricardio gives Jadeanu and Luke a hug, but Ren refuses.

"So cowardly," Ren mumbles under his breath.

"Now Jadeanu, you could have this too," Lightwalker says.

"No, I'm over it. I've got a mission to complete with the people that need me," Jadeanu answers.

"Well, Ricardio, Annabelle," Lightwalker continues. "If you two are ready to go, I'll take you back to your home." "Yeah let's get on. This goodbye stuff isn't my thing," Ricardio says. "You guys take care."

Jadeanu smiles and nods farewell to his old friend.

Lightwalker lifts both Ricardio and Annabelle with his telekinetic abilities, wraps them in light, then sends them away, in which they both are just blasted off at light speed into the air.

"So, 'Angel of Opportunity,' if you can send people away at that speed, could you take us to the powerful person Northeast?" Jadeanu asks as he gives the lamp to Luke.

"I could but I'm not interested. You'll find things much more rewarding by going on foot. Now I've got to go. Hahaha."

Lightwalker then flies away swiftly.

"So now it's just the three of us," Jadeanu claims.

"I can't believe he would betray us like that!" Ren protests. Everyone continues walking.

"Well, think about it. That's his wife, the woman he shares his soul with," Jadeanu gives his perspective.

"He lost her and was given the once-in-a-lifetime opportunity to get her back. You've got to understand he's got an obligation to her. An emotional rollercoaster that he would never want to end. He loves that woman. Do you know what that's like? Have you ever had a woman to give your all to?"

"No. Most women don't tend to be attracted to me," Ren answers. "I have a girlfriend or rather had, but you know what that's like for me. I guess I'm just not as cool or good-looking as you. Just look at you and look at me. You've got muscles and even Luke is cool with all the shields and such, all big brother-like. I don't know what it's like to have someone to give your all to. But I do know about giving yourself to your mission. Isn't that just as important?"

"It is, and that's why it's such a hard decision," Jadeanu admits. "But that's why I chose to stay here. The universe has to keep going and so do I."

"The universe?" Luke wonders and then an idea pops into his head.

"Jadeanu! You remember when Will told us that the rest of the Blessings, we could likely find wherever our instincts lead us on their whereabouts? Well if there is a god of the Universe then I think I might know where the Blessing is. It's the only one I could think to find."

"And where would that be?"

"Up there," Luke says while looking at the stars above.

"How do you propose we get up there, let alone find a Blessing in that huge place?" Ren demands.

"I don't know," Luke answers. "Well I think I can get up there, but... I just hope I can sense the Blessing's power without having to go too high. After all, I'm the only one with the power to jet upward."

"That's suicide," Ren says. "Maybe, but it's the only lead we have so I have to try it. If no one else has got the Blessing, then it's probably in a place no one would want to go if they ever even thought of it. This might be our best shot."

"Well, if you're going to do it then I suggest you take this with you," Jadeanu says, handing Luke his right gauntlet which Luke responds by giving the magic lamp he's still holding to Ren.

"The Willpower Blessing will keep you going, and you'll be unable to touch the naked Universe Blessing without the gauntlet," Luke takes the gauntlet and puts it on his arm. "I'm only going into the atmosphere, not all the way out there you know."

"Be warned of the lack of oxygen and note that if you fall, we will try our best to catch you, so don't go too far," Jadeanu advises.

"Don't worry, I've got this," Luke says. He takes a deep breath and rockets himself straight upwards. After several seconds of blasting off, he realizes how hard this would all be. The more distance he covers, the more energy he would have to shoot down in order to keep blasting up. Luke starts to sweat from exhaustion.

"Wow, this is really stupid. But I've already started, so I've got to keep going," Luke gets extremely tired fairly quickly, yet he keeps going as the oxygen supply turns thin. "Crap! It's getting hard to breathe," Luke starts to go nearly unconscious. "Is he really doing this?" Ren says in disbelief. "Will he be alright?"

"I sure hope so," Jadeanu worries.

Luke really starts to struggle once he gets so high that he can't even be seen by one's naked eye staring from the ground.

'Is this what it's like to die from a lack of oxygen?' Luke resists. He then suddenly starts breathing normally again. He soon realizes that he is now floating in an area that looks like outer space. There is nothing but stars around, but he wonders how he is able to breathe? From the ground, Jadeanu strangely lifts up and is tossed up to the Earth's atmosphere by some unknown force.

"What the...?" Ren asks, concerned.

"Well, sure, just leave me behind. Don't die up there." Jadeanu floats to where Luke is. They both make eye contact with each other, confused.

"Jadeanu! How did you...?"

"Where are we?"

Many stars move and outline a figure in the empty space. The figure is shaped like a person. But the person is completely transparent or rather is made of small stars, blending in with the environment around it. The being's eyes open and it has no pupils, only bright whites. This being does however, have long luxurious transparent hair. Whoever they are, one can tell that they're supposed to be beautiful.

"Greetings, Jadeanu and Luke Stroyem. I am Universe," the being says with a slight British accent. Jadeanu bows in respect and asks, "You summoned us?" "No. For I am not even fully here now. I am merely in your minds, and you are in one of my pocket dimensions. But no, your souls have called upon my Blessing, and it has come to you," Universe gestures at Luke's arm covered in the gauntlet which is clenched closed.

He opens it and notices a black orb with small white sparkles on it. It resembles outer space. Luke has a look of surprise on his face with his mysterious accomplishment.

He prepares to grab the Blessing with his other hand.

"No!" Jadeanu panics.

"Here, let me," Jadeanu then grabs it with his left gauntlet and prepares to place it on the rightmost empty socket of Luke's right gauntlet.

"Not there. The one in the middle," Universe tells them. Jadeanu adjusts and places the Blessing on the slightly bigger engraving at the center of the gauntlet.

"He who touches the Blessing and removes it from its natural habitat summons the attention of the respective god," the Universe foretells.

"I am here to judge he who calls upon my power." "So by just touching a Blessing untouched by another, we may talk to the other gods?" Jadeanu wonders.

"Yes, but they will not actually be present. They may speak but not aid you."

"But how does that work?"

"I control the entire universe. I am capable of being everywhere and anywhere all at once. I am busy working elsewhere while implementing myself into your mind now. All gods can do such but through their own flow of power. For I am here, over there and even here."

A hand touches both Luke and Jadeanu on their shoulders. They both look back but see nothing there.

"You see, I am the all yet the one. The center that branches through all things within a constant cycle of bounding communication," Universe continues.

"This world and all on it connect. That is the bind that holds us all together. Everything has an extension to another. Every cause has an effect, every action has a consequence. He who understands that has true power.

For the deaths of those who have passed, create a path for those alive. All deaths, no matter how tragic, bring something new to be ventured whether through evil or good. Rather than grieving the past, one must move forward through the upbringing of strength. One must forgive the past but never forget it, thus dawning the creation of power through the confused setting of the wise. Always remember that every death has a reason. You should consider how the deaths you've seen so far have made you stronger. How they have led you on your journey and here to me. How have you responded to such? For that also speaks volumes of who you are.

The way one does one thing is the way they do everything. Even the smaller things are direct messages that lead to your soul. But connections stem further than events. Everything you touch and feel grants you a connective figure. Your connection to another. A gift granted through our image. An intuition. A connection derivative from your hair. Your hair branches to the world as your soul branches to another's. A gift steadier in women than men, yet it works the same.

Similar to soul empathy is the feeling for another and the energy they give off. Whether positive or negative, but neither are evil, such as the enjoyment of another's misfortune. It is not evil nor detrimental, but a pleasure connotation of negative energy. That is a collective madness that all possess one way or another. It is only a matter of energy shift due to the resonance of your spirit. A resonance that may be altered by many things but you have control over it. Your control is at its finest when you detach yourself from the material things of the world and learn to live without need. This control of energy shifting can also be heightened by a gift of man. That gift is music.

The soothing sound is pleasant not to the ear but to the familiarity of the soul. Whether from an instrument or the sweet sound of a woman's voice as an inspiration to her husband. It all tickles the power hidden in your spirit. The being of you that doesn't belong to you. These ventures will provide power where none seems present. This is my wisdom to you."

"Thanks Universe," Jadeanu says in appreciation. "I ask you then, do you think that I really can beat Death?"

"Do you think you can beat me? The god of the universe, with objects of the universe?" Jadeanu frowns in disappointment.

"I'll show you a glance at my power," Universe mentions as he waves his hand and Jadeanu turns into dust. Then Universe clenches his fist, and the dust turns back into Jadeanu.

"As you can see, there is no true way to defeat a god. Especially not in their own kingdom."

"Their kingdom?"

"Yes, nearly every god has one. A god's kingdom is the dimension they reside in. It is balanced with that god's power. The bigger a god's kingdom, the more they influence and the weaker the god is physically. The smaller the kingdom, the stronger the god is. I am the strongest god because I have no kingdom at all. Yet the universe is mine, so one could say I have the biggest kingdom. But nonetheless, a god's strength is partly bound to their kingdom.

Despite that, a god's power is unlimited in its rawest form. There is a way to tire a god's spirit. For all life has energy. When a god is in his kingdom, that energy does not expire. But when they are not, they may enter a stasis of energy recharge known as a stalemate. That is when a spirit that cannot die is unable to move nor use much energy as its body needs to recharge. This will occur once one is hit with a normally fatal attack."

'So that's what happened with Javean and Vermunya,' Jadeanu thinks.

"You see, Death is no longer in his very small kingdom, but he is in Life's. Watching the show of Earth. He can be stalemated but not beaten. If with the powers of the Blessings, you can stalemate Death, he will likely call it your win. You are not his enemy; you are no true threat. He may kill you, but he won't just erase you or dishonor you. You have a chance. But you'll have to give it your all."

"Thank you Universe."

"I warn you Jadeanu, the Blessing you have just received can be just as dangerous to you as it is to others. It allows you to manipulate the universe to your will, but it can also destroy your universe. Be wary of something as simple as teleportation, which is applicable mind you, which causes you to eliminate the current position of your molecules and move them elsewhere. But if you do not recreate all of your molecules exactly, you could miss something vital; permanently. I would suggest you use it sparingly if at all." "I will."

"Farewell, Jadeanu and Luke. You will have my guiding hand. Things may not happen as you want, but always as they need," Universe fades away into the void of space, and Luke and Jadeanu fall from the sky but glide down slowly when they reach the ground.

"What the heck happened up there?" Ren demands. Luke takes off Jadeanu's gauntlet and shows Ren the acquired Blessing before giving the gauntlet back to its owner.

"We met the considered to be 'most beautiful god there is.'"

"He was truly interesting," Jadeanu says.

"Ren, before we start back on our journey, do you mind if we pray for a guided journey?"

"Pray? Well since we've gone on this journey, we've seen a lot in so little time and things always lead us back to the Heavens. So sure, there's no harm in praying," Ren responds. The three men sit on their knees and give a prayer to the graceful gods.

"Dear essential gods, I am grateful for the many blessings you have given to me," Jadeanu voices. "I humbly ask that we receive more guidance on our journey so that we may grow and traverse safely. Thank you for listening." After that, the boys all get up.

Chapter 9:

A King's Limit

"Well guys, just know that this prayer doesn't promise anything. All our wants will have to be pursued by ourselves," Jadeanu informs his crew. Everyone nods. "Now let's continue." They all keep moving forward for a while.

"Hey guys? You think that Mishu knows all of his former mercenaries are never coming back?" Jadeanu wonders. "He's probably just sitting there wondering when they'll report back to him."

"That's kind of cruel," Luke responds.

"Serves him right for trying to kill us," Ren says.

"I was referring to our loss of Blast. To think you'd bring his death up as a joke about Mishu."

"Well it's alright. It was just a thought," Jadeanu admits. "As long as we no longer have to deal with him anymore, we should all be fine."

"Well we're all out here in Nevada. He's still in Texas. I doubt that he would have, let alone could have followed us," Ren remarks.

"Well we've got worse things to worry about now," Jadeanu says.

They all approach the end of the trail and beyond it sits a road that has an intersection leading to a towering, large double-door stone gate ahead before continuing around west and east. The gate shields a place guarded by an enormous thick brown stone wall spanning as long as the eye can see. The gate is guarded by two men in armor with glowing red eyes.

"You think we might need to fight them?" Luke asks, concerned.

"I hope not. They look kinda creepy with that armor," Jadeanu replies. "The wall seems pretty big. I don't think we can just walk around. It's better to cut straight through the place." Jadeanu walks up to the guards.

"Hello, um, we just need to pass through here if that's okay."

"The way around is unnecessarily lengthy," one of the guards says. "You may pass; however, we must warn you about this place."

"This is the great city of Elko. Ruled by King Elcero. Once you enter this place, make it known that you all are just refugees," the other guard says.

"Citizens of this place are not allowed to leave. This gate is only to let people in, never to let people out. The only other exit is known by the king himself."

"King Elcero won't let anyone out of it or even know where it is unless you are a refugee. You have to ask the king if you want to pass through. I wouldn't recommend you go around. As I said, it's unnecessarily long and dangerous. Do you still wish to pass?"

"Yeah," Jadeanu answers.

The guards then open the thick gates with their seemingly colossal strength, allowing for passage.

"But may I ask why can't anyone leave here?" Jadeanu asks.

"Nobody knows the answer to that. You have to ask the king

yourself. Do be aware that his strength is like no other. No one even denies his rule out of fear and out of respect. Good luck in there," one of the guards answers.

"Thank you," Jadeanu says as he leads everyone inside through the big gates.

Inside, there is a large, beautiful city full of attractions and huge well-constructed buildings flanting the architectural genius put to use here.

"Whoa, what is this place? It's...beautiful," Jadeanu says, mesmerized.

"It's so peaceful and put together, unlike most places we've been so far," Luke acknowledges.

"If it's like this all around, why would anyone want to leave?" Ren asks. "That's what I'm worried about," Jadeanu says, concerned.

They all walk forward and look around at the peace of the hopeful city. There are children, women and families playing catch, tag, and just indulging in everyday activities. It's as if the Death Spiral never occurred here. Or rather it's as if people have just accepted it as part of life. After all, some people still had strangely colored eyes. They undoubtedly had powers.

"It really makes you want to stay here doesn't it?" Luke says.

"Sure do, but Seinaru and Kinra didn't die for us to stay here," Jadeanu retorts.

"Right. Our mission is to find the king and get past this place," Ren says. "Let's ask around."

Ren leads everyone to a pretty and young woman.

"Hello young lady. Surely you are a noble, perhaps a queen. You must know where the king is, do you not?"

She looks at Ren confused and responds, "No, I am not a noble."

"Well I couldn't tell, because your beauty is truly royal," Ren flatters her. She laughs a bit and smiles. She has an adorable gap in her front teeth and sports a slight Mexican accent. She is clearly Hispanic.

"Thank you, but I have a husband." She then flashes her ring. "And the king lives in a huge castle far up ahead. You can't miss it."

"Thank you young lady."

Ren walks away with a smile on his face.

"Whoa there Ren, what was all that about?" Jadeanu teases him.

"Well I just thought it would be nice to find someone to love like Nature said. I've still got a life to live you know? Despite my issues with my old girlfriend," Ren responds.

"I don't blame you. Keep at it. You'll find someone who actually deserves you eventually."

"Hey guys, it's getting late. You wanna find a place to rest? We can find the king tomorrow," Luke suggests. "Yeah sure, there's got to be an inn around here somewhere," Jadeanu agrees.

"But do we have enough money to spend the night is the real question," Ren says.

"Maybe we won't need to," Jadeanu says. "Most places don't really need money anymore. But then again, this place seems pretty normal. I guess we'll just have to find out."

Jadeanu and company walk through the place on the sidewalk so as not to be hit by any moving cars still operating in the area. Most of the people here seem to have working cars. The boys walk through the brightly lit-up city hoping to find a place to stay.

"Hey guys. I don't mean to be that guy, but we haven't eaten in a while. Can we get a bite to eat?" Ren asks. "Well if you go to sleep, you wouldn't be hungry anymore would you?" says Jadeanu.

"Yeah but–"

"I'm just joking. Let's get some food. I miss having a good fast-food meal."

Jadeanu walks through the door of the first restaurant he sees. There is a small line leading up to the ordering counter. They wait through it and approach the cashier. "How may I help you?" he asks.

"Hey, I just saw the last guy give you cash. You still take money here?" Jadeanu questions him.

"Oh, you three must be refugees. Yes, we only take cash here. Other places are chaotic and full of criminals who steal and such, but not here. We are organized."

"Well we don't have any money," Jadeanu says.

"I don't know what else to tell you," the cashier replies.

"Oh I'll take their tab," an older woman says from behind.

"You three can get whatever you want. I'll pay for it; you don't have to worry about it," she continues. "Why thank you ma'am," Jadeanu says, thanking her.

"It's nothing. We people have to stick together during these rough times."

After they all order their food, they eat and thank the lady again.

"Hey, by any chance, do you know where an inn is around here?" Ren asks.

"Yes, there is one close by. It is across the street, and you should see it on your left," she answers. "I appreciate your help," Ren expresses. They all leave the restaurant and follow the woman's instructions to the inn.

Once they enter, they see the innkeeper behind a desk.

"Aye, you three need a room?" he asks.

"Yeah," Jadeanu says.

The innkeeper grabs a key from behind his desk. "It's upstairs first door to your right."

He then gives the key to Jadeanu.

"We don't have to pay for this?" Jadeanu asks, confused.

"Nope. Everyone is welcome to sleep here if they need. Especially refugees."

"Well thank you," Jadeanu says in gratitude.

"Sleep well," the innkeeper says as the boys go to their room.

"I really like this place. Everyone seems so kind," Ren says.

"Maybe. Or maybe something sinister is happening here," Jadeanu says. "After all, the king won't allow anyone to leave. Consider that."

"But you still can't deny the wholesome treatment," Luke adds. "Let's at least enjoy it for a moment."

They all enter their room and soon drift off to sleep.

Several hours pass and morning comes. Jadeanu and his two companions awake.

"You all slept well?" Jadeanu asks.

"Yep!" Luke answers.

"Like a baby," Ren responds. "It's been a while since I slept like that."

"Well we've got a mission to complete," Jadeanu tells them. "Aw come on. Do we have to start immediately?" Ren complains. "Of course we don't! Let's enjoy this place!"

Suddenly, a rumble fills the floor. "What the heck is that?! An earthquake?!" Ren exclaims. "Maybe it's an Ancient," Jadeanu hypothesizes. "Let's go check it out," Luke says.

Jadeanu puts his gauntlets on and grabs his sword. Luke brings the genie lamp. Ren fetches the room key. They all head downstairs. Ren immediately gives the room key back to the now-alarmed innkeeper.

"What is that noise?" Jadeanu asks.

"It's probably just another one of those giants," the innkeeper says calmly.

"It's close by but it shouldn't be a big deal."

"No big deal?" Jadeanu asks in disbelief. He then rushes outside, sword in hand. Luke and Ren follow behind. There is an Ancient about the size of the one Jadeanu and the others had once fought.

There is a woman with blue colored eyes firing an energy blast at the Ancient. A guy with red eyes comes forth and tells the woman to launch him. The woman stops blasting the Ancient and leg lifts the guy into the air, supporting him with a weak blast to boost him into the air.

"Are they...fighting the Ancient?" Jadeanu says with surprise.

"That's not important. Let's help them," Luke says rushing toward the scene.

"Now!" the red-eyed man yells. Another guy, who is close to the Ancient, then throws a sharp piece of the Ancient—he must have ripped off of it—toward the other guy. The guy in the air does a few hand motions and the sharp Ancient piece positions its sharp part on the Ancient's head. He must have telekinetic abilities like Mishu. He spins the sharp Ancient part with exceptional speed. The piece starts to drill through the Ancient's hard skin. The other guy climbs up to the Ancient's head, jumps up and smashes the piece deeper into its skull. He must have had super strength, beyond the casual strength gained from just having powers.

Soon the Ancient falls to the ground dead, before transforming into red particles and vanishing. The three who stopped its rampage then go home like nothing happened. "They actually...beat it?" Jadeanu asks, surprised and confused.

"I guess it really was no big deal."

"Hey look over there," Luke says. There is a small crowd looking at something. Luke, Jadeanu, and Ren all run over to the scene.

There's a man with a house on top of his legs, the rubble crushing them as he shrieks and moves frantically from pain. The Ancient must have knocked it down on him when he was trying to leave his house. The guy has red eyes signaling power.

"Hey. Someone get Edd! He's the one with the super strength," someone from the crowd says.

"Jadeanu, how are we going to help him-" Luke begins before he's interrupted by Jadeanu.

"Stand by," Jadeanu warns. "You two get ready to grab the body." Jadeanu then walks up to the house and firmly plants his feet on the ground. He puts a sword into the ground and strengthens his hands with red energy. He places his fingers under the roof of the collapsed house. He then lifts with all of his might. The house starts to rise up.

"What? Jadeanu's strong enough to lift a whole house?" Luke says in disbelief. "Well isn't that something."

Jadeanu's muscles bulge, and his body shakes vigorously from the strain. The house lifts up a little more. Shock and surprise can be heard from the people around. Jadeanu shouts a war cry as he completely lifts the house up to eye level. "G-go...Now!" he says, grunting from the pressure.

Ren quickly uses Jadeanu's shadow to snatch the man from under the house. Jadeanu then slowly eases the house down and lets go of it. Everyone around starts cheering and then they go home. Jadeanu pants as he looks at the guy he saved.

"Thanks stranger," the guy says. "I swear this is the last straw. I'm going up to that king and giving him a piece of my mind."

The guy gets up, then snarls and falls back down. "Sir your legs!" Luke worries. "Don't worry too much. My legs are heavily damaged, but they're not shattered. The added strength from having power saved them."

"Then I can heal them," Jadeanu informs him. "Really?"

Jadeanu nods and then points the now glowing Nature Blessing at the guy and his legs start to rejuvenate.

"What's your name?"

"Stellar Gilga."

Stellar is a rather fit white-skinned guy wearing a black long-sleeved shirt and tracksuit pants. He has black hair that extends down his neck, followed by a black bead necklace. He also has a very friendly-looking face.

"Well Stellar. We're going to see the king. Do you wish to travel with us?" Jadeanu asks.

"Sure. You guys seem cool."

Soon Stellar's legs completely heal and he's able to stand up on his own. "Hey thanks...um...what are your names?"

"I'm Jadeanu."

"Luke."

"Ren."

"Alright! Let's go to the king," Stellar says excitedly.

"Hey before we go, may I ask what your power is?" Jadeanu asks.

"Check it out." Stellar holds out his fist and out comes a red-light staff figure from the part of his hand where his thumb is.

"Whoa, that's pretty cool," Luke says. Jadeanu picks up his sword and gestures at Stellar's light sword saying, "May I?"

"Go ahead," Stellar says. Jadeanu swings his sword at Stellar's and they both collide with sparks.

"Oh that's so cool," Ren admits. "Makes me want to get a sword."

Ren then creates a thick shadow sword connected to his shadow with a dense and flexible string of black shady energy just for the heck of it. He soon lets it dissolve back into his shadow.

"Nice Stellar. We can use power like that," Jadeanu tells him.

"We should get going now," Luke urges them.

"Okay come on," Jadeanu takes the lead. They all walk for a while through the sidewalks of the city, then conversation springs up.

"So Stellar, what's your beef with the king?" Jadeanu wonders.

"I've never met him in real life, but his rule is obstructing," Stellar says.

"You must be refugees. So you must not know. He doesn't allow anyone to leave here no matter how bad things get. He'll let us all die before opening up that front gate. So I just kind of accepted it; and things weren't that bad, but stuff would happen. After all, I had a house on my legs from being forced to stay here. Those huge things pass through here often and there is a woman that attacks our city once every few days. She kills hundreds and we still have to stay here and take it. It's likely to keep us controlled. I want reform. We have to overthrow the destructive rule. His power is thought to be supreme but with all four of us, even great strength can be overcome. The problem is, if we go against the king, he is bound to have guards and supporters. That will be the problem."

"We'll just have to fight through them all," Jadeanu says. "If you want change, you'll have to fight for it. No matter how harsh the odds are."

"That's true."

Several minutes of walking pass and the king's palace is nowhere in sight.

"Hey guys, you know not everything here is all bad. We've got time right?" Stellar mentions.

"Yeah. What's up?" Jadeanu asks. "There are a couple of great places around here. It sucks that you can't travel by car and mine was destroyed along with my house, but we can still make things interesting if you're willing to walk. Come on!"

Stellar leads everyone into a building.

"What is this place?" Luke wonders.

"It's an old school. It was closed down for obvious reasons and of fear of the Death Disease spreading," Stellar explains. "It's open for anyone but hardly anyone comes in here. So I decided to make the place my own."

As Stellar says that, he switches the light on in a room, revealing a large gymnasium. There are a bunch of cut-up softballs on the ground as if someone had a grudge against them.

"I usually use this place as a training ground. In case I need to fight something or someone," Stellar admits.

"But there is another use for it. Anyone up for some dodgeball?"

"Bring it on! I'm gonna wipe the floor with you," Jadeanu boasts. Some time passes as the boys play competitive dodgeball, and then move on to basketball and then target practice through the attacking of soft balls that they throw at each other. They all eventually get exhausted and take a rest.

"It's good to have fun and exercise every now and then. Makes me feel young," Ren claims.

"You're only in your twenties dude," Jadeanu says. "I know, but all this work I used to do really gets to my body."

"Got that right. It is nice to feel like a free-spirited child again. A luxury many adults forget about thanks to all the responsibility we inherit. Many tend to think of that as maturity, but true maturity comes with an understanding of what's better for you. Being free to be loose is sometimes what an adult needs," Luke says.

"If you guys are done with this place there are a few others we can go check out," Stellar proposes.

"Sure, let's check them out," Jadeanu agrees. Stellar leads everyone out of the school and into another yet not abandoned building. Yet Luke is filled with so much adrenaline that he leaves the school empty-handed, though he hadn't entered that way. The building they enter is a place of entertainment. There is bowling, laser tag, and arcade games, all for free.

The four men spend a lot of time there doing all they can to have some innocent fun in this tragic world they now live in. Then Stellar takes them all out for food. Ren even hits on another woman. He fails miserably, which is hilarious for everyone but him.

Later in the afternoon, they all leave for the adventure once again.

"So Stellar. You planning on staying here in Elko after we're done meeting the king?" Jadeanu asks.

"Maybe," Stellar answers. "The place isn't bad, but I just want to be able to leave when conditions become unlivable you know? Now why are you guys looking for the king?"

"We just want to pass through here."

"That was a mistake. You would have been better off going around."

"Do things really get that bad here?" Jadeanu asks.

"My house fell on my legs today."

"Fair point," they all say.

Silence fills the air as the group walks for a while in the sunlit city. "Hey there's the castle!" Luke points out.

In front of them in the distance, stands a vast giant castle. The building is absolutely luxurious with gold and purple designs scattered beautifully throughout the grey stone walls. Definitely a place fit for a king.

"You can't deny, no matter how corrupt the king may be, he's got good taste," Ren admits.

"We're not far now. You guys ready to fight?" Jadeanu asks. Everyone nods.

Soon they all approach the castle. There are two guards with red eyes watching the entry gate. They both are holding spears and wearing armor like the ones the guys saw guarding the entrance to the city.

"This place is off-limits to civilians unless you have a reservation for an audience with the king," one of the guards says.

"I have permission to meet the king," Jadeanu claims. The guard approaches him. "I'll need to see proof." "I have your proof right HERE!" Jadeanu then punches the guard in the face with red energy on his fist, then he readies his sword.

The guard slams into a wall on the side of the castle. He then spits out blood and stands back up.

"So it's going to be like that huh?" The guard smiles and his spear starts glowing red. He then swings his lance forward, and a red crescent of energy goes forth. Jadeanu dodges and rushes forward. The other guard calmly pushes a button on the castle and brings his lance forward. His spear glows red and fires pellets of energy out of it like a gun. The energy travels toward Luke and Stellar. Luke makes a small shield around himself to block, and Stellar cuts through some of the energy pellets with his light swords. Luke's shield cracks a little as he is pushed back.

Jadeanu swings his sword at his guard. The guard blocks it with his spear. Jadeanu withdraws his blade and attacks again, expecting a different result. The guard blocks him again.

"You're a rather strong one," the guard says. The guard then knees Jadeanu in the stomach and punches him in the face. Jadeanu goes flying back, landing on one knee. The guard then swings a crescent of energy at him. Jadeanu throws his energy-filled hands up which blocks the attack, but it sends him backward with its force.

Meanwhile, the other guard continues shooting energy at Stellar and Luke. Ren guards Luke with a massive shield out of Luke's own shadow. He adds a shield around Stellar as well. After soaking up the attacks, Ren moves Stellar's shadow shield into a crescent which moves toward the guard and then forms into a huge projectile that hits the guard then slams him down. Stellar closes in.

The guard charges up his spear and fires a thick laser at him. Stellar puts his light swords together and blocks the laser, then he slips one of the laser blades into the guard's shoulder. He then positions the other for the guard's face and pushes it down aggressively. A black box appears in front of the guard's face and blocks the laser saber. Ren closes behind Stellar and grabs his wrist. "We don't kill people. That's not our thing," Ren informs him as he dismembers the shadow box. The guard is petrified and unable to wield his spear due to his shoulder wound.

"Look at him. He's not a threat. No need to kill him." "Fine," Stellar agrees.

Jadeanu and his guard are now going toe-to-toe, sword against spear. Luke comes in and shoots the guard with a blast. The attack hits the guard away, yet he stays standing. Luke and Jadeanu stand side-by-side. Jadeanu swings his sword, and the guard blocks it with his spear. Luke deploys a shield and throws it at the guard's legs, thus tripping him. Jadeanu catches his fall with an uppercut to the face. Luke hits the guard with an energy propulsion to the stomach and Jadeanu moves to the side and punches the guard straight in the cheek. His red energy emits a shockwave that sends the guard hard into the castle wall. The guard falls down unconscious.

"You know Luke, I could have handled him myself," Jadeanu complains.

"I'm sure you could have. But we're not here for your pride. We're here to see the king without unnecessary injury," Luke retorts.

"You're right about that," Jadeanu then opens the castle gate and leads everyone inside. Inside there is an alarm going off and an abundance of people waiting for the four intruders.

"Oh crap! So that's what that button the guard pressed did," Luke realizes.

"You guys ready for this?" Jadeanu asks. Luke creates a shield for all three of his allies and one for himself. He then forms a giant one above all of their heads.

"So exactly how many shields can you make at a time?" Jadeanu wonders.

"It seems to be only five which is definitely an improvement considering I used to be able to only do one," Luke answers as he somersault kicks the overhead shield into a small crowd.

Ren concentrates and lifts his hands up. Luke, Jadeanu, and Stellar's shadows rise up and form another version of the person respectively. Each shadow mirage grabs the shield of their person and protects their caster. Ren forms the same thick blade he had made once before and prepares to fight.

"Holy crap Ren! When were you able to do all this?" Luke questions.

"That's not important," Ren replies. Stellar streams two more light swords out of the bottoms of his fists, thus making a dual saber on both of his hands. They all commence the fighting.

Luke throws his shield around and shoots blasts and gas energy balls. Jadeanu swings his sword around, slicing enemies but not killing them. He hits those he can with his free fist. Stellar swings around his light blades also injuring people but not killing any. When overwhelmed, he sucks his light blades into his hands and the pinky side of his fists ignites with masses of red flame, balanced and contained. Stellar would either attack with the flame blades or aim them at someone and extend the fires toward them in an explosive burst. Ren attacks with his blade, changing and reforming it as needed. He also ensures that the shadow mirages of his allies attack the enemies and defend their respective human counterparts.

Soon enough, all the enemies are lying on the ground in defeat. Ren returns each shadow mirage back to the ground as just shadows once again. Luke vanquishes all of his shields. Jadeanu grabs the nearest guy and asks, "Where is the king?"

"All the way up those stairs behind us and just straight from there," the guy says. Jadeanu leads everyone up some large circular flight of stairs while the alarm still rings.

Once they all reach the top floor, they move forward, and a few more guards show up to stop them. Jadeanu and company prepare to fight.

"Everyone please halt!" an unfamiliar voice calls out. The guards immediately relax and take several steps back. The alarm suddenly stops.

At the end of the room stands a tall man with purple royal robes on. He has black straight hair down past his shoulders and he has two long braids stemming from the sides of his hair down the front of his shoulders. His eyes glow light blue with a hint of silver within them.

Truly an enchanting sight to see. He has two guards next to him; one on each side of his shoulders.

"You all are no stronger than the guards on the lower levels. Sending more of you would just cause more unnecessary injury. They're after me. You all stand down," the man says.

He is undoubtedly King Elcero. All the other guards stand down with their backs to the wall revealing a clear path to Elcero.

'His eyes are blue? That would mean his powers came from a noble person,' Jadeanu thinks. *'I always expected him to be some kind of tyrant, but he seems to be rather decent so far.'*

"What do you see, Lord Elcero?" one of his personal bodyguards asks.

"Two fifty and two sixty percents. How interesting. No wonder they were able to take out the lower-level guards," King Elcero responds.

"That's all? I believe we may be able to take them out, but I respect your will Lord Elcero," the other guard claims.

"It is true that you two are my only sixty percents. Strong guards are hard to come by. But I'm afraid I cannot sit idly by and let you fight my battle," King Elcero states.

"For your information, when we say percent, we are referring to your combat strength," the other guard tells Jadeanu and crew. "Everyone has two power identifiers. One indicator is to show how well one is versed with their spirit and therefore, power. The other, which is the one I speak of, is to verify one's combative abilities. We rank people's strengths by comparison to our king. In respective values, Lord Elcero has identified a collective distance between the power of people. Each graphed in contrast to him. For he's the only human to receive a ranking of one hundred percent. All others are at a relative distance from it. He is the peak of what is thought to be humanly possible. And when we say percent, we don't mean that is the strength comparison. It's more of a number ranking out of 10.

Our king is the only 10 out of 10. Us two personal guards are 6 out of 10. These number jumps are drastic. It is rare to see someone above a six because of that. But anyway, just because one is 50% and the king is 100% doesn't mean the 50 is only half the king's strength. The number process is a bit difficult to measure, but I would say that the difference in power would be 33% of one who is one number or 10% from another. So, 50% will be half the strength of one who is 80%. Meaning the 50 could never win on his own because he'll only be half the other's strength. The king is the only one who can feel and calculate these numbers though."

"It is interesting how you four are made of two sixties and two fifties. That's rather strong in comparison to many others. I'm impressed," King Elcero says.

"What is it that brings you all here?"

"We want to dethrone you! Your oppressive rule of forcing people to stay here against their will must come to an end!" Jadeanu yells.

"That's not at all why we came up here," Ren exclaims. "Hehe. Fine then," the king responds. "If you wish to enforce your will, come. I suggest you all attack me together."

Jadeanu rushes first, sword in hand. Elcero motions at the ground, and a thick sword forms from the earth, and flies into his hand. He and Jadeanu clash swords.

'*What!? My blade should be able to cut straight through that stone. It must be his energy that's holding it together,*' Jadeanu wonders. Elcero and Jadeanu's swords fight intensely without faltering. Elcero ends up with the tip of his sword close to Jadeanu's handle, then he knocks the weapon clean out of his hand.

"Good, I prefer you unscathed," Jadeanu claims, adding energy to both of his gauntlets.

Elcero drops his blade and wraps the earth around his hands like gauntlets. Then both earth gauntlets ignite on fire. Elcero and

Jadeanu throw punches, dodge and block whenever they can. Jadeanu takes the energy from one of his arms to one of his legs and he tries to kick the king. Elcero evades the kick, then adds fire to one of his legs and kicks Jadeanu in the face. He then closes in with an uppercut to Jadeanu's chin, thus knocking him far back.

Stellar comes in next with three light swords on each fist. One protruding from the thumb opening of the fist, another from the pinky side and the last from the knuckles of the fist.

"So you're coming at me one at a time to start off. Fine by me," Elcero says as he mimics the look with stone rods coming from each identical section of his fists. He lights each rod with fire. He and Stellar go at it perfectly, with precision and swiftness. Elcero pierces through Stellar's ribs and throws him afar.

Luke shoots two gas balls at Elcero, who responds with fireballs of his own. His fireballs cancel out Luke's, then he fires one more. Luke deploys a shield to block it and he fires a blast back at Elcero. Elcero crafts a shield of the earth to avoid the attack. Luke closes in with a bubble on his fist, riding a shield to throw at the king. Elcero crushes Luke's shield by dropping his own on it. Then he dodges a punch from Luke, and surrounds his own fist with a bubble using a concentration of the air around, and he hits Luke away.

Ren is the last one left, and he comes in with his shadow sword. The moment he comes close to Elcero, he creates another human-sized mirage of Elcero with a sword out of the king's shadow. Both Ren and the shadow attack. Elcero stomps the ground, which lifts a rock sculpture of a person with a sword. His sculpture combats Ren's shadow puppet. When the shadow changes, so does the rock image to combat the shadow. The shadow Elcero swings its blade at Elcero, and the rock sculpture blocks with a sword of its own. The shadow forms a scythe and attacks, and the rock sculpture forms a scythe immediately and blocks.

Elcero forms his rock sword again and defends against Ren's big blade. Ren tightens his shadow to his feet and does a backflip, extending the shadow energy toward Elcero's chin. Elcero dodges the attack and tightens earth onto his foot and does a backflip. His foot crashes into Ren's chin, launching him into the air. As Elcero lands, he extends a pillar of rock into Ren's stomach, hitting him away.

"Augh, did we just get beat by a mimicry of our own attacks?" Jadeanu questions.

"You see? My power is much too great for you all," King Elcero claims. "Even restricting my ability to fit your own, I still rise above. Now I will show you a glimpse of my true power." Elcero then holds out his hands and a huge gust of wind pushes against Jadeanu and his allies.

"This again? First Javean, now you?" Jadeanu complains. "But at least Javean's had breaks in it."

Elcero takes a deep breath and pulses his hands which makes a stronger wind current come forth. Ren, Stellar and Luke are pushed back to the entrance wall. Jadeanu goes back a few feet but puts his sword into the ground to stop himself. He pushes strongly against the wind and takes one step forward.

One of the guards comes and whispers into the king's ear, "He took a step forward. Do you think he could ever become-"

"No. He is much too weak for that," the king answers. "He may not seem like it but he's one of the weakest of his whole team. He is still rather strong; he must have grown much on his journey here. But he'll never grow to what she was on his own. I reckon his resolve comes from an outside force. Undoubtedly those glowing things on his gauntlet."

King Elcero tenses his muscles, and a stronger gust of wind goes forward and immediately sends Jadeanu and his sword back to the entrance wall. The king stops his wind. "Do any of you know why it is I do not want to kill you?" There is a pause, and no one says anything.

"It is because I understand your resolve. The reason I do not allow anyone to leave my city is because when you value something, you won't dare just let anyone take it away. You see, if there is a rich man with many homes and a poor man with a single home, when the wrecking ball comes to destroy their home, the rich man wouldn't care as much, but the poor man must fight the odds even 'till death. When one has little to lose and can escape tragedy, things will lose value. But when you can't run from the problem, you'll give everything to protect what you have because you'll appreciate what you have much more. I don't let anyone leave Elko because if you could, this wonderful city would be no more. All the hard work to make this place would be undone. And people would have learned nothing but comfort and laziness. But being forced to stay here, the people will naturally protect their land and take care of one another."

'So that means these people choose to be good people on their own?' Jadeanu thinks. *'Wow. Our journey must have been that rough. To be suspicious of genuinely good people. It is good to see wholesome people again. Thank you Elcero. You're not such a bad guy after all.'*

"I admit that I'm a bit stubborn, but I want to see people being responsible for the things they care about," Elcero says. "I don't want my people to run from their problems; I want them to fight, just like you all. You didn't like my rule, so you've come directly to the source to settle your problems. That is accountability that I can admire." "Thank you King Elcero," Jadeanu says in appreciation. "I apologize for the trouble."

"It's nothing."

Immediately after those words escape the king's lips, a loud alarm suddenly sounds.

"What is that?" Jadeanu asks.

"It's the city alarm. Something big is happening outside," Elcero answers as he bends a piece of the roof downward, revealing the dusky sky.

"Come," he commands as he lifts himself through the hole in the roof with the air around him. Luke takes Stellar up there with his gaseous energy propellant. Ren lifts himself with his shadow, and Jadeanu super jumps up there.

Now with everyone on the roof, Elcero replenishes the roof with the missing piece. They all gaze upon the beautiful city to see what's wrong. In the distance, near the now-destroyed entrance gate, there is an enormous Ancient waddling toward the castle destroying everything in sight. Many buildings turned to rubble and many people running for their lives hoping to not be crushed. The king takes a deep breath and then cuffs his hand over his mouth. He then says the words, "Everyone evacuate closer to the castle at once."

He uses his wind manipulation abilities to spread the message to everyone in the city by resonating his sound waves with the wind current. The Ancient is so big that it is able to completely crush homes by simply stepping on them. The Ancient has two stubby legs and a large fish-like body. It has an enormous face with a huge trunk above its wide mouth full of sharp teeth. It also has two colossal fins on its side, and it has a long wild tail attached to its back.

"That's the biggest one I've ever seen. And it smashed through the front gate. I hope the guards made it out," Elcero expresses.

"Everyone, combine your attacks!" he yells at what seems like no one. But then the guards and citizens that have gathered toward the front of the King's Castle all start attacking. They mix their energies and throw all they have at the Ancient. Their attacks slow its progress forward.

"Looks like he brought company. Those of you who can throw projectiles, I recommend you throw them," Elcero suggests after seeing a few more much smaller Ancients also progressing forward. Luke begins throwing his energy balls and beams at the big Ancient while some of the townsfolk attack the other Ancients. "We're really gonna fight that thing?!" Jadeanu questions.

"It's our best course of action," Elcero answers.

"Even an evacuation wouldn't work. People won't be willing to move past that thing to the entry gate and my other exit won't be able to get everyone through. Now I could pull down the surrounding wall and let everyone go, but our city will be destroyed, many will die, and the survivors will harbor hatred. Plus, it will be exhausting for my body. I likely won't be able to move much, and I would probably die in the process. And this great beautiful city will fall. I cannot allow that. The least we can do is try to kill this thing!"

Elcero takes a stance. "Now you'll get to witness the full power of the king."

King Elcero prepares to attack, and a white aura surrounds his body.

'That power. If I had felt that before, I never would have thought we could actually win against him,' Jadeanu thinks.

'He's definitely stronger than anyone we've faced so far. A perfect 10 out of 10 huh? I have no doubt that he's the strongest human.'

"What are your names by the way?" the king asks.

"I'm Jadeanu."

"I'm Jadeanu's older brother, Luke."

"Ren."

"And I'm Stellar."

"I am King Elcero. I'm sure you know who I am, but we have never formally met. I thank you all for coming up here to help me. And it is rude of me to ask this, but I desire your assistance if you will."

"Sure! I don't want to see this great place get destroyed," Jadeanu agrees.

Elcero tosses up five boulders from the ground and throws fire on each of the rocks, thus lighting them on fire. He tightens the fire around the rocks and then throws a strong wind on them, launching them with extreme speed and strength like cannon balls. The fire boulders hit the Ancient on the face causing evident damage.

"The thing's skin is-" Jadeanu starts.

"Really tough. I know," Elcero interrupts.

"Everyone in the city knows that. The bigger the monster is, the tougher its skin. There's no way we can pierce through that. I'm trying to do impact damage to the thing and damage its internal organs."

"We can at least cut out its eyes right?"

"Absolutely not. That will only make it go insane and destroy everything even quicker."

Elcero lifts up a house-sized boulder from the ground and lights it with fire. He then makes several hand motions gathering up the air in concentration and sends the massive amount of air at the huge rock, thus propelling it with intense speed at the Ancient's face. The hit visibly hurts the gigantic Ancient and halts its path for a moment. The Ancient spreads its fins and wildly swings them in frustration. It destroys many establishments, knocks back all the rest of the smaller Ancients, then continues forward.

'He's actually hurting it,' Jadeanu analyzes. *'I hit a much smaller one with all my might and it didn't do as much damage as this. This guy is truly amazing.'*

"There's got to be something we can do," Stellar says.

"I'm afraid not," Elcero responds. "But if you get any ideas on how to kill this thing, I'll hear them out."

The king then bends two separate vast ponds on opposite sides of the Ancient. He compacts as much water as he can from them both and slams them into the Ancient's sides. The attacks almost rock the beast over then flood the area knocking around the surrounding Ancients. Luckily all the pedestrians either would have already gotten away from the area or have already died, only for their bodies to be swept up by the current.

"Hey maybe we can drown the thing," Jadeanu brainstorms.

"We've tried. These things don't need to breathe oxygen," Elcero says. "I'm not sure how that's possible nor what they even are. Good thought though."

Elcero uppercuts the Ancient's underbelly with several pillars of rock, then creates a powerful force of fire and blasts the beast through the extension of the blaze with a mass concentration of air.

One of Elcero's personal guards jumps up onto the roof of the castle and calls, "Lord Elcero!"

"Have all the remaining citizens moved near my castle?" Elcero demands.

"Yes sire."

"Good then. I can finally release it," Elcero closes his eyes, and his white aura increases in concentration around him.

"What's going on with him?" Jadeanu asks. "Remember when I told you, he was one hundred percent, the peak of human strength?" the guard starts then the king finishes, "I have also found a strength that transcends that. Strength beyond the classification of human."

Elcero then opens his eyes and there are no pupils. Only pure bright white sockets. Elcero clenches both of his hands forward and flicks both wrists. Two distant buildings tumble and fall on top of the Ancient, thus harming it and slowing it down. Elcero bends his knees and pushes against the air as if lifting an imaginary heavy object. In the distance, a huge skyscraper is lifted and slams into the Ancient with crazy speed.

Elcero lifts up all the water in the Ancient's area into a huge tsunami and clashes it onto the Ancient's body. The Ancient still perseveres forward with the intent of destroying everything. But now even the king's mound of destruction can compete with the Ancient's. Yet the king mostly destroys what the Ancient has already.

'Wow. To think that the king is able to command and destroy his entire city without too much effort,' Jadeanu ponders.

'I could only barely lift a building.'

The king sends a strong wind to slow the Ancient's progress even more. Then he circles the wind into a large tornado that in turn, sucks up the nearby water and doubles in size.

Elcero conjures up a massive fire and wraps it around the twister but not touching the water. He also sends several large boulders to orbit the massive elemental tornado. He then pushes it toward the Ancient with exuberant speed and power. The tornado smashes into the Ancient's face and continues through its body.

The attack does the most damage to the Ancient, but it still isn't enough. Elcero sends the tornado into the Ancient again and again, yet it still doesn't do any fatal damage to it; only bruising and burning its resilient skin. He dispels the tornado, then lifts up two giant boulders from the ground and rapidly breaks off pieces of them and launches them like bullets, shredding down the remaining Ancients and further harming the big one.

Then soon, Elcero falls to his knees, and his eyes return back to light blue. He starts panting out of exhaustion. "We need something all-powerful to take that thing down," Elcero comments. "All-powerful?" Jadeanu wonders. His face then lightens up with hope.

"Luke, do you have the genie lamp?" Luke's face fills with fear. "I think I left it at that abandoned school." "What!?" "Don't worry, I bubbled it." "So? I'm pretty sure that thing can break through your little shield pretty easily."

"No, it hasn't made it to the school yet. And what I mean is I can telekinetically bring it back to me. I noticed when we were fighting the guards of the king's castle that I could always summon my shields back to me. I'm hoping I can do the same with my bubbles even while they're guarding something," Luke explains. "Good then. Give it a try."

Luke concentrates and holds out his hand and soon, a genie lamp trapped in a blue barrier flies to Luke's hand but stops right before touching it. He grabs the bubble and then pops it.

"Now why do you want it?"

"Here, I want to see something," Jadeanu responds, gesturing for Luke to hand him the lamp. Luke gives it to him. He holds the lamp with both hands. "Okay, now a spirit connects to another," Jadeanu tells himself. Jadeanu closes his eyes and concentrates. Then he starts to hum ever so gently. The Universe Blessing starts to glow. "His will for power is the same as mine yet altered by reason." Jadeanu opens his eyes.

"We can beat that thing." "How?" Elcero concerns. "Inside this lamp, there is a warlock ready to transform into a powerful genie. He'll be big enough to fight this thing once his transformation is complete," Jadeanu explains. "You've had access to that thing the whole time?" Elcero questions. "You see, we have a friend who's also trapped in there," Luke adds. "And Jinzen isn't exactly a good guy." "If that monster attacks Jinzen, they'll fight. And Jinzen will likely be able to beat that thing. If not, he'll at least damage the thing enough to where it won't be much of a threat. It's already hurt so it's our best bet. We ought to give it a try," Jadeanu assures.

"And if Jinzen wins?"

"If he remembers us, we can possibly lead him away. And if not, Jinzen will still be a human right? My blade should be able to cut right through him," Jadeanu says.

"Whatever's in that lamp has a lot of power. It may just be able to save the city," Elcero mentions.

"But Stougma and all the others inside will die," Luke worries. "Yet everyone in this city will live," Jadeanu states.

"I don't want to seem like a jerk but everyone in this lamp has fought Jinzen and failed. They're already pretty much dead. But the people in this city still have a fighting chance. Look at all these people. Look at them!" The guys all take a look at the thousands of people gathered up, trying desperately to stop the Ancient with their powers. And the ones that can't attack are protecting and shielding their loved ones. Their crying kids, their elderly relatives, and their significant others. All gathered together with a contagious fear of certain death marching their way. "If Stougma knew that his sacrifice would save all of these people, well I've never really known him much, but I think he would approve."

Jadeanu suddenly feels a chill down his spine. "I...I just felt something nostalgic." The Universe Blessing glows for a second then returns to normal. "It felt like Stougma's energy. Like a positive vibe from him. Like he's speaking to me telling me it's okay."

"Then you have no reason not to free Jinzen," Ren says. "He's guiding us and has been here all along. Thank you Stougma. I'll ensure never to forget you," Jadeanu says.

Jadeanu grabs the top of the lamp and lifts it up. A yellow energy swirls from the top of the open lamp. Jadeanu throws the lamp as far as he can toward the Ancient. The energy then projects an image. A reanimation of Stougma turning into a ball of flesh. "What in the..." Elcero starts. "Those are the people trapped in the lamp," Luke establishes. "Let's just watch."

The image above the lamp, now laying on the dirty road, shifts to a man being transformed into a bunch of pieces of paper and then folds into another colored orb. Another guy was burned to ash and then blown away and reassembled as a colored orb. A group of three were diced into pieces and combined back together as three individual colored orbs. Then the last and probably most disturbing. The last guy was manipulated like a puppet and stabbed himself multiple times. After all the images, the energy turns orange and grows to a massive size.

A detailed picture of the woman Jinzen was once acquainted with named April flashes the scene. Jadeanu looks at it sympathetically. All of the colored orbs unlock themselves from the lamp and orbit the energy. They then separate into energy auras and combine into the current of power, creating a beautiful rainbow colored swirl of pure energy. The energy then forms a giant man, taller than the Ancient but not as wide. The lamp under Genie Jinzen explodes, revealing his lack of legs. Just a torso with fire beneath his waist.

Jinzen is shirtless but not at all how one would think an old man would be built. He actually looks young. His face resembles how he must have looked in his late twenties. He has a black mustache and beard, as well as long black hair. He also has a full six-pack, and his body is covered in a yellow-orange aura. His eyes still glow with a sinister bright red.

"Bwahahahaha!" Jinzen laughs. "Power!"

The Ancient hits Jinzen on the side due to Jinzen being in its way. The weight of the swing knocks Jinzen to the side. He catches himself on top of someone's house. He rebalances and punches the Ancient in the face. "They're actually fighting," Elcero's bodyguard says in shock. "That genie," Elcero begins. "He's got to be at least double my strength. I never thought I'd see the day."

"Jinzen must have been a pretty handsome guy back in his day," Luke blurts out. Stellar looks at Luke in horror. "Uh, I'm saying that because he was all old when we first saw him," Luke explains. "It would seem like he hates something regarding his look," Jadeanu adds. Stellar, Ren and Luke gaze at Jadeanu in curiosity.

"I looked into the energy surrounding the lamp he was in. All I felt was constant blazing hatred. He has some kind of inner hate concerning that his decent looks weren't enough to save that woman whose face was shown to us all just moments ago. I believe she was the one he told us about back when we were at his house. He wasn't just telling us a random story about himself. Her death is likely what pushed him to be the monster he is. It must have driven him mad with rage that he can now express after all this time. It doesn't excuse his deeds though, but I think I can understand him"

Jinzen goes for another punch but the Ancient opens its wide mouth and bites Jinzen's arm who aggressively grunts from pain. The Ancient's mouth soon lights up and it releases its grip on his arm. Smoke streams from the Ancient's mouth. Jinzen pulls his arm out and shoots a stream of fire at the Ancient from the palm of his hand. The Ancient gets angry and spreads its fins then spins around a few times. The sharp tips of the Ancient's fins slice through Jinzen's abs. "So he can be cut," Jadeanu analyzes.

The Ancient then bashes Jinzen with its fin, nearly knocking him down. Jinzen grips the ground to catch himself. He lifts the earth from the ground and fills it with lava, then throws it at the Ancient. He connects a fierce left hook that knocks the Ancient down on its back. Jinzen lifts his hand up and a meteor forms in midair and crashes into the Ancient's face. Jinzen then keeps wailing on the Ancient before forming a flame sword and shoving it into the beast's throat. The Ancient now lies dead before turning into red particles and evaporating into the atmosphere.

Jinzen's long black hair swings back as he turns to the king's castle. He then starts moving toward it. "Crap! He's coming for us," Ren worries. Jinzen's left-hand fills with a fireball that he chunks straight toward the castle. Luke creates a huge barrier around the place. Elcero supports his shield with a rock wall and masses of air. The fireball gets through most of the defense but still doesn't make it all the way through. Jinzen sets the entire floor around him ablaze by blasting it and all the nearby houses with fire. The fire brushes ever closer to the living citizens of Elko.

Elcero gets angry and his eyes return white. "Wait, King Elcero!" Jadeanu calls. "Your body's exhausted. You won't last!"

"And!? What good is a king that can't protect his own people!? Even if that means death! It'll be worth it if I can just damage him a little. So that my people will be inspired to finish the rest if I can't!" Elcero uses the wind around him to accelerate his movement to an exceptional speed as he runs and jumps off of his castle roof, using the wind to make his body fly. He speeds himself toward Jinzen, preparing a halfhearted strike due to exhaustion. Jinzen swats him like a fly, and Elcero crashes against a building and falls unconscious.

"Did he just one-shot the king?" Jadeanu asks, fear now present in his heart. Ren puts his hand on Jadeanu's shoulder and says, "Welp, you're our only chance of beating him."

"Hey Ren, didn't you say you wanted to use a cool sword? Well now's a good time," Jadeanu jokes. "No, you've got it. If you fail, everyone here will only die." Jadeanu's body now shakes, knowing that he is the only one who stands in the way of Jinzen's destruction. He takes several deep breaths and then jumps off of the castle roof, sword in hand.

As he bravely approaches the towering genie, suddenly Jinzen is hit with something powerful enough to knock him down on his back. Three white-winged beings show up on the battlefield. They are angels.

"Zeus, you get the citizens out of here. Azrael, you hold him off," the leader orders.

"Yes Metatron!" the other angels accept the orders. Jinzen stands back up only to be electrified by the angel known as Zeus before the angel goes to organize the crowds of civilians. The angel known as Azrael grips the sword on his hilt and draws it. He goes forth and cuts

Jinzen's arm clean off before diving down and punching the ground. Once his fist touches the ground, four giant sharp bones in the shape of tusks explode from the ground and stab Jinzen.

The leading angel who has pale skin, sparkly silver eyes, black hair that extends past neck length and a strange black cube-looking necklace, known as Metatron, turns to Jadeanu and says, "Jadeanu Stroyem. Thank you, all of you for holding these monsters off for so long until we got here."

Fireballs suddenly come toward Metatron while he's speaking. He doesn't even turn to them. He simply throws his backhand toward his side where the fireballs are approaching. Once the fireballs reach his vicinity, an electric field appears and destroys the fireballs on impact. Metatron counters by waving his hand, and long sharp icicles form and jet into Jinzen's body.

"We were a little late. We had other Ancients to deal with. But the universe called for me to protect you. And now your work is done. We will handle the genie now. You need not worry about it anymore."

Jadeanu notices that Azrael and Zeus have their swords with them, but Metatron does not. The thought that he must be **some** angel to fight without a weapon, crosses Jadeanu's mind.

Azrael forms a giant skeleton man with a sword made of bone to attack Jinzen on near-even terms as Zeus leads the people through the rubble to the front entrance of the city.

"I want you to leave," Metatron commands as he forms a strange carpet out of what seems like nothing. "Gather your group on that carpet and bring the king as well. You all need to escape this place. Once everyone is on, just yell the word 'go', and it'll take off. Now please evacuate."

Jadeanu runs to the front of the castle and yells for his group members to get on the magic carpet. They all follow his direction. Jadeanu then runs to King Elcero's unconscious body and lifts him up, then brings him to the carpet. Once he gets on, he screams, "Go!" The magic carpet immediately moves. Jadeanu and the others watch the scene from the comfort of the moving carpet. "April, I wanted the power you had. The bravery to take on the world," Jinzen claims as his mind flashes memories of his old friend. Metatron throws two personal fireballs at Jinzen to get his attention, then he forms a huge saber and lunges it through Jinzen's brain. "I just wanted to be like you," Jinzen speaks his last words before tears fall from his eyes.

Lastly, Metatron waves his arm with force, and a huge gust of wind rips Jinzen's body to dust, scattering it in the wind.

"Wow! Those angels took Jinzen down in like three seconds," Luke claims in amazement. King Elcero soon wakes back up with a sudden motion as the boys ride through the city filling a calm wind on their skin.

"I lost. But what happened?" he asks.

"Some angels came and killed the genie and gave us a ride," Jadeanu explains.

"So my people are safe. Good." The carpet suddenly stops in front of a huge stone gate disguised as a piece of the wall around the city.

"It led us to a dead end?" Stellar wonders.

"No. It's my secret exit. Only I can open it," Elcero claims.

"I guess now is the time to say it," Jadeanu starts to confess. "We, except for Stellar, are refugees. We merely wanted to go through your city and keep going northeast. It wasn't originally our intention to overthrow you."

"So I see. Then you are where you need to be. Even without being native here, you saw a problem and you worked to solve it yourself. I commend you for that."

Everyone gets off the carpet and it vanishes. Elcero bends the stone gate open, revealing the real gate made of metal.

"So I guess this is where we depart," Jadeanu says. "I guess so," Elcero agrees.

"Unless you want to come with us."

"No thank you. I have duties to this city and its inhabitants. But besides that, Jadeanu, it must suck to have to carry around that big sword all the time."

"Yeah it does but it's alright."

"Here."

Elcero bends some stone onto Jadeanu's back and shapes it into a small U-shaped figure. The stone makes small piercings into Jadeanu's shirt and then folds in like a staple. "You can place your sword there now."

Jadeanu places his sword through the hole, and it holds up. "Thanks King."

"The gratitude is mine. I am truly grateful for your labors. You all may come back to my city anytime you wish."

"I may stop by one day. But Stellar, where are you going to go?"

"Hmm, that's a good question," Stellar admits. "You could come with us. We could really use your abilities," Jadeanu appeals.

"Maybe I could, and I don't have a place to stay now that my house was destroyed."

"You know my castle isn't just big for luxury and defense," Elcrero says. "Those loyal to me have a living space there if you're interested."

"Well then it's settled," Stellar concludes. "Sorry guys, but I like Elko. And I've caused the king a lot of trouble. Now that I see that he isn't such a bad guy, I can use my power to serve the king of my city. I'll be one of your-no I'll be your best guard, Lord Elcero. Thanks for showing me this path guys. You all seem cool, but I love Elko. I will protect my home."

"Well it's just the three of us again," Luke says.

"Hold it," King Elcero calls out to them. "You all will be going forward from here?"

"Yeah," Jadeanu answers. "Then I must warn you. Surely you've heard of a woman who attacks my city quite often, yes?"

Jadeanu nods. "She lives in a not-so-distant city in the direction you will be going. Controlling it from underground. Before my kingdom was what it is now, she broke into my castle with no struggle and confronted me directly. She wanted to fight me and so I obliged. I took her on the same way I did you, by using her own power against her. That was my first mistake. Even with my wind enhancing me, I couldn't keep up with her speed.

Her strength was formidable as well. I had to go all out on her. I even had to go into my unleashed state. In the end though, neither of us won the fight but I managed to push her back enough and we eventually called it a draw. At first when I fought her, I knew she was exceptionally strong, but she grew even stronger and stronger the more we fought. That's what terrified me.

After we were done, she told me to get stronger. She said she would too and then come back to defeat me. The problem is, I haven't gotten any stronger since then, so I fear her return. And now she attacks my city rapidly to remind me of those words. And I can't do anything about it. She's always gone before I can act. In fact, the only reason why people even know that she's here is because there's chaos and female laughter."

"Doesn't your wall keep her out?" Jadeanu asks.

"She can jump right over it," Elcero informs him. "Now I tell you all of this because she's dangerous. If you couldn't even scratch me, then you'll have no chance of beating her. You should avoid her at all costs. If you see her, you should avoid eye contact and definitely hold no hostility toward her.

But you know, her fighting capabilities aren't what shocked me the most. It was her beauty. She's remarkably beautiful. It's truly jaw-dropping. She is much too gorgeous to be going around fighting people like she does. I never thought I'd say this to another man, but you'd be lucky if you never get to see her beauty. If you do end up meeting her, you'll know it's her if she's probably the most attractive woman you've ever seen. I know how that sounds, but believe me, her presence is unique. You'll know it. Either that or you'll know if you see a woman with a demonic right arm and a golden necklace with a ring on it. Be careful."

"You like her don't you?" Jadeanu points out. "I say it's impossible not to," Elcero responds. "She's absolutely alluring and the only woman who can give me an equal fight. Appealing in every manner. Nearly fit to be my queen, but she's much too diabolical for that and therefore I cannot be with her. I have duties to my city, the very one she disrupts. She is no queen. If nothing else, remember this; a leader is born but a king is made, such as a parent to a real father. You need works to verify your title whatever it may be."

"So what's her name?" Jadeanu asks.

"She made sure to tell me after leaving my castle. She said her name is Ava."

"Thank you King Elcero. We must be going now." "Farewell then. I wish you good luck. Come Stellar, we have rebuilding to do."

Chapter 10:

The Eighth God

"Ravah no!" an angel with an orange aura says to another angel of whom is known as Ravah. The random angel is down to a kneel; he has been stalemated.

"What are you trying to become? Some kind of Messiah to them?" the angel asks. "You think you'll be able to do this with no consequence! You will fall!"

"Will I? Fate will occur as it does, and you are clearly in no place to oppose," Ravah claims while standing over the other angel. "What exactly is your aim here?" the other angel asks.

"I see no reason to tell you. Yet if it was one's desire to intrude on my ambition, sending you alone was a miscalculation." "If you are going to kill me, go on ahead. But know that punishment will catch up to you."

"I need not kill a lowly angel such as you. You are no threat."

Ravah looks elsewhere and begins walking away.

"And by the way, I aspire to leave punishment behind." Ravah then flies away from the defeated angel.

Meanwhile, Jadeanu, Luke, and Ren wave goodbye to Stellar, King Elcero, and the City of Elko before they walk through the exit of the city wall.

"I kind of feel bad for Elcero. He has to deal with so much for his city," Luke sympathizes.

"Yeah. I'm guessing that's part of why he has everyone cooped up in there. He doesn't want to lose the people he cares for," Jadeanu agrees. "He even has this route sealed off to protect people from that Ava chick."

"Speaking of her. What are we going to do about her?" Ren suggests. "What do you mean? We're staying away from her," Luke says. "It's the safest option."

"I agree with you Luke, but something just doesn't sit right with me," Jadeanu claims. "Sure, maybe staying away from her is the safest option, but she's a murderer. She kills dozens of innocent people every few days. You saw those wonderful people. And we'll pass by her city and not do anything about it? We serve the gods. The least we can do is take her down."

"I get that, but you heard the king. There's no way we can beat her. Maybe we're not fated to fight her."

"But we'll never know if we don't fight her. Well how about this, when we pass by her city, if we see her, we'll fight her. But if not, we may not be destined to combat her, and we'll leave it be."

"That'll work, but I still say we should leave her alone for the time being."

"Is that because you can't hit a girl?"

Ren starts to chuckle. "That's not the only reason...." Luke claims.

"Dude you can't hit a girl?" Ren questions. "I mean I get it, but surely you've got to be able to if necessary, right?"

"Don't let society stop you from duty," Jadeanu says. "I think I could hit a girl if she threatened you two's lives," Luke admits.

"You've got to be able to really hit her though," Jadeanu adds. "Some of these girls need it. They didn't get enough spankings as a teenager, and now they need a new form of discipline to protect them from themselves. Sometimes you just got to AAH! You know what I'm saying?"

"Okay, don't listen to your brother," Ren advises.

"Hey. I'm the only one of us who was married. Think about that."

The three dudes end up in an area with a few buildings and many trees and bushes. A guy is wandering along the path with red eyes. Jadeanu and the others just plan on passing by the guy, but the moment the guy sees them, he yells, "Eradicate!" An energy beam suddenly shoots from his eyes toward Jadeanu, who dodges just in time.

"What's wrong with him?" Ren asks. "Obliterate! Exterminate!" the guy says before letting out another laser beam. "He's possessed!" Jadeanu and Luke blurt out. Luke creates a shield to guard his two allies. The laser beam hits the shield but can't go through it.

"I forgot people could get possessed by their soul's will," Jadeanu confesses.

The guy adds more energy to his beam, and Luke's shield cracks a little.

"The objective is to just snap him out of it," Jadeanu says. "On it," Ren says. Ren uses the guy's shadow to trip him and then binds him to the floor using shadow-like ropes. The guy starts screaming and struggling severely while his heat vision continues into the air.

Luke vanquishes his shield, and they all cautiously gather around him. "Wow, I just realized how much this looks like a crime scene," Jadeanu says. The guy aims his gaze at Jadeanu, who uses his gauntlet to block. Jadeanu uses his other hand to punch the guy in the face hoping to snap him back to sanity. But instead, the guy is knocked unconscious.

"Oops. Well... let's just get out of here." They all quickly leave the scene. They all continue walking through the calm and quiet area, gazing at the appealing environment. The world is truly a wonderful place full of interesting things. They look at the night sky, the casual squirrels, and other animals finding rest. They watch the ants laboring for their queen and feel the gentle wind graze their bodies.

The walk is a short peaceful one, then suddenly Ren says, "Hey it's getting late. We should get some sleep."

"You're right. Maybe we should," Jadeanu agrees.

"And also, I'm pretty dirty. I'm pretty sure we all stink," Ren says.

"Oh yeah, right," Luke says. He pulls out one of Nature's water bubbles from his pocket. "I forgot I even had these." Jadeanu unsheathes his sword and slices the bubble.

Water comes out and cleans everyone and all their things. "Well we're all nice and clean. Let's prepare to get back dirty when we lay on the ground," Jadeanu reveals.

"I guess we didn't really consider that," Luke admits. "But we'll be fine if we stay on the grass. Now all we need is to make a fire. I don't want any of us catching a cold. And fire will scare away any predators,"

"Do any of you guys know how to make a fire?" Jadeanu asks. "Nope," Ren and Luke answer. "Then I guess we'll be cold. I miss Ricardio already." "Well I can use the shadows to make a cover around us," Ren says. "Of course, it will only be temporary because once I doze off...."

"What if that possessed guy comes back?" Luke asks. "I'm sure we can survive his laser vision hit. Then we'll take him down again," Jadeanu jokes.

"That's a horrible plan," Luke claims. "It's always a risk out here. We can just hope for the best," Ren says. "Let's just get some sleep."

Soon they all sleep, and the night zooms by. The morning approaches, and they all wake back up. They greet each other and continue their walk. The sun is relatively high in the sky, so it is not early in the morning. They walk for a while, then Jadeanu stops. "Ravah is nearby," he says. "So we're finally going back to the original mission; getting all the Blessings!" Ren exclaims.

"How would we win though?" Luke concerns. "Sure it's a new day, but yesterday we got our butts handed to us by the King of Elko. Then we watched him lose to a genie who was easily beaten by a few angels. Our chances of winning are low." "Well we've got three blessings. I've been reluctant to use them since I heard they can kill us," Jadeanu reassures. "But I can still use the Nature and Willpower Blessings. Plus we've got to get the Knowledge Blessing from him eventually."

"But if we fail, we die," Luke re-establishes. "Maybe we can pass by this time and come back when we're ready." "But what if he attacks us before we're ready?" Jadeanu claims. "We should just fight him and be done with it. We don't actually have to stalemate him; just get the Knowledge Blessing and escape." "Stalemate?" Ren questions. "It's what happened to Javean and Vermunya when we beat them, and they didn't die." "Well then, I hope you're ready for this," Luke says with a slight shake in his voice.

"You think I'm not afraid?" Jadeanu says. "I'm terrified. And that's why we have to do this. The sooner we get the Knowledge Blessing, the sooner we can complete our mission and not have to worry about Ravah. It's time to man up and just do this!" "Fine, let's go then." "He's up ahead."

They all continue walking, and soon they witness a gigantic crowd of people just outside a church, standing there seldomly speaking to each other. "He's in that church," Jadeanu points out. "What's with all those people? There's got to be at least a thousand of them," Luke calculates. "Let's find out," Jadeanu says. He walks to the closest guy and asks, "What are all these people out here doing?" "Waiting for the new to get their blessings from the 8th god," the guy says. "The 8th god?" "The god of enlightenment. The Light-bringer, Lucifer." "You mean Ravah!" "Yes. The enlightened wisdom spreader. He gives us the knowledge that's been kept from us for so long. Now we are getting what we need to prosper in this sad world."

"He is no god. And you shouldn't listen to him!" "You're an anti-Lucifer! Everyone! They want to kill our god!!!" the guy calls, and at least a hundred people in the crowd turn to Jadeanu and the crew. Most of the people have colored eyes and now an angry expression on their faces. "INTERLOPERS!!" everyone starts screaming, slowly spreading their message to the attention of everyone else in the crowd.

"Oh crap," Jadeanu notices. "We don't have to kill or fight them all. We just need to get past them into the church." "I can create a giant bubble around us, and then we can run." "Well you might want to START!" Ren suggests noticing the growing hostility of the crowd of over a thousand enraged people. Luke hurries and shields everyone.

The guys all then start running through the aggressive people with the shield pushing away those who are in its moving path toward the church. The people attack the shield as the boys run through them. Ren uses the crowd of folks nearby shadows to keep them away as much as possible by making waves to push them back. Some people get their attacks in any way. Others attack from the sky. Those people usually have wings. One shoots laser beams from his hands at the shield. The barrier cracks more and more.

"Guys, the shield won't last. I need to get rid of it for a sec before we get swarmed in!" Luke says. "If it breaks, it will take longer to bring back! If I get rid of it, the cracks will heal!" "Then hurry up!" Jadeanu cries. "You guys ready?" Luke says before letting his shield down, allowing a swarm of angry people to invade and surround the guys.

Ren creates shadow mirages of each of his allies to support in fighting. He uses his own shadow to attack. Luke shoots beams and energy gas balls at the people. Jadeanu adds red energy to his arms and hits the people with shockwaves from them, knocking them back. Luke battles the few flying people with his projectiles. He gets past most of them, but one more is able to counter Luke's projectiles with his own. Seeing this, Jadeanu grips Luke's arm, and they trade opponents.

Luke tosses Jadeanu into the air. The arm that Jadeanu was grabbing of Luke's glows red with energy. Luke fires a gas ball from that arm at the people Jadeanu was originally fighting. A pink energy gas ball comes out and hits Luke's target. The explosion is double the size it normally is and blows back multiple enemies. The red glow in his arm disappears after the attack. He looks at his arm with fascination.

Jadeanu's arm has a much smaller glow on it, but it returns to normal energy soon after. He blocks the attacks from the airborne enemy with his gauntlets, then punches him in the face while still using the momentum of his ascension. The guy falls down into the bulk of the crowd, and Jadeanu lands next to Luke as they continue fighting.

"Bro! Did you see that?" Luke says. "No. What happened?" "Your energy went into my arm and made my attack stronger." "Really?" "Yeah but anyway, the shield's ready. Get everyone out of our circle." Ren makes a miniature wave out of all the shadows nearby, which pushes everyone except for his allies away. Luke recreates his huge barrier, and everyone starts back running.

Soon, they all approach the church door. "We're almost there," Luke says in anticipation of finally reaching a sense of safety. Then suddenly, Luke's shield breaks. "What just…" Luke says. He turns around, and Jadeanu and Ren follow suit. "Everyone stand back!" an unfamiliar voice says. A man without wings levitates down in front of the crowd. All the people do as he says and stop pursuing the guys.

"It's Aire! Those three sacrilegious fools are screwed now!" a crowd member says.

The guy known as Aire has red eyes with a hint of yellow in them. His right arm is encased in yellow energy, and at the end of his arm is the tip of a spear being held in his hand. It's likely what he used to pierce Luke's shield. "Those three can't stop you Aire. You can defeat them," another crowd member says. "Perhaps they can't; then again, perhaps they can," Aire responds. "But they definitely can't stop Lord Ravah. If they wish to face him, let them. They cannot halt his will, and they won't return alive. We are not Ravah's protectors. Unless that is what you desire to be. But then, it is your job to see your own will through if you think you can rise to the challenge. But if you are unwilling to commit to your cause without someone having your back, then withdraw, for you are unworthy of such an honor. Ravah can handle himself."

Jadeanu, Luke, and Ren enter the church, and no one tries to stop them. They see a small crowd of people standing in the church and hear a soothing, familiar voice. "Your struggles deem worth. They are not vain," the voice of Ravah speaks to the people. "The turmoil you face in life may hurt, but it is all for good. It is what makes your spirit strong. And the tides of your life grow and branch off in collective response to that trouble subconsciously. That is where the path of your life shall lead you. The traumas of what you've seen inspire a will away from or towards it.

That is your power. And you should use it to create the life you want. Nothing should stand in your way of accomplishing your goal. For that is righteous. You are not ONLY human. You are a strength in mankind. That is a marvelous nobility. As a human, you have such power. The power to command your world. The ability to heal wounds. The ability to gain and use everlasting knowledge. You are created in the gods' image. You have the power of a god. The ability to grow in whatever field you desire. The ability to grow stronger from any damage done to you. The ability to use otherworldly power through the form of intuition.

These powers are unique to all humans and should be used, not harbored. Humans are simply amazing and powerful. Allow me to guide you all to a proper world where all knowledge is given to the world's inhabitants. Keep faith in the gods, for we will lead you all to paradise."

"He's wrong! You're just trying to get people to fight and wage wars for their own selfish sake. People will only hate each other!" Jadeanu yells out. "Ah, Jadeanu. Well I certainly did not expect your acquaintance. But do you not agree that love and hate are one and the same? Just two sides of the same coin. One cannot exist without the other. They are both essential and must be expressed."

"And? Do you think that justifies murder?" "Of course not. But murder and killing are different concepts. Murder is the unnecessary and unlawful life-taking of another, whereas killing is merely the process. But you understand that there are exceptions to the laws under the gods. All separated by the flow of time. If one attempts to invade your home and slaughter your family, would you be condemned for killing the invader in defense? Has it not been done to kill those who block out a necessary will? For it is not murder, merely sanctifying what is yours. The messengers of the gods perform such."

"But you know that people aren't always noble and will go out and act out against the will of the gods! You know these people will act chaotically!" "Perhaps, but I prefer not to judge in such a manner, for false judgment creates more issues than silence. Yet order must prevail. Your works must never be confused with self-indulgence but rather righteousness. A proper vengeance is justified and should not be looked down on. Anger is good and should not be held in. Use it to get what you need and hold it tightly. But allow me to guide all goodwill. Allow me to be your shepherd."

"Have you ever heard what these people call you? You're full of it!" "I have little control over their words. They may speak as they will. Words have an untapped power behind them. Words are like a connector to the universe. They bring an unforeseen power that shapes and twists the fabric of the conscious world. Names and titles are the same. What they call me is a receptor of my energy and a redirect of it from them. Names shape a being.

Names and words have energy. Once a parent names their child, that may be a sign of blessings or curses. And it ripens the child. A fool would aim to materially change their name and run from who their energy dictates. But whatever the people title me strengthens my collective energy. It shall make me whole. After all, you're not the gift in your life; your mindset of change is the gift. And a fitting name only solidifies that purpose. For without purpose, your life is meaningless."

"I don't know what you're trying to gain here, but I'll stop you!" "Lord Lucifer, may we silence that man?" a guy asks Ravah. "No," Ravah answers. "If he wishes to oppose me, allow me to guide him.......to death. For a man's work is constant, never at rest. Such as the burning of the stars signifying a quantity as numerous as life. They burn with everlasting resolve. A man must walk through that flame and bend their own will with their own force. Randy, take everyone and evacuate them all to the western city."

The guy known as Randy leads everyone out of the church and does as Ravah instructs. Of course Jadeanu, Luke, and Ren stay behind. They angrily look at Ravah, who is scratching his little pet on his shoulder under the chin with his long sharp nail. "How dare you give incomplete knowledge to these people. Knowledge is power, and not all people should have that power! They will misuse it!" Jadeanu argues.

"Do you mind if we postpone our fight for a few minutes?" Ravah proposes. "This fight could get dangerous, and I don't want any innocent people to be killed. Let's just talk for a moment." "Fine, but what is it that you have been teaching these people?" "Many things. Such as the belief in the gods is what is needed to reach salvation." "That's it!? No works or life's devotion to goodwill?"

"Well their knowledge is their own. They need to gather what they will on their own." "You left all that out on purpose didn't you?! They've got to be real idiots to believe that that's it, yet they do. And you just let them." "Thousands of them believe it. And I'll need much more to complete my goal. It's not my fault that they choose to self-indulge in only what is given to them."

"But it is your responsibility. And you will pay for it." "But shall I? I will not rule out the possibility. For that is a nobility in itself. I have been enlightened by the fact that true greatness is achieved by special people. And those special people change the world, not conform to it. And because of that, they make the greatest sacrifices to stay on track. I am aware of the sacrifices I must make for such a noble opportunity. And I shall take them wholeheartedly. But who are you to stand in my way Jadeanu? You are but a common folk. I am an angel. Superior to you in every way. I am stronger, faster, smarter, and nobler than thou. You cannot stand to me."

"Well Javean and Vermunya were angels, and we managed to stop them." "Javean is an ignorant newbie, and Vermunya is arrogant. You were capable of weakening their will because of it. But I am what it means to be a true angel. Nearly perfect at all turns. Such a trick won't work on me. For an angel can't truly be stopped by a human. You can postpone us a few times, but no matter what, we'll eventually get you. And I assure you now, you will either give up those Blessings of yours or face me, in which I intend to grant you a punishing death.

You see, all life and, more specifically, angels can attack with more than power. Power can attack, and its energy can defend, but one's soul or raw spirit is always open for attack. That direct attack is given to those with higher nobility. The more noble a being is, the easier it is to attack in such a way and bypass power. You can be as powerful as you will, but a more noble being is sure to win eventually."

"Well we'll see about that." "You know, your powers; I've seen them before. I've seen yours and Ren's before. The power to strengthen certain parts of your body. You have a limit of two parts at a time. Ren has shadow manipulation." "How did you know? Were you watching our fight with-" "No. Your red eyes signify it all. They came from my realm. I can control a dimension called the abyss.

The abyss is the worst of many hells. It is responsible for many things but mainly for torturing evil inhabitants with every evil thought ever to be contemplated by any being. Imparted with my energy and my dominion. It is no understatement to say that I can unleash Hell on Earth. Of course it is forbidden, but I can still do it. Your powers came from Hell. That means the person who thought of them has had evil thoughts about them. And so…"

Ravah then summons a portal to the abyss and puts his hand in it, which causes his other arm to glow with red energy, and his shadow comes to life. "I can do them as well." Ravah then gets rid of his portal, places his shadow back where it belongs, and his red energy subsidies. "But Luke, yours are unfamiliar. But I can sense your protective nature."

"It doesn't matter what you can do! The will of good will prevail!" Jadeanu challenges. "You truly are magnificent Jadeanu," Ravah congratulates. "Your resolve is unshakeable. A trait not so common in many humans. That's why many are weak and roam like white sheep. Humans are like children. They don't change, only alter what was already there. For no one can change what you are born into. You might as well accept it.

People get angry when things don't go how they want and hail to aggression. They know they are small so they yield to a superior but most hate the thought of a higher life. And so they run. Run to a higher source of sloth and convenience, unknowing that it only leads to another form of domination. But rather a controlled one to escape consequences. Humans fear consequence because it is out of their control. Ever so hypocritical they are. Humans are so fascinating to understand. Due to their adolescent behavior patterns, they call me their parent, their god, all on their own. And whether my influence creates good or evil, I shall give the humans knowledge. The knowledge that was kept from them."

"I've seen the harm of too much knowledge. People think they want it until they get it. It's enough to drive them completely insane if they don't have the will or tools to understand it. You said humans are like children, and there is a reason you don't tell children everything about the world because it will hurt them beyond repair without proper preparation. You give them raw knowledge but not the wisdom to guide it," Jadeanu hypothesizes. "That is the flaw in your rule. You know Ravah, I don't doubt that you are a great leader by birth, but a king is made. You were not made to be their king. And now I must dethrone you."

"Hmhmhmhmhmhmhm. Well then, I suppose we'll have to settle this now. Those people are likely gone by now. We can fight." "Good then." "But before we go at it, let us see how you do against my pet." Ravah picks up his little pet creature on his shoulder by its sides. "I'll have you know that he is an Ancient. All Ancients come from my abyss but were released with the Death Spiral. But they belong to me, and many wish to return to my similar aura. The objects of the abyss can shrink or grow to whatever size I desire. Now I shall return him to his natural size. Ravah creates a purple portal in front of himself and tosses the miniature pink rhino into the portal, then closes it. Within a second, he makes another bigger portal in front of Jadeanu. The Ancient jumps out as a much more giant monster, towering over Jadeanu and the others. Showing its clear pink crystallized spikes covering its head and body.

"You may attack me if you think my pet isn't up to your speed," Ravah announces. He stands back, watching his Ancient work. Ravah's pet lunges toward Jadeanu with its sharp pink rhinoceros horn. Jadeanu narrowly dodges out of the way and pulls out his sword. He charges toward Ravah directly with energy in both of his arms. He jumps and swings his blade down. Ravah slowly reaches his hand up and catches the blade with his fingers. "Wha..?" Jadeanu questions. "A very strong sword. I presume crafted by a god," Ravah states. "Capable of cutting straight through me. But all I've got to do is keep the blade from touching me."

Ravah slowly reaches his other arm's pointer finger to Jadeanu's face and forcefully taps him on the cheek. The strange strength from Ravah's touch knocks Jadeanu back all the way toward Luke and Ren. Jadeanu gets back up, touches his face, and looks at his hand. There are several drops of blood on his gauntlet. He looks back at Ravah and charges again with rage in his red eyes. He runs and jumps. Ravah doesn't even move. Jadeanu does a twist in the air and aims his blade toward Ravah's side. His attack is suddenly stopped again by Ravah's three gripping fingers. This time, Ravah flicks Jadeanu's forehead, which sends him tumbling back again. Ravah's sharp nail cuts into Jadeanu's flesh causing his face to trinkle blood.

Jadeanu pulls himself up and analyzes Ravah. He remembers how Vermunya told him that Ravah and Javean walk around with their weapons. But Ravah looks nearly weaponless. Other than his elbow spikes. Jadeanu also recalls how Ravah's cloak turned into a weapon when he first attacked him. Maybe Ravah's clothes are the weapon, he ponders. He turns his attention to the Ancient.

"Hey Jadeanu, the pink spikes on the Ancient are even tougher than Ancient skin," Ren says. "So how do we damage it?" Jadeanu asks. "We're still figuring that out," Ren claims. Jadeanu jumps on top of the Ancient and stabs his sword toward the Ancient's skull. The crystallized skin on the Ancient deflects Jadeanu's sword.

Ravah's pet swats Jadeanu off of it with its bulky hand, then it performs a frontflip towards Jadeanu with its sharp back aimed to impale him. Ren snatches Jadeanu away, and the Ancient lands on its back. Luke surveys the Ancient's body and notices it has regular grey skin on its underbelly. "Be careful. This one is really agile," he says. Ravah's pet flips back on its feet. "We can go for its eyes," Jadeanu strategizes. Ren uses his shadow sword to go for the right eye, and Jadeanu goes for the left. Ravah's pet bites Ren's sword and tosses him away. Then the pink crystals on the Ancient's back light up and a 360-degree vertical blast emits and knocks Luke and Jadeanu far back.

"I should tell you that he is not like most Ancients," Ravah says. "There are a few that have magical powers. But they are rare." Ravah's pet throws a bunch of pink energy crescents from its horn at Ren and Jadeanu. They both dodge the attacks hastily. Luke approaches from behind and attacks to distract the Ancient. The Ancient throws an energy crescent from his tail at Luke, who defends with a shield. The shield cracks severely but sustains.

Immediately, the Ancient's sharp tail breaks through his shield and smacks him forward. With everyone in front of the beast, it throws a horizontal crescent the same size as its first energy attack. Luke, Ren, and Jadeanu brace themselves and are knocked through the church wall. They all bang themselves on the church steps outside.

The Ancient jumps out of the church, trying to land on its enemies with his colossal feet. They all roll and evade out of the way. The Ancient lunges with his sharp teeth to bite Ren, who narrowly escapes. "Wow! This thing is relentless!" Ren grieves. Ravah slowly walks out of the church with a face full of amusement as he watches the showdown.

"So exactly how are we going to damage this thing?" Jadeanu demands. "If you notice, Ravah's pet only has those crystal spikes on its back. Its underbody is the same as any other Ancient of its size," Luke analyzes. "Impact damage won't be enough, but its chin leads directly to its brain. We'll have to pierce through it. Now is a good time to try out your strength-spreading ability. Ren can make a drill, but you'll need to strengthen it. The hard part is making the Ancient stay in the same place." "That won't be hard," Jadeanu responds. "We just need to take out its legs." "Let's go then!" Ren calls.

Jadeanu dodges a pink energy crescent from the creature and places both of his arms around Ren's wrists, and channels his energy into him. Energy drains from Jadeanu's arms and adds to Ren's. Jadeanu's arms recharge, and he looks at his older brother Luke. "You ready?" "I'll go for its left. You get the right," Luke plans as he launches himself with barriers on his fist. Jadeanu runs full speed, resheathes his sword, and comes at the Ancient's leg with his red arms. He and Luke crash their fists against its legs simultaneously, hitting it where its skin is still grey.

Ravah's pet's legs collapse and the beast tumbles forward. Ren creates a huge drill under the Ancient's chin with its shadow. The spinning drill glows red, signaling Jadeanu's added power. Ravah's pet lands directly on the drill, and blood spews on the floor. The Ancient quickly tries to stand up. "Crap! It's getting up," Jadeanu notices. "Who cares? The drill is in! All we have to do is push it in deeper!" Luke resolves.

Jadeanu and Luke rush to the bottom of the Ancient's head. Jadeanu takes the energy from his left arm and moves it to one of his legs. He jumps up toward the ascending drill preparing to punch it. Luke comes from behind and fires a weak blast at him, which hits Jadeanu in the butt and pushes him forward even faster. Jadeanu hits the bottom of the drill deeper into the Ancient's chin and soon, Ravah's pet falls down and turns into red particles that dissolve in the air.

The sound of flesh slamming together in celebratory cheer erupts in the air. It is the sound of Ravah clapping. "Bravo! Excellent performance!" "You knew that we were about to kill him. Why didn't you jump in to save him?" Jadeanu questions out of curiosity. "He was not essential to me. I care not if he was to live or die." "You inconsiderate piece of...Don't you care for your allies?!"

Suddenly Jadeanu's vision darkens, and he feels a sharp pain all over his face. In less than a second later, his vision returns to him. He notices that Ravah is only two feet away from him, with his hand covering most of Jadeanu's face, gripping his flesh. But most appalling is that they both are surrounded by fluffy black clouds, and above all other surrounding buildings. "You shouldn't talk so boldly," Ravah quotes.

Fear consumes Jadeanu's heart in realization of the trouble he's in. Ravah lets go of Jadeanu, who reaches towards Ravah rapidly. Jadeanu nearly panics when the wind hits him during his descent toward the far ground. "Catch him!" Luke commands Ren. They both position themselves below Jadeanu. Luke creates a huge shield for him to land on. Ren creates a shadow trampoline from his and Luke's shadow. Jadeanu's body crashes straight through the barriers and lands on top of Luke and Ren. The shields stopped his excessive falling force, allowing Jadeanu to be hardly injured. "Ow!" Ren shouts. "Your sword hit my back." "Oh sorry."

Ravah flies back down, landing on his feet in front of his downed opponents. The three guys struggle to get up. Ravah flaps his wings, and his powerful aura hits the three. They all immediately fall back down to a kneel. "Darn it! He's strong!" Ren announces. "Guys... get up. Quick!" Jadeanu commands. "In case you haven't noticed. Your face is painted red with your blood," Ravah says. "That is because nearly every part of my body is a weapon. My skin is sharp like little needles." Ravah walks up to Luke and lightly touches his face with his finger. "My touch is like several razors ripping through flesh." Luke feels the sharp pain and blood dripping from his face.

Ravah takes a few steps back, allowing Jadeanu, Luke, and Ren to stand to his aura. "Are you all ready?" Ravah asks. "Let's go!" Jadeanu yells as everyone else notices the blood painted all over his face. Jadeanu and Ren draw their swords and attack from the sides. Ravah blocks both of their weapons with the spikes on his elbows. With his brute strength, he knocks both of them back.

Luke fires a blast at him while he's distracted. Ravah moves quick enough to dodge the blast then the spikes on his elbows detach and spring toward Jadeanu and Ren. They both barely block it as Ravah moves toward Luke with blinding speed and claws at Luke's chest. Luke narrowly dodges the slash, and Ravah's elbow spikes fly and reattach to his elbows.

Luke seizes the opportunity to punch Ravah in the face. Regret immediately fills him as he realizes that Ravah has taken unnoticeable damage and Luke's fist is now bleeding. Ravah smiles his sinister smile as he stabs through Luke's stomach with his sharp nails. He then turns around and slices through Luke's flesh while ripping through the air. Dark pink liquid flies from the attack, then it quickly swallows Luke's body, wrapping him inside a dark pink sphere.

Ravah grabs one of the bottom pieces of his cloak, which comes off with no rip, revealing it to be a hidden miniature scythe. He swings it overhead towards the pink sphere. Jadeanu gets worried and comes to tackle Ravah, who dodges him and slices through a section of the pink sphere. The dark pink liquid vaporizes once cut, and Luke's body flies out of the sphere with a large cut on his side. "Luke!" Jadeanu yells. "Are you okay?" "What just happened?" Luke wonders.

Meanwhile, Ren attacks Ravah with his sword. Ravah's superior strength goes right through Ren's weapon, which liquefies it as a shadow leaving his scythe to graze Ren across the chest. He quickly recovers and moves everyone else's shadow to surround Ravah and stab at him rapidly. "I was floating in a large dark space," Luke explains to Jadeanu. "You were trapped in a weird pink orb," Jadeanu says. "But you said it was large on the inside?" "Watch out for Ravah's nails. The pink substance on them is what did that." Jadeanu starts healing himself and Luke's wound with the Nature Blessing.

"Can you guys hurry up?!" Ren calls. Ravah cuts through the shadow spikes all around him with speed and elegance. Now Ren's shadow manipulation is temporarily useless. Jadeanu keeps healing Luke with his right hand but picks a boulder from the ground and throws it at Ravah. Luke supports with a beam.

Ravah cuts through the rock with his cloak scythe, dodges Luke's blast then reaches for his crown. He grips the purple crown on his forehead and detaches it from the rest guiding his face. He throws the sharp crown piece like a boomerang, and it flies toward Jadeanu, who blocks it with his sword. "Every part of his body really is a weapon," Jadeanu says.

The boomerang crown returns to Ravah, and he places it back on his head. He flies up and aims one wing at his enemies. Several feathers jet out like bullets. Jadeanu stands before Luke and spins his blade around to deflect the feathers. Luke creates a huge shield to guard them both. The feathers go through Luke's shield and are only stopped by Jadeanu's blade. A feather gets through, and pierces straight through Jadeanu's shoulder, and continues toward Luke, who dodges it. Soon Ravah stops shooting feathers.

Luke looks at Ren, who he just noticed didn't have anything protecting him. Ren is covered in blood and holes. He spits out blood and falls down. "You... you demon! You killed Ren, you MONSTER!!!" Jadeanu howls, and all three blessings on his gauntlet light up. Jadeanu uses the Willpower Blessing to chunk a huge boulder at Ravah. Ravah dodges it and flicks his hand up. A nearby skyscraper is grabbed by two giant hands coming from the abyss, and they uproot the large building and toss it to Ravah, who catches it with one hand and lifts it over his head as if it weighs nothing.

"Hey Jadeanu! It feels like Ren still has a pulse!" Luke announces. "We can heal him!" "Great! But that's second to the giant building coming our way!" Jadeanu responds, noticing that Ravah tossed the skyscraper toward them. Luke picks Ren up gently and rockets himself over the projectile. Jadeanu stares at the incoming building in shock, then the part of the building coming his way suddenly splits in half.

The Universe Blessing stops glowing. Jadeanu runs through the sudden rip in the giant structure. Ravah's two sides on his waist apron of the cloak move around his body vertically on opposite sides of each other. He then spins around like a moving wheel with the blades moving with him. He jets toward Luke, who narrowly dodges the eviscerating attack due to his momentum of propelling. Ravah stops spinning and returns his cloak scythes back to where they belong. He turns around and flies straight toward Jadeanu. "Where do you think you're going?"

He grabs Jadeanu by the back of his neck and grips him tight. His needle-like skin piercing Jadeanu's neck, sending acute pain into his nerves. Several small abyss portals open around Jadeanu's face. The Universe Blessing glows, and then the Blessing of Willpower, and suddenly an explosive shock wave emits from Jadeanu's body, knocking Ravah back. "Wha…" Jadeanu looks at his gauntlet as the two glowing Blessings return to normal.

"The Universe Blessing must have connected with the Willpower to defend me. I didn't even know that was possible," he concludes. "That means I can use the Universe Blessing to manipulate the others." Ravah stands and reaches inside his cloak and pulls two rapiers out of what seems like nowhere as he says, "Now you shall have a taste of my designated weapons. Prepare yourselves."

Jadeanu prepares his sword. "Connections and contrasts are the fields of the universe, which triggers all metaphors," Jadeanu states. "I am but a tree, and you a storm. I may not be able to stop you, but I can stand tall for my sapling. I will fight the storm and branch off to mend and nourish you with my sacrifice." The Universe Blessing glows, and then the Nature Blessing. Ren's wounds begin to close without Jadeanu having to point the Blessing at him this time. Jadeanu charges at Ravah, and they begin their sword clashing. Due to Ravah having two swords, he gets a few cuts and slashes on Jadeanu. Each laceration makes Jadeanu think of a tree getting its branches blown off by an intense storm. And due to Ravah's superior strength, each sword clash knocks Jadeanu back several dozen yards. Jadeanu receives multiple send backs due to Ravah's relentless pursuit.

Luke carries Ren and tries his best to keep up with the others. Ravah approaches Jadeanu and swings his blade. Jadeanu dodges to the side instead of taking the strike. Surprise hits Ravah as he stops himself from fully swinging. A strong wind comes from Ravah's sword and severely blows the nearby area. "Whew. I almost destroyed that nearby city full of people. I can't allow that," Ravah says.

Jadeanu counter attacks with his sword, but Ravah quickly reaches and grabs Jadeanu's face. The miniature blades on his skin pierce through Jadeanu's flesh as he pushes him with intense force letting the wind take him for a ride. Jadeanu flies back for a while before Ravah closes in and clashes his blade against Jadeanu's, thus sending him in the air. Ravah quickly flies even higher into the air and brings one of his swords down on Jadeanu, who blocks and is sent back down to the ground.

By this time, Ren's wounds are completely healed up, but he remains unconscious. "Amazing. It looks like you'll live Ren," Luke admits. "We could have died so many times, but it's like the Universe doesn't want us to yet. Maybe it's from the Universe god or maybe our Universe Blessing. Just having it seems to bend the whole world in our favor, like a good luck charm. But rather specifically for our wants and needs. Our prayers are coming true. Thank you, Universe."

Ravah slams his swords into Jadeanu's, which sends him blasting into a huge old castle. Ravah opens a portal and steps through it to immediately teleport into the castle after Jadeanu. Luke carries Ren and rockets through the hole in the castle. "Ah. In a vast citadel, you shall make your final stand," Ravah expresses, referring to Jadeanu.

Ravah then flies to the only exit of the fortress and summons a giant hand from the abyss that pushes Luke back towards Jadeanu, who is struggling to stand up from the impact of his crash.

Luke starts shaking Ren and slapping him to wake him up. "Huh, wha...Ravah! Is Ravah…" Ren panics. "You're okay; you just lost a lot of blood. But we're still fighting him," Luke says. Jadeanu charges Ravah and swings his sword. Ravah effortlessly blocks with one of his swords. He then casually looks down at Jadeanu's gauntlets. "So you have all the other Earth-bound Blessings," he points out. "All I need is to take those, and one set will be complete." Ravah then pushes against Jadeanu's sword, launching him to the back of the castle. Ravah places his swords back in his cloak.

Luke and Ren attack from both sides. Ravah holds out his hands, one toward each attacker. He then closes his fists. Immediately, Luke and Ren are grabbed by giant hands from the abyss, which holds them in place with its fingers completely wrapped around the two. "Oh my. My hands are occupied," Ravah acts. "Whatever shall I do if attacked?" Ravah then unclenches his fists, and the abyss hands continue crushing Ren and Luke. "Oh! Would you look at that? They hold on without me."

Ravah then aims one of his hands at Jadeanu, and his nails shoot off like little rockets. Jadeanu barely dodges and pursues Ravah, who regrows his nails and charges back. He swipes his claw-like nails at Jadeanu constantly, and Jadeanu takes special care not to let Ravah's nails touch him, as Luke advised. Jadeanu counters Ravah's assault with his sword. Ravah guards effortlessly with his nails, and his thick pink abyss liquid moves and grabs Jadeanu's sword. He yanks the sword out of Jadeanu's hand and throws it to the side.

He goes for a flurry of powerful kicks as the blades on his boots tear through the air anticipating when they'll feel the warmth of human blood. Jadeanu dodges all of the well-performed kicks. Ravah does a somersault kick toward Jadeanu's chin. Jadeanu dodges back, and Ravah uses his wings to keep his body above ground as he comes back around and sweep-kicks Jadeanu into a spiral off his feet.

Ravah lands on his and palms Jadeanu hard in the ribs. There is a crack in his rib bones as he flies straight to the nearby castle wall. There is a large impact sound as Jadeanu's back slams into the wall. Unfathomable pain consumes Jadeanu's backside and ribs. He clenches them both while struggling to breathe.

Ravah turns to Luke and Ren, who are still trapped in the giant abyss hands, struggling to break free. "The pain, can you endure it?" Ravah claims as he closes his fists, making the abyss hands crush even harder. Luke and Ren scream loudly. Their horrible ear-piercing screams are interrupted by an even louder crash. Ravah turns to see what it is and beholds a hole in the castle wall, and Jadeanu has his sword and runs away, holding his side. Ravah stops squishing Luke and Ren and turns to Jadeanu. He creates a small portal and sticks his hand through it. A portal opens under Jadeanu, and a hand grabs his leg. Ravah quickly yanks his arm out of the portal, and Jadeanu is pulled directly in front of Ravah.

Jadeanu smiles and lets out a precharged crescent of Blessing energy at Ravah from point-blank range. Ravah narrowly dodges the unexpected attack giving Jadeanu enough time to get away. His ribs are already healed, and he runs and cuts Luke and Ren out of the abyss hands with his sword. "Whew! That sure took a lot!" Jadeanu reassures. "Clever boy!" Ravah says almost proudly as he replugs the castle hole by filling it with rubble by destroying the top of the exit with his abyss hands.

"But you see, you're using the Blessings like an amateur," Ravah announces. "In the right hands, you can do so much more with them. Allow me to enlighten you." Ravah grabs the Knowledge Blessing out of his pocket, and a small orange crystal appears on his forehead. The crystal lights up, and a powerful orange laser beam emits out of it and travels toward Jadeanu, who jumps out of its way.

"Okay guys. We've clearly bit off a heck of a lot more than we can chew," he states. "You think?" says Ren. "I've got a plan," Luke admits. "What?" Jadeanu asks while dodging another laser beam, followed by a flurry of many more to keep them all on their toes. "All we've got to do is give him the Blessings, and we get to walk away right?" Luke wonders.

"Yeah, but we're not just gonna do that." "That's not what I'm getting at." "Okay then." "If one of us has the gauntlet with the Blessings, he'll attack that person. The others can escape. The only problem is that as long as he has the Knowledge Blessing, he can find us. One of us will have to use the Blessings to fight and somehow steal the Knowledge Blessing from him and toss it back to the others." "It's suicide, but I guess it's the best we've got right?" Jadeanu agrees. "Who's gonna be the one to fight him? We've got to decide-"

"I'll do it," Luke accepts. "When I thought of the plan, I knew I would have to be the one to do it." "But you don't have to. If you do this, you'll die," Jadeanu says. "Yeah Luke. Let's think this through," Ren suggests. "My mind's all made up. He's playing with us and still kicking our butts. We don't have a lot of time before he stops messing around. And...you know, there isn't a better way for me to die than protecting the both of you. Ren, I wouldn't dare ask you to die for us. And Jadeanu. My little brother. If one of us dies, the other will continue the mission. You know that. I was put on this Earth to protect people. To protect you. That's what my powers are for. And I failed Kinra and Blast. Stougma's death helped so many people. That's what I want mine to be like. Please allow mine to not be a tragedy for you. But a reason for you to continue. Complete your mission without me. Take care of Ren and save the world."

"If only we just left Ravah alone...." "But we didn't. Because we have people to save, and that's something to be proud of. Now take off your gauntlet." "If Ricardio was still here, he could think of something else..." "But he isn't. He made his choice, and now we must make ours. I need that gauntlet Jadeanu."

Jadeanu starts tearing up as he takes off his gauntlet and gives it to Luke, who puts it on. "Do me a favor and win," Jadeanu tells him before giving his brother one last hug. Luke smiles as tears run down his cheeks. "I wouldn't want things any other way. Here, take this last washing bubble, you'll need it more than I will," Luke responds while giving Jadeanu the bubble still in his pocket. "Now both of you run! I'll send the gauntlet back to you if I...no when I win. NOW GO! GET OUT OF HERE!" Luke yells.

"Bye brother," Jadeanu says as he and Ren take off toward the exit at full speed. Luke shoots a blast at both of their backs to boost them out. He also blasts forward toward Ravah, using those blasts to propel himself. Ravah opens up his hand and tries to stop Jadeanu and Ren but is interrupted by Luke, who approaches with a punch with his gauntlet-coated hand.

Ravah dodges the attack and closes his hand toward the palace exit. A huge abyss hand grabs the wall and crumbles it making the place temporarily inescapable. But Jadeanu and Ren had already made it through. "Humph. A noble deed to sacrifice your life for theirs," Ravah says. "But I have no reason to let you get away. Prepare for my power."

Ravah flies into the air and charges up a Knowledge beam. In the air, several abyss portals open up, all aimed at Luke. Meanwhile, Jadeanu and Ren run from the castle. Jadeanu takes a deep breath and then, "AAAAAHHHHHHH!!!!! DAMN IITT!" Ren looks at him sympathetically but says nothing.

Ravah fires his Knowledge beam from his forehead, and each of his portals unleashes a large Knowledge beam out of them as well. Luke war cries as he dodges each of them and proceeds towards Ravah. Another beam comes from Ravah's head. Luke instinctively creates a shield around himself. The beam goes straight through the shield and slices Luke's left arm clean off. Luke holds his bleeding stub as Ravah descends, saying, "Are you ready to submit to your fate."

Ravah throws his right hand up, and a mimicking abyss hand appears, hovering above Luke. Luke notices the Blessing in Ravah's left hand. "You know, it would be easy to give up now. But I'm not submitting to that," Luke claims as he dashes forward just as Ravah makes the huge arm smash down. Luke continues talking as he attacks.

"My job isn't to go down! My job is to complete what I'm set out to do! Things were never built to be easy. And I accept this challenge! Because that's what life is all about! Moving forward with what little power we have! We've lost many along the way, but we, the alive ones, must keep going! Because I believe that there is better out there! And I'll be damned if a monster like you can ruin it! I fight for this world and for my allies! And if my death means their life, then I would die a million times over! So let's do this! This is my choice! And I won't turn back!"

Luke approaches Ravah and throws a punch toward him. Ravah dodges but Luke counters with a kick coated in gaseous energy. Ravah jumps back and draws his swords. He rises into the air above Luke and dives down, swords extended and spiraling downward. Luke evades and swipes his arm toward the currently defenseless Ravah who's swords are drilled into the ground. A huge gassy energy crescent comes out towards Ravah, who narrowly avoids the attack.

Ravah puts his swords back in his cloak, leaving the Blessing of Knowledge as the only thing in his hand. Luke uses his legs to rocket up the back of the castle, and he does a backflip, kicking another strong crescent of energy at Ravah. Ravah dodges it and then notices Luke approaching quickly from his left. Ravah does a spin to avoid Luke, then he kicks him with the back spike on his boot.

"Interesting. He's growing stronger now that he's accepted death," Ravah analyzes. Luke grabs his now cut side and emits a strong 360-degree blast from his body which blows Ravah back. Luke closes in, and circles to Ravah's left again. He shoots a beam, and Ravah dodges it, making it hit the front wall that used to be the exit. At the same time, he kicks with energy on his leg, forcing Ravah to dodge it as well. Before Ravah could counter, Luke kicks a shield at Ravah's legs causing Ravah to jump. Luke brings forth a crescent of energy with his arm, and while Ravah is occupied by the damage of getting hit, he finally kicks the Blessing of Knowledge out of his hand.

He snatches it with his gauntlet coated hand, and blasts away with his legs, hitting Ravah's blocking wings with the blast. He moves to the nearest wall, then throws the Blessing up and catches it in the socket of the gauntlet with the wall. He closes his eyes and concentrates. An orange crystal materializes on his forehead as he shoots a Knowledge beam at Ravah while blasting himself to the crumbled exit.

"Now where are they?" Luke asks the Knowledge Blessing while concentrating on it. His eyes turn orange, and he looks through the hole he made in the rubble with his previous beam. "There!" he exclaims. Luke uses his power to blast the gauntlet into the night sky. "There you go Jadeanu. I did it; now I leave the rest to you," Luke says as he blasts back to Ravah, preparing to continue fighting to buy more time.

As soon as he comes to Ravah with a punch, he feels a sharp pain in his gut. Ravah pierces through Luke's stomach with his sword. Luke smiles as blood comes up from his mouth. He stands proud of his sacrifice and now he feels a sense of ease in his heart telling him he can die in peace. Ravah looks down at Luke's arm and notices that the gauntlet is gone. "Well done, Luke Stroyem," Ravah congratulates. "But I have no intention of letting you die peacefully. As you said, you'd die a million times; let's see just how long your body can last."

Ravah throws Luke off his blade and to the ground. Immediately, Ravah makes an abyss hand grab Luke and take him into the dark dimension. In about one second, Luke's body comes right back out, completely bound by hands and pink abyss liquid. He's not even able to lift a finger. "Witness my abyss burial; where you shall be stranded on your tomb," Ravah says as several sharp nailed hands come out of little portals all around Luke. Ravah starts laughing in a maniacal high-pitched laugh as the hands rip Luke apart piece by piece, making sure to keep him alive as long as possible. Luke screams like never before with sheer pain feeling the embrace of true torture.

After the abyss burial is done, all that's left of Luke is a skeleton with chunks of flesh here and there. A small blue image of Luke comes from the corpse, and Ravah sends it upwards with a motion of his hand. "You get to go up there now Luke. Rest in peace," Ravah states.

Outside the castle, Jadeanu and Ren find the gauntlet sitting alone in a spot of dirt and appreciate Luke's work, giving thanks to his brave final effort. Jadeanu picks it up as they approach the nearby city. The city where Ava awaits. But now is the time for the rest of the two physically and mentally exhausted men. They both find a safe place to rest, then let slumber take their conscious.

Chapter 11:
Ava Ramada

"Hello. I am Ava Ramada. And this is my story." Ava is a tall, 5'10 woman with long black straight hair down to her thighs. She has light brown, almost yellow skin. Her skin is perfect, radiant and has no blemishes in it whatsoever. She is 39 years old despite a youthful appearance. Age can't touch her type of beauty. Her fingernails are long, sharp, and painted a sensual red. Her eyes are a beautiful purple, like the rare dawn sky. She has thick sharply curved eyebrows. Her eyelashes are long and elegant, as is her physical charm. Her lips are plump and well-hypnotizing. She has a preference for wearing the color black over her body.

She blesses one of her all-black entire-body one-piece jumpsuits with the honor of covering her body. The suit has a front cut out of a heart right where her boobs are, showing a bit of skin but not much. Her breasts are a perfect shape. Plump, not too big, not too small, but just the right size. Her curves move sharply down to her hips and buttocks, which are nice and round.

Her body is flawless, and her clothes highlight every inch of her aesthetic. Indeed a sight to behold. Her shoes of choice are black block heels which complement her feet nicely. She wears a necklace as well.

At the curve of the necklace holds a beautiful diamond ring. "This is my wedding ring. I was married to a wonderful man, but he passed away on the day of the Death Spiral exactly a week and one day ago. I still hear his voice echoing through my ears sometimes. I embrace his ring close to my heart to symbolize my love for him."

Ava stands up and looks at herself in the full-body mirror on the wall of her room. She is truly a sight to admire, as the King of Elko said. The best part is she is all-natural. No fabrications are needed on a being so perfect. She walks to her bedroom window and looks out the blinds. "It seems it will rain soon." She grabs an umbrella from her large walk-in closet and leaves her room. She tiptoes down her huge flight of stairs past her luxurious chandelier. She reaches her front door and opens it.

Ava ventures outside, ensuring to lock the door. She walks through her front yard with bushes full of blooming roses. There is a front gate towering over her entire yard. She unlocks it and lets herself out. She walks the path outside her home, which doesn't have many neighbors, especially now. She walks into the bulk of her city.

The rain starts pouring down from the blackened clouds, and Ava shields her hair with her umbrella. She walks through a shortcut to her destination through an alleyway. It is a pretty common alley to pass through, considering that people are seemingly unhesitant to go through there. A guy is walking by on the opposite side of the small corridor. He makes eye contact with Ava. She locks eyes with him. His cheeks turn red as he blushes at her astonishing design. "Hey... um, ma'am. I'm sorry to bother you, but I must say, um, wow, you are the most beautiful woman I've ever seen."

"Oh thank you! You're not so bad yourself," Ava compliments. The guy is an average-looking white guy in his early thirties. He is slightly shorter than Ava and has a rather fit physique. He's wearing a jacket and has his hood on, but his face is present. He has very clear red glowing eyes. "Why don't you come under my umbrella? Let's talk," Ava suggests. "You sure? I could be a predator you know," he responds. "But a predator wouldn't tell me he is. So yeah, I'm sure."

The guy comes close to her under the shade of her umbrella. The first thing he notices is her delightful aroma. *'Wow, she smells like roses and strawberries. It's intoxicating, but it doesn't smell like perfume. Maybe it's her soap?'* "Hey, I hope I'm not intruding on something. Where are you headed?" Ava asks. "Oh I was just walking home from a peaceful walk around. I love the city in the morning. It sometimes lets me forget about the horrors of the situation we're all in. But no, you're not intruding." "Good then. Do you mind coming with me to my job? I won't be long. Then we can go on a nice date. How does that sound?"

Ava's voice is strong with a deep feminine charisma. Her tone has an underlying sexual appeal behind it. It's pleasant to the ears. "Well I would love to, but my money's kind of short." "You don't need to worry about that. I'm the founder and CEO of Dynine Physical Flights. The clothing design company that institutes health and yoga. Have you heard of it?" "Yeah I have." "Well, I'm trying to say that I don't mind paying since I have plenty of money. Although that's not the job I mentioned earlier," Ava informs. "Congrats, um…what is your name?" "I'm Ava. And you are?" "Chris."

Chris's face starts to position towards the floor. "You know you're not any less of a man just because a woman is paying on a first date," Ava states. "I know, but it…just feels weird." "You'll get over it. After all, I asked you out, so let's just have fun and let go of any bad thoughts." Ava and Chris stand side by side, walking for a few blocks. Ava stands about an inch and a half taller than Chris.

There is an awkward silence that Ava fills with a soothing hum. She then starts to sing.

'The angelic tears come pouring down. Hitting the floor with sympathy's sound. A cloud of water hinders our sight from a great new world full of delight. Buuttt rain isn't for sadness. Rather a deliverance from madness. For rain makes flowers bloom, so the storm is no reason to gloom.'

Ava's singing voice is angelic. "Your voice is amazing. Do you sing? Like professionally?" Chris wonders. "Not really. I do put on a nice song for people in exchange for money sometimes though. It's just, the rain makes me think. I like to sing when in thought." Soon they both are face to face with a large building. "Hey this is that karaoke place right?" Chris questions. "I guess you could say that. But it's more than that. C'mon." Ava walks Chris inside.

Meanwhile, Jadeanu and Ren walk through the city in the morning's peace. Rain slams against their uncovered heads, drenching their hair. Jadeanu seems deeply bothered by yesterday's event considering the loss of glow in his eyes. "You know Jadeanu, I don't know what it's like to lose someone who's been here all this time like that. But I miss Luke too," Ren empathizes. "He was like a big brother to all of us." "It's okay Ren. I'm not sad; he did what he needed to do," Jadeanu responds.

"If Luke didn't do what he did, we wouldn't have the Knowledge Blessing, and Ravah's corruption couldn't be allowed to continue. I'm proud of that, and it's the way the universe needed things to be. I wouldn't want it any other way. Luke looked so sure of himself." "Well then, now that you have the Knowledge Blessing, what's our next move? We could keep going Northeast to see what's up, or we can use the Knowledge Blessing to locate the other three Blessings." Jadeanu concentrates on the Knowledge Blessing for several seconds. "There are two Blessings not far from here. They are just up ahead, past this city. We'll follow them." "Alright then."

Back to Ava and Chris. Upon entrance to the building they arrived at, a young man with red eyes greets Ava. "Hey Ava. We were waiting for you. And who is this young man?" "He's a friend of mine." Ava reaches into her pocket and pulls out a little slip of folded-up paper. "Chris, sorry to ask this of you, but can you give this to that security guard over there? I've got to go. You can take a seat; I will be back soon." "Sure no problem." Chris takes the slip of paper and starts toward the lone surveying security guard with red eyes. "Hey, I was told to give this to you." The guard grabs the paper with a little hostility as if expecting something.

Ava follows the guy who greeted her up an elevator, and Chris finds a seat near the entrance. Immediately, a few people gather around him, asking questions like, "How do you know Ava?" "Is she your friend?" "What's she like outside of work?" Chris answers the questions the best he can, saying, "I only recently met her, but I think we're friends. I can say she's a wonderful person. So kind and sweet." The questions keep pouring in, but the interviewers are careful not to overwhelm Chris, yet he likes the attention. "Do you trust her?" "What's her secret to smelling so good?"

Meanwhile, Ava rides the elevator up alongside her co-worker. "So Ava. Are you excited? Everything's finally coming together," the guy says. "All is well on my end. But I'm far from finished," Ava replies. "How are things for you Jeremy?" "Everything is clear. No surveillance, and no one even knows that you are the idea that started this company. Soon this city will be all yours." "Good."

The elevator stops at the top floor and opens. As this happens, the guard Chris gives the paper to, opens it up, and reads some words placed on it. He gets exceptionally angry and burns the paper with his power which is evidently fire. He goes into another room and starts yelling at some other guy. The guard is out of Chris's sight and he can't even hear all the commotion due to his distant proximity.

"So you think it's funny to make jokes about things like that?!" the guard yells. "I think it's priceless! Especially looking at your face now," the other guy says. "Hey guys, cool it. You aren't even supposed to talk to each other," another guy says. "I don't care about that distance rule!" the guard says. "Officer James-" "No, I think the officer is right. We should settle our own differences like the single childless men we are. Oh wait!" the other guy exclaims, looking at Officer James.

"But...Steve!" "Out of the way Craig, this is the last time Steve will ever speak! I'm gonna kill your insensitive ass!" Officer James says with fire on both of his fists. "Must suck to have your child and wife die if it turns you into such a sap!" Steve says with his hands lighting up colorfully. "But come on! It's about time we settle this."

There is screaming and lots of loud noises, which starts to concern Chris, but he doesn't dare intervene. A few minutes pass, and the employees at the place are all gathered in shock at the scene. Officer James is on the floor, dead. Steve is also hurt and bloody, with burns on his clothes. "I quit! Let me pack my stuff!" Steve screams and goes over to his workstation. A few people drag out the body as if it's just normal to see a dead person. The rest get back to work in their own personal cubicles. Chris misses it all.

Meanwhile, Ava enters a meeting room. "Hello!" Ava waves to a bunch of people sitting at a large table. "Mrs. Ramada. Please take a seat. We couldn't start without you," a guy says. "Thank you for having me, Mr. Ford." "Please, call me Jefferson." Ava and Jeremy take seats at the table. "So Ava. It has come to my attention that you want an audience with our mayor. Please elaborate as to why," Jefferson states.

"We are all aware of the constant casualties we face. The people are scared, and so you've all come up with the idea of using this place as a way to get away from the horrors. But I have endorsed and made the place greater, creating happier faces; yet it doesn't change the fact that people are dying. The mayor must understand that the ruling office needs more strength. This is a matter of life or death, and people will keep dying without proper regulation. With more power and stricter laws, we can stop this hysteria. Late night curfews to stop the violence no one gets to see. A police system. Consequences to those who encourage violence. The mayor has the power to make those things happen yet neglects to use it. I must see him about it. Does anyone have an objection to my plan?" Ava explains.

A guy raises his hand, but everyone else stays neutral. "Things are already chaotic as they are," the man states. "The Mayor can only keep things organized for so long before violence wins in the end. I believe it is better to leave things be so that end won't come sooner." "Good thought, but I like to believe that trying is better than letting the worst happen. We'll meet and discuss that dilemma after this meeting. I'd like to see if I can change your mind," Ava advises. The guy nods and puts his hand down. "So how are we to ensure you mean no ill will?" Jefferson demands. One of the other guys raises his hand.

"She is well-liked by everyone in this building. Well respected and honorable. The employees on the first floor, which is the one she operates, trust her with all their hearts. I heard about it a few minutes ago. She even has a friend down there talking about how much he admires her. Plus, she doesn't have powers which makes her not as much of a potential danger." Ava cracks a light smirk.

"Well then Mayor McKenzi will be here tonight. We'll speak on your behalf, and you'll meet him no later than tomorrow. He loves to sing and dance," Jefferson informs. *'Oh I am well aware of that,'* Ava thinks. "Thank you Jefferson. It is an honor." "Dismissed." Ava stands up and takes the elevator along with Jeremy and the guy who raised his hand in objection to Ava's plan earlier.

Ava stops on a certain floor and tells the other guy to come with her. Jeremy manually stops the elevator and waits patiently for Ava to return. After several minutes, Ava returns to the elevator with Jeremy. "So things are looking up," Jeremy conversates. "They sure are. I appreciate your cooperation. I do hope I never have to use your assistance again," she claims. "Indeed." Jeremy agrees with a troubled expression on his face.

The elevator stops on the first floor, and they both get out. Jeremy goes to another room, and Ava goes straight to Chris. "Hey Chris." "Hey Ava. I thought you were going to leave me for a sec."

"Of course I wouldn't, silly. Now I've got to check on my guys okay?" "Take your time." "Sorry. But it won't be long." Ava then moves to another room.

She notices Steve packing up his work materials and approaches him. She leans close, and in a low voice says, "So you took care of James?" Steve nods. "Good. Now he can't get in my way." "Why'd you choose me to do it?" "I could feel your energies. I knew you would be able to kill him. Plus he's a hot head, and you're even-tempered. You had every advantage over him." "Thank you Ava." "You've served me well Steve." Steve smiles and walks out of a back exit.

"Hey Ava," someone else calls, and she turns to him. The dude points at the telephone he's holding. Ava takes the phone and puts it up to her ear. "Hello. This is the manager….Oh my, that's terrible. We'll get on that right away…I'm so sorry that that happened…. Thank you, bye." Ava then hangs up the phone. "See what you can do about that. If nothing is easy, then ignore it," Ava tells her employee.

"Hey Ava. Did you get in?" another guy calls. The guy has a chevron mustache, and he is rather short and overweight. "Your spies have done me well, but what exactly are you doing William?" Ava responds. "I just don't see a reason to tell you." "Watch your tongue, Ava. Acting all high and mighty like that. I'll have you know I've secured your image. Now we are closer to getting the mayor."

"Hey it would be really nice if you assemble all of your spies to watch over the mayor and his guards when he gets here tonight, don't you think?" William frowns. "You're always the one talking about effective order right? Everything must be flawless," Ava includes. "Fine." William angrily storms off. *Trying to manipulate me into doing her dirty work and trying to pass it off as my idea. It wasn't even clever.* "Haha, bye William."

Ava returns to Chris and holds out her hand. "Come on. Let's go have some fun." Chris smiles, takes her hand, and they both go outside. They both go out for food, then after the rain stops, go-kart racing, bowling, painting, and lastly, they chill out by a pond watching the sunset. Ava had beaten Chris at all the competitive games. It was like she was good at everything. They flirt a lot while enjoying the ease of each other's company. If one was viewing their bonding, they'd certainly say that love was in the air.

After the sun sets, she walks Chris home and then starts her walk, which isn't that far away. As she walks on the sidewalk, a man and his son look into Ava's dazzling eyes. "Hey, you're Ava aren't you?" the guy questions. "What's it to you?" Ava responds. "You remember that your company took money from me and my son with faulty equipment, and you told me that you'd get right on it. But nothing happened!" "Oh, so that was you," Ava says with an expression of pure boredom.

"I don't appreciate people lying to me and taking money from my son and me!" "Listen. I told you we'd get on it, and so we did. We never promised a refund. But think about it, we already have your money. Why would we go through all that effort just for you? We'll only lose money and time, and I hate waste." "You wretch! You know what? Hey son, stand back and watch me. I'm gonna show you how we should deal with injustice in the world. Learn from the consequences of her mistake."

The father takes off his jacket and cracks his knuckles. He and his son have red eyes, so they both have powers. "Hahahaha!" Ava laughs. "What's so funny?" "Oh, we've needed some blood! And apparently so did you, looking for the first chance to cope with your world using violence." Ava's eyes suddenly start to glow red, and her right forearm starts to look demonic. It is coated in pinkish-red crystalized spikes similar to the spikes on Ravah's pet.

"I'm going to enjoy this!" "What in the…." In a matter of seconds, the guy is on the ground bleeding out from a massive rib wound. Ava's demonic arm moves as if it has a mind of its own. It yanks Ava's body toward its victim in a desperate attempt to finish him off on its own. Ava just smiles maniacally as she lets it happen. "Stop!" the boy yells to defend his father. "Awe, how cute," Ava responds as she stands back up. Her voice having a slight echo in it. "I don't want you to live with hate in your heart child. That wouldn't be good. So it would appear that father and son will die together!"

Ava grabs the boy by the neck with her demonic right arm. The boy squirms and squeals like a trapped guinea pig as Ava just stares. He goes completely limp as Ava snaps the boy's neck and then proceeds to tear his head off with her demon arm's claws. "HeheheheHaHaHa!" she laughs as she quickly returns to the dying father and slices him in half vertically with her sharp claws. She looks at her monster arm now stained with drops of blood. "You naughty thing, wanting to fight me for control of my own body. Hehe. All you want is to cause death and destruction. Well I can't have that," Ava says as her arm returns to normal, and her eyes return to their beautiful purple color.

She takes a towel out of her pocket and carefully cleans the blood off of her hand. She balls up the towel and places it back into her pocket; then continues walking and soon ends up at the darkened alley leading to her house. "A girl as pretty as you shouldn't be wearing things like that," a strange voice says out of the darkness of the ominous alley. Ava turns to see a shady-looking guy standing in the darkness with red eyes peering menacingly at her. "A sexy woman isn't safe out here with no powers. Don't worry. I won't hurt you too badly." "HaHaHaHa!" Ava laughs as her eyes return red and her arm returns to its insidious look.

Back to Jadeanu and Ren, who walk through the big city. There is the sudden sound of a creature's movement in the darkness of the sunset sky. They both look in the direction of the noise in caution. They see a stop sign pole in a dark corridor where it's not supposed to be. And under it is a man with blood under his lips.

"Help...me!" he calls out. Jadeanu and Ren rush to the guy. He is the very man who had spoken up against Ava's plan during their meeting. The stop sign is embedded deep into the ground through the guy's abdomen. His arms are gone; they look as if they were cut off. "Uh, let us remove this pole," Jadeanu suggests. "No! Don't!" the man yells.

"The person who did this….I didn't even know she had powers. I've never seen anyone turn them on and off like she did." "Who did this?" "Her name is Ava. She stabbed this pole through me for speaking out against some plan she had. She…filled it with some explosive energy. If anyone attempts to pull it out of me, she says it will detonate. The explosion won't just kill me but the noble rescuer and everyone even remotely close by. It'll be big enough to kill everyone around this block. She…made sure I couldn't do it myself by ripping my arms off and patching them up so I wouldn't bleed out.

Even if you were to rip this sign out of me, I think it's in my abdominal aorta, or so she said. If the pole is removed, I'll bleed out in seconds. She thought of everything. No matter what anyone does, I'll die. She didn't want me to have an easy death. Either I could be selfish and kill everyone around or sit here until I'm torn apart by wild animals or dehydrated to death…or possibly killed by someone else. Don't try to be a hero here. Please kill me. Please."

"Where is Ava?" Jadeanu asks. Ren stares in surprise. "I…don't know. I just know she works at the song and dance station. Oh no. The mayor! He…he's in danger! You have to save him. But first, please kill me." Jadeanu draws his sword. "Jadeanu, I thought we didn't kill people," Ren quotes. "Yeah but what Ravah said makes sense to me now," Jadeanu claims. "Rather, we shouldn't murder, but killing isn't such a bad thing. After all, the law was made to guide us, not restrict us. I think it's better to end this guy's suffering rather than turn our backs on him while he's in need." "I guess you're right about that."

Jadeanu hesitantly brings his sword down on the guy's neck, staining his blade with dead human blood for the first time. "I'm sorry it had to be this way," Jadeanu sympathizes. "So what are you thinking?" Ren questions.

"I'm thinking we find and kill Ava."

"Are you sure?"

"Yes. I know Luke wouldn't want us to, but she must be taken down for what she's done."

"But can we do it? Remember what King Elcero told us." "We beat Javean and Vermunya. I think we can take her." "Sure, but can you actually kill her if given a chance?" "As of now, I think of her like I thought of genie Jinzen. She is no human and must be destroyed. Now let's find clues about her whereabouts."

In the meantime, Ava walks away from her alley, in a fit of laughter. Behind her is the unrecognizable corpse of the creepy predator. "Well while I'm out, I might as well go back to my job." Ava returns to her place of work and enters the building. She enters a few busy rooms full of people doing karaoke and other things. She notices the mayor singing a duet with his wife. Ava smiles in triumph, then is tapped on the shoulder by Jeremy. "Hey Jeremy." "Come outside."

Ava follows Jeremy outside. She ends up getting in his car with two other guys. One of which is Steve. They drive to a specific location and get out. "You see that giant building? That's Mayor McKenzi's place of business," Jeremy says, pointing to a huge building. "Then we shall make preparations. Gather a few dozen people for the event. I'll need an audience," Ava directs.

While this occurs, Jadeanu finds a person to ask about Ava. "Do you know a woman named Ava?" "Everyone knows Ava." "Do you know where she stays?" "Nope. All I know is that she's crazy rich. So she probably lives in one of the rich folk neighborhoods." "Thank you."

Later, Ava returns to her home's front gate. She notices a black cat walking past her feet. The cat stops and looks at Ava. She smiles and says, "Hey cutie." She bends down and pets the cat. "Are you hungry?" The cat meows and rubs up against Ava's hand. "Okay, wait right here." Ava hurries into her mansion and later comes out with a half-eaten baked fish. She throws it down toward the cat and it immediately starts eating. "Sorry, it's a bit cold. It was last night's leftovers." Ava reaches down to pet the cat's soft fur again. "You enjoy that. Bye!"

Ava stands up and re-enters her house. She walks through her house and goes into a big room with a chin-up bar and a big TV underneath it. Other than that, the room is mostly empty. Ava starts punching and kicking the air in flawless form. A left jab followed by a right hook, then two spinning kicks. A sweep kick to a backflip, then a right twirl with a strong back-fist. She continues practicing her fighting technique for a while.

She later goes into push-ups, sit-ups, squats, chin-ups, and jogging in place for several minutes at a time. She sweats profusely, but the air around her only smells like roses and strawberries. She later does some yoga. Afterward, she lifts her leg up so high she is able to kiss her thigh as a stretch. And she does it effortlessly, maintaining full balance; then she switches legs.

Interestingly enough, she does all of this without even using her powers. She takes a deep breath and lets her leg down. She then goes to a huge mirror in a nearby room and looks at her sweaty body.

She grabs the ring on her necklace and clenches it close to her heart. "I miss you," she says. "No matter how much I sweat and radiate heat, I'm still cold inside." She lets go of her necklace. "But tomorrow I will overthrow the mayor and seize control of the city. And soon, my city will fight yours, King Elcero. And I will beat you and conquer your city. Then after that, I'm coming for you, my son."

Ava takes a shower and changes into a T-shirt and sweatpants. She looks at her right arm and envisions her demonic arm. "The sooner I get to bed, the sooner tomorrow comes. We've done enough for today." Ava gets in her two-person bed by herself and drifts off into slumber.

Concurrently, Jadeanu and Ren continue wandering through the city. "These people really seem not to know that Ava has powers," Jadeanu tells Ren. "Yeah, I think she's like Jinzen. She can turn them on and off at will. How is it that they can do that?" "I've got no clue, but we should rest now. It's getting late. We'll need rest if we're going to take on a woman like that." Jadeanu and Ren find an abandoned home and take a rest in it.

Morning arrives, and Ava wakes up. She gets out of bed, and she is still a masterpiece in looks. She then prepares to get ready for work. She brushes her teeth and combs her hair. After that, she picks out her outfit. "Today makes me feel as if darkness is coming." She grabs one of her favorite black full-body jumpsuits. It complements her body well, showing a little cleavage to enhance her sex appeal. She throws on some black flats and holds her wedding ring necklace tight.

"I know you wouldn't approve of this, but the combat of your warmth is no longer here, and the monster inside must act." She looks out her window and notices a beautiful sunny day. She heads down her stairs and enters her kitchen. She cooks herself up a nice wholesome breakfast. She makes pancakes, oatmeal, a salad with fruit in it, and a fruit smoothie. After she eats, she washes her dishes and cleans her counters.

"The haunt of this echoing house, haunted with memories of the past," she says with a sigh as she walks in front of a mirror and gazes at the ring dangling near her breasts. "I love you, but I don't want you back. This is how things are now." Ava walks out of the door of her mansion. Then through the gate around her yard.

She walks to Chris's house, which isn't far. She doesn't knock or anything; she just sits down on his porch. Soon, she moves her pupils to the right and sees Chris coming her way. She stands up and puts on a wide smile. "Hey Chris!" she says in her enchanting feminine voice. He panics for a second, then he notices Ava. "Oh, hey Ava." "I knew you were coming, so I waited for you." "You remembered my address? Well anyway, what's up?" "I want to ask you on a date after I'm done with my work. I want you to come to my mansion after sunset. I'll come by and pick you up. Sound good?"

Chris is perplexed by the amazing look of Ava's glimmering purple eyes in the sun's light. "Um, yeah. I would love to." "Well great! I've got to go now, I'll see you tonight!" Ava walks away. Chris breathes in relief due to an abrupt collection of nervousness in his heart. He smiles and enters his house. Ava continues walking to work.

As she passes through the alleyway, an average-built guy with glowing blue eyes looks Ava up and down. Ava notices him and he starts to become a bit nervous. "What are you looking at?" she replies. "Ava, I presume," the guy says. Ava nods. "I don't know what you're trying to achieve, but I know you're up to no good. You probably want to overthrow the mayor and become some kind of dictator, don't you? I've also noticed that people tend to die when they're around you."

"Is that so?" "Plus if you want to be an inspiration to others, you shouldn't walk around dressed like that. It's degrading. H-having your breasts all out and clothes tight enough to parade your body to everyone." "Aww, are you saying that because you like what you see?" "Of course not!" "You don't have to lie to me. You're definitely staring all at my voluptuous body. Is it pleasing to you? You strike me as unpopular with women. The little stutter in your voice says it all." "S-so what? I prefer quality over quantity anyway." "Oh, but am I not quality? One touch of my body will make your nose bleed won't it? You don't have any quality women to divert your attention from me."

Ava walks closer to the guy, and he starts slowly backing up. She gets close and leans in to his ear and whispers, "You want to know why I wear clothes like this? It's not to impress boys or get attention. I do it because they don't restrict my movements when I kill, and blood washes off the skin pretty easily. So the more skin I show, the better."

The guy jumps back quickly in shock. "That's it; I'm taking you off the streets. Your rose and strawberry scent of death won't curse anyone else." "Hehehahaha!" Ava laughs as she turns her eyes red, and her right forearm returns to its insidious look. "I knew it! You are something to be feared!" the man claims as he throws a punch at Ava. She sidesteps it easily and moves in. She takes special care to ensure that her boobs graze his extended arm in her motion. He retracts immediately in embarrassment, then his vision goes dark for a moment.

He feels something cold on his cheek. He tries to grasp his environment, but his vision is now slightly altered. He notices something to the side of him. He looks to see what it is, moving only his eyes. He notices a huge pair of legs. He follows the legs up to see the rest of the person. He sees a rather tall, looks like, male figure. He scans to see the face of the towering guy, but he instead views the guy's bloody neck with no head on top. It doesn't take long for him to realize that the guy he is looking at is his own body. He then notices Ava in front of him, smiling triumphantly at his severed head. Her eyes return to their natural color, and her arm returns to normal. She walks away as the man loses consciousness and his body falls down.

Later, she ends up at her job. Jeremy is the first to greet her. "Ava, the company's bigwigs are all on their way to see you." "Great! Everything's in order then." "Hey Ava!" William calls. "You didn't tell me you were going to see the mayor today! That was OUR plan!" "I told one of your spies I borrowed from you to tell you," Ava responds.

"You were supposed to give me the heads up yourself beforehand!" "Tough luck big boy, but it looks like I run the show now. It would behoove you to get out of my way William." "Do I need to remind you that my wife died because of the mayor not doing anything to help our city? We were supposed to oppose him together." "Must I tell you that I'm the one who killed her because I knew you had hate in your heart and resources that I could use?"

William gets increasingly angry. "Raphael! Anthony! Seize this woman!" he calls, and now everyone in the room starts paying attention to the hostile situation, but they are all still too far from the two to make out what else they are saying, yet no one makes a move despite hearing William's first command.

"Aw. Looks like they don't listen to you anymore. But I've got an idea. Why don't we just do our jobs and pretend this whole thing didn't happen?" "You mean I do all the work, and you profit by going to meet the mayor without me. Sorry, but I'm done being belittled by you. You're lucky you're a woman, or I would punch you in the gut and watch you writhe in agony and repent for what you did to my wife."

Ava smiles. "Oh would you? You'd hit me in the gut? Well hit me then. By all means, try; it's all you can do when in the presence of superiority. It's the least you could do to avenge your blood stain of a wife. Turn your fantasies into reality! Hit me! Go on. You gonna do it, or are you going to do your job like a good boy?" William rages and punches Ava in the stomach with all his force.

Due to William not having powers, he only pushes Ava back and toward the ground with his force. She holds her gut upon going down. She smiles and lands on the tips of her toes. She's really concealing her arm as it shifts to its demonic claw, and her eyes turn red. She lunges at William and rips through his neck like it's made of paper. She looks at her arm and pretends to be scared. She turns to William's dead body and forces herself to nearly gag. She conveys herself convincingly enough that everyone runs to comfort her.

"I didn't, I didn't…William's…he's…." Tears stream down Ava's cheeks, and she displays herself as a beautiful crier. On the inside, she's really laughing. "Ava it's okay," the people comfort. "You've just awoken your powers. You must not have had control of them." "What is going on here?!" Jefferson says, coming to the scene.

"Ava awoke her powers and accidentally killed William," Jeremy informs. "Ava. Are you in control now?" Jefferson asks. "Yeah." *Sniff* "I hope so. I don't want to hurt anyone else." "You'll be alright Ava," Jeremy reassures. "Once you awaken your powers, I don't think you can lose control again."

"Get yourself situated Ava. We'll take care of William. You've still got a meeting to attend if you're up for it," Jefferson tells. Ava wipes her false tears and smiles sympathetically. "Yeah, okay. I still want to go but are you sure it will be safe for me to?" "I trust your opinion. After all, it's your body. You'd know that better than I would." "Thank you Jefferson." "The Mayor of Brigham City is waiting for you at Town Hall. Do you need a ride?"

"I'll take her," Jeremy volunteers. Jeremy takes Ava to his car, and they both get in. "Hmhmhmhmhmhmhmhm," Ava laughs. "It's good that you chose now to show your powers. Genius planning as always," Jeremy claims. "You ready for this?" "Greatly. Have you got them?" "Yes, everything went even better than planned. And still, no one suspects that you created the karaoke company."

They drive up to Town Hall and get out of the car. Ava goes up to the building, opens the doors, and enters with confidence. Her gaze immediately meets with the mayor's from across the room sitting at a desk with two guards with red eyes, one at each of the mayor's shoulders. She struts across the room with her captivating red eyes never leaving the mayor's eyes. In the room, there are several guards lined up side by side holding guns of all kinds on the side walls of the building, ready to shoot if Ava was to try something.

"Mrs. Ramada. It has come to my attention that you want to speak with me about our city's well-being," Mayor McKenzi states. "I go to your karaoke place quite often. I love the atmosphere. I feel inclined to speak with an unsatisfied manager." Ava blinks slowly and flips her hair.

"Yes, you see. I'm afraid your rule must come to an end." Ava raises her arms. "You are no longer needed, McKenzi." Ava snaps her fingers, and both walls lined with guards explode, killing them all. The mayor stands up and tries to make a run for it, but he bumps into Jeremy, who is holding two knives painted in blood.

Both of the mayor's personal bodyguards are also dead with slits in their throats. The mayor turns to run the other way, but Ava is already in his face. She points the claws on her demonic arm at the mayor's throat. "Don't kill me!" he cries. "Don't worry, I won't. As long as you announce me as the leader of Brigham City and resign." "You are the new leader of Brigham City." "Not here. Come with me."

Ava leads the mayor outside only to see dozens of people, some of which have cameras. Ava ensures to look as nonmenacing as possible to allow what is about to happen to look natural. "Now say it!" Ava demands silently. "People of Brigham City. I hereby resign from my duties as Mayor. Please accept Ava as your new leader."

The people erupt in cheer, and some wave signs in support of Ava. Some of the signs say, "Mayor Ava!" or "We love Ava." Many of the people yell, "Queen Ava! Queen Ava!"; with certain glee. Ava smiles triumphantly at her supportive people. She has successfully conquered an entire city, and no one even seems to suspect any suspicious behavior. In fact, people think of her as a queen. Steve and the guy known as Raphael are both in the crowd and give her a thumbs up. She also notices that there is a middle-aged tall white guy with combed-over black hair trying to make his way through the crowd to get to Ava. That person is Jefferson.

"What is this Ava? You overthrew the mayor! That evil arm of yours must have gotten to you!" he says. "The only thing in control of Ava is herself," Jeremy says. "If this arm was controlling me, you'd be dead now. Be thankful for your life," Ava states. "How dare you talk to me like that!" "I'm sorry, who are you again? Merely the "founder" of a karaoke business. I'm the Queen of this city. How quick it was to go from under you to mountains above you. Oh, and by the way, I'm the one who started your little business anyway." "Now you speak nonsense! I founded the place and made it the hope of the people."

"Do you remember a week ago? You were just a businessman out of a job. You were walking to your house to attempt suicide when you heard, *'There was a huge place so fun, it gave people stability and hope. Hope that things could get better, so they went there every day to forget their problems.'* Do you remember those words?"

"No…" Jefferson says, not to answer Ava's question but in the realization of something mentally controversial. "Those words weren't said by me, but it was a child's voice that I placed there for you to hear. And you took the idea along with a suggestion of a karaoke place by hearing my singing voice. You thought it was an angel showing you a way and saving you from suicide. But it was me, using you. It's amazing how humans indulge in self-delusions for their foolish pursuit of salvation. I made you, Jefferson. Now I don't want to destroy you, so enjoy your position as the head of my company. I'll no longer be needing it."

"Well then, Jeremy, you're fired for this treachery." "Great! I don't need you either. I have Ava." Jefferson stomps off, feeling powerless. Ava and Jeremy walk through the crowd. Everyone paves a path for their new leader. She waves at Steve and stops when Raphael steps in her path. He looks at her sparkling face, and then his eyes travel down to her cleavage.

"They're real," Ava says. Raphael immediately fills with embarrassment. "For helping me get this recognition, you can touch them if you want." "No. I'm sorry, I shouldn't have been-" His sentence is interrupted as Ava grabs his wrist and places his hand on her boob. She laughs as she lets him go and walks past him. Raphael just stands there looking astonished. He looks back at Ava, who is looking back at him while walking forward with a sly smile on her face, and her hand on her hip, conveying her authority.

She continues walking through the crowd until she sees Chris at the end of it. She tells Jeremy to wait in the crowd. "Hey Chris!" "Hey Ava! Someone told me that you were going to become the new Queen of the city, but wow. You even have powers! It's all amazing to see! I'm happy for you." "Thank you. Now I told you I would take you to my house right? Just let me talk to my friend real quick okay?" "Yeah no problem." Ava goes back to Jeremy.

"So Ava. It's been fun, but this doesn't have to be goodbye does it?" Jeremy asks. "Can I work as your advisor or something?" "Jeremy, you have helped me a lot. You're the only one who was an actual ally to me. I will never forget your help, but I prefer to work alone." "I know that, but there's got to be room for me. I don't want to leave your side. I know that you could have done all of this by yourself, but please-"

"I'm sorry Jeremy. But I must go alone. You're free now. This world must kneel before my lone superiority. You can still serve me but only at your own leisure, okay? I will no longer give you orders. Now I've got to go." Ava leaves Jeremy and goes to Chris. "Now let's go." Ava takes Chris's hand, and they begin walking. Jeremy just stares in silence.

In a far distance, Ren wakes up in the morning on his own. He looks at Jadeanu's bed and notices that he's not there, but his sword is up against the wall. Ren grabs the weapon and searches the house. Eventually, he hears something from outside. It sounds like a male voice singing.

'There is so much chaos in this land we call Earth. A heart so warm but grows so cold by the storm that girths. All our twists and spins are mementos of where we've been. But now our journey together has come to an end. And I will never see you again.' Ren comes outside to see Jadeanu singing those lyrics and his voice actually isn't bad. "Jadeanu, are you going to be okay?" Ren questions. "Yeah, I just had a dream, and Luke was in it. It made me think. But I'm fine. No more sulking.

I have a mission to complete." Jadeanu grabs his sword from Ren. "You ready to keep searching for Ava?" Ren nods.

Later, as the sun begins to set, Ava arrives at her home with Chris. She and he walked all the way there. Wow, your house is huge! That's all yours?" Chris wonders. Ava nods as she opens her gate and lets Chris into her yard. Then she ends up unlocking and opening her door to let him inside her home. "This place is beautiful!" Chris appreciates looking at the spacious and luxurious home. "Come with me Chris." Ava leads Chris through her house and into her mostly empty training room.

"We're done. You can go home now," Ava tells him with a hint of callousness in her tone. "What!?" "Your assistance is no longer necessary. You remember your way out right?" "If you're kicking me out, why did you even bring me here?" "I said I'd bring you here, and I did. I have other reasons though." "But what do you mean we're done? Did I do something wrong? We never even got the chance to be together."

"Listen, Chris. I never liked you and I never will. In fact, it's rather insulting that you even thought someone like you would even have a chance with someone like me. I'm greater than you in every way. I was merely using you. You've done great in raising my peer relation with my co-workers and your excitement for my upbringing brought many supporters to my inauguration. I manipulated all of that, and you fell for it when you fell for me. Men will do a lot for a woman they love, but now I no longer want you around. Your exile from my life will be better for both of us."

"So I meant nothing to you?" "No one means anything to me." "Not even your employees?" "Nope, all just pawns in my game. And most of them know it. They just adore me enough to stick around. My husband was the only one who ever had my unconditional love." "You were married?" "So caught up in your emotions, you've never once seen my wedding ring dangling next to my tits."

Chris starts to experience evident shame clearly on his face. "Now I'll give you a chance; leave my house!" Ava commands. "No! Just... not yet. I-I'm not going to let you do this to me!" Chris responds. "Then you forfeit your ability to leave my house alive. If one enters my life and has no use for me, their existence is no longer necessary." "I gave you all that time, all I had left to give, and this is what you do to me! No! I'm not just going to leave!" "I thought you might say that."

Ava pushes a button on the wall of her room next to the light switch, and music starts to play. The song is slow and romantic, but it is only an instrumental so there are no words. Ava smiles and starts moving her body with the rhythm of the song. She grabs Chris's hand and tries to get him to move with her. He stands and lets her do all the moving; he is too appalled to struggle.

"I'm going to fight you. To the death," Ava whispers in his ear. "It's not good to hold in that anger. That malice is building in you. Release it on me, and don't disappoint." Ava twirls around Chris, then dances away from him, letting go of his hand. "Consider yourself lucky. I usually don't fight people. I usually go straight for the kill." Ava knees Chris in the gut, then uppercuts him with her demonic arm. Blood spurts out of his mouth as he rises high into the air and lands headfirst on the marble floor.

'I can tell by the look in your eye. That you want your heart to be mine,' Ava sings while dancing closer to Chris. He starts to stand up while wiping the blood from his face. Ava kicks him and hastily moves past him, clawing into his rib with her claws. He grabs his bleeding ribs.

"If you don't fight back, I'll make sure you suffer for it." "How could you be so evil?!" "That is a question many men have to ask women. The truth is that you men give us women too much power over you. The sad truth is that we women weren't made to use power in noble and responsible ways, so we use it to get what we want or what we think we want. The blame is on both of us though. We women generally use power selfishly, and you men give us that supremacy.

Afterall when a man gets wealthy, he usually thinks about how to use it to provide the best for the people close to him. But when a woman gets wealthy, the first thing they think about is how they don't need men and typically detatch from them and provide only for themselves. Destroying the mental health of the very sex that made them. Which only destroys us both in the long run. It's not like it's a secret. Just take a look around you."

Ava cuts Chris across the back, then backhands his spine hard enough to push him several feet forward. Ava starts singing again. *'Commit to someone who you can listen to. Commit to someone who's just like you.'* Ava rushes to Chris and knee's him in the nose, drawing blood and sending him backward. Ava keeps up with him and grabs his arm, breaks it at the elbow, then cuts it and pulls it off, making a bloody mess all over her brown marble floor. Chris whimpers in pain holding the stump that was once his arm. "Why...me?" Ava smiles. "Because you let me."

Ava kicks him to make him lie on his back. She slowly presses her five sharp demonic fingers into his stomach. He screams and then kicks toward Ava. She dodges, and Chris stands up and then throws a punch. Ava evades it and socks him in the nose with her demonic claw. "Hehehe." "Stop laughing!" Chris demands with sheer rage in his voice. "HeheheHAHAHA!"

She stabs one of his eyes and then claws through his face in the same motion. "AAAhhUUuGGhh! You monster!" he screams in a mix of anger and pain. "I never said I was human." Ava grabs Chris's shirt firmly and punches Chris in the liver with tons of force from her demonic arm. He crumbles to his knees, gasping for air. "Please….. kill..me." he says with absolute defeat in his voice. "Gladly!"

Ava cuts Chris's head clean off. "Hahahahahaha! That was fun, wasn't it arm?!" The arm starts to glow as if communicating to Ava.

She looks at Chris's dead body. "I guess I'll have to clean that up." Ava grabs the body and takes it outside, and soon comes back without it. She returns to her training room and turns off the music. She turns her powers off and gets to scrubbing the blood off her floor.

Eventually, she ends up cleaning the floor till it shines. "All done. Now I haven't eaten since this morning. I'm not that hungry, but I could eat. I guess I'll treat myself to some quality food. Hmm, maybe that fancy restaurant, Le Nonne." Ava walks out of her front door and goes through her fence. She starts to her usual alley shortcut. She notices two guys with red eyes seemingly waiting for her. Those two are Jadeanu and Ren.

"You're Ava, aren't you?" Jadeanu questions. "That's right. Now who are you?" Ava responds. "I'm Jadeanu, and this is Ren." Ren looks at Ava with astonishment clear on his face. His heart is currently beating intensely in admiration of Ava's inhuman beauty. *'The King of Elko wasn't kidding. She is definitely the most beautiful woman I've ever seen.' 'What's up with weirdos appearing in this alley in these last two days?'* Ava thinks.

"What do you two want?" "We want to put an end to the evil you cause. I can't pass through here knowing that you're out here killing and torturing people, along with spreading fear and manipulating these people," Jadeanu claims. "The person who led us here didn't even know how monstrous you are. It's sickening." "Listen Jadeanu. Earlier today, there was a guy who wanted to do exactly that. To "stop me." It didn't end so well for him. And second, Ren doesn't seem to be concerned about stopping me. It must suck to be lovestruck when first meeting someone. Even though it's not love you're feeling. Rather just admiration of my aesthetic."

"Ren!" Jadeanu calls. "I don't like her!" Ren exclaims. "Liar," Ava reveals. "Anata wa watashi no karada o aishite iru dakedesu yo ne? (You love my body, don't you?)." "What?" "Haha, I'm just playing with you. But if you are do-gooders, I can appreciate your desires. However, I don't want to kill you, so it would be best if you stay out of my way." "I'm not going anywhere and you'll be the one to die," Jadeanu responds. "And how do you propose you'll kill me? Those little Blessings of yours?"

Jadeanu's heart drops. *'How does she know about the Blessings?'* "Yeah, we'll crush you with these." "Please. I can hear the doubt in your voice. You haven't mastered them, and even if you did, it would take time to use one of them. Their powers are finite. In the time it would take you to attack with one of those things, I could kill you both five times over. But you know, I don't have a problem with do-gooders like you." "And why is that?"

"Because the concepts of good and evil interest me. Most people want to be good, but they have no idea what good even is. People nowadays only look for what is best and most convenient. Afraid of resistance. They go against each other with vanities, hoping to find an easy path to follow. They either look for the best or try to destroy it because it's what's easy for them. And because they want the best, they always end at my feet.

They follow me, disregarding all other beliefs in their own pit of weakness. Do you want to know what I believe? I believe that good and evil are one and the same. Just two sides of the same coin, like love and hate. Those who would do the greatest good could also do the greatest evil if prompted enough. It doesn't matter how good you are. It can all be changed into the very thing you despise."

"Yeah right. The line between good and evil is clear. You're wrong to think that the good of the gods is anything like your diabolical behavior. You're just trying to justify the horrors you've caused." "You don't believe me? Well then, you don't like manipulating people into doing your bidding right? That's just such an evil, inhumane thing, isn't it? Well think about your journey. Surely a feeling of fear has driven you to trick someone into defeating themselves, right? You've manipulated someone into the very thing that defeated them; tell me I'm wrong."

Jadeanu thinks back to his first encounter with Jinzen and how he tricked him into getting into the genie lamp. He realizes that she is right about that. "How? How do you know that?" he asks. "I can see it in your eyes," Ava responds. "They say the eyes are the windows to the soul, and I see your soul clearly. Your eyes tell me your entire journey leading up to me. You can learn a lot about a person just by looking at them.

You've had some hardships, seen amazing things, and lost a lot of people, even someone dear to you. I'm guessing you were married, and the Death Spiral turned you into a widower. You lost her, and it hurts doesn't it? Like you've lost a part of yourself. You feel like trying your best to find peace with it and move on. Trying to find some light in your darkened life. Though I'm guessing a part of you wants to just join the one you've lost despite being afraid to die. You know you're willing to accept it; that's why you put yourself through nearly impossible situations hoping that something will finally lay you to rest. But the fear of death keeps you going, am I right?

But I see someone else. There was someone else who kept you going, but then they were recently killed, and that loss is just ripping you apart isn't it? And deep down inside, the cure to it all, the thing you want the most is just to feel the soft, embracing lips of the woman you've promised your life to. But you know you'll never experience it again, so you stay fighting.

I can see that you both are strong. You've grown strong on your journey. I can admire that. Neither of you are as strong as I am, but you're strong in your own right. And because you're strong, you have my respect. I despise weaklings. I can tolerate them, but I can't care about them. Their deaths are meaningless to me. And yeah, I know that makes me sound evil, but in truth, I just don't care. All that matters to me now is my will. And I will see it through."

"And that is why you must go down. Weaker people still have a place in this world." "You see, weaklings are consumed by fear and too afraid to freely live their lives. They are trapped in their own spiral of death, so when this one happened, it was just too much for many to handle. That's why they get in the way. They are just burdens that we strong people have to carry. They cause problems and can't dare fix them.

Sure they have a place in the world, but not in my world. And they will realize their sin of weakness in the wake of my strength. Getting in my way, causing nothing but a bunch of problems. Because they have little concept of the future, only the present. I despise weakness and burdens, but I just simply can't care enough about the people who create them to hate them."

"So what if they get in the way sometimes? They can be good and do good. Just that is worth fighting for. It doesn't matter how much they screw up and how many issues they create; in the end, we all have to continue fighting for what we want. Sometimes their problems are set here to make others stronger. So we can give purpose to their flaws!"

"I like you Jadeanu. You are quite perceptive. If I had a daughter, I'd let you have her hand in marriage in a heartbeat. I'd rather leave you alive and let you run free. But I've got things to do. All that matters is power. And with it, I will be supreme. I will rule over the weak, so they will know their place. If you stand in my way, you will suffer the consequences."

Ava's eyes turn red, and her arm goes into its demonic form. "You know, I don't really care about what is good and evil. I've got things to do on this Earth. I won't be cursed on it with no promise of a desired afterlife. My power is all I need to create whatever I want. A power that many women have specifically. We women have so much power but little room to control it. That's why we search for the guidance of men. Due to the insatiable desires of women, they lose sight of their power, and so they want more. But I know my power, and I will use it. So much power that women have and don't know it. It's truly amazing. But I won't lose sight of mine. So I hope you are ready Ren and Jadeanu. Here I come!"

Chapter 12:
Survive

Ava moves towards Jadeanu, slightly looking down at him, conveying her height of about two inches taller than both Jadeanu and Ren, who are the same height. Jadeanu swings his blade, and she blocks it with her demonic arm, which deflects his attack. She counters with a swift left hook then a right three-inch punch to his stomach. Jadeanu flies and hits the side of the building next to him. Ava turns to Ren, and his heart starts beating exponentially. She vanishes and appears behind Ren, then touches his back with her normal left hand. Ren nearly panics. *Is she able to teleport?'* he thinks. "Whoa!" Jadeanu says astonished. "She moved so fast that it looked like she teleported. That could be troublesome."

Ren hurries and turns around to attack with his shadow. Ava moves behind Ren again. "You move quick," she says before she palms his back, sending him far forward. Jadeanu runs to her while her back is turned, charges his hands with energy, and swings his sword. She turns around quickly and blocks the sword with her demonic arm, then brings her claws toward Jadeanu's throat, stopping just inches in front of it. She retracts her hand, and Jadeanu swings his sword again. Ava blocks it and attacks his neck again, stopping short once again. They continue this several more times. Ava never killing Jadeanu then and there.

'She's fast enough to attack twice with that arm before I can attack once. She's just mocking me. She could kill me at any time,' Jadeanu thinks. *'Even with my added energy for speed, I can't compete with her. Swinging my blade isn't gonna do me any good.'* Ava back fists Jadeanu right on the nose with her demon claw which knocks him on his butt.

Ren uses her shadow to sneak attack her in the back with a spike. Her demon right arm immediately grabs the spike. She turns and looks at it, then squeezes it until it liquefies back into her shadow. *'Her arm moved on its own,'* Ren hypothesizes. "Ava. Is that arm of yours alive?"

"Yes it is. He can move on his own but only when I'm not using him," Ava answers. "He can't talk but he can communicate with me with energy waves. Rather I can feel his energy with my intuition and translate it. With that, he tries to take over my mind. His thoughts are usually the same. Death and destruction. Also defending me. Don't worry, me letting you know this information won't affect me much."

Jadeanu sneaks behind Ava and swings his blade. Ava moves at incredible speed and seemingly disappears. "Where'd she go?" Jadeanu asks Ren. Ren shakes his head. "You don't listen well do you?!" she yells. Jadeanu and Ren look up and see Ava on top of the skyscraper in front of them. She jumps down. "What? No human, even with powers, can survive a fall like that," Jadeanu says as he backs up, giving Ava room to go splat.

She aims her demonic hand's pointer finger toward the ground. The moment she lands, a red explosion wave comes from her arm and hits Ren and Jadeanu. It doesn't cause much damage to them, but it was certainly painful to feel. The wave clears fast, and Ava's finger is drilled into the ground. Her body is standing upside down with her finger as the foundation holding her up. Smoke emits from her body, but she is unscathed. She flicks the ground which frees her finger and tosses her up enough to front flip back on her feet.

"Well now she's just flexin' on us," Ren points out. Jadeanu attacks again with his sword. Before he completes his attack, he is tackled into the other nearby skyscraper. She sends him through the wall and then up all the floors. In just three seconds, she jumps through the ceiling of the giant building, holding Jadeanu by the face. She then walks to the edge of the building and jumps off, holding Jadeanu's face towards the ground. She has a wide smile across her face as they both descend.

"I can catch him," Ren says as he leaves the alley and moves to the street where Ava will land. He looks and notices that Ava's pushing Jadeanu down. "No I can't! I'm sorry, but I think you're on your own Jadeanu." Jadeanu tries to attack, but all he can see is the glow of Ava's demonic arm covering his eyes. All he can feel is the fast-moving wind on his body. Jadeanu decides to aim his sword toward the ground. As he is about to hit the ground, his sword goes into the pavement, taking all the momentum. It's fortunate for Jadeanu that his sword is nearly indestructible.

An explosive wave emits from Ava's arm and consumes Jadeanu. The explosion is only big enough to cover both of their bodies. Jadeanu falls next to his sword with steam radiating off of him. Ava lets go of him and stands up. Her shadow attacks her with spikes that she hastily dodges. Jadeanu's shadow attacks and Ava spins elegantly away from it.

Ren comes close and attacks with his shadow sword. Ava limbos under it and slices through all three shadows, rendering Ren temporarily powerless. She flexes her left leg, which bulges with a non-feminine amount of muscle, and then kicks Ren in the jaw, nearly breaking his neck in the process. She grabs him by the face and slams him into the concrete hard enough to crack it. She then lifts him and tosses him hard against the same skyscraper she dived from. Ren's body makes large cracks in the wall. He falls with blood dripping from his nose. Jadeanu struggles to get up after healing himself slightly with the Nature Blessing.

"Oh! You ready for some more?" Ava says. She slowly reaches her demon hand towards Jadeanu's face. He powers both of his hands with red energy and pushes against Ava's demonic arm. His elbows start bending in, and his arms move toward his face. Ava is overpowering him. *'Come on! I'm pushing with both arms here and I'm still not strong enough.'*

She grabs him by the neck with her other arm and lifts him up. Ren runs to save Jadeanu. "Stop right there Ren! Or I'll drill my hand straight through his stomach," Ava tells. Ren stops running in his tracks and wipes his still-bleeding nose. "Listen, both of you. Do we really have to fight? This is senseless. Neither of us has anything to gain by killing each other." Ava lets Jadeanu down. "You two are strong. There is no need for me to kill you. Are you two really set on stopping me?"

"We must stop you Ava," Jadeanu says. "You are a tower of evil influence. We have friends in Elko that you want to kill. We are instruments of the gods, and I can't pass up an evildoer. You must go down no matter what!" Ava smiles.

"Well then, let's make things interesting," she says. As she speaks, Jadeanu uses the Nature Blessing to heal himself and Ren. "How about we have a test of strength and honor. Let's fight and really fight. You two against me. Whoever is beaten to the point of being unable to defend themselves, may be killed. Only when beaten. No instant kills. No outside forces, no Blessings. Only our powers and weapons, so you may use your sword Jadeanu.

If you two may defeat me before I defeat you, you may kill me. That'll make things fun won't it? Do we have a deal?" Jadeanu and Ren exchange looks. "Um…" "What's the matter? Don't you trust this face?" "No!" both boys yell. "Hahahahahaha. Let's begin! Let's fight as if our lives depend on it because it most certainly does!"

Ava smiles, and a powerful red aura envelopes her body. "That pressure. She's definitely stronger than that assassin we faced," Jadeanu says. "I should add that any breaking of the rules will result in immediate death," Ava adds. She lunges at Jadeanu who does the same. They both slam their right fists into each other's. Jadeanu retracts his energy enhanced fist. *'If I didn't have this gauntlet on, my bones definitely would have been shattered in my hand.'*

"So your power is the ability to strengthen certain parts of your body," Ava claims. "That means you actually have to be able to fight to use your powers. Just like mine." Ava sweep-kicks Jadeanu, then grabs his face again. She slams him into the concrete and then tosses him into a brick wall nearby. The moment his back hits the wall, she dropkicks him through it.

She turns to Ren. Her shadow grabs her feet and sows them to the ground. Her shadow comes from the ground as a mirage of herself and puts her into a chokehold. She looks around to study the situation, then at Ren. Ren is holding a shadow bow and arrow with four arrows on it. "Oh, clever," Ava says.

She destroys her shadow self and dashes out of the way of the arrows. She front flips, and her legs land on Ren's shoulders. She grips his head with her knees then backflips, tossing him toward the broken wall where Jadeanu is. She runs over there and catches Ren by the collar before he lands. She looks at his face and says, "Hey," before tossing him on the ground.

'Her breath smells like spearmint,' Ren thinks. Ren and Jadeanu stand up. "Plan. Without that arm, she has no power. Let's restrain it," Ren plans. Ren uses his shadow to grab her demon arm and spring himself to it. He tries his best to hold her hand down as she lifts it at him. Jadeanu runs to try to help restrain her arm. She simply snaps, and an explosive wave covers the whole area. All three of them steam, but only Jadeanu and Ren are damaged and fall down.

"It's even worse than Javean's," Jadeanu establishes. "It doesn't push you back; it just burns you." They both stand back up. Jadeanu adds energy to his left leg and does a Thai roundhouse. Ava ducks and tackles Jadeanu's other leg. Once she pins him to the ground getting ready to pummel him, Ren uses Jadeanu's shadow to attack her from the side with a hammer. She rolls off of Jadeanu and Jadeanu gets up.

"New plan," he starts. "She moves too fast for us to hit. But she has long hair that can't move on its own. We should be able to grab and yank it to get a hit." "Great idea. She won't see it coming." Jadeanu moves in and attacks. He goes for a low kick. She jumps back. Ren gets behind her and uses his shadow to try to grab her hair. Her demon arm instantly moves and slices the shadow. She looks in Ren's direction, causing her hair to flip towards Jadeanu, who immediately grabs a handful of her hair.

He wraps it around his arm and yanks her down. Instinctively, her demon arm grabs his arm and squeezes exceptionally hard. Jadeanu still perseveres. He goes for a punch to Ava's face. She smiles slyly and brings her legs up. She places Jadeanu into a triangle choke and brings him toward the floor with her downward momentum. She squeezes his neck so hard with her thighs that they bulge with extreme muscular definition.

'My goodness! She smells like strawberries mixed with some kind of flower. It's so good,' Jadeanu thinks. He doesn't even try to get out of her hold. *'I've had whiffs of it while we were fighting, but being here, this close to her, it's amazing.'* Jadeanu's airways have been blocked for a short while. Time is running out for him. *'You know, dying like this doesn't sound so bad.'*

Ren attacks Ava with her shadow. Ava slaps the ground with her demonic hand and blasts herself into the air away from it. She releases Jadeanu, and he can breathe again. He gets up quickly and throws a punch toward Ava, red energy on both of his hands. Ava's demonic arm consciously catches his fist, to which he responds with another quick jab. It lands but Ava tanks the hit and then smiles as she hits Jadeanu with a counter hook from her demon fist, knocking him to the ground. "It's about time I landed something," Jadeanu mentions triumphantly.

Ava's smile gets wider, and her pearly whites become visible again. Her demonic claw grows and gains more pinkish-red spikes. "Good. Now I can go all out!" she exclaims. "Ah crap. She's getting stronger. So this is what King Elcero was talking about," Jadeanu recognizes. Jadeanu and Ren stand side by side.

Ava reaches her demon arm out towards them, then triggers an explosion blowing them both back. She comes up close to them and punches downward towards Jadeanu's descending face. Jadeanu moves his head just in time. Her demonic fist cracks the ground on impact. Jadeanu stands up and pulls Ren up, adding energy to his arm.

Ava and Jadeanu go hand to hand, which ends up with Ava dodging one of Jadeanu's attacks and counters punching Jadeanu into a building. *I'm too slow when I use my shadow as a weapon. I can't fight on their level like this,'* Ren thinks. *'Oh wait. Yes I can!'* Ren says while making shadow gauntlets around his hands. Ava turns in his direction and is face-to-fist with a stretching shadow gauntlet.

Her demonic arm extends to her side, and it seems like she is yanked along with it. Ava closes in and kicks Ren on his left thigh. He starts to fall but holds his ground despite the pain. He throws a punch with the arm that Jadeanu had strengthened with energy previously. She grabs his arm with her demon arm and clenches it tight. Red energy runs through her arm to her palm. The shadow gauntlet continues to extend past Ava. It makes a turn, then comes back and hits Ava on the head. The red energy from Jadeanu's enhancement disappears with the connected attack.

Irritated, Ava lets go of Ren's arm, which is now coated in red energy, and kicks Ren's thigh again. This time, Ren goes down but still holds up on his other leg. Ava kicks that leg too. Ren falls to his knees, facing the ground. He looks up only to see Ava's leg above his face and next to her own. She lets her leg down with force on top of Ren's head, forcing him to eat the concrete. She steps on Ren's head in triumph as Jadeanu approaches. She picks Ren up and tosses him at Jadeanu, who catches him. Ava snaps her fingers, and Ren's red glowing arm explodes on both him and Jadeanu.

Ava dashes past both of them and places her demonic hand on the floor. She adds a massive amount of energy to the ground, then gets up and runs. Jadeanu and Ren stand up. Jadeanu adds energy to Ren's right arm but excludes the left one because it is all burnt up from the explosion Ava put in it. "You okay?" Jadeanu asks. "I've been through worse," Ren responds.

They start to give chase but notice the red energy on the floor as they run. Ava picks up a car with just her demonic claw, fills it with energy and chunks it at her pursuers. Then she jumps up and places her demon arm into the side of an occupied skyscraper. She clings onto the wall about seven stories in the air and fills the place with energy as she holds on. Jadeanu and Ren avoid the car which explodes once it gets close to them, nearly catching them in the blast. Then they approach the combustible floor.

"As long as we go nowhere near it, we should be fine right?" Jadeanu asks. "I don't know," Ren answers. Jadeanu leads Ren around the land mine. They both run as fast as their hurt bodies will enable them. The moment they come close to the building, Ava jumps off of it, and the part she was holding onto explodes into a large burst of her energy, knocking the boys back. The building catches on fire and then comes crashing down toward Ren and Jadeanu.

Ava soars and flips away from the carnage but then comes back and saves the boys. She takes them both away from the chaos by their collars. People start running out of the building, some on fire yet they all scream in horror. Ava just watches and smiles. The building crashes on top of all survivors, filling the area in smoke and blood.

Ava starts laughing and drops Ren and Jadeanu. "You monster!" Jadeanu calls out. "All those people!" "Oh, please! If they weren't so weak, they would have lived!"

Jadeanu throws a punch to Ava's cheek. She catches it and counters with her normal hand. She starts wailing at him constantly. He guards the best he can, but then Ava picks him up by his neck with her demonic hand and triggers two small explosions before slamming him down and triggering two more while laughing maniacally.

She doesn't plan on stopping at two, but Ren attacks her with spikes from her shadow. She claws through the spikes and turns to Ren with the ravenous smile he's ever seen. She lunges at him, and fear strikes his heart. He tries to stay calm as best he can as he uses Jadeanu's shadow to move him away as he claps his hands together.

With that, he gathers all of the nearby shadows to surround and skewer Ava from all around, but not the head in order to keep her alive; only for her to be merely in a state of defeat. She simply holds out her hand and blows up all the shadows. Ren falls to a kneel due to a loss of energy from the final resort attack he just pulled. Ava moves in and grabs Ren by the face, and spirals elegantly into the air. She then crashes his face into the ground, causing an explosion of power. Ren's vision starts getting blurry as blood leaks all over his face.

The Willpower Blessing starts glowing as Jadeanu stands up. He coughs up blood. "Hey Ava! Don't forget...about me," he says. "Hmhmhmhm. Looks like someone can't defend himself," Ava claims, pointing her demon arm's finger at Ren's head. Energy gathers up to her finger, and the energy seems to be ready to fire. Jadeanu runs and tackles Ava. A thin laser beam shoots from her finger, but thanks to Jadeanu's tackle, it misses Ren and hits the distant concrete and travels up a restaurant building. The beam cuts straight through the concrete like it's paper and slices through the restaurant. Then soon, everything touched by the laser explodes. Jadeanu looks at the devastation, hoping there was no one inside the restaurant.

He turns to Ava, whom he is now on top of. "You like being on top of girls like this?" Ava teases. Jadeanu goes for a punch. Ava thrusts her pelvis, knocking Jadeanu forward, off of her. She gets up and clips his leg with her arm, then she punches him in the face. Blood spews from his mouth, but he stands his ground. She charges up another beam and presses her finger into Jadeanu's side. He sidesteps it as the beam comes out and counters with a punch. She deflects his arm with her other arm. They both jump back and take a fighting stance.

'Okay, all I've got to do is hold out for long enough,' Jadeanu plans. *'But...long enough for what? For Ren to get back up, so we both can get pummeled again? Then die? Heck, I probably would have died already had it not been for the Willpower Blessing keeping me going. Speaking of which, why hasn't she called me out for its glowing. Is it because she knows that I'm not actually using it? But how would she know that?'*

Ava goes for a Sparta kick. Jadeanu dodges it and throws a right punch. Ava blocks his arm with her demonic claw and Jadeanu hits her in the ribs with a left hook. She counters with a left uppercut. Ren watches the fight from the ground, panting from pain and exhaustion. *'Come on. Don't pass out. Don't pass out or we'll die,'* Ren says to himself.

Jadeanu takes the uppercut and grabs Ava's thigh and slams her down. She locks her legs around his head and positions herself on top of him. She throws two punches to his face. He rolls her over and takes the mount. He prepares to throw a few punches, but she starts kicking him and then does a back roll away. She and Jadeanu stand up as quickly as they can.

"You're good," Ava compliments. Jadeanu spears Ava, but she locks her arms under his chest and lifts him into a powerbomb. She drops his head into the concrete. He gets up immediately and gets behind her. He locks his arms around her waist and suplexes her into the ground. She does a headspin breakdance move to kick Jadeanu off balance. She does a backflip to quickly get up. She grabs Jadeanu and body-slams him. He lays comfortably just sitting there, considering his wounds, but he sees Ava preparing to kick him, and he moves. Ren, on the other hand, starts trying to get up.

'Come on Ren. If you can move, you can stand,' he says pushing his hands against the ground. 'Ah! My left arm.' Ren starts to get up and nearly does but then stumbles downward, catching himself with his shadow. He stands up completely and starts limping toward the fight using his shadow as a cane.

Jadeanu stands up and Ava jets to him so quickly it creates a trail of afterimages behind her. She socks Jadeanu straight in the nose with her buff demon arm. Blood springs straight from his nose. 'Now I'm sure my nose is broken,' Jadeanu claims, holding his bloody nose.

"Now that sure was fun Jadeanu!" Ava expresses. "I haven't fought like that in a while. But now you must die." Ava smiles very wide, and the demon arm spreads all the way to her shoulder. She becomes even stronger. 'She just keeps getting stronger and faster,' Jadeanu grieves. 'This is just like our fight with Ravah. A fight that could have been avoided, but my goodwill forced us into it. And now we might die, and it'll be my fault again. But I can't think like that! We got away from Ravah; we can get out of this!'

Ava runs and hits at Jadeanu. He blocks with his gauntlet yet is still sent back several feet. 'Just one more burst should do it,' Ava strategizes. She runs up to the nearby building and jumps from it. "Get back!" Ren shouts at Jadeanu as he snatches him back with his shadow. Ava punches the ground and causes an explosion at least two houses long. Jadeanu and Ren are barely out of its reach.

Once the explosion wave clears, Ava vanishes. Jadeanu feels a punch in the stomach. Ava had moved so fast he couldn't even see her. The excessive force from her attack launches Jadeanu several feet back. He spits out more blood. "Awe crap!" Ren concerns.

Ava starts laughing maniacally and her left forearm turns completely charcoal black with lines of pinkish-red energy. Turning it into another demon arm. Ava laughs extremely hard, and yet her laughter has a waver of a whining sadness in it. She starts to cry and laugh all in one. Tears of blood stream from her beautiful eyes. The saddened look in her eyes reflects a subtle internal struggle. The blood tears make a slight design on her face. They fall down her cheeks but don't drip. They turn black with a pink line of energy in the middle of each.

"She...she looks like a demon," Ren points out. "She was so beautiful; what has she become?" "Volevo solo prendere qualcosa da mangiare! Volevo solo trovare qualcosa da amare! (I just wanted something to eat! I just wanted to find something to love!)" Ava speaks before laughing again and then vanishing with her super speed. All that can be heard is semi-demonic feminine laughter echoing through the darkened streets. Jadeanu slowly approaches Ren. He puts his arm around Ren, and they both walk around together.

Ava reappears behind them and fires a beam from her right demon arm. Ren notices it, and they both separate to avoid the blast. They both look behind them and see no one there; Ava is on the move again. Jadeanu looks back to his front, only to see Ava with her left demonic arm's finger in his face charging up a laser. He can't dodge in time and is hit directly with the laser in the forehead. He is blasted back but isn't sliced up. Her left arm's laser must be different from her right arm's, lucky for Jadeanu.

She doesn't even look at Ren when she grabs him by the face and passes him to her left arm. She explodes him with her reddish-pink burst of energy and then slams him on the ground. She stomps on him and then aims her right arm at him, charging up a beam. Jadeanu tosses his blade at her, which her left arm instinctively catches. Jadeanu comes up after and dropkicks at Ava. She quickly moves back, stopping the charging of her demonic right arm. She charges up a beam from her left arm, releasing the sword.

Jadeanu grabs the sword and moves to Ava's left. Ren uses his shadow to snatch himself to her right. She unleashes a huge blast from her fingertip, about the size of Blast's Mark 3 Pyro cannon but much stronger, incinerating everything in front of her. Jadeanu and Ren go for an attack. She grabs both of them by the face before they can. Jadeanu brings his sword down towards Ava's left bicep, which is not guarded by her demon arm. She releases Jadeanu and jumps back.

Ren kicks Ava in the leg, which does nothing to her. He manipulates both his and Ava's shadows to try to stab her legs. She jumps away from the shadows and places her claws into Ren's back, lifting him up above her head. She bolts upward, then claws all the way through his back with both demonic arms scratching in opposite directions, making it rain his blood as she laughs like a lunatic. Jadeanu catches Ren when he falls.

"She...she spared my life. But I won't live long like this," Ren faintly tells Jadeanu. "You have...to do something. The...rest is...up.. to..you." "Hold on Ren! You've got to stay with me." Ava laughs again as she fires a laser from both of her demonic claws. Jadeanu puts Ren on his shoulder and jumps away.

'I just might die here.' Ren keeps his mind active so as not to give in to death. *'But what a way to go. Dying by a woman so beautiful. I never even got to fall in love and start a family with a good woman. But it's okay.'* "Hey...you know, if I die here, please let me into Ava's arms. I want to be kept under her bosom. I just want to hold her tight and lay my head on her breasts to get the feel of cherishing a beautiful woman one last time. She can do whatever she wants to me after that." "I'm not gonna let you die!" Jadeanu responds.

Ava jumps in front of Jadeanu and punches him in the stomach. She socks him again in the face, and he drops Ren. She continues a constant assault on Jadeanu, and all he can do is guard himself by putting his arms up. Ava laughs constantly as she continues. *'Lamento hacerte esto pero quiero vivir. Pero yo...no...(I'm sorry to do this to you but I want to live. But I...don't...)'*

She switches to slices and cuts into several parts of Jadeanu's flesh. *'È passato un po' di tempo dall'ultima volta che ho visto il volto di uno dei miei. Hai fatto così bene. È sei cresciuto tanto. Non è bellissimo figlio mio? Per avere questo ballo finale. (It's been a while since I've seen the face of one of my own. You've done so well. And grown so much. Isn't it beautiful my child? Having this one final dance.)'* Ava says. *'I can't understand anything she is saying? Has she lost touch with reality?'* Jadeanu wonders.

In the next second, she disappears. Absolute fear consumes Jadeanu as he looks around, breathing heavily. He looks at Ren, who is unconscious on the floor. He bends down to him and starts smacking him. "C'mon Ren, wake up!" Ren's eyes slightly open. "C'mon," Jadeanu picks Ren back up on his shoulder. A strong wave of wind passes by again, and a few cuts appear on Jadeanu's inner thighs. He squeezes his legs together. "Did she just go for my balls?" Jadeanu's fear increases even more.

"You were worried about your friend when you should have been focusing on me!" Ava's voice echoes through the atmosphere. She comes from behind and punches Jadeanu in the back. *'Mon cher garcon, maman est si fiere de toi. (My dear boy, mama's so proud of you.)'* Ava conversates. She then goes for a claw under his legs. Ren starts to fall but he moves Jadeanu forward to avoid Ava's hit using his shadow. As Ren falls, the cuts on his back crash against the concrete, and his vision starts to go black.

Jadeanu turns around to guard an aggressive onslaught of Ava's attacks. *'Bienvenido a casa hijo! (Welcome home son!)'* Ava exclaims. Jadeanu's guard weakens, and he starts to drop it, but if he does, he dies. "Listen to me Ren," he starts. "I need you to attack. Please. It's all I have left to ask." Ren peers at the situation and can barely see Ava, but it's all he needs. He attacks her with weak spikes from her own shadow. She dodges the attack. While she's distracted, Jadeanu immediately takes out Nature's wash bubble Luke gave him. He impales the bubble with his sword, and a giant wave of water flows around Jadeanu, Ren, and Ava.

Ava looks around, confused. *'The water should null her demon arms' senses.'* Jadeanu quickly moves in and stabs through Ava's chest. "Aaugh!" she screams in pain. He twists the huge blade in her gut counterclockwise. "Aahh!" *'huff' 'huff'* Jadeanu slices through Ava's left side, cutting her left bicep off in the process. Blood would splatter everywhere, but it is all washed away by the water.

Once the water disappears into thin air, Ava looks Jadeanu dead in the eyes with the last bit of life she has left as she falls down. *'Gracias por librar al mundo de este monstruo. Dile a mi hijo que lo amo. (Thank you for ridding the world of this monster. Tell my son I love him.)'* she thinks. A triumphant smile spreads on her face as the life in her eyes fades away. Jadeanu looks horrified at what he has done. He falls to his knees and screams with anger directed at none other than himself.

"What's wrong Jadeanu?" Ren questions. "I'm a failure! Nothing but a piece of garbage! I don't deserve to continue this mission," Jadeanu responds. "But you saved us and stopped Ava's evil." "You don't get it do you? No offense, but you've never been much of a noble guy. But you see, I disgraced my honor. We had a deal with Ava that we wouldn't use any outside force nor go for an instant kill. But I did both! And it wasn't out of nobility, but it was out of fear. I was afraid for my own life, so I just... took hers in cold blood.

She proved her point that those who can do the greatest good can do the greatest evil. She committed to her guidelines. She was honorable and could have killed us several times over, but she didn't. But look at me; I killed her the first chance I got. Now I'm the manipulative murderer. She may have been evil, but as of now, during this fight, she was innocent."

"What do you mean innocent?" "Think about it, Ren. If you saw your enemy having dinner with his family and being kind to people, would you take this time to kill him when he's not expecting it, or would you wait when he's being evil to take him on fair? Ava wasn't doing anything wrong, just following the rules she guided us with. And I, an instrument of the gods, have exploited them like a coward." "You know, I'm bleeding out. Can we talk about this after we're healed?" "Oh, of course." Jadeanu starts healing Ren.

"Oh yeah, that feels so much better. I'm glad that the water bubble doesn't go into my wounds, or I would have bled out already. You know Jadeanu, you're only human. You did what you had to do. It may not have been the most noble thing, but it sure saved your life and mine. That's enough." "I need to be more than a pathetic human if I take on the god of Death. I'm much too weak as I am now," Jadeanu expresses. He finishes healing Ren and then himself. They both are going to live another day.

Chapter 13:
Spirit Animal

Jadeanu and Ren stand up and take a look behind them. They gaze at Ava's dead body lying peacefully on the ground, still with a smile spread across her face and her eyelids softly covering her eyes, then they look back ahead. "So where are we going now?" Ren asks Jadeanu. "I don't know," Jadeanu replies halfheartedly. "Well we're still going on our mission right? We can't just stop halfway through." "Yeah I know. I owe it to Luke, but I just need to think." "Well while you're thinking, think about all the good you've done. All the people you've saved. Maybe you just need to sleep to clear your mind. It is getting late. Hopefully things will be fine in the morning." "Yeah."

Ren and Jadeanu enter an abandoned home and get some rest in a room with two beds on opposite sides. Morning comes around, and Ren wakes up. He notices that Jadeanu is up already, sitting on his bed and staring at the wall. Ren does a stretch then suddenly stops. "Ow. My body is sore. That fight took a lot out of me. It must have done even worse to Jadeanu," he says quietly to himself.

"I guess we're lucky for always being able to heal our wounds. Most people don't have that. One bad call and they die. You know that right Jadeanu? We're fortunate, and that's a reason we must go on. We've got fortune on our side." "You're right. No point in being stagnant." "We don't have to start our mission immediately though. I've got an idea if the Ava incident is still bothering you." Jadeanu looks at Ren with curiosity. "Follow me."

Ren leads Jadeanu out of the house. He continues walking through Brigham City until they reach a nearby nature canyon area. "Back when we used to work together, you always talked about how much you like taking walks through nature, and I've always paid attention to that, so I thought this would be peaceful for your mind," Ren admits. Jadeanu smiles. "Thanks Ren, it's nice here. You mind if we walk around for a while?" "Of course."

They wander around the canyon, gazing at the beautiful scenery of narrow valleys, split by mountainous orange and brown rocks. Then they notice a single house surrounded by several plants such as ferns, bushes, and palm trees. The door to the house opens suddenly, and a tall man walks out. The man has white skin and straight black hair extending past his shoulders. He wears a blue vest over a black undershirt, followed by black and blue pants. He has blue eyes with a hint of green and a very thin sword in his hand. He points his sword at Jadeanu. "I sense turmoil in you. Please come to me."

Jadeanu and Ren cautiously walk toward the man. "That pressure. You're really strong!" Jadeanu claims. "That is unimportant. My name is Spirit Haiwan. I have the ability to feel and contact spirits. Yours is breaking. I suspect it has something to do with that woman in that city." "How do you know that?" "Your spirit is calling out to me. Do you mind if I touch your forehead?" "Um, sure."

Spirit touches Jadeanu's forehead with two fingers. "I see. You've succumbed to fear, and now you feel shame. You have also lost what you love. And you have been kind to nature, even helped by it. I can restore your fighting spirit if you allow me."

"Sure. But with all due respect Mr. Haiwan, if you know about Ava and her mischief, why didn't you stop her? You're definitely strong enough to give her a fight." "She is none of my business. She is kind to animals, and so I have no grievance with her. But those who harm nature will be persecuted by my hand. Despite that, there's no promise that I could win. She's a devourer. I could give her a good fight yes, but winning is a whole other concept. Not to mention failure would result in my death. Then who would protect the natural world and its inhabitants?"

"I see; so you're an animal lover?" "Yes. I can connect to them on a spiritual level. I can speak to them, feel their ancestry and feel their entire life's energy and struggle. That's one of the powers I was given in this Death Spiral. I can do the same with people as well, but they are a bit more difficult due to the interference of the soul. Now come with me. I will show you the light. But first, are you hungry?" "Yep."

Spirit welcomes them to his house. He feeds them all fruit and pastries. "I guess I should say that although I am a vegetarian, I don't mind those who eat meat. After all, meat was made for people to enjoy. Killing animals in necessity is alright with me; only when animal harm is unnecessary is when I have an issue," Spirit assures. "Please tell me your names." "Jadeanu." "Ren." "I see; now let's not further speak as we eat. Enjoy your meal as it will grant wonders for your spiritual harmony."

They all eat then Spirit takes everyone outside. Spirit leads Jadeanu and Ren on a lengthy walk around the canyon. They reach the highest peak of the rock and then stop. Then the three boys all look off and see the faraway structure of the city of Brigham. Tall buildings, people walking around, and many destroyed structures, some of which were created during Jadeanu and Ren's fateful encounter with Ava. "Now, can you see the city in its entirety?" "Yes." "Gaze upon it and think of what you did for it. You have defeated the tyrant who planted an ill will in it." "But I didn't defeat her."

"Then think of it as an intrusion of destructive plans. You've replaced her darkness with hope and truth, which should never be overlooked. These people won't know it, but you've done them justice.

You've done what was necessary for that. Consider it a lesson. Learn from your mistake, don't sit in it. You have ambitions to complete. You've brought shame to yourself, but shame is temporary. You can beat it with your will. So continue to have goodwill, and your shame will be not but a faint memory. Now let us sit and meditate."

Spirit, Jadeanu, and Ren all sit Indian style and put their fingers together. "Now close your eyes Jadeanu. Focus on the good and the evil you have done. If your good outweighs your evil, then continue your path," Spirit continues. "Think about the people you love. Feel them, connect with them. Why is it that you love them? Is it something you can be proud of? Then continue it. Feel the world around you. Hear the birds. Smell the air. Feel your heartbeat; let it flow with the soft wind. Feel the warmth of the sun; let it calm your heart. Take a deep breath.

You want to do good. You want to help others. You've succeeded, haven't you? But you do more than help others. You fight for this world as well. You aim to fight the god of Death to return balance to this world that people won't make themselves. Even without the people you're with, you'll fight for the world. Because you love it. So you'll do whatever you must to protect it. Yet you walk the path of purity. That is something to be proud of.

Now imagine dancing with this world as it shall dance with the beat of your pure heart. You can do evil, but you do good. And so, there are necessary evils that may be done but for a will that is good. And that evil will be met with forgiveness. But first, you must forgive yourself. Now open your eyes."

Jadeanu and Ren open their eyes. Jadeanu starts to smile at the beautiful nature around him. Spirit lifts both of his hands up to his sides, forming a cross with his body. Several birds gather around. "Come. I have one more thing to give you." The birds all work together to lift Spirit, Jadeanu, and Ren and bring them back around Spirit's house.

The birds drop Spirit on top of a tree stump and drop Jadeanu and Ren in front of him. "Ren, you'd best stand back; this isn't for you," Spirit advises. "For you, Jadeanu, forget about the little bonding moment we just had. I don't want you to think of me as a friend but now as an enemy. We will fight, just you and me. And be warned, if I am disappointed, I will kill you."

Spirit throws his left arm to his side, and a huge bird appears on his arm. The bird has short wings and a sharp beak and talons. The bird is about four feet tall, with green and blue feathers decorating its body. Jadeanu draws his sword. The bird opens its mouth and shoots blue energy balls out of its mouth. Jadeanu blocks them and is sent back by each hit. "That's stronger than I thought," Jadeanu says. The bird then flies directly at Jadeanu with its beak ready to pierce. He blocks it and is knocked down by the sudden force. He gets up quickly and adds energy to both of his hands.

The bird comes from behind and scrapes its wing against Jadeanu's side. The wings are sharp and cut straight through his flesh. The bird stops not far from him and covers itself with its wings. It charges up some energy that sparkles around its body and spreads its wings. A strong field of energy encases the bird and hits through Jadeanu's sword, and knocks him several feet back, tumbling into the dirt. Jadeanu stands back up with blood all over his body. "That's one tough bird."

Spirit stabs his sword into the ground, and a wolf appears out of the floor and then sprints towards Jadeanu. A katana forms out of the wolf's mouth that it grips with its teeth. It swings the sword at Jadeanu, who blocks it with his sword. The wolf's force knocks him back and onto the floor. The bird flaps its wings toward Jadeanu, and lightning strikes the ground. Jadeanu barely gets out of the way.

"Can I help him?" Ren asks Spirit. "No. It will be worse for his spirit if you do. Hey Jadeanu! You are starting to disappoint me! I expected more from you! But you're pathetically weak!" Jadeanu gets angry and runs towards Spirit. "Well why don't you come to fight me instead of letting your animals do all the fighting," Jadeanu rebuttals. Spirit throws his sword straight at Jadeanu's face. Spirit teleports to his sword and stops it from going into Jadeanu's skull. "I can kill you at any time, don't test me boy," Spirit threatens before throwing his sword back to his tree stump and teleports to it, landing back on the stump.

Spirit's bird shoots lightning out of its mouth at Jadeanu. He dodges it, and the bird fires a laser from its mouth. As Jadeanu dodges that one, the wolf swings its blade at him. He blocks it and is sent backward to the ground. The wolf's blade vanishes, and ninja stars fly out of his mouth and strike Jadeanu in the legs. The bird fires another laser beam. Jadeanu stands up despite the pain in his legs and evades.

He jumps up and swings his sword at the bird. His blade crashes into the bird's wing, which causes sparks to fly, and the attack fails. The wolf shoots knives at Jadeanu after he lands. He swings his sword and blocks but is still sent back a bit by the force. Jadeanu jumps up even higher than before and swings his blade at the bird. Its wing blocks Jadeanu again, but this time, he lands on top of the bird and jumps off of it to attack the wolf from above. Massive blades emit from the wolf's fur all around its body. Jadeanu frantically tries to stop himself from landing on the sharp weapons, but his momentum is too much.

Also, the bird hits him in the back with an energy ball which blasts him straight into the sharp objects. The wolf retracts its weapons and Jadeanu falls down, impaled in several areas but alive. The wolf spawns four huge blades making it the shape of a large ninja star. It jumps toward Jadeanu, then starts spinning in midair. He uses the Willpower Blessing to move the rock under him out of the way of the attack. Jadeanu lands on his feet and stumbles, catching himself on his sword.

"He's still sore from last night's fight!" Ren announces. "That'll be good for him," Spirit recognizes. "Not if he dies!" "He won't," Spirit reassures. "The real fight is just beginning." Jadeanu stands up, and now the Willpower Blessing is glowing. "Now tell me Jadeanu, what are you fighting for?!" "I, I fight...for the whole of the world!" Jadeanu responds with an aggressive tone of determination in his voice. "This world! The very one I stand on! It will prosper because that is my will!" "Good, then prove to me that you can!"

Jadeanu runs to sword-fight the wolf. The wolf forms a katana into its teeth. Their swords clash several times, each one sending Jadeanu back from the wolf's extraordinary strength. The bird sneaks behind him and calls thunder to strike him. He moves immediately behind the wolf, causing the lightning to hit it instead. The lightning somehow doesn't damage the wolf at all. "Okay then." Jadeanu closes his eyes and focuses on the Knowledge Blessing. He then opens his eyes and dodges several attacks from the wolf. "What? I can't sense their minds when they attack," Jadeanu admits.

He continues sword-fighting the wolf while dodging the bird's attacks. He eventually dodges one of the wolf's attacks and the bird's, ending up on the wolf's side. He swings his blade toward the wolf's neck and then hesitates. "Go on! You may proceed!" Spirit calls to him. "You control the animals with your mind, don't you?" Ren demands. "That's right." "And you let him get that attack in." "True. He could never truly beat my animals at his level. This is all a test."

Jadeanu slices the wolf's head off, but no blood comes out. The wolf just falls down and is immediately encased in a bubble. "Huh? What's this?" Jadeanu questions as he strikes the bubble with his sword. His sword is immediately deflected. The bird takes the time to tackle Jadeanu down, stabbing him with its beak. The bird then unleashes an explosive wave right on top of him.

The attack leaves Jadeanu all bloody on the ground, gasping for air. The bird flaps its wings above Jadeanu's dying body then it charges up a laser beam. "No. I'm not going to die here!" Jadeanu stands up, and all four of the Blessings start to glow on his gauntlet. The Nature Blessing heals his wounds, and the Willpower Blessing keeps him alive and fighting. The Universe Blessing mixes with the Knowledge Blessing's power and somehow makes all nearby birds attack Spirit's bird.

The wolf's bubble suddenly pops, and the wolf is fully healed and ready to fight again. Jadeanu uses the Nature Blessing to blow the wolf against the side of the canyon with the wind. He then hits the wolf with a huge boulder using the Willpower Blessing. "Yes! Don't forget who you're fighting though!" Spirit yells.

Jadeanu turns to Spirit, standing on his tree stump with only a thin sword in his hands. Jadeanu runs to him, jumps, and swings his blade toward Spirit. Spirit blocks with his sword but doesn't move at all despite Jadeanu's momentum. "Good. Now we can truly begin!" Spirit praises. He snaps his left hand as he says, "Come to me."

His bird and wolf turn into spirits of light in their same distinct structure. They are then absorbed into Spirit's body and blow Jadeanu back with the venturing bright blue and green shockwave. Once the light depletes, Spirit emerges. He has short blue transparent wings on his back. His sword is now almost as thick as Jadeanu's giant blade. The design of the sword is also different. The handle is more decorated and has wings on its guard as well. Spirit's eyes become even more greenish but still blue. He levitates off of his tree stump and in front of Jadeanu.

Jadeanu attacks with his sword. Spirit counters with a faster swing which hits Jadeanu's sword and knocks him back several feet. Spirit's sword vanishes as he creates multiple swords with the wave of his hand. Each weapon radiates with Spirit's blue energy. He telekinetically throws them one by one at Jadeanu, who dodges them all. When the swords hit the ground, they explode like bombs. Spirit throws out his left hand, and his bird flies out as his wings disappear. The bird flies towards Jadeanu and turns into a bunch of smaller green birds made of energy. The birds follow and swarm Jadeanu and then attack him with headbutts, wing bashes, and kicks. Each attack severely impacts Jadeanu, ripping his clothes and drawing blood from his mouth and body.

Jadeanu falls down with more blood oozing from his body. The birds fly back into spirit, and his wings reappear. He flies up and over Jadeanu and resummons his sword. Jadeanu opens his eyes to see Spirit descending with his sword facing down. Jadeanu uses the Nature Blessing to throw wind at a diagonal slope toward the ground, which sends him away from the attack. Spirit throws his sword into the ground, which creates a shock wave around the area. "As far as strength, it's hard to say who is stronger," Jadeanu analyzes. "Spirit and Ava are really close in strength; I can't tell who's stronger. But still, none of them are quite as powerful as King Elcero was."

Spirit flicks his sword upwards, creating a huge crescent of greenish-blue energy towards Jadeanu, who dodges it. Spirit deletes his sword and summons two blue energy spears in his hands. He throws them at Jadeanu while summoning a new one to throw each time he throws one. Jadeanu avoids most of them, but a few of them stab into his legs. He jumps up to avoid the rest.

Spirit quickly respawns his sword and throws it at Jadeanu's face. He teleports to his sword, stopping it from killing Jadeanu yet again. Instead, he does a spin and swings the sword at Jadeanu's neck. Jadeanu blocks and is sent into the side of the canyon.

Spirit slowly descends to the ground. He charges blue energy onto his sword and throws two smaller crescents in an X shape at Jadeanu. Jadeanu launches himself away from the attack with a rock. He turns to Spirit and fires a Knowledge beam from his forehead. Spirit dodges it and shoots energy balls out of his hands. Jadeanu avoids them, and Spirit smacks his sword against the ground, creating a pack of energy wolves to stampede and trample over Jadeanu.

He evades most of the wolves but is run over by one. Jadeanu gets up and spits out blood. Spirit has a smile on his face, and his wolves merge back into energy and are reabsorbed into his body. He runs at incredible speed and meets sword to sword with Jadeanu. "Ugh, you're fast!" Jadeanu compliments.

Spirit's overwhelming force pushes him back. Spirit's wings curl around him as he charges up energy. Jadeanu already knows what's coming, so he jumps back, using the wind to accelerate his movement. Spirit's wings open up, and a huge explosive shockwave emits from his body. Good thing Jadeanu moved in time, or he would have certainly been eviscerated.

Spirit flies behind Jadeanu and swings his blade. Jadeanu blocks it and is sent back. "Now tell me! Who are you?!" Spirit yells as he throws crescents and energy balls at him. "I am Jadeanu Stroyem! The master of the Blessings of Existence! And the man who will save the world!" Jadeanu calls back as he dodges all the attacks, then moves in on Spirit. He swings his sword. Spirit catches his sword with his fingertips.

"We're done here. Good job Jadeanu," Spirit congratulates. "Are you okay?" "Yeah." "Then I've got one more thing for you." "What is it?" "First, come. I'm sure your friend is worried about you." Spirit takes Jadeanu's wrist and flies back to Ren. Spirit takes a deep breath, and his wings disappear as his sword returns thin.

"You guys done?" Ren asks. Spirit nods. "Jadeanu. Take off your left gauntlet," Spirit commands. Jadeanu obeys. "Now touch the Willpower Blessing." Jadeanu places his hand on the Blessing of Willpower, and nothing happens to him this time. "Amazing!" Jadeanu celebrates. "You can touch them all now. You are now truly their master now that your soul has aligned with their divine guidance. You're welcome for that."

Jadeanu touches all the Blessings and is truly unaffected by them. They finally judge him worthy thanks to the new wisdom he has attained for himself. "Thank you so much Spirit!" Jadeanu thanks, as he puts his gauntlet back on, then starts healing himself with the Nature Blessing. "You've been a great help. I'm glad we ran into you when we did." "Perhaps the gods led you to me, and I was placed here to meet you one day." "Maybe but how about you come with us on our journey. You'd be a great help."

"I can't do that. I love my home, and I must take care of this place. Your journey is dangerous, even for me. It is your calling, not mine. And now that you have taken out the woman with the demon arm, this place can prosper, and I have no one here strong enough to beat me now. I can spread my spirit to anyone who ventures here without fear. For that, I will always remember you. And you may visit me anytime you wish." "Thanks, we may just."

They say their goodbyes and go their separate ways. "He sure was kind," Jadeanu expresses to Ren. "He beat you up," Ren responds. "But look at what that did for me. He replenished my spirit that Ava almost broke. And now it will never break again." "That's not the only thing she broke," Ren jokes. "Yep. She broke a lot of our bones too. Perhaps more than anyone else. Good thing the Nature Blessing can restore bones." "I was referring to my heart. But she did break a lot of bones. I'm surprised you were even able to fight after all that."

"You sure liked her didn't you?" "Well like Elcero said, it's impossible not to. She was wonderful, but I couldn't be with her. She was too monstrous for my taste. I just want a nice, caring woman." "You know, our mission is coming to an end. We just need three more Blessings, and then we'll need to find the god of Death. What do you plan on doing once we're done here?"

"I don't know. Maybe I will try to live a life I can be proud of. Marry a woman. Have a kid and pursue my career as an actor. What about you? I'm sure you've got everything figured out, right?" "I don't really know. I guess I'll gaze upon the new beautiful world that I would have helped create. Maybe just make more friends and appreciate the joy people will now have. But that's even if I can beat the god of Death. I'll need to get a lot stronger before that."

"That's true. But do you even have to fight the god of Death? Once you have all the Blessings, won't you be powerful enough to undo the Death Spiral alone?" "Possibly, but I have no clue how to do that. Maybe I'll just have to ask him when I get to him. I'll likely get my answer through force. After all, he could just do it again." "Aw yeah, I didn't think of that."

"Now, there are two Blessings somewhere up ahead. We also get to see whoever's up here with the power of life and death if we're lucky. Objectives will be completed one at a time." "We've made it far. Let's see how things pan out."

Jadeanu and Ren continue walking through the city in the direction of the two other Blessings. Things seem to be looking up for the two.

Chapter 14:

Life and Death

Jadeanu and Ren walk through the city of Brigham. The place seems so abandoned, with many buildings filled no longer with the sounds of human enjoyment. Just how many people have lost their lives in this once lively place? Yet there are still people. Most walk around with a look of pure despair in their eyes. Like the weight of their lives has broken them beyond repair. The few that aren't, usually have to visit Ava's karaoke business for a chance at some form of happiness.

"This place had potential. It's sad to see a place like this become so worn out," Jadeanu empathizes. "Well our fight with Ava sure did a lot of damage," Ren recognizes. "Maybe I'll visit this place once I'm done with our mission and see what I can do for the people," Jadeanu states. "I wonder how the people will react to seeing Ava's body," Ren wonders. "Most of them really seemed to like her." "Oh well. This is all just a memory now. We have much ahead of us now."

They continue walking until they see a shady man approaching. The man's wearing a hoodie and has a beard along with red eyes. "This could be trouble," Jadeanu predicts. "Hey you!" the guy calls. "Give me that sword on your back. And I'll take those gauntlets along with anything else that you have that's valuable." "Why is it that you feel you must steal?" Jadeanu demands. "There's so much more you can do with your power." "That's none of yo business! Now give me your stuff before I have to use force." "Please walk away."

The guy pulls long chains out of thin air. He puts them into the ground, and they spring up and restrain Jadeanu and Ren. Jadeanu stays calm as his arms light up with red energy. "Wow, you're really weak," Jadeanu insults as he breaks out of the chains with little struggle. Ren flicks his restrained hand up, which makes his shadow form a blade that cuts through the chains. The guy gets angry and swings a chain at Jadeanu. Jadeanu backfists the chain, which breaks it. Ren ties the dude up in chains made from his own shadow. They both continue walking as if nothing happened.

Jadeanu puts his hand on the man's shoulder. "You shouldn't go around robbing people. It's clearly not your thing. Had we not been so kind, you could be dead." Jadeanu and Ren continue walking past him. Once they get far enough away from the guy, Jadeanu speaks to Ren. "You can free him now. It would be foolish for him to follow us." Ren releases the dude, and he does not pursue. He just stands there in defeat.

The two boys continue past Brigham City into an open road with a rocky plain around it. The place is beautiful. Not very heavy on the nature side, but pleasing to gaze upon nonetheless. They walk for a long time. "When you said the next place is close by, I didn't expect it to be this far," Ren speaks his mind. "Uh, sorry about that." "It's okay; I've grown used to all the walking."

Soon they see a guy in the distance running toward them as if running away from something. The guy has red eyes. "Hey! Hey!" he calls out. Jadeanu and Ren stop. The guy stops a few feet in front of them. He puts his hands on his knees in exhaustion, but there is no sweat on him. "There is a powerful demon in the city behind me," the guy claims. "I've been running from him. But you guys came from somewhere else. Could you escort me there? I feel much safer traveling with other people."

"Yeah right. You just want to rob us like the previous guy," Ren assumes. "What!? No. There really is a demon back there." "I believe that, but you're dodging my statement," Ren continues. "You plan on stealing from us when we help you. I know a backstabber when I see one, trust me. Your eyes never once met ours for more than a second. Stop acting!"

"Fine then. You caught me, but now we can't avoid conflict," the man responds, now standing up straight. "Why is it that you steal? It's not like money is that important now, despite the few functioning communities," Jadeanu questions. "It's fun to take things from others," the man answers. "You're right. Money isn't that important; power is the new wealth. You can just take whatever you want." "That's in the mind of a dysfunctional member of this world." "But even so, being able to take power from someone else and gain power yourself is all I want. So hand over everything you've got before things get ugly."

"Hey Ren, you want to handle him?" Jadeanu asks. "Sure." "Don't you ignore me!" The man throws a punch. His arm, along with his sleeve, stretches towards Jadeanu like a rubber band. His hand grows in size for added damage. Jadeanu's left fist lights with red energy. He punches the arm's extended wrist, which forces the man to retract his arm in pain. "Ha! Your greatest strength is your greatest weakness," Jadeanu taunts. "When you stretch, so do your organs, and so they are a bigger target. Your powers say a thousand words."

Ren uses his shadow to imitate the guy's stretch with a shadow fist. His hit lands, and even if it didn't, he was never in any danger, unlike his opponent. They both create giant fists to punch each other. Ren's superior strength nearly breaks the guy's knuckles causing him to howl from pain and quickly retract his rubbery fist. Ren uses the man's shadow to trip and smash him with a giant shadow hammer.

Ren places both shadows back where they belong. The man lays flattened on the ground, hurt and covered in his own blood. "I think we're done here," Jadeanu establishes. As they start to walk, the man stands up, his legs shaking from pain. "You two aren't worth it," he says as he forms himself into a parachute and flies through the air. Ren forms a bow and arrow with his shadow and aims it at the dude. "Go on and shoot him down," Jadeanu permits. Ren releases the arrow, and it hits the guy in the arm. He comes crashing down.

Ren and Jadeanu beat him up, then tie him up with his own stretchy arms. "Okay, now you will be kind to others and never steal from anyone again," Jadeanu dictates. "Okay fine! Just please let me go," the guy pleads. "Your words are empty. And now you shall wait for someone else's kindness to set you free," Jadeanu quotes. "Let's hope that the next person you meet will be kind and not like you, or you'll suffer your karma."

Jadeanu and Ren walk away. "You know it sucks that we have to force people to do what's right," Jadeanu conversates. "Yeah, especially now that people think it's the end of the world. They've only gotten worse," Ren agrees. "But things will get better. We'll make sure of that." They continue walking, and soon a city filled with large buildings nearly reaching the indigo afternoon sky peers into view. There is another guy running in their direction. He looks frantic. His eyes are that of a regular human with no powers. He doesn't even slow down when approaching Ren and Jadeanu. He bumps into Jadeanu and is forced to stop.

"Hey what's wrong?" Jadeanu asks. "There's a monster! In the city!" the man responds. "I thought my brother was strong enough, and I told him to fight the monster, but he was just fodder. I got my brother killed!" "What's with this monster?" "He-he has the power to command death and life. He can bring people dying to full life or kill them with foul darkness." "That's the guy we're looking for! Thank you." "You plan on finding that thing? Good luck!" The man continues running past them and out to the open field.

Jadeanu and Ren fearlessly pursue the upcoming city. As they continue, they notice that the city looks nearly abandoned. Most people are dead, and the living ones seem broken and distraught. Jadeanu and Ren find someone walking around. They approach him. "Excuse me, but do you know where the powerful being that can control life and death is?" Jadeanu asks. "You mean that powerful angel judging our civilians?" the guy responds. "He's behind me to the left, then proceed forward. He's always in that open field proving his divinity to any who objects. I believe he's definitely the one who started the Death Spiral. All to test us humans and see just how good or evil we truly are." "Thank you."

Jadeanu and Ren continue and follow the guy's directions. They end up in an open area surrounded by buildings, most of them abandoned. In the open space, there's a guy being stabbed through the heart by a much, much younger male who doesn't exactly look male to the untrained eye. He has a strongly effeminate and petite design, but if you were to look closely, you could definitely tell he's a guy.

The younger guy looks about 14 at most. The young teenager has light brown skin and is about 5'3 in height. He has considerably long brown hair down almost touching his shoulders. He's remarkably good-looking, especially for his age. He has very stylish-looking white and black clothes and two identical swords in his hands. The swords are mostly purple with red at the edge of the blade and in other places for design. The kid's eyes, though, are an interesting story. His left eye glows white, while his right eye glows purple.

The kid takes his sword out of the other guy and lets him fall down dead. "What's with that child?" Ren wonders. "I don't know. But he's definitely the one we're looking for," Jadeanu responds. "That energy, I think I get why everyone says he can control life and death. It's all so clear. He has the Life and Death Blessings. They're in his blades, at the handle."

The kid does, in fact, have a white orb socketed inside one of his sword handles, and a purple orb in his other sword handle, slightly sticking out from his hands. "But he's touching them, and nothing's happening to the kid. Something's up here." "So are you two just going to stare at me, or are you here to fight me too?" the kid says in a high-pitched voice that sounds like a twelve-year-old just now starting puberty. Jadeanu and Ren walk slowly toward the kid while conversing quietly.

"Should we fight him?" Ren asks. "Well we need those Blessings," Jadeanu replies. "But can't we ask him?" "Considering that people say that he can command life and death means he knows how to use them. He won't just hand them over, plus he might think we're just thieves." "We're not going to kill him right?" "I hope not. But if it comes to it, we may have to."

Jadeanu then turns to the kid. "It seems many people think you started the Death Spiral. But I know that's not true. So what is going on here?" "Humans are pathetic weaklings who believe what they want no matter how much you say otherwise. That's why I KILL them. He...he...he. They think I'm a monster." "Well we are here to fight you despite all of that. There's something we need from you. As a reward for victory in battle, we'll walk out of here with what we need." "It's rather cold out here isn't it? Oh well, let's go."

The kid takes a stance where he spreads his arms to his sides and his swords are facing diagonal to the ground, and his body is perfectly symmetrical. A white aura consumes his body. His aura hits Jadeanu and Ren, which almost makes them fall from the pressure. "What the...That power is...inhuman." Fear instantly consumes Jadeanu and Ren as they look at their opponent. The kid has a wide crazy looking smile on his face. "You know, you shouldn't pick a fight if you're afraid," he advises.

"He's much stronger than King Elcero. If King Elcero was as strong as what's humanly possible, then how on earth is this kid so strong? It's just not human," Jadeanu thinks. "What's up with this guy?" Ren wonders. "And what's with his eyes? People that have powers are supposed to have either red or blue eyes, but his are white and purple." Jadeanu draws his sword. Ren creates his.

The kid walks up to Jadeanu and swings one of his swords at him. The moment his sword hits Jadeanu's, Jadeanu flies several yards backwards, landing on his back. The kid moves his pupils to look at Ren then he slowly turns his face. Ren nearly pisses his pants, then sums up enough courage to run at the kid. He brings his sword down on the kid, who blocks effortlessly and stares at Ren with his lifeless white and purple eyes. The kid's left sword vanishes into the air, and he lightly puts his palm on Ren's chest. Ren tries to move the kid's hand by jerking the kid's wrist, but he can't make the boy move even a little.

Once the kid moves his hand on his own, there is a white insignia on Ren's chest. Then Ren is sent back by force from the kid's blade being pushed into his. As Ren is sent back, the kid snaps, and the insignia on Ren's chest explodes. Once the smoke clears, Ren spits out blood and falls to the ground. "Ren!" Jadeanu shouts, then starts trying to heal him with the Nature Blessing.

The kid throws one of his swords toward Jadeanu, who can't block it in time, and the sword stabs him in the ribs. He stands up and looks at the blade in his body. The kid suddenly appears behind him. "Hi," the kid says creepily before stabbing Jadeanu in his lower back on the left side. He pulls both swords out, puts them on the back of Jadeanu's neck, and swings them.

Immediately, Jadeanu is yanked out of the way by his shadow. Ren is still on the ground but is able to move a little bit, at least enough to use his shadow bending to save his ally. Jadeanu crashes into the ground due to the sudden movement. The kid suddenly appears in front of him and kicks him in the face, which sends Jadeanu far into the building in the distant front of the kid. "He doesn't seem like an angel. And he's definitely not a god. Is he truly human?" Jadeanu says as he flies into the building. Blood flies out of his mouth.

The kid scrapes one of his blades across the ground and into the air in a vertical direction. A thin wall of light comes from the attack and proceeds towards Jadeanu, who bends earth with the Willpower Blessing to move out of the way. The thin light cuts the entire building clean in half. "Glad I didn't get hit by that," Jadeanu relieves. Ren uses the kid's shadow to attack the kid with a spike. Without even looking, the kid stabs the spike, and it returns to his shadow. He then throws his sword at Ren, who blocks it with his sword. The kid's sword goes straight through Ren's shadow sword and pierces through his chest, barely missing his heart. Ren's shadow re-liquifies, and now he is nearly defenseless. The kid holds out his hand, and his sword instantly flies and returns to it.

He then aims both of his swords at Ren and fires bullets made from light at him. Ren freaks out and looks for the nearest shadow. There is a shadow of a nearby building that he uses to move his body away. "If I get hit by one of those, I'm probably dead," Ren exclaims. Ren keeps using the building shadows to keep moving and the building itself to take the bullets. He then moves to the building that was split in half, where Jadeanu is recovering.

The kid starts walking forward while shooting. The bullets start crashing into the building, blasting off large chunks of concrete with each hit. Jadeanu gets on the move too. "Why'd you bring the fire to me?" he questions. "I need to use your shadow," Ren replies as he clings to Jadeanu's shadow. Jadeanu uses wind to move forward. Then the bullets stop and appear in front of them, thus pushing them to move backward. Then the bullets just stop altogether. Jadeanu is fully healed now, thanks to the Nature Blessing. He starts healing Ren while they have a break.

The kid palms the ground with both hands and twists, which creates a giant insignia on the battleground. Then he resumes shooting.

"If we touch that, we're dead," Ren informs. "Then we'll just have to stay in the air," Jadeanu resolves. He continues to use the air to get around, and Ren gets a free ride in Jadeanu's shadow.

They travel around the battlefield while the kid continues shooting at them. Jadeanu's wind manipulation diverts some of the bullets to keep the boys safe. Jadeanu throws a boulder at the kid with the Willpower Blessing. The kid does an elegant spin out of the way and resumes shooting. "We're not strong enough to beat him. We've got to retreat," Jadeanu concludes.

He continues and heads towards a skyscraper. The kid stops shooting and draws a circle of light with his left sword in midair. He then stabs his right sword through it, which creates a thick and powerful laser beam toward Jadeanu and Ren. They nearly get hit by it but crash into the building just in time as the beam incinerates part of the structure. Jadeanu rides a rock and continues his retreat. Ren, who is now healed, uses his shadow to skate forward.

A ball of light flies into the building after them and stops directly in the center of the room. The ball of light then turns into the kid. He puts his arms overlapping each other across his chest, creating the Lazarus sign, but while holding his blades. It seems as if the whole world has dimmed in light when he does this. Jadeanu and Ren exit through the other side of the building. They proceed into another skyscraper by jumping straight through the wall.

The kid unwraps his arms, and a giant pillar of light engulfs and vaporizes the entire skyscraper on contact. "Wow, that's some power!" Ren realizes. The kid then turns back into a ball of light and moves to the next building with lightspeed. He creates the Lazarus sign again, and the atmosphere dims again. Jadeanu and Ren barely make it out of the building in time, but they do and enter the last consecutive skyscraper in the path.

After a single second of charging, the kid unwraps his hands again, creating another powerful, thick pillar of light that obliterates the whole skyscraper once again. He repeats once again with the third skyscraper. "We're not going to make it!" Ren screams. Jadeanu uses the rock he's on to throw himself forward fast. He grabs Ren's hand, and they both accelerate out of the building. But not quite quick enough. Due to the sudden acceleration, Ren's left arm is sticking out.

The kid's light pillar hits his forearm and completely decimates it along with the huge building. Ren screams from the intense pain of getting his arm completely singed off. Yet he and Jadeanu both make it out. The kid decides to stop pursuing now. Jadeanu and Ren continue running until they find and enter an abandoned home where they both take a rest.

Ren continues grunting from pain. His left stump is burnt to charcoal black. "You okay Ren?" "Ugh, please heal it." Jadeanu starts trying to regenerate Ren's arm with the Nature Blessing. The Blessing glows, but nothing happens. Ren's arm doesn't start healing. "What's going on?" Ren starts to panic. "It's not working. I don't know why, but your arm just won't heal." "So this is it?! I've lost my arm for good?! Augh, it hurts!"

Jadeanu finds some cloth in the house and wraps up Ren's arm to keep it from infection as much as possible. "We lost, and he let us escape," Jadeanu reflects. "With that speed, he could have easily caught us, but he didn't." "What's up with that kid? He was insanely strong, could stop healing, and he seemed not all there. He's crazy."

"I wouldn't say crazy, but something's definitely off about him. He's noble enough to hold two Blessings in his bare hands. His soul has a strange but familiar essence to it. And his eyes are so dark and lifeless. I've got to find out what it all means. I'm going to fight him again. We've got to get those blessings. If we can't, we might as well give up. But that's not happening. I didn't come this far just to fail. You don't have to come; you're injured." "No, I'm coming. You have a better chance with me there with you. Even with my injury. Let's at least finish healing and resting; then, we should go get some food for energy."

They do all they said they'd do, then proceed in the direction of the kid. They get to the last building before the kid's field. Then Jadeanu feels something haunting, a chill down his spine. "Something's telling me that we shouldn't go past here. We should turn back while we can. But I have to keep going." Jadeanu and Ren walk back to the open field. The giant insignia that was once there is now gone, but there are blood stains all over the ground.

The kid has several people in front of him, all wanting trouble. They say things like, "You think just because you're a kid that I won't kill ya?" "You caused the Death Spiral; you better change things back!" "You think all of this is some kind of game?" "I'll bash your little skull!" The kid looks around with the look of fear in his eyes. But he's stronger than all these people, so what's he afraid of? The kid starts to speak as well.

"Awe man, there's more of them. It's cold in here isn't it? We could play with them for a while, but I don't want the darkness to consume me again. The guy yesterday sure was funny." "What is wrong with you kid?" "You crazy or somethin'?" the people continue. The kid speaks again. "I hate people. But it's okay because with my power, I can blow them all away."

The kid raises his sword and performs a diagonal slash which emits a strong light that cleaves through and kills everyone in the crowd except for one person who was far enough away to avoid the blast. The one person immediately tries to escape. "You can't get away. You have to deal with your fears like I do." The kid throws his sword, which goes through the other person's skull. His sword then flies back into his hand. "That's better, no more noise. It's all quiet now."

Jadeanu and Ren cautiously approach the kid. "Hey kid, I've come to fight you again. And this time, we have to beat you," Jadeanu tells. "You again? I let you go, and you come right back to me like they always do," the kid responds. "I thought you'd be different though. I guess it was foolish of me to think that. Oh well, I guess I'll just have to kill you this time. No more running away." The kid's white aura advances. "That's fine by me!" Jadeanu claims. "I'm Jadeanu Stroyem, and my friend here is Ren Torilase. What's your name?" "Rahricu Ramada. Ren and Jadeanu huh? There's not much use in learning the names of the people I'm gonna kill."

The kid states firmly, now looking completely serious. His voice also changes drastically. He now sounds like a grown man. His voice is deep, and one could tell he's not faking It. *Did that kid's voice just change from sounding like a child to a grown man?* Ren thinks. "Hey Jadeanu. Rahricu is much stronger than us, faster, pretty good at using his powers, and he has two Blessings that we just can't take. Please tell me you have a plan on beating him." "Nope. All we've got over him is strength in numbers, but that won't do us much good here." "Well that's just great!"

"You know, fear and all emotions are all in your imagination," Rahricu informs. "All just figments of your reality created in the brain. Isn't that neat? Okay, die now!" Rahricu scrapes his sword across the ground and launches it toward the air. "Lightwave," he says. Light comes from his blade in vertical wall form again. "I'll take whatever you throw at me, RAHRICU!!" Jadeanu announces as he blocks the light wave with his sword, causing an intense amount of sparks to fly as his feet drag back unwaveringly. He is sent back as far as the attack goes, which is rather far from the battlefield.

Ren creates his shadow sword. He swings it. Rahricu swings his, which goes straight through Ren's and scrapes Ren's cheek. He then starts stabbing both of his swords toward Ren rapidly. Ren has no choice but to dodge. He keeps dodging left and right. Rahricu speeds up to a speed Ren can't keep up with. He stabs Ren multiple times in both of his shoulders until he falls down from pain and impact.

Jadeanu throws a crescent of energy from the Universe Blessing straight toward Rahricu from far away. Rahricu simply charges the Blessing of Life's energy into his blade and throws a crescent toward the attack. Both attacks cancel each other out. Jadeanu advances towards Rahricu using a levitating rock. He extends his sword to attack. Rahricu lunges forward and makes an X shape with his blades to block Jadeanu's sword. He separates his swords hard while pushing against Jadeanu's sword. The force of his attack pushes Jadeanu far back. Rahricu opens his arms up to his sides and leans back in an unnatural position. He also throws his swords toward Jadeanu's legs in the same motion. Jadeanu barely dodges.

'He went for my legs! He must know that I can't really do much with my powers without them,' Jadeanu hypothesizes. *'So he's rather smart too. There really is something about this kid, but I just can't figure it out.'* Rahricu's swords start moving and attack Jadeanu on their own. Rahricu turns to Ren.

"Bye-bye...Ren." he says as he draws a circle with one of his hands and punches through it with the other. Ren uses Rahricu's shadow to move himself away before the thick laser beam comes from his fist. Ren controls the shadow solely with his feet as he can no longer use his arms. Rahricu tries to follow Ren with the laser and purposely hits his own shadow to throw off Ren's movement. Ren quickly switches to skating on his own shadow and continues behind Rahricu. Rahricu stops his laser and redirects his swords to stop attacking Jadeanu and attack Ren instead with a motion of his hands.

Jadeanu seizes the opportunity and swings his blade at Rahricu. The moment the blade even comes close to Rahricu, it suddenly stops. Rahricu blocked it with his arm; no armor, just skin. The blade couldn't even pierce the skin; it was like metal. Jadeanu's heart immediately sinks. "You'll never be able to beat me. Not with an attack like that," Rahricu expresses with his voice sounding like a twelve-year-old again. He summons his left sword and thrusts it at Jadeanu, who dodges it.

'So we're unable to guard and even cause damage? How strong is this kid?' Jadeanu thinks. Ren appears behind Rahricu and attacks

his head with a shadow spike on his foot. The attack strikes Rahricu's head but does nothing, not even make Rahricu flinch. "You see? You can't beat me. You should just give up," Rahricu claims. He turns around and places his palm on the defenseless Ren's chest as he falls from momentum. Rahricu twists his palm, which makes a huge insignia covering Ren's whole body.

Rahricu dismisses his blades and prepares to snap. Jadeanu hastily throws a Universe crescent slash at Rahricu's arm. Rahricu does a twirl around the attack and punches Jadeanu in the face. Jadeanu's jawbone shatters, leaving his jaw hanging open. The excessive force launches Jadeanu several yards away, and he bounces on the ground with blood coming from his mouth. *If I take a full-force hit from him, I'll die. Luckily, he seems to be barely hitting me,* Jadeanu considers.

Rahricu prepares to snap his fingers again. Ren hurries and moves his right and only hand, despite his shoulder wound. He makes his shadow turn into spikes and makes them stab at Rahricu's eyes. Rahricu dodges the spikes and says, "Hehehe, you fell for it!" Rahricu summons his sword and stabs Ren's chest, then summons the other one and aims it at Ren's heart. "Ren!" Jadeanu yells to the best of his ability with the broken jaw that he's healing. "Jadeanu," Ren calls in a low, dying tone. "Before I even met you, I merely wanted to...gain power by using people. But...this journey and you changed me... You helped me see the value in more...than just the physical things. You helped me see how fragil and valuable lives can be. You showed a selfish man like me kindness and understanding, so that I could do the same for others and see its benefits bring the world together. You gave me a journey I could never forget. Now I can finally say... I'm proud of myself and my life. It's thanks to you. You have the power to change people...don't forget that."

Rahricu waited for Ren to say all of that before stabbing his other sword into Ren's heart and slicing him open. Ren falls to the ground with his eyes still open wide, though the life in them has finally died out. Now Jadeanu is all alone against this monstrous kid.

Rahricu smiles maniacally. "Hehehehe." A purple aura surrounds his body. "What!? His power is rising!" Jadeanu announces. "At this rate, there really is nothing I can do. He was already tough enough."

Rahricu's eyes glow red, and his hair gets slightly longer. His suit colors turn from black and white to purple and red, and he grows black bat wings. He turns to Jadeanu and says, "Your turn," in his deep adult voice with a demonic echo behind it.

He moves to Jadeanu so fast that his movement isn't even evident. He swings his blade, and Jadeanu manages to block it and is sent far back, no longer on his feet. Rahricu appears in the air, several yards ahead of his path. Rahricu slowly lifts his blades up and crashes down on Jadeanu, who guards that as well.

The force sends Jadeanu into the concrete, a few inches deep. Rahricu aims his hand at Jadeanu and lights it up with purple flame. *Those eyes, his smile. The way he talks and moves. It means something, but what? What does it say about him?'* Jadeanu examines. Jadeanu uses the Willpower Blessing to move the rock underneath him, launching him away from Rahricu. The purple flame hits the ground and explodes into a huge beautiful purple fire. Rahricu emerges from the fire unscathed and with smoke coming from his body.

"That fireball was a heck of a lot stronger than the assassin's," Jadeanu compares. Rahricu quickly flies into the air above Jadeanu and slams his blades downward. Jadeanu barely dodges. Rahricu repeats this several times, narrowly missing Jadeanu each time. He gets up and throws a punch at Jadeanu. *He's got to be about double his previous strength. One hit from him now will obliterate whatever he hits.'*

Jadeanu blocks with his sword and is sent flying immediately. Rahricu adds purple lightning to his hand, which he throws into the air. Out of fear, Jadeanu instinctively bends the wind to move himself from the coming attack. "Dancing lightning!" Rahricu calls. Two thick purple lightning bolts fall from the sky. The two bolts wave around the area then they spin around each other like they are dancing. The bolts would have incinerated anything in the area if there was something to hit. Then they disappear as quickly as they arrive.

Rahricu moves beyond lightspeed towards Jadeanu, then stops abruptly. He swings his blade downward, and Jadeanu holds his sword horizontally with both hands to block. "Hehehehe!" Rahricu laughs as he brings his sword underneath Jadeanu's and brings it up toward his chin. Jadeanu dodges backward. Rahricu does the Lazarus sign, but this time, his swords slightly levitate from his hands. The entire field goes dim, then really dark. Jadeanu can barely see anything around him.

A sword proceeds from ahead of him, dashing blade-first. The sword moves at a near undodgeable speed. Jadeanu is lucky enough to block the sword but staggers back from the force. Another sword comes from behind and goes straight through Jadeanu's ribs, handle and all. Jadeanu falls forward, holding his side. Jadeanu sits down, guarding his vital parts with his gauntlets and his back with the sword he leans on.

Swords come from all directions one at a time eight more times. Jadeanu is scraped a few times, but he's overall safe. The darkness fades, and Jadeanu can see again. Rahricu slowly descends, and Jadeanu notices with evident fear that he is still in Lazarus' sign position. He then opens his arms up, causing a pillar of light to engulf him, and several come from the ground incinerating whatever they touch on contact. Jadeanu is lucky enough to not get hit by one. Or perhaps it's the charm of the Universe Blessing.

Seeing that Jadeanu is still miraculously alive, Rahricu snaps his fingers, detonating the insignia still on Ren's corpse. The sudden large explosion distracts Jadeanu, allowing Rahricu to hastily stab him through the chest. Purple energy surrounds the blade and then disappears. Jadeanu is then paralyzed and can't move. Rahricu swings his other sword at the defenseless Jadeanu's throat.

'I know I can get it. What it all means. I can see it all in your eyes, just like Ava said,' Jadeanu thinks to himself. As Jadeanu confidently and desperately stares into Rahricu's eyes, the atmosphere changes around him. He is suddenly surrounded by darkness and can't see a thing. A strong cold breeze hits Jadeanu, making him shiver and fill with goosebumps. Jadeanu looks around and taps his foot on the floor. It's marble tile that he's standing on; he must be inside a building. He walks around, looking for a light switch. He bumps into something, and the sound of glass breaking fills the quiet atmosphere.

"Don't try looking for light; there isn't any here," the voice of Rahricu says with its light childlike tone. Jadeanu looks in the direction of the voice and sees Rahricu with his white and black clothes on in the fetal position sitting on the ground. "If you keep trying, you'll only break things," Rahricu continues. "What is this place?" Jadeanu asks. "This is my home or at least the place I belong." "But it's so dark in here. There's nothing you can do." "That's right. Doing nothing is the best plan." "I don't think so. You've just got to find the light."

Jadeanu's body starts to light up, and it reveals that the place is a huge, beautiful castle with gold, jewels, and many beautiful structures covering the place from head to toe. "No, stop! Get out of here with that!" Rahricu panics. "No way! This place is wonderful!" Jadeanu holds out his hand toward Rahricu. "Come on. Let's explore this place together!"

Suddenly Jadeanu reappears in the battleground, still paralyzed. Rahricu is swinging his blade to kill him. "Rahricu! The darkness inside of you won't last forever!" Jadeanu yells. Rahricu stops his blade inches from Jadeanu's throat, and his eyes return to white and purple as his suit returns to black and white. "I get it now. You're not crazy or evil; you're just alone in this cruel world. You're suffering on the inside, and it's almost unbearable isn't it? But you keep holding on. And nobody cares or values you enough to listen to you. But I will!"

"No, you don't have to. It's best if we don't." "No I must! I think I understand you now." Jadeanu gains the ability to move again, and he immediately hugs Rahricu. Tears swell up in Rahricu's eyes. "The problem is, no one's ever taken the time to understand you. They were so quick to label you but never listened to you. Making your mind go to a dark and lonely place. But I'm here. I don't want to fight you anymore. Let's just talk." "About what?" "About you and why you're doing all of this." Jadeanu stops hugging Rahricu and instead just smiles genuinely at him.

"Uh, um, well, I don't know where to start. But I guess I c-can start w-with this," Rahricu starts with fear evident in his voice. His whole body trembles severely. "It's okay Rahricu. Take your time, then just please be open with me. I'm listening, and I see you. Now let me get to know you."

"Well, um, I'm the son of a woman named Ava Ramada. She's a woman walking around with a strange demonic right arm."

Jadeanu looks at Rahricu in shock and sympathy, knowing he's the one who ended her life.

"You're Ava's son?" Jadeanu asks.

"Yep. Do you know her?" "Yeah. But I ended up with no choice but to...end her life. I'm so sorry about that." "It's alright. I don't really like her anyway. Plus she had it coming to her. But it is sad to know that she's finally gone now. But you don't need to be sorry; after all, I did kill your friend, so we're even, right? But anyway, when the Death Spiral happened, I was the only one I knew who somehow got powers from both Heaven and Hell. One couldn't beat the other, so I got both powers. And look."

Rahricu rolls up his right sleeve and reveals a large gash on his forearm. "I also have the Death Disease. I was able to get the Blessings of Life and Death to hold it back from growing, but I can't cure it. Death can't be cured. It will always be there. So I just keep it under my sleeve to not spread it to other people. I don't want to hurt people. I just wanted to have a little fun and express myself but when I used the Life and Death Blessings, people thought I was the one who started the Death Spiral and they attacked me.

No matter what or how much I tried to tell them otherwise, they kept feeding into their own delusions and never believed me. So I had to kill them to defend myself. I don't like killing them, but my darkness likes to take control of me. I don't know whether what I have is a blessing or a curse. I guess it would be both, but that doesn't matter because I've got nothing for this world. My life doesn't amount to anything. I've got nothing, nothing to fight and live for, and nothing worth dying for. That's why I believe it would be better for me to just let the Death Disease take me, and I disappear."

"This world may not know it, but you have a place in this world. I'll show you. Please come with me as I ask…Will you be my friend Rahricu?" There is a long pause and a look of unease in Rahricu's eyes. "S-sure, I guess so." "Now I want you to tell me your story. I want to truly understand who you are. Don't hold back and tell me everything you feel comfortable with." "Okay, here it goes."

Chapter 15:

Rahricu's Troublesome Childhood

Well I should talk a bit about myself. First off, I'm nineteen years old. I don't look or sound like it, but I assure you I am. The thing is...I'm always afraid. That's why my voice always sounds so light-pitched and shaky. There's not much I can do about it because I'm so scared of interacting with others which is an almost everyday occurrence.. I'm terrified of having to deal with other people, and I'm not really afraid of anything else. I've always been horrible at social situations, but the fear strengthened with the help of my mom.

She's a horrible person, as you should know. She's cruel, monstrous, and manipulative. Many people know how dangerous she is, but I was the one to experience her evils firsthand for several years. She didn't hold back even on me, her only son. My mother, Ava, was so cruel to me. She terrorized me for so long.

As you should know from meeting her, she enjoyed watching people suffer. She adored hearing screams of terror and the mental and physical torture she put people through. Torturing me was one of her favorite hobbies. It all started when I hit the age of six. She acted to break me in every way she could. I vividly remember the scary smiles she would have on her face when I suffered.

She was the one person who knew the most about me, and she made sure to use that information to make my life as horrendous as she could. By the age of six, I was forced into household chores, and for many of my small joys, she made hellish for me. She took away my joyous childhood first. I had to handle the trash around the house, wash the dishes, clean the tables and counters, dust the place, sweep the floors and later on, clean my room, fetch the remote for her when I was busy doing other things, cook and more all while juggling school work.

I don't know if you know this, but my mom is rich, so we lived in a mansion. My mom is a minimalist and doesn't like spending unnecessary money because doing things yourself builds character, so she doesn't have a maid to do the housework. I have to do most of it instead. Very rarely would she help me.

Most of the time, she would make messes for me to clean on purpose just to use me as a slave. And of course, if I didn't obey her every whim, I was a disobedient, unappreciative child who didn't love his mom, and I needed to be corrected. But I really couldn't love her, or at least I couldn't feel like I did. I wanted to but it's hard to love someone who treats you so bad.

And if I didn't obey her, she would yell at me and call me names. But the things she would say to me, she really tried to destroy my soul with them. She always knew just what to say to hurt me. She discouraged anything I would do for myself and tried her best to embarrass me in public. Whenever I would ask her for anything I needed, she would make me do the worst and most humiliating things just to get them. Even for things as simple as getting some regular pairs of shoes.

And she belittled me at every turn. I was nothing more than a stupid, ignorant child who didn't know anything to her. If I ever spoke up, that's how she shot me back down. *'I don't know what I'm talking about'*, she said. *'I'm just a boy, and my life is nothing but a burden for her; the least I could do is make myself useful and do some chores'*, she said. *'I have lived, grown, and been where you've been, but you haven't gotten to where I am, so you can't tell me anything because you don't know anything, and you shouldn't ever dare step to me like this again boy or I'll kick you out of my house and show you how dangerous the real world is'*, sh-she said. She said it all so much. And it hurt so bad every time I heard it. What kind of parent says such detrimental things to their own children?

She would even say and do some of the most disturbing things. Because I have a face that resembles hers which is very feminine, of course, she would use that against me as well. She would always point out and compare my size and skinny body to others as well. She would say I was so pretty with a face both boys and girls were attracted to. She would always make disturbing jokes about me gaining a bigger body because many people would try to grope and harass me if I didn't. She was right though, but I still didn't want to think about that when I was young, and she drilled it in too. I was forced to think about it a lot.

My fearful look and light voice would draw more predators, she said. She also assured my insecurity of never being able to find someone to marry one day. I would end up alone because no woman is attracted to a frail man with a voice like mine. Unless I like guys, but I don't. I only like girls; I'm just no good with them, like she said. She really teased me about it. She was very brutal with it, claiming I'd never be able to please the ideals of a woman. She's not wrong about it though; I've never had a woman look at me twice outside of pity or fear.

She claimed I was lucky to have her. She was as close as I would ever be to a woman caring about me. Oddly enough, my mom actually liked hugging me. She was a hugger, forcing me to hug her and say I love her even if I didn't feel like it. It made me really confused at first. When I got to around the height I am now, she would like to hug me and place my face directly on her boobs. Sometimes I couldn't breathe. Sure, that's something many guys would probably want, considering how beautiful my mom is, but I obviously didn't want that and it seriously ticked me off.

She would sometimes do things like that to confuse me. So that I wouldn't see her as my mom but as just a beautiful woman. A beautiful woman I could never have. Just to tease me with a constant memory of the life I'd forever live. She'd even make small gestures like forcing me to look her dead in her eyes as she would give me the most seductive glare she could. She knew what she was doing and used it to further ruin my perception of life. Trying to damage my youthful mind anyway she could. I know that because she would always laugh and then walk away afterward knowing that thoughts like that would stay in my young mind.

Another thing she would do is force me to dance with her. It was okay because I like dancing just like she does. But things got really weird for me when she taught me how to slow dance. Because, of course, I had to dance with her, and due to my size, I usually had to be the "female" in those parts. Making me make feminine gestures and be led around, knowing I am a man. But that was alright; I learned a lot while doing it. But it didn't help that she took extra care of me, such as manicuring my nails to make them pretty like hers.

Despite her not liking me, she was also overprotective. She never let me do anything that could allow me the ability to become independent from her, either. I never learned how to drive, I never got much money from her despite her slightly spoiling me, I depended on her for food, I didn't have any friends or family outside of her, I never had a phone and I never even learned how to swipe a credit card. I couldn't escape from her even if I wanted to. Finding me would be no issue for her, but the punishment she would give me when she caught me. It definitely wouldn't be worth it.

I couldn't do many common things, and I had no way to learn, at least without suffering for it. So I was stuck, stuck depending on her for everything. I couldn't survive in this world without her. I was made to work for her, never securing the life I wanted for myself. Nothing in that house was my own to her. She always enforced her power to take anything away from me, even if I earned it. If I objected, she was always so clever, enough so to somehow shift blame for anything that frustrated her onto me.

Even with her frustrations, she rarely ever hit me. She knew I could take the hits, so she focused on my mental and emotional suffering, which is much worse and more long-term. She would rarely slap me for "being disrespectful" sometimes when I deviated from whatever she wanted to use my time for. Outside of that, I've not really been hit by her many times.

Well, we are a family of fighters, so when she trained me to fight in the many martial arts forms she mastered, she would hit me. But she always held back a lot. She's actually insanely strong, especially for a woman, so she knew to be disciplined in sparring with me. But she would commonly force me to test my skill against her even when I was busy doing something else, and she would only hurt me to punish me for something I may have done "bad." I liked learning how to fight, but I hated fighting her. She was so hard on me. She tried to use my anger to motivate me, but I just wanted to relax sometimes.

My mom was very interested in fighting techniques in the past and she traveled to Japan, where she learned karate and participated in many competitions, such as a Kumite tournament. And she was brutal but able to fight freely because here in America, such things are less common and less fun, so her inner bloodlust had time to build up. I saw how terrifying that is firsthand. I'm sure you have too, Jadeanu.

She killed a few people during those days, but she actually didn't like to. Odd right? She was a small-time murderer even before the Death Spiral. And she mainly killed with her bare hands; that's how strong she is. She absolutely loved the process of taking a person's life, even if she didn't want to. Her bloodlusty smile when she did so is truly chilling. Her kicks were famous in underground fighting you know. Her legs were exceptional. She had a kick so swift and strong that just one could kill a person. And not just any person, but a trained male fighter. I remember one time she kicked me in the arm for doing something "wrong." She held back of course, but I couldn't feel my arm for a whole day. And it hurt for a whole week.

She always made sure to hold back whenever she put her hands on me so as not to kill me. One of the reasons she didn't like killing was that she preferred to break a person's spirit instead. Killing a person on the inside and forcing them to surrender to fear and constant mental turmoil. A fate worse than death. That's what excited her the most when it came to these things. Death is her mercy, and she didn't want me to rest yet. And neither did I.

I was so scared of doing anything even remotely wrong because she was so terrifyingly crafty with her punishments. Whenever she punished me for things that she didn't like, the scariest thing about her was how different and creative her punishments were. That, mixed with the haunting smile she would give me while scheming something, was terrifying. I lived in constant fear of the things she would do to me. I never knew what to expect.

I was born an introvert, and I've never really liked talking to people. I could handle everything I needed to by myself. But thanks to the severe fear my mom put into me, I developed powerful social anxiety. The fear and ever enclosing doubt of every social interaction I have from now till the day I die. I couldn't, nor did I care to make friends. So I had no one. I have no one except for the darkness inside me. He helps me through everything, but I don't want his help sometimes. I could do it all alone and shut out my want for companionship, but I just don't want to. My heart would just freeze over and I couldn't take it.

There was this one time my mom ended up buying a pet chicken, who was only a baby chick at the time. He was in danger of being put down, so my mom ended up adopting him to save his life because my mom likes animals. She gave him to me to soothe my loneliness because only she knew me enough to know I suffered from it. It was a great, kind gesture. I gladly accepted him, but I did have one concern.

You're probably wondering where my dad is in all this. His name is Raiyane. He was killed by the Death Spiral. Before that though, he was a good man who was just phenomenally good-hearted. He served in the military special forces. We were a military family, so we also moved around a bit which made it easier for my mom to do horrible things to me. And because my dad was gone a lot, he never really got to know me very well, nor did he know that his wife did these things to me. He was mainly there for me financially but nothing else. Not really his fault though.

The interesting thing is how my mom's behavior changed whenever her husband was home. It would seem as if all the darkness inside of her melted away when he was around. She became so nice and lost all her inner brutality with him. She truly loved him, and her happiness was contagious. She became an entirely different person when he was around. I loved when my dad was home because those were the only times when I was happy because my mom was happy. Oddly enough, Ava's not a bad mother; she chooses to be horrible to me. I've seen the light of her personality, but it was just so close yet far away.

My mom buying me that baby chick was a sign of her inner kindness. The thing is, my dad doesn't like pets like me and my mom do. But he likes humans like me and my mom don't. My dad has a strong disdain for pets and is completely against them in the house. Mainly due to insecurities set by his military involvement. He just couldn't trust an animal in his home. But I didn't want my baby chick to die. And neither did my mom, so she bought the chick secretly while my dad was away training. She insisted that it would be good for me and that I could keep him as long as I kept him a secret and took care of his needs as well as cleaned up after him.

I knew my mom was likely planning something sinister, but the chick was bought, and there wasn't much else that could be done. I gladly accepted, thinking that I would finally have a friend. Even if he was an animal. I raised him for a whole year, and I loved him so much. I named him Kevin. He was so funny and so cute, and he was there for me through my struggles. He gave me companionship.

But as I expected, my mom manipulated everything using the fact that I was the one who did most of the housework. She planned for the house to run out of food and in need of restoration on the very day that my dad would be coming home. My mom always likes to have food prepared for my dad whenever he returns home. But there wasn't any to prepare, plus she had already confirmed to my dad that I would have food done before he arrived. So I would get the blame if that didn't happen, and I would get in serious trouble, at least I would with my mom. We were pressed for time, and our lack of food would be an issue. But there still was something that could be cooked, my chicken.

My mom made me a deal saying that either I would have to cook him, or she would tell my dad that I had an animal in the house that I wouldn't give up. Of course, that meant I would have to kill Kevin then I'd get in trouble for the lack of dinner and hiding an animal. If I decided to cook Kevin, she would keep my secret and help me make dinner so I wouldn't be in any trouble. Either way, my friend Kevin would have to die by my hand.

The choice was easy, but it was just so hard for me to carry out. I-I very hesitantly decided to kill Kevin and defeather him myself. My mom helped me prepare him and fry him. I remember crying the whole time. How could she make me murder my only friend?! As my parents ate him, my mom smiled at me menacingly as she picked him apart with her teeth. I couldn't bring myself to eat any chicken for a while for very obvious reasons. It was all just so horrible.

I was so afraid of her every day. And almost every day, I was haunted by her smile. Her enjoyment of my scared and troubled face. I was so lonely, and it all hurt so much. So bad that I began to feel my emotional pain physically. It was maddening. My darkness entered me, and I felt it so deep in my heart. Slowly ripping away my humanity. Making me feel like I might go crazy.

Unfortunately, I was born with a brain too strong to be able to become completely insane. A brain too aware to ever get lost. I laughed at my pain. I started to get so used to it that it started to feel good, even though I knew it shouldn't. It was just so funny how no matter how much I tried, where I went, or how good my intentions were, I would always end up crawling back to my dark feelings.

Hahahaha, nothing ever changed, and nothing ever would. No matter how much I wanted to leave, I would always get sucked back. I honestly didn't even care about going back. I was so used to those horrible dark feelings that it didn't even feel so bad anymore. I couldn't care. It was the only thing that I was entitled to. I cried soo much. I shook violently with pain as I lay in bed wishing my fantasies of freedom would finally come true. My heart filled with hatred. But I couldn't do anything with it.

I am so used to losing. I've lost soo much. Every time I would gain anything small, I would lose something much more valuable. I wanted something real, but no. Every time I even got close to something that I really wanted in life, it was always snatched away right when it was at my fingertips. I was always reaching for something I knew I would never gain. I learned nothing and gained nothing for the hours of time I would dedicate to my crafts. I worked so hard and have nothing to show for it. Nineteen years of endless torment, and it's always in vain. It's all meaningless. My efforts, my life.

I want to live, but if my life and work never amount to anything, I want to die! Stop being a meaningless burden on this lovely planet. If there isn't anything for me to gain, let me rest in peace. I've felt what it's like before. In here, my heart. All that's left is for me to feel it all over my body and be tortured to death. That's what I want as an atonement for wasting this planet's resources with my pathetic life, filled with so much talent and potential that I could never use. Never making any meaningful fruits for my endless laboring to become a great person. It always amounts to nothing.

To be honest, I always thought I would die from the severe pain I always felt in my heart. I thought it was only an amount of time before my body just gave up. And it wasn't just my mom making me feel that way; it was everything in the universe…

I am afraid of interacting with people; it's the worst fear I have. People tormented me. No one understands me, and no one cares to. No one sees the pain of who they think is privileged. I realize that I'm alone and no one cares about my suffering. But I don't want pity or sympathy; I just want someone to understand. I had hoped that by acting troubled enough, someone would actually care.

I guess I was stupid for thinking that. I've always wondered. If I killed every single human on this planet, would I finally be free? Could I finally experience the happiness that people constantly stole from me? Now that I have the Death Blessing, I can do exactly that with ease. Kill everyone. But as you can see, people are still alive, so I never truly made up my mind. All because I never wanted to hurt anyone.

People only tried to bully me, but they couldn't. I was too strong for that. Instead, I just carried the weight of other people's sins, trying to do right by them no matter how they treated me. I carried the weight of this cruel, senseless world all on my shoulders alone and was promised nothing in return. I was okay with that though. I've always wanted to use my abilities to help people, but people don't like being helped. They hate people who are greater than them. People are truly horrible enough to bring down stronger people.

Just like crabs in a bucket. Pulling down the one closest to freedom. Bonded people hate free people. They want everyone to be the same, so they are quick to label someone without knowing who they are. One of the only ways for that one great crab to get out of the bucket is to kill everyone holding him down, then go out and reach their new heights. But that crab would be the one to be called evil for doing so in this dispassionate world. No one ever even took the time to understand just how much danger they were in for pushing someone like me.

All I wanted was to love the world and the people in it, but people are horrible and undeserving of help. They keep pushing me to hate them, but I don't want to. And I've never felt what it's like to feel loved, so what am I to do? Just disappear? No, because I've seen love. I've seen the light trying to illuminate my soul. I know something better is possible; I always have. I just need to prove to the world that I was here and that I've done something with the years I've been given.

But over time, my heart has grown bitter and unsympathetic towards humans. I was always so cold, with constant chills filling my body no matter how many covers I wrapped myself in. Soo so cold because it didn't come from outside; nope, it came from inside. Right here in my heart. The shivers even extended to pain in all my limbs, making them numb and feel so weak sometimes.

Even my soul is shrouded in darkness and dry from the loss of water that my tears have used up. I don't have anything to live for and nothing worth dying for. There is nothing, and that's factual, not just a dark and depressing thought. But all I have left is hope. A hope that gives me the strength to continue to wonder if anyone will ever actually need me. Hope that never pays off. But I carry the weight of the world's sins anyway.

Even if it's like I am an island paradise, each time I move to another island in the hope of finding travelers, the island just goes further away, and I'm stuck in the middle of the ocean alone. All I want is to have something meaningful that won't just be taken away from me. It's all I've ever wanted. But I'm sick of always being afraid. There's nothing I can do about my fear of social situations except to just deal with it no matter how tragic the outcome is. Because it's a fear that's constant and will never go away. It has no cure because it's an ever-adapting fear. You can never truly conquer it because every encounter with it is new. Nothing else scares me, not even my mother.

But you know, she wasn't always a bad person. My mom may not seem like it, but she was actually not a bad person. She's even read a lot in the Chako; she's well-versed in spirituality. After all, her strength should have said it all. The strength of your powers is an identifier of how spiritually strong someone is. And she was a rather strong person, as you should know. I guess I should tell you where it all started, huh?

There is a reputation regarding Ramadas, which is my and my mom's last name. As far as what's been recorded, my ancestors originated somewhere in Thailand. Several generations ago, the first recorded Ramada, although I don't know his name so let's call him Elder Ramada. He was a pretty good kickboxer in Muay Thai. It was always a known stigma that we Ramadas are born with a few strong traits through genetics.

Elder Ramada learned that he was born unnaturally strong and had other strong traits. With that, he began to wonder and think about philosophical ideas. One of his most prominent thoughts was a prediction. He predicted that based on what he knew about our world, there would come a day when chaos would break loose. And when that happens, society would shift to a state where people would either conquer or be conquered. The strong would conquer while the weak would be forced to bend to those who are strong. Natural selection would rule. Survival of the fittest.

He knew how powerful his genes were, and he wanted them to survive and never grow weak. He wanted his family to survive and always remain the masters of their fate. So he adapted the practice of selective breeding. He decided to find a wife who he could see eye to eye with. A woman that was his equal and could complement where he lacked as well as strengthen what he had. Then when they would have a child, that child would be born with the strengths of both parents but without most of the flaws. And the family would continue that over the generations until they created offspring so undeniably great that they would be sure to never become a subject of anyone else's will other than their own.

There were always a few concerns, the main one being the fact that all Ramada, even Elder, are all born with two dark traits in our blood. Bloodlust and power hunger. All Ramada are born with that, even me; it can't be helped. Out of concern that those dark inner traits could corrupt our family down the line, Elder Ramada wanted to instill discipline and kindness into the hearts and souls of his children. He taught his children martial arts to keep them strong and disciplined.

He wanted his family to grow strong, stay good-hearted, and one day create a perfect human. Great in every way but humble. So the Ramadas ensured to be spiritual and marry the one they desired before mating with them. They wanted to stay healthy mentally and physically and never overvalue their spouse. That means the women were not to chase the best man, only the man who they deserved and vice versa.

But eventually, after Elder Ramada passed away, the family eventually forgot their roots, and some Ramadas started to become toxic. Feeding into their power hunger and even being jealous of the fact that their children would quickly surpass them. Their unwillingness to accept that, led to a lot of issues regarding the family. Causing corruption and separation of the family. In an effort to escape the toxicity of the parents and find compatible companions, the generations moved to Taiwan and then Japan. One man, in particular, was born there in Japan.

That man eventually moved to America after being pushed by power-hungry parents. He found a beautiful black woman who he found was compatible with his energy. And together they made my mother, Ava. My mom turned out to be the first selective breeding project success and the first woman born into the Ramada family. And because of it, she received a lot of backlash from her own relatives. Many envied her because she was perfect in every way. Beautiful beyond description, smart, marvelous personality, and humble attitude. She was just a bit more...how do you say... curvaceously endowed.

She was born a Virgo in her zodiac sign and she embodied the idea of that sign. She was a good child and very obedient. She never once did anything bad, but that doesn't matter much when your parents are flawed. Her parents were cursed with the ongoing Ramada toxicity and still found ways to punish her for things that weren't bad. My mom lost love and trust for her parents first and then the world.

She eventually came of age to look for at least someone to love, but she couldn't. She had no friends because they were all inferior to her. She didn't need them and they couldn't understand her complex mind anyway. She, just like me, was considered weird to most people because of it. Boys were only concerned with her looks and body. Rarely wanting her for her. The ones that did were too weak for her taste. Couldn't really bring anything to the table that she didn't already have. She ended up growing independent and self-reliant.

She was trained in martial arts by her father. That was one of the few times she bonded with her family. She rarely saw her other family members because of the curse of their toxicity. Her cousins and aunties were also jealous of her and wanted her downfall. She also received a lot of negativity for her skin color in the family as well.

Lacking love from and for her family, she only cared for a few things. Power, dancing, singing, fighting….and killing. But she had never killed before; she just liked the violence of it. That's something all-natural-born Ramada can relate to, including me. Yet because she was female, her emotions were stronger than other Ramada, and she was known for having it the worst. She enjoyed watching people suffer, but not because she was evil, she just had a love for violence through DNA.

At the age of sixteen, she started her own business. She wanted to escape her tortuous parents as soon as possible. At the age of eighteen, her business became a success, and she became wealthy. My grandparents weren't very wealthy, largely by choice. In order to have a humble background, they stayed a low middle-class status. Ava knew she could do much better, and she did. She moved out of her parent's house and bought a mansion far from where her parents lived. She lived there alone for a while.

The problem was that life was too easy for her, and soon she became a multimillionaire all by herself. She used her charm and loveable personality to get ahead. That helped her get power, but what use was it without some way to use it.

She thought about violence to keep her bloodlust in check while showing her gained power. But the thing is, in her time, picking fights and killing people was heavily frowned upon, so she had very little outlet. She didn't want to be a criminal, so she decided to forget about the small pleasures of it and began looking for the one thing in which she could find true joy. The one thing she couldn't control with power. Love.

But she had no one. In her pursuit of a lover, she occupied herself by taking a side job as a singer and dancer and pursuing mass philanthropy, considering that she rarely used her own money. She's a minimalist, and money means nothing to her especially considering that she makes her own luxuries. She enjoyed doing things for others, but it never amounted to much for her. People weren't always very grateful or ended up squandering her blessings. But with her singing and dancing, she had more luck. She loved the idea of captivating an entire crowd. It was a graceful way to show her commanding power and she enjoyed it.

At one of her small-time singing shows, she managed what she thought was almost impossible. While she was singing for a small crowd, she locked eyes with a man, and she was captivated by what she saw. She had finally done it. She found what she had spent so much time looking for. My mom told me about this day several times over. Her face just lit up whenever she would tell the story like it was one of the happiest days in her life.

Ironically, she was singing a love song while staring into this man's eyes throughout the whole show. My mom was always good at reading a person through their eyes, so she could see a lot about this man just from doing that. For the first time in over eighteen years, her heart fluttered with excitement. After the show, my mom made it her mission to track down the man she locked eyes with during her performance. She eventually found him, and they spoke with one another. That man's name is Raiyane, and not long after, he became my dad.

He was only a year older than her, and when she turned nineteen, she married Raiyane. I know that sounds early, but my mom knew herself, and she knew what she wanted. It didn't take long for someone of her caliber to learn that everything that she saw in my dad while on stage was a reality. And he was the first man to make her happy. All of her inner strength finally amounted to a great catch. She fell in love, and he loved her.

My dad was an amazing man. My mom saw him as her equal in nearly every way. They complemented each other well with their good hearts and great abilities. Raiyane never even lusted for my mom; he was much too ambitious to be controlled by hedonistic desires. He was a military man though.

He had military-style combat; she had martial arts. He had a style of fighting she hadn't explored yet, and she craved the power of learning it and added it to her arsenal of combat. They complemented each other in other ways as well. They were a perfect power couple. And after my dad left for training, he left my mom a little present. My mom had become pregnant with me.

Raiyane ended up taking Ava's last name due to her pride as a Ramada and her desire to keep the Ramada name flowing, considering that she never had any brothers or sisters. Despite my mom not liking her family, she still wanted to honor the will of her family's tradition. She deeply wanted me to be a selective breeding project success like she was. She stayed healthy and never once did anything that could damage me while in her belly. She must have been so excited to create an even more perfect child. It was one of the things she wanted the most.

I was born when she was twenty years old. And she really loved me. She took care of me to the best of her ability, but she was kind of thrown off by the fact that I was small. I was only five pounds at birth. This was strange because my dad was a tall man over six feet. My mom was also tall for a woman. But I was a rather small baby. My mom was a bit disappointed, but she decided to love me anyway.

My dad was gone a lot because of the military, so my mom had to take care of me mostly on her own. And things were truly looking up for her. After eighteen years of a miserable life, she finally had a break from it and could find inner happiness. By the way she spoke of it, these were undoubtedly her greatest years.

My mom was never much of a happy person, so it was always special to see her with a genuine smile on her face. Because of it, I've always kind of been able to feel when she was happy, even if I was too young to remember. The problem was that her happiness never got a chance to last and sit for a while to let it mature to the point of being unconditional. Her husband wasn't always there, and I was a hope for her. She wanted me to be strong more than anything else.

As I grew to four years old, she trained me in every form of fighting she knew. Even sword fighting, which she learned from a master swordsman in Japan. She trained under his wing until she surpassed him. Then she left him, but he chased her, and she ended up killing him. Which highlights one of my mother's most powerful skills that truly makes her scary. She was able to surpass her master in swordsmanship in just a few days. That doesn't sound very possible, but I assure you it's not for my mom.

One of her special skills is the ability to evolve as she moves. It's not just adapting; she's able to completely strengthen herself extremely quickly with everything she does with her genius analytical brain. That gives her the ability to learn something efficiently and extraordinarily quickly.

For instance, there was one time recently, during the first few days of the Death Spiral. I was watching TV to understand what was happening around the world. Apparently, the world-champion American kickboxer got stranded in our town, and he had no powers. I heard he had a record of 63 wins and zero losses. Not long after that showed on the TV, my mom suddenly left the house. I already knew what was going to happen. She loves conquest to satisfy her power hunger. American kickboxing was a form of combat she didn't have. She was going to go learn it.

Soon she came back through the door, and the news stated that the world champion was knocked out by a woman with no powers. I don't know if you know this, but my mom is the only one I know who could turn her powers on and off at will, so I have reason to believe it was her. The world champion ended up becoming so devastated that he gave up on fighting and was soon killed by other challengers. She told me about the new form of fighting she had just mastered, all in just participating in that one fight.

I knew my mother well, so when I was four, I was really concerned about her power hunger with her inner brutality. I knew that without the light of contentment filling my mom, her inner darkness would show itself. I figured that with my mom's conquesting mentality, if I allowed her to see that I was a selective breeding project success, her instincts would lead her to want to claim my power for herself which would ruin me in the process.

If I was to ever show her that I was greater than her at anything, she would challenge me and end up outdoing me in everything before I had the chance to mature. Then there would certainly be no reason for me to exist, at least not for the reasons I want to exist. There really would be nothing for just me. I would be a failure as a Ramada. I didn't want that because I am a miracle child.

I inherited my mom's looks, so I am beautiful to both males and females. I only like women though. I also inherited my mom's genius mind, but mine works largely differently from hers. Mine is centered on memory and mental assimilation through my strong imagination. I am a tempered man, strong. Other than my height, I am essentially perfect; I am near sinless, other than the killing of these people, but even that, I can justify. I am short, likely because of my recessive Japanese genes, but that's not important.

I knew I could never let my mother know how great I was. So I didn't. I lessened my scores in academics, and I never went all out on almost anything because I knew how much it would cost me. It's like if you want to become the best professional football player, you of course, will put all you have into it. Years of training and dedication. The last thing you would want is to have your mother go out there and beat you in football horribly in a matter of minutes. That would completely destroy your will to continue because now your entire life's work is meaningless. That's what she would have done to me in everything. She would have completely destroyed my soul.

My mom has always been a spirit breaker which means she would destroy everything you hold dear until you are obsolete. As I've said before, everyone that she doesn't kill, she breaks their spirit.

But anyway, I held back on everything I could do to avoid her going after me. The only thing I went all out on was fighting. I knew that I could never beat her at that.

Because of my "weakness," my mom grew increasingly disappointed in me and even herself for making such a weak child. And when I reached the age of six, she stopped loving me. It was so sad because I could tell that she really wanted to love me, but her heart was just incapable. Similar to how she thought of everyone else, she thought of me. She couldn't hate me, and she couldn't love me. I just sort of existed to her. She felt nothing, and I felt the same towards her.

Although she still didn't give up hope in me. She wanted to see my growth through. That's why she didn't make any brothers and sisters for me. She wanted to see if I could grow to be greater than her like I'm supposed to be. But I never let her see that I already did. I knew the price if I ever had.

Had my dad been around more, she would have never maintained the bitterness in her heart. But she also didn't want to hold back his ambitions for that, especially because she considered him more attractive for being so invested. Because of his lack of being there, he could only try to be a good dad. He didn't know enough about me to really be a help to me, and he was never able to see Ava's horrible side because she lost it when he was around. He'd never believe anything I'd say over her, so I had no power when my mom became cold and cruel to me.

When my mom stopped loving me is when she started ruining my life. Being such a monster to me. She knew that we Ramadas were all mentally strong, so we were all known for becoming much stronger from adversity rather than ever giving in to it. She hoped that being a huge bully to me, would make me stronger.

It worked, but I kept that to myself too. I just couldn't bear what she would do to me if she ever saw how strong I was. She remained cruel and not even because it made her feel better. There was another thing that made her grow even more ruthless. My mom isn't an idiot; she was fully aware of the possibility that I may be holding myself back for whatever reason. It made her more sadistic in an attempt to make me give in if her hunch was right. Which it was, but I kept going.

She remained so cruel over the years, since I was six, till recently. Thirteen years of torment by her hand. Even if the time was sometimes good. Sometimes with my dad, we ended up moving to different countries, and I got a chance to see the world. My mom would usually be so kind and sweet during these times. It was beautiful.

We went to Mexico, Italy, and Japan, just to name a few. My mom became fluent in the language of every country we visited. I had some fun times and some bad times, but I'll never forget the lights in my mom I saw during those times. It kept reminding me that she did have a good heart. It never lasted too long though, and seeing her go from warm-hearted to freezing cold was always scary and sad.

When the Death Spiral happened, I managed to become much more powerful than my mom, but I still couldn't let her know that, not with a learning and evolving demonic arm at her disposal. The most shocking and life-changing thing happened as well. My dad was one of the people who randomly dropped dead, thanks to the whole thing. When my mom found out, she was so distressed that she demanded to see the evidence because my dad wasn't home at the time. When my mom finally saw her husband's dead body, I remember seeing just the saddest look in her eyes. Like the last bit of life she was holding on to just vanished.

In that instant, she lost the one thing she held dearest. The one thing that could make her happy. The one thing she loved. There was nothing left but coldness in her heart. A strong mound of ice that lost its counteracting fire. All that was left inside of her was her inner darkness. She had suffered for so long, she no longer wanted to hold back the monster inside her. With the help of her demonic arm, she became more cruel, bloodthirsty, and power-hungry.

She gave me more time to myself as long as I would continue her bidding. She used me to help her create a company and control it as I would be one of her spies. I told her about my Death Disease, and she told me to find the Blessings to stop it. I was lucky to find the Death Blessing, but I had to talk to the God of Life to get the Blessing of Life. Kinda scary to think that my mom could have had her hands on them if she wanted them.

Once I had the two Blessings, people started to misunderstand me again like they always do. They thought that I was the one who started the Death Spiral. So I had to kill them to defend myself. And when I came back home, my mother somehow just knew I had killed people. She asked me creepy questions about it, and I really didn't want to answer them. She asked me if I had enjoyed it and wanted more. I did enjoy it, but I didn't like that I enjoyed it. I didn't want to kill anymore. But when do things ever go my way?

Eventually, my mom made me infiltrate her company to kill someone who she claimed was in her way for her new ambitions. But I didn't want to kill, especially not for her, so instead, I killed one of her spies, and I enjoyed it. It was the first time I'd ever boldly gone against my mother. Later, when I got home with her, she started yelling at me and calling me names. Then out of her frustration towards me, she even questioned why she kept me around for so long. She then swung her demonic claws toward my throat with the intent to kill me.

And for the first time, I showed her my power. I blocked her attack, then grabbed her by her face and tossed her through the house, literally. She went through several houses actually. It was the very first time I'd seen my mom take complete defeat, and it was by my hand. It felt good to do that. Too good, and that's when my dark form showed itself. I ran away from her and ended up here. I never saw her again since then. I knew she would eventually come for me to gain my power, but she would need more power herself to do that. I came here and killed everyone that the Life and Death Blessings told me I could.

But you know, I always took pride in the fact that I was the only one who could make my mom mad. It showed that she still didn't completely see me the same way she saw others. It showed that deep down inside, my mother really loved me. I know it doesn't seem like it, but all she really wanted was for me to be strong. I know she must have been proud of me but was just unable to express it. She couldn't feel the love she had for me, but it was still there. There were times I saw it. There was one time that really meant something to me.

My mom's not much of a crier. She only does so when something really important to her is at hand. I've never seen her tears, but I have heard her weeping just once. She was locked in her room when I heard it. I listened, and I knew that I was the subject of her crying. It sounded like she was praying to the gods, asking them to ensure that I would grow strong and set my life up where I needed it. She was sincerely begging them to watch over me and make sure I would have a good life. It was really sad but reassuring to hear. To know that my mom cared about me even if she rarely expressed it. That's kind of why I feel sad that she's dead now.

Jadeanu, tell me, did she cry or smile before she died? "A bit of both actually." I see; then she really wasn't such a bad person after all. Well she wasn't always evil. In fact, if my dad had never died, she likely would have been your ally. Afterall she only wanted to make the world more suitable for stronger people so we wouldn't have to suffer so much. I believe she would have done great for your team. And your friend likely would have never died by me. Funny how even small things that have nothing to do with one another are still connected. The irony of life.

Speaking of which, what exactly are you after? "Getting all the Blessings and then finding the god of Death to reverse the Death Spiral." I guess you'll be needing these two Blessings then. "But won't you die?" No. I use the Death Blessing to stop the disease from spreading and the Life Blessing to slowly heal the skin. But it only works when I make it. Otherwise, it's not always working, such as right now.

"Then if you come with me, you'll be fine. Don't worry, Rahricu; things will get better. Sabbath day is coming tomorrow; it's a religious day of rest. We can use it to bring you the peace you deserve."

It seems my mom must have passed her torch to you. "What do you mean?" You haven't figured it out yet? This is just a prediction based on the fact that my mother both cried and felt bliss when she died, but if I had to take a guess, I'd say my mom wanted you to meet me or rather knew you would, and that we would become friends. Knowing her, she probably laid out a plan for you to pick up where she left off. She was a woman broken by despair. I don't know what happened when you two met, but I know deep down that my mom wanted to be laid to rest. It would explain why you managed to survive the encounter with her but she didn't.

My mom wanted to make the world a bit better, even if it was only for strong people. You also want to make the world better, so she must have seen that and decided it would be better if you made the change instead of her, so she can finally be at peace. You'll end up helping the strong people once you've met me anyway. You were able to understand me from looking into my eyes, a trick I'm sure you learned from her. And I'll bet she said a few things to you that implied she saw herself in you right? That you both had similarities?

'Jadeanu begins to think about when Ava mentioned that their powers were somewhat similar in regards to the need of being able to fight in order to use them. He also thinks about how she also was widowed like he is; realizing that everything she said about it back then, she was actually talking about herself. Jadeanu starts to realize that Ava truly did see herself in him, sending a chill down his spine.'

Can you tell me what her last words were? "Sorry, she spoke them in some other language, I have no clue what she said." That's alright, although it does make me curious as to what the last thing that went through her head was. I guess I'll never know. But it is comforting to know that she didn't die in vain. So if I can help you in any way, I'd like to be of assistance to your mission if I can.

"Oh, you said you also spoke to the god of Life? Do you know where he is? I need to speak to him about getting to Death. Or just about reversing this thing." Yes, I know where he is. "Please lead the way."

Chapter 16:

Lights of Life

Rahricu takes the Blessings of Life and Death out of his swords and sockets them into Jadeanu's left gauntlet. He only needs one more, the Blessing of Spirit now. Then he would speak with the god of Death, possibly even fight him. The thought of it sends a shiver down Jadeanu's spine. Yet he follows Rahricu in the direction of Life.

"You know, each Blessing has a direct correlation to their god. They can be used to locate their creator if he's not far," Rahricu informs in his deeper voice. "And also, I'll need my two back whenever we're at a resting spot. To control my Death Disease." "Fine by me," Jadeanu responds. He drifts off into thought. "Something's concerning you. What is it?" Rahricu asks.

"It's just. I would never have thought I would become friends with a guy whose mother I killed. And the guy who killed my last friend." "I would say I'm sorry about that, but it wouldn't mean anything. Not to me nor you." "It's cool. His death yielded a great reward. I have you now! Not to sound like a jerk about it."

"Well it's good to have you as well. It's nice to have a friend for once—someone to care about. I'm not used to it though. Not used to having to feel, considering that my darkened heart has severely weakened my emotions. All I can feel are things I call feelings. The soul, not the heart, feels them. Hate, insanity, love, care, and real happiness are to name a few. Like my mother, I can only resonate with feelings but not emotions; our hearts are too cold for anything else. She and I really aren't so different after all."

"How do you tell the difference between emotions and feelings?" "Feelings are stronger, more permanent, and harder to explain. Emotions are just simple temporary feelings that everyone has, such as contentment, sadness, anger, and excitement. I have to make myself 'feel' those even though they aren't real when I do that. Feelings just hit you. You can't really control whether you get them or not, such as empathy or bloodlust. In simpler terms, you can master emotions because they are distinguished by your brain. They're just tools. But feelings are reactions of the soul, driven by your instincts. That's the nature of your passion."

"You're quite wise kid." "I'm sure I'm not much younger than you." "You're right. It's only a six-year difference." "Then you shouldn't call me kid just because I'm short and look frail. I've been more mature than most adults since before my age even hit the double digits." "Sorry." "It's alright. Just please refrain from doing so."

They continue walking through the city. "You know, Life is actually kind of far. We should get some rest; it's getting late," Rahricu suggests. "Also, so that you know, my birthday is May 3rd. It passed not long ago, so I'm a recent nineteen year old. It's June 30th now. The Death Spiral started on the 20th." "Same day as my marriage." "Oh, you were married?" "For like an hour. Then the Death Spiral took her away." "So I see. Is that why you've decided to confront the god of Death? Her death lit a fire in you that made you want to act."

"That's exactly it. You know, I'm a bit nervous about fighting Death." "Of course you are. No offense, but you couldn't even beat me, and I was taking it easy." "Oh come on. You don't have to say that!" "Hahahaha. Sorry."

Rahricu leads Jadeanu to an abandoned house. "This is where I stay now that I left my mom." "All right then, let's rest up." They both enter the building. Jadeanu nurses Rahricu's Death Disease then they take showers and rest.

The good atmosphere between the two creates good dreams. Jadeanu has a dream about his wife and all the people he lost on his journey. They all seem happy, and they motion for Jadeanu to take care of his new friend. Rahricu dreams of freedom from the binds of his mother's limitations and a bright new future.

Rahricu symbolically walks away from some chains that were once holding him back. They break as Rahricu journeys towards a strange light where Jadeanu is waiting. "Rahricu." a familiar feminine voice calls from behind him. He turns to look at who called him. His gaze immediately meets the gaze of the beautiful violet eyes of his mother. Rahricu immediately jumps in nervous fear. "M-mom!" "It's okay dear. Please don't be afraid," she reassures.

Ava smiles a smile of contentment as she stares into Rahricu's worried eyes. "I just wanted to tell you to take good care of your new friend," she continues. "And I also wanted to tell you I love you. You don't have to say it back though. I totally understand if you-" "I love you too mom," he responds with a smile on his face. "Rahricu! D-do you really mean that?" "Of course mom. I don't personally hate anyone. Not even you. I wish you well too, wherever you're going." "You always have been better than me, haven't you? I'm so sorry for taking so long to realize how great you are." "I really wish I could see you again mom. So we could have this conversation face-to-face. But I know you're gone. This is just in my imagination." "That's right. I'm where I belong; you're where you belong. But you know, she wishes she could be here and talk to you too. But fate has allowed us to drift apart. Now I finally get to be with your father again."

As Ava says this, Raiyane, her husband, suddenly appears beside her. He stands a few inches taller than her and has straight brown hair in a similar style that Rahricu has, falling past his handsome pale-skinned face down past his army-camouflaged clothed shoulders. He puts his hand around Ava's waist and just stares at Rahricu with a smile on his face.

"You know Rahricu, I'll really miss you and that cute little face of yours," Ava says. "To be honest mom, I wish I could say the same. But honestly, I'm glad we aren't together anymore." "Hahaha! Awe man, that sucks to hear! But it's what I get for being such a horrible mother. It's my greatest and only regret. But you've got better things to pay attention to, so you won't be a failure like me. The day is waiting for my son. Go. You have a whole life ahead of you. It's time for you to forget about me and live it. Live a life you can be proud of with your new friend."

Ava's eyes water as tears run down her cheek, passing by her quivering yet smiling lips. She and her husband both turn around and begin walking away toward a field of darkness, standing as opposed to the field of light behind Rahricu and where Jadeanu is still waiting. Rahricu sheds tears as well, as he turns to look at Jadeanu and then back at his parents. "Hey mom!" he calls. Ava turns to Rahricu, still with tears in her eyes.

"Thank you," he says. "For what?" "For him," Rahricu says with a slight nudge toward Jadeanu. "I'm not stupid mother. I know he couldn't have killed you at his level. So thanks for letting him live." "You're welcome, my sweet child."

"Bye mom."

"…Goodbye Rahricu."

Rahricu turns to Jadeanu and the strange light in his dream and walks toward it.

The early morning sun shines outside, and both men awake early in the morning with smiles on their faces. Rahricu wakes up with tears in his eyes. He quickly wipes them before Jadeanu can even see them. "Today's going to be a good Sabbath day. I just know it!" Jadeanu exclaims. "You want to spend it with Life?" Rahricu asks. "Sure!" Jadeanu and Rahricu walk out of the house, and Rahricu treats Jadeanu to a home-cooked meal. Then he continues leading to the god of Life.

They leave the city and move on to the next. Rahricu starts to sing in quite an amazing voice. He's definitely Ava's son with his great vocal talent. "You sing really well," Jadeanu compliments. "Thanks, but I-I'll stop if you want. S-sorry, so sorry, but I like to sing when I'm happy." "No, it's okay. Keep going. I sometimes sing too. But I do it mostly when I'm sad." "Well singing is good for your soul." "So I've heard." Rahricu continues singing until they reach the next nearby city. The city still seems in decent shape, but it is still a bit run down, likely from devious people ruining the place with theft and vandalism.

"Hey Rahricu. Do you want to help people and bring happiness to them?" Jadeanu questions. "I'm sure the people of this city could use that." "But wouldn't the work profane the Sabbath day?" "But isn't it relaxing to do such a thing? Taking a break from the main mission and just having a bit of relaxing fun. We won't do any major work, just a little. After all, a little work for a good purpose, I say it's a good reason to disobey. Which isn't disobedience considering that the spiritual law was made for us. Whatever is of comfort to us is permitted on this day." "Fine then. Since it isn't out of our way."

Rahricu and Jadeanu happily enter the city. The streets are vacant and quiet. Most of the people seem to be inside their homes. There aren't many people or cars out on the streets. The boys walk through the place and notice three big guys with red eyes surrounding another guy and a teenage girl who both have red eyes. The girl is holding an ice cream cone in her hand, evidently trying to enjoy it, but she hesitates to take a lick of it. "Hey buddy! Your kid has an ice cream cone. That means you have money. You better give it up before we have a real problem here," the leader of the group says.

"I just wanted to get her something nice for once. But I'm broke! I swear!" the guy says. The gang leader punches the man in the stomach and then says, "Don't lie to me." "Leave my dad alone!" the girl yells. The gang leader then snaps his fingers, and his two goons smack the ice cream out of her hand and pull a knife out, and put it on her throat. "Wait! Please don't!" the guy pleads. "Hey! That's enough!" Jadeanu shouts.

Rahricu spawns one of his blades and points it at the leader. "Put it down. I'll handle them," Jadeanu tells Rahricu. "I don't want you to accidentally kill anyone." The gang leader tells his goons to wait, and they stand by his side. They turn and size up Jadeanu and Rahricu. "A tough guy huh? Big mistake," the leader says, then claps in a specific rhythm. Several rough-looking guys come from the nearby buildings. There are about 10 of them in total, all with red eyes. Some have pipes, chains, and even swords in their hands.

"How about this? Your lives for hers," the gang leader suggests. "Fine by me," Jadeanu claims. Rahricu stands there silently, emotionless. Jadeanu runs through, and one hits KO's almost all of the goons. The leader comes for Rahricu and hits him with all of his force. There's the distinct sound of bones breaking. The leader's knuckles are broken. With his other arm, he attacks Rahricu, even kicking him in the nuts.

Rahricu is unharmed; the gang leader's foot, however, is aching. Rahricu thumps him on the forehead, and he falls straight to the ground in pain as he holds his now bleeding forehead. Rahricu looks up at Jadeanu, who is standing around several hurt thugs. "One of them is missing," he points out. "There were ten of them. I took out their leader, and there are only eight bodies around you." Jadeanu looks around for a runaway while Rahricu concentrates. "He's up there." Rahricu points to a guy on top of a building, pointing a gun at Jadeanu.

"Give me a boost," Jadeanu directs. He runs at Rahricu, who cuffs his hands for Jadeanu's feet, then launches Jadeanu up on top of the high building. The gang member is startled, then he shoots his gun. Jadeanu blocks the bullet with his guantlet and attacks the guy. All he hits is a stream of wind. The guy had moved at super speed away from Jadeanu. He pulls the trigger again. Jadeanu luckily catches the bullet and then throws it back hard, piercing the guy through the leg.

Jadeanu closes their gap quickly and grabs the guy by the neck. He brings the guy to the edge of the building and then jumps off with him. Rahricu doesn't hesitate to catch them. "Are you alright?" Rahricu asks Jadeanu. Jadeanu nods. The gang member is too frightened to fight back. Rahricu puts them both down. "Now listen, all of you," Jadeanu says to all of the gang members. "You all will leave this city! And you will never do these destructive things again! Do you understand?"

No one says anything. "He said, do you understand?!" Rahricu repeats. All the gang members, even their leader, say, "Yes sir," in fear. The gang leader leads all of his followers out of the city in a hurry. The man that Jadeanu and Rahricu saved starts clapping. Then a bunch of people come from the nearby buildings and clap as well. Rahricu starts to get really nervous as he looks around, only to see attention from all around closing in on him. "Thank you!" the guy appreciates. A few members of the crowd take pictures of their two "saviors." A guy in a suit comes toward Jadeanu and Rahricu and shakes their hands.

"Thank you," he thanks. "You two have saved our city. Those bandits came here and took over when the Death Spiral started. They've taken the money out of all of our pockets to maintain power. Please take this money. It's the least I could do."

Another man shows up with stacks of cash and gives it to Jadeanu. "We were planning to raid their money stash for a while, but now that they're gone, we just did it anyway." "Thank you, um, that was fast," Jadeanu expresses. "Their stash isn't far, nor is it guarded now," the guy explains. "You guys are welcome. Just doing my civic duty," Jadeanu states. "Now we've got to go."

Meanwhile, a teenage boy with a white and tan beagle dog comes outside after seeing the gang running away. His little dog runs towards the bandits barking intensely. The boy restrains the dog with its leash. But the dog is strong, and the boy has a poor grip on the leash. The dog wiggles aggressively and eventually gets away. The dog runs towards the bandits, then notices the crowd of people gathering around and is startled by the noise. With all the people in the way, the dog loses sight of his owner. He continues through the crowd hoping to run into the boy again. But he never does.

The boy, in turn, looks for his dog but the white and tan of his furry friend never crosses his gaze. The dog ends up leaving for another area, finding a shady-looking man without any special glow in his eyes. The dog tries to get his attention with whimpers and soft barks. The guy is frightened by the dog and starts kicking at him. The dog dodges most of the attacks but takes a kick to the stomach then he runs but takes a sympathetic look back at the shady guy. The guy runs at the dog waving his arms to scare him away. The dog runs away in fear.

Meanwhile, Jadeanu and Rahricu go around giving their money to the people that need it more than they do. They eventually make it to the very same shady guy who was fearfully attacking the dog. "So what's your story?" Jadeanu demands. "Huh? What?" the guy responds. "He means, what events led you to stay out here?" Rahricu restates.

"Oh! It was that gang. They robbed me of everything I had, and I ended up being stuck out here." "He's not lying. You may help him," Rahricu claims. Jadeanu takes a few hundred-dollar bills from his pocket and hands them to the guy. "Here, this should be enough to help you get back on your feet. I suggest you arm yourself and go find a job." "Oh, thank you so much! May the gods bless you both!" "You're welcome."

Jadeanu and Rahricu continue walking. "Oh, wait! Before you go...I was recently attacked by a dog. Even though it wasn't much of an attack, it just seemed helpless and lost, like me. I kinda... overreacted and chased it off. If you can find it, please help it if you can." "We'll see what we can do," Jadeanu replies.

Jadeanu and Rahricu both walk around the city. "So, we've helped out most of the people in the city. We don't have much money left," Jadeanu conversates. "Helping all those families sure was nice." Rahricu brings up. "We should go try to find that dog."

"Well can you fly up and find it?" "No, sorry. I can only fly when I let the darkness consume me. And I can't control my body when I'm like that. I'll end up hurting you and everyone else by mistake. We'd best look for it on foot." "Fine. If we see it, we'll help it." "That's the best plan. And by the way, I could learn how to control my dark form if I let it run wild for a while. Then I'd learn to master it. But that would cost many innocent lives, and I can't allow that."

Meanwhile, the dog continues walking around the city, lost. His tummy rumbles and so he goes to find some food to fill it. He walks up to a restaurant and enters when someone opens the door. He harasses a few people for their food by rubbing up against them aggressively or even jumping on their laps. Of course, they didn't share. Instead, they attack and hit the dog for ruining their dining experience. The manager of the establishment runs the dog out of the building with aggressive taunts. One of the workers approaches the manager in sympathy saying, "He just wanted some food." The manager ignores the worker's comment and continues on.

Soon, the worker takes a tray of leftovers outside. She sees the dog and calls to him. "Hey. Hey. I've got something for you. C'mon." The dog hesitantly comes closer to her. "That's it. C'mon." The dog approaches and she puts the tray down for him. The dog puts his face on the tray ready to finally have something in his empty belly. "What are you doing out here Rachel?!" the angry manager of the restaurant yells as he springs out of the building. The dog immediately turns and runs for safety without even taking a bite of the meal that was brought for him. "Get back in here and get to work! Quit messing around with that animal!" the manager continues. The worker managed to catch a glimpse of the collar on the dog, noticing that his name was Bucky. "Sorry Bucky," she mumbles. Bucky continues out on his lonely road. He barks for someone to aid him, for someone to come to his rescue. But he only gets told to shut up by the few that hear his desperate cries.

In the meantime, Jadeanu and Rahricu walk triumphantly through the city. They are approached by the very man who gave them the money that they gave away. "Hey you two. You enjoying your small fortune?" he questions. "We gave it all away to the people who need it," Jadeanu answers. "I had a feeling you'd do that. I'd like to ask you two if you would like to run this city with me," the guy states.

"So the money wasn't just a reward for chasing away those bandits," Rahricu adds. "I suppose you could say that. But that doesn't matter, the people now have that money, and they'll spend it on business. I am a businessman. That means their money comes back to me and I'll have all the power. But I'll need your strength and influence to run the city."

"You have no powers on your own and these people are not for you to control," Jadeanu expresses. "So I see. You sure you won't change your mind? Just think of all the-"

"Yep. We've got things to do. You take care now!" Jadeanu and Rahricu leave the guy and continue through the city.

They hear the distinct sound of a sad dog barking echoing through the lonely streets. They both follow the noise. Before finding the dog, they see a lost dog poster on a wall for Bucky with an address, number and picture. "Rahricu, you think you can remember the address?" Jadeanu asks. "I already memorized the address and number. Let's go!" Rahricu exclaims.

They follow the barking of the dog and soon see Bucky running. As he comes into the street, a car comes straight for him moving too fast to stop in time even if the driver wanted it to. Rahricu uses his light transformation to speed himself in front of the car. He stops the car from hitting Bucky by holding his hand out and physically stopping the car with his strength. He creates a massive dent in the front of the car and the sudden impact causes the man inside to spring forward. Good thing the driver was wearing a seatbelt and therefore did not eject out of the vehicle. The dog continues running.

A guy walking the street has a plate of meat in his hand ready to give to Bucky. He sprinkles rat poison on it then puts it down for the dog to eat. Bucky goes toward the food with drool streaming from his mouth as he prepares to feast. Rahricu quickly vaporizes the food with a light bullet which makes Bucky only more scared and angrier now that his chance of eating was just ruined. Rahricu and Jadeanu corner the dog, making him aggressive and ready to bite. He barks and growls at the two boys.

Rahricu puts his arm near Bucky's mouth and Bucky chomps down, but Rahricu feels no pain. He just lets the dog hang onto his skin which isn't even pierced. "Now let's find his home and while we're on the way, let's get him some food. He must be hungry," Rahricu suggests as he picks the dog up gently. He goes to get food for the dog from a nearby store, and Bucky soon develops trust in Rahricu.

After some petting and playing, Bucky and Rahricu create a good bond. Bucky falls asleep in Rahricu's arms as he carries him to his home. Jadeanu rings the doorbell and there is no answer. "Should we wait here?" Jadeanu asks. "Can you use the Blessings to manipulate rock?" Rahricu questions. "Yeah, why?" Rahricu summons one of his swords. He strikes his blade around the side of the door. "I'm going to need you to repair the damage that I'm making."

Rahricu cuts the entire wall around the door with one hand as he holds Bucky with the other. Once cut, Rahricu removes the whole door with his free arm and lets Bucky inside his home. Rahricu repositions the door and Jadeanu uses the Universe and Nature Blessings to reseal the door to the wall, leaving no trace of it ever even being cut.

The duo both continue through the city, following Rahricu's directions toward the god of Life. They eventually find a zoo. The place is unoccupied as no one goes there now, especially now that business was ruined by that gang. There are still some animals in there with looks of defeat and despair in their eyes. They still get food sometimes from the people who pass the zoo by but barely, so the animals there are undoubtedly hungry. But many of the animals are still all in cages. "Let's free them," Jadeanu suggests. "You think you can contain them?" Rahricu considers. "With the Blessings, yeah." "But where are we going to lead them?" "Good question."

Jadeanu concentrates on the Knowledge Blessing which glows in respect. Jadeanu then creates a large path of smooth rocks with the Willpower Blessing. "It leads to an open field," Jadeanu informs. "I've got a plan. You're fast right? I need you to free all the animals at the same time. With the Nature Blessing, I'm going to make all the animals violent and chase you. You will have to lead them along the path to the open field. It shouldn't be too hard and you won't have to worry, all the animals with powers escaped on their own. These are just the regulars." "It wouldn't matter anyway. None of them can catch me or hurt me. Now let's go."

Rahricu shoots bullets at each cage that has animals in them, bursting them partly open. Then a bunch of different types of animals immediately break out and run toward Rahricu. Elephants, giraffes, lions, donkeys, meerkats, penguins, alligators, and birds. Rahricu turns into light and moves quickly along the path. Jadeanu immediately jumps on the back of a giraffe to keep up with the animals.

Rahricu stops every so often to allow the animals to keep up with him. Jadeanu takes care that the animals don't fight each other and that the big animals don't step on the smaller ones by bending their desires with the Nature Blessing. Soon they all reach the open field. There is grass and beautiful white, and red lilies as far as the eye can see. The sun is setting behind some distant hills, illuminating the scene in a fascinating manner. All the animals plunge into the field and Jadeanu stops their aggression towards Rahricu with the Nature Blessing. He jumps off the giraffe and lands next to Rahricu.

The animals immediately mind their own and gaze around in the field. Jadeanu calls upon the Nature Blessing and creates a dip into a part of the field. The hole soon fills up with water which creates a pond there for the alligators and for the animals to have water. He fills one part with swamp water and the other with fresh water, separating them with a dam of rocks. He does another split in the freshwater and fills one side with glaciers. He then creates several different types of trees, some with fruit so the herbivores can eat. "And one last thing." Jadeanu holds up the Willpower Blessing and it glows, and its energy branches off and lightly touches each animal.

"What was that?" Rahricu wonders. "I just lessened the ravenous will of all the animals. Now they can live in peace with each other. Or at least they won't try to kill each other without a good reason." "That's good." "It's beautiful, isn't it? All these animals are free now to enjoy this land. And we did that for them. And we've restored this city as well. They all have a fighting chance to help their own world." "You're just missing one thing." "And what's that?"

"More species of aquatic animals to feed what you put in those waters. This is where I come in. You'll need to use the Life Blessing to create and give life to some fish. Close your eyes and concentrate on the inner beauty and purity of yourself in the world around you. Feel the fact that you're alive in this world and focus on your breath." Jadeanu obeys what he's told, and the Blessing of Life starts to glow. "Now imagine fish, then extend your soothing breath into them." As

Jadeanu does this, he opens his eyes, and they glow with a white hue. He summons multiple types of fish in midair and then throws them into the water sources telepathically.

Jadeanu and Rahricu smile at the beauty they have caused. "You ready to go see Life? He's just past those hills over there," Rahricu comments. "Not yet. We've made many people happy, but there's still something we can do to make people **really** happy. Or rather a certain group of people."

"What?" "There are tons of beautiful flowers around here. I say we pick one beautiful flower for each female in the city. And we go door-to-door and just give one specially picked flower to the female of each home." "Sure, but how are we going to know where to go and how many lilies to pick?" "I'm sure that businessman we met will have an idea. He seems to know a good deal about this city and the gang must have had a system to keep things on lock. I'll ask him. You can stay here and pick some flowers."

Jadeanu starts walking back toward the city. "And only pick the best-looking ones! And no shortcuts!" he calls back. After several minutes, Jadeanu comes back with a piece of paper in his hand. "There are exactly 314 females in this city. I even have a map of each of their homes. Seems that gang really had the place mapped out. No wonder the people were cautious about fighting back." Rahricu stands there holding dozens of lilies. "I already have 37 of them. The most beautiful of the lilies I can find," Rahricu informs. "Good, we just have a bunch more to pick." Jadeanu jokes.

"What exactly are you hoping to achieve here?" Rahricu questions. "Just think. How would things have changed if only someone stopped to give you a flower." "I see. Then we have 277 more flowers to pick. Come on."

Rahricu and Jadeanu pick the most stand-out flowers they find in the field while enjoying the relaxing atmosphere. "Let me tell you a story Jadeanu," Rahricu says. "There once was a small rat. The rat was smaller than all the others, and so he was shut out from all the others. The small rat was exceptionally skilled in combat. He went out to fight big rats to show his strength, hoping that someone would actually acknowledge his feats. And he would always accidentally kill the big rats, but he didn't like having to kill them. But because the bodies were all that was left, no one recognized the small rat's efforts, thinking it was always a farce.

And so, he had no mate to look in his direction. So he continued fighting bigger and stronger rats, killing them all by mistake. Yet no one would still believe the small rat. The small rat wanted to prove his legacy, but he didn't want to kill anymore because it wasn't what he liked, and it would scare away any female rats. So, he purposely held back on all of the rats. And because of it, no one believed in the small rat's abilities even more.

So the small rat left and stayed in the darkness alone and became a demon. Even though all he wanted was to become an angel for the other rats. Things didn't have to be like that, but the rats were incollectively ignorant and now all who are not must suffer."

"But with another rat as the small rat's friend, he has more to look forward to. He doesn't have to stay a demon." "And if he doesn't, he still never had a chance to be near a female rat. He's no good with them and they make him run away." "Well that's okay Rahricu. A good woman won't require you to prove yourself with games." Jadeanu puts his hand on Rahricu's shoulder. "I've learned from an angel named Ravah, the most special people make the biggest sacrifices and suffer the most. But they make the greatest changes if they hold on. There is something out here for you. You'll become great. I know you will. People will remember you for generations. And if not on its own, I'll make it happen!"

"Thank you Jadeanu. I've always wanted to be human. But I believe that no man is complete without a woman. Yet I am beyond man. I have other options, but I don't want them. They won't do me any good." "I guess we'll see how you do with women when we're finished picking all these flowers." "Oh gosh…"

Nearly an hour passes and now Jadeanu and Rahricu have a huge vase full of lilies. Jadeanu had created the vase using the Willpower Blessing. "And this makes exactly three hundred and fourteen flowers. You ready for this?" Jadeanu expresses. Rahricu smiles. "Yeah."

They both go door to door giving each female that they see a flower. Each girl smiles and thanks them. Something as simple as a flower has made these girls' day. It's just what they needed as a light in these dark times. A simple gesture that shows that at least someone cares about them. The boys go up to one lady's home and the beautiful woman who owns it immediately catches Rahricu's eye. The woman is rather tall for a woman and has long, pretty dark brown straight hair and bright yellowish-brown skin. She has a gorgeous face and a small mole near her mouth on the left side under her lip. She has perplexing brown eyes meaning she has no powers. She sports a black button-down long-sleeved top with casual dark blue jeans. Rahricu blushes slightly when he sees her.

"Here, please have a flower. Let it be a sign that someone cares about you," he says. "Oh thank you," she thanks with an enchanting voice. Her eyes lock with Rahricu's as she smells her lily. "Mmm. Smells nice. You truly have made my day. May I ask how old you are?" "Um..uh, n-nin-nineteen," Rahricu stutters. "I'm 23," she informs. "You know, it's a bit lonely out here when you're a girl like me. When you're young and mature, there aren't many good guys who are like-minded."

Rahricu starts shaking in nervousness. "Y-yeah well…good…luck with that. I…I…I've…gotta go now." "Are you alright?" the woman says, concerned. Jadeanu puts his arm on Rahricu's shoulder. "Come on. You've got this. I'm sorry miss. He's just nervous." "That's alright," she considers.

"You know, you two are the reason I am able to spoil myself a little. You two got rid of those thugs and donated money to my house when you gave money to that family that supports financially independent women. So how about I take you two out to eat. I know you're hungry. It's the least I could do."

Rahricu grabs his fidgeting arm and looks down. "Sure. We can...go out and eat." "C'mon. Get in my car. I'll take you to a place I know," she commands as she brushes past Rahricu. Her breast hits Rahricu's shoulder which makes him space out. She grabs his wrist and brings him to her black Toyota Camry. She opens the passenger car door and waits for Rahricu to get in before she closes it. She moves to the driver's seat. Jadeanu brings the vase of flowers and gets in the backseat. They all strap on their seatbelts and the woman starts the car then drives off.

As she drives, her eyes stare at Rahricu with a sly smile on her face. "You should keep your eyes on the road," Rahricu advises. "I guess you're right," she responds and looks forward at the road. They continue in silence until they arrive at a restaurant. "This is the place," she tells. They all get out of the car, and Jadeanu brings his vase. The woman grabs Rahricu and clenches his hand as she walks to the entrance of the restaurant. Jadeanu smiles as he follows behind.

As they enter, someone notices Rahricu with the beautiful woman. He approaches. He also has red eyes signaling his powers. "Hey kid. A woman like that wants a real man, not some stiff walkin' loser like you," the guy says. The woman's eyebrows arch in annoyance. Rahricu silently balls his fist. "What!? You gonna hit me?" the guy taunts. Rahricu takes a deep breath and opens his fist.

"Ha!" The guy punches Rahricu in the face and hurts his hand. Jadeanu grabs the guy's shirt and lifts him up. "Hey! What's your problem?" "Forget this. You can have her!" the guy exclaims. Jadeanu lets him down and he speed walks out of the building. "You've got a good friend," the woman compliments. After that, they are all seated at an open table, given menus and time to figure out what they will get to eat as the waiter leaves them to themselves.

"I don't know what kind of foods you guys eat but they have lots to choose from," the lady suggests. "Don't be shy and get whatever you want. I'll pay for it all." "Thank you miss. Um, can you tell me please you-your name?" Rahricu says with nervous energy just radiating out of his mouth. "Hahaha! Weird way to state your question," she responds with a jokingly teasing tone. "My name is Huana. Haha! And you are?"

"Rahricu." "Well Rahricu, you wanna make our meeting more formal with a handshake?" Huana jokingly says while holding out her hand. "Oh, um…yeah, sure." Rahricu panics and slowly reaches his hand towards hers. "Dude, I was kidding!" Huana assures while withdrawing her hand. "Oh, was I not supposed to?! I, I-I'm sorry. I just…I didn't-" "Rahricu calm down. Here, gimme your hand." Rahricu fully extends his hand as Huana grabs it. Then she lightly grabs his hand with her other hand as well. "It's okay. You're not good at these things, I get it. It's nice to meet you Rahricu," she says as she slowly shakes Rahricu's hand which calms him down.

Then they both return their hands to themselves. Huana takes a look at Jadeanu and asks, "So what's your name?" "I'm Jadeanu." "Oh that's neat, you both have a 'U' at the ends of your names." "I never actually thought of that. That is pretty interesting," Jadeanu responds. "Well anyway, let's focus on what we want to eat before our waiter returns and makes things awkward," Huana suggests. "This place isn't super fancy, but it has high-quality stuff. The chicken and waffles in here are to DIE for. It's what I'm getting. But there are many more things here, if you have any questions, just ask me. I'm the expert."

Some time passes and everyone finds out what they want, and soon the waiter comes out with it. As everyone eats, conversation springs up once again. "So what kinds of things do you guys do for work and fun?" Huana asks. "I'm a bit of a simple guy," Jadeanu speaks up. "I used to work for an insurance company, but for fun, I kind of just go with the flow of things. Go out on random outings, find some fun, and exercise."

"I don't work, but I like to sing, dance, watch anime, play video games, draw and read books," Rahricu answers. "I also like to help others whenever I can." "I like to dance around my house naked like a lunatic," Huana states. Rahricu starts to chuckle at the thought, and Jadeanu follows suit. "I'm joking. No, I'm a bit of a practical person. I like to watch movies, and I **love** to read. That, we have in common, Rahricu."

"Ooh, what kind of books do you like?" Rahricu asks. "All of them." "Have you read the Percy Jackson books?" "Oh yeah! I love that series." "So do I." "You know, I get to read a lot. I work as an editor and a library assistant. So being around books is my thing. Plus, I love helping others find what they need. Those two jobs are why I have a good amount of money to spend like this. Although most of it was taken by that gang you guys disposed of.

Unfortunately for me, those guys took from everyone except for businessmen. Everyone else was left broke and depended on the mercy of the gang to get anything. And they definitely picked on you when you wanted to go out for anything other than the necessities like food. So recently, I've been mostly stuck at the house so as not to create any trouble with those guys. After all, who knows what would have happened if those guys had singled me out.

Anyway, I had food and supplies at my place, so I decided to make things work there. And I'll tell you, I can throw down in the kitchen. But now I have money again. The good thing is that people still like to read books, so I'm not out of a job and I'll be able to get back on my feet in no time. Then I can live a good luxurious peaceful life and continue to aid others who need just a little push in the right direction.

Speaking of which, Rahricu your drink is looking a little empty. You know they give free refills here." "Oh, really? Do I ask the waiter?" "Yeah." Rahricu immediately gets frightened at the thought of talking to his waiter. Huana notices the slight change in Rahricu's expression and gets the waiter's attention, and asks him to give Rahricu a refill herself.

The three eat the last of their food and soon the waiter comes by with the check, preparing to give it to Jadeanu. "Over here. I'll be taking this one," Huana corrects. The waiter gives Huana the check and then the customer copy of it as well. She pays the check and then writes something on the back of the receipt with the pen she was given.

"Well this is where we go our separate ways," Huana says as she and the guys all stand up and prepare to leave the establishment. "Man I am soo freakin fat," she continues. "It's been a while since I've gotten so full. I'm glad we were able to do this."

"I am too. Thanks for the meal," Rahricu appreciates. "It was the least I could do. Well Rahricu. Please take this." Huana gives Rahricu the, now folded up, customer copy receipt. Rahricu opens it up. It says, "Call me, handsome," then a ten-digit number. "That's for my landline phone. I know phones with service aren't really abundant, but if you can, please call me. Or pay me a visit whenever you can," Huana suggests. "Do you need a ride?" "No thanks. We are exactly where we need to be." Jadeanu says holding his map.

Huana leaves after saying goodbye to the boys. Jadeanu and Rahricu deliver the rest of their flowers to the remaining women in the city. Rahricu has a genuine smile on his face with the light of what has all occurred and the hope he has nurtured on this day. Then they both walk back along the path that leads to the field of lilies. They notice a billboard with both of their faces on it saying, "We will remember our heroes." The city now has a chance for everyone in it to live a peaceful life.

Somewhere in the city, the boy who had lost his dog, is happy with his dog's sudden return. His family also had a donation of Jadeanu's reward money. Because of it, the boy had a decent allowance. He takes his dog, Bucky, for a walk, ensuring to hold his leash tight.

Bucky ends up noticing a teenage girl walking by on the sidewalk and then moves to try to sniff her. The boy tries to restrain his dog. "It's okay," the girl says. She bends down to pet Bucky. He continued sniffing then moved toward the girl's butt. "Hey! Hey Bucky! That's not appropriate!" the boy calls. "No. I think he wants this," she states while pulling out a lily from her butt pocket.

The dog follows the flower. The girl is, in fact, the very girl being harassed by thugs when Jadeanu and Rahricu first came by. She gives her lily to Bucky and then smiles at the guy. He blushes then says, "My dog seems to like you." "Hehehe well, I'm pretty good with animals," she starts to blush a little too. "Well you lost a flower, so how about I buy you some ice cream to compensate," he mentions. "That would be awesome," she replies.

Jadeanu and Rahricu continue walking through the peaceful field of lilies admiring what they have done. When they get close to the tall hills, Jadeanu stops walking. "We should get some rest here," he suggests. "But we're close. We could miss Life," Rahricu considers. "It's Sabbath day. He likely won't move much. We can catch him tomorrow," Jadeanu plans. "Plus I'm a bit scared. The closer we get to getting the last Blessing, the sooner I have to face the god of Death."

"Well we're in this together. I won't let anything happen to you." "Haha. You sound like someone I used to know. My brother Luke. He was like a protective parent and a great friend." "Well what happened to him?" "He...he died saving me and my friend that you had killed. He was so happy to die for me. You sort of remind me of that resolve."

"Thanks I guess. It's unfortunate that you lost someone so close to you." "It's okay. It's why I'm alive now. It's why I met you.

I wouldn't want it any other way." "Good. Then you shall have no regrets. It's healthy for your Spirit. Let's go ahead and get some rest."

The boys set up a little camp by the hillside. Jadeanu starts to sing a little. *'A man's gotta do what a man's gotta do. If that means that I stand here to fight you.'* "Singing a remix of a song I've heard somewhere before. You're imagining a stressful scene while doing so huh? Well I'll leave you to it. Goodnight." Rahricu goes to sleep first, then Jadeanu. The bright morning sun wakes them both in its supposed time by blasting them with its bright gaze.

"Come on, Life is close by!" Rahricu starts. "Shouldn't we get some food first?" Jadeanu suggests. "We can get food later. C'mon, let's go!" Rahricu leads Jadeanu past the hills and there is a trail of beautiful and various plants. "I can feel it, the presence of everlasting life," Jadeanu announces. He and Rahricu move through the trail, excited to see the very god who aided in the start of the Death Spiral.

They both continue until they see a man with tan white skin and brown hair down his neck. He wears an all-white robe with a strong white aura surrounding him. He's undoubtedly the god of Life. His eyes are silverish-white, and he has his white rapier drawn.

He is speaking to someone who is on their knees, likely because of his strong presence. The other person is a man with a beard, wearing lots of makeup and has long, straight hair. He is wearing a dress and high heels. And he has a voice of which poorly mimics natural femininity as if he wants to be a woman.

"You are the one who made me like this! You should accept me for who I am!" the crossdressing guy says in a loud and agrivating voice. "But you were not made this way. This is what you chose to become. An abomination," Life says in his iconic Australian accent. "I am free to be whatever I want," the crossdresser claims. "And free you are. But that doesn't exclude consequences. Of which you shall suffer," Life responds.

"You are a man and you shall always be. Run all you like but you are male due to birthright. For it is the gift of life's many surprises. You have the responsibilities of a man. You must not run from your counter differences from a woman. You must accept your reality. You are held to a greater standard than a woman, for your actions encourage that of future life. For life is pure and innocent. Yet innocence is stolen by your decisions.

Preying upon the pure to enforce a will they cannot even comprehend. Torturing them with the responsibility that they ought not have. The unnatural position of youth is the start of a destructive, unnatural future of regrets that they would have never had a chance to yet understand. You are a stain on the innocence of life. Filling people with the binding of a mental death out of your own fear. Respect what you have and be the man you are. For all you do is lie. Lie with your face and lie with your words. And speaking of this is no use to an abomination such as you."

"Then why are you saying it?" "For them." Life gestures toward Jadeanu and Rahricu. He then stabs swords into the crossdresser 's skull, thus killing him. He turns to Jadeanu and Rahricu then steps forward. Each step he takes causes a plant to sprout from the ground. His aura knocks Jadeanu down to a kneel and even makes Rahricu stumble. Rahricu kneels in respect and then stands back up. *He sure isn't holding his aura back, is he?'* Jadeanu thinks. "Stand up," Life commands.

Jadeanu slowly stands up. "Hello Rahricu. It is good to see you again." "It is good to see you again as well." "And Jadeanu. Greetings." "Hello Life." "You have come to me for guidance, have you not?" "I have. I want to better understand the Death Spiral. Why did it happen?"

"You don't know how it occurred, but you know why. It is merely a time in which a new aspect of the Universe was given to the Earth. A time when life will be in its rawest form. A struggle and purity such as the Blessing you hold." Jadeanu looks at the Blessing of Life. It is half white and half orange all spiraling like a yin-yang sign.

"Death sits where I once sat. It has created a disbalance in your world. For it connects to you as all spirits are connected. Such is what Universe represents." "So we are all connected somehow, but exactly how? And you killed that person, but you are Life. Please enlighten me as to your reason if I may ask."

"Well, do you believe that you are different from Rahricu? That man? My angels? Me? Or even these plants around you? We all live. We all have a spirit. I am the great tree that all of you branch from. I and my angels are greater than you but not better, for we are one in the same. You are the smaller spirits from my great spirit. You all live. You all breathe the same air. We're all on this Earth breathing together. I am your father, and you all are brethren. Having different struggles and different lives but all ending up the same.

For we all exist together. All just branches from the same tree which is me. Some branches are bigger than others but all branches nonetheless. But there are values within those branches. Do you feel sympathy when you squish a bug? You do not think that you may have killed another life form's father who was out only for food to take care of his young and you just ruined that. Although your lives are the same, your worth is what pushes you from sympathy. The bigger branches are more valuable, and so the smaller ones are less significant but should still be regarded as an equal life. This is the cycle of significance.

All things should be a life for life unless there is a collective judgment of one's worth. Yet that is not a permit for selfish revenge. One rotting branch must be cut from the tree or its rot will spread to more branches until it covers the tree, and all will experience death. That is why we must all judge life and extinguish what is necessary to extinguish.

Such as this tree." Life states, motioning toward a nearby tree. "It springs a single apple. A life it gave to another. Yet you must kill it for food. For its life is not as great as yours and it shall provide a nourishment for your life. And so, its life is still significant, even in death. For one's death means another's life. That is the work of the Universe and why it shall remain eternal. Time and death do not separate us. We are always connected in some kind of way. For with an open mind, many advantages become possible."

Life positions his sword as if about to cut the apple from the tree. In less than half a second, the stem of the apple is cut, and Life catches the apple. "It looks as if I moved really fast to cut the apple from its tree. However, I did not. I merely willed for the apple stem to be cut and so it did. I need not touch it with my blade."

Life holds the apple and concentrates on it, and it splits perfectly in half. He gives one half to Jadeanu and the other to Rahricu. "Your mind is a powerful tool. It connects to your entire body, and it connects to your spirit. And through it, you can harness your spiritual power that comes from us gods. All you need is to open the door to opportunity and the path of your life will follow. And with the power of a god, what does that make you? You understand your importance now do you not?"

"I do." "Good then. If you wish to confront Death, you'll need to get to the Heavens. I can take you to him, but I require that you attain the Spirit Blessing to complete your journey first. Only with all seven Blessings will I let you travel to the Heavens. Spirit is not far from here, we traveled to Earth for the same purpose, and we remain close in doing so. Once you get the Blessing from him, return to me. I will remain here as he will remain until you complete your task. Go on, Jadeanu, you are nearly done with your mission."

"Thank you Life." Jadeanu and Rahricu move forward. Jadeanu concentrates on the Knowledge Blessing to locate Spirit. He leads the way. Not much time passes before Jadeanu and Rahricu find Spirit standing in an open pasture filled with the residue of a scorched stadium. Spirit has long brown hair down past his shoulders. His eyes are red, and so is his aura. He wears white robes as well and carries a flaming sword in his hand.

There are many dead bodies around him, signaling that he slaughtered hundreds of people. Jadeanu and Rahricu are unsettled upon approaching him. "Um, Spirit?" Jadeanu calls. Spirit gazes at them, and his strong aura hits both of them. They don't fall however. They hold their ground. "Yes?" Spirit answers with a deep voice. "I desire to wield your Blessing." "Humph. Well you and your friend are pure. You do not give in to your pleasures. You are well and do well for others. Your intentions are noble, and you both have suffered much. You have my favor."

Spirit spawns the Blessing of Spirit and gives the red orb to Jadeanu. "Complete your mission, for I have one to complete. I don't have much to say. I am not a spirit of guidance. I am a spirit of judgment. Your journey here has given you the wisdom of your soul and shall continue through your experience. Good luck."

Spirit grows huge white wings ignited with fire. He quickly moves in front of a city full of people then he flaps his wings, which creates a giant flaming tornado to ravage the city. Jadeanu sockets the last and final Blessing into the empty carving on his left gauntlet. His mission is nearing an end. Jadeanu feels the misfortune of understanding that all the others he was once companions with won't see it. "I'm not ready to fight Death yet," Jadeanu claims. "I need to meditate on all the Blessings first. I need guidance, power, and control. I'm going to pray first." Jadeanu sits down in a crisscross and closes his eyes.

Chapter 17:
As Perfect As A Human Can Get

'I want the power to complete my mission. I must get rid of fear. I need power and wisdom to guide it. I need to be better,' Jadeanu thinks as he concentrates deep into his mind. *'I must leave all behind. All that matters is my mission! I will complete it! No regret, no fear. Let it all dwindle away. Dear gods, please grant me the power I need to perform my task. I am Jadeanu Stroyem, and I must become perfect.'*

All seven Blessings glow, and all of his chakra points stemming from his spine light up a bright white alignment as his body starts to change. His hair grows down past his shoulders. His muscles become more defined, and his face suddenly becomes more handsome yet uniquely his own. He is surrounded by a bright rainbow aura as his power rises substantially. He opens his eyes, and there are no pupils, only glowing white all around.

He stands up, and it seems he has grown a whole foot taller with him towering over Rahricu now. His clothes stretch to fit him perfectly. All the Blessings stop glowing. "Come Rahricu. We shall finish this," he says in a slightly deeper voice. Rahricu looks at Jadeanu in shock, then he nods.

Far away, back in some other land, Knowledge looks into the air as if sensing something. "Well Jadeanu, what Ravah had said was incomplete," Knowledge says. "You are an ordinary man. But you are special because you wanted to be, and you have become the only man to awaken the power of the original humans. The generations have weakened over the centuries of sloth and convenience, but you awoke your native strength and maintained your intellect. That makes you special. You asked for power and guidance; now you have it."

Jadeanu and Rahricu continue walking through the open area. Animals from around the wilderness all move to Jadeanu and bow their heads at him. Jadeanu looks to his left side and sees a lion sitting down with its head bowing in respect. He pets the lion's soft mane and continues. Some people also bow at Jadeanu in respect of his godlike presence. "A god!" someone shouts. "No. Not a god," Jadeanu corrects. "I am but a human like you. For this form is attainable by all." Some people feel devalidated by the thought of a human being so great and decide to attack.

Someone with red eyes punches Jadeanu in the face. It does nothing. Jadeanu grabs the guy and snaps his neck. Another guy swings a sword at Jadeanu. The sword breaks into pieces, and Jadeanu draws his. He slices the guy in half without hesitation, causing blood to spray all around. A group of people roll in a cannon from what seems like nowhere. They aim the cannon at Jadeanu and fire. The cannonball shatters on impact with Jadeanu's skin, leaving the shooters dumbfounded.

Jadeanu swings his blade, which causes a strong wind that shreds the people completely in a large radius. The surrounding animals all get angry at Jadeanu's attackers and start chasing them off. Everyone else runs for their lives. Suddenly, a giant hand comes from nowhere in the sky and descends quickly with force in an attempt to smash Jadeanu and Rahricu. They both separate and dodge the attack. Then they both look at the sky and see Ravah there flying above them.

"I could feel the power of the Blessings from far away," Ravah announces. "Now I shall kill you and claim all the Blessings for myself. I will gain the power of a god." Ravah draws his blades and charges Jadeanu. Jadeanu places both hands on his huge sword and blocks Ravah's attack. He is sent backward by a few inches but overall holds his ground.

"Hmm. That strength. What form of power is this?" Ravah questions. Rahricu throws one of his swords at Ravah, causing him to back up from the collision with Jadeanu. Rahricu jumps next to Jadeanu and reclaims his other sword. "Who is this guy?" Rahricu asks. "This is Ravah. The angel I've told you about. We'll have to defeat him if we are to continue." "Hmhmhmhmhm. This is interesting," Ravah expresses. "Jadeanu and Rahricu. Your number of allies sure has dwindled. Rahricu, a perfect mind and body alongside Jadeanu, an ideal soul. But none of your perfections shall equal the perfection of a true angel. Prepare to gaze upon your ultimate fate of death."

Ravah flies up and aims his wings at his opponents. He fires a barrage of feathers. Jadeanu blocks with his blade with swift hand speed. Rahricu does the same. "Watch out for his nails. They have special powers," Jadeanu warns. "He's strong right? That means I can finally go all out," Rahricu admits with a smile on his face.

He finds a chance to aim one of his swords at Ravah and fires light bullets at him. Ravah moves to the side of Rahricu and dashes at him with a sword. Rahricu blocks it but is pushed back by the force. Ravah moves to Jadeanu with a claw from his sharp nails. Jadeanu dodges and balls a fist with his left hand. His hands light up with white energy instead of the usual red. He punches Ravah in the face, which causes a great deal of damage. Ravah grunts from pain and counters with a punch to Jadeanu's face, which does a similar amount of damage in addition to cutting his face with his sharp skin. Jadeanu swings his cutlass forward, and Ravah blocks with his sword. Jadeanu's force knocks his opponent back a little; he is actually overpowering Ravah.

However, Ravah simply draws his other sword and pushes against Jadeanu's force with both of his rapiers. Jadeanu grips his blade with both hands to equalize Ravah. Rahricu moves behind Ravah and swings his blade. Ravah dashes to the side, and Rahricu responds by dragging his blade across the ground to create his piercing light wave wall attack.

Ravah dodges. Jadeanu points his right gauntlet, and the Universe Blessing glows. Space itself bends around Ravah in an attempt to collapse on him. Ravah opens an abyss portal to escape. He reappears far above his attackers. "So the Universe Blessing truly does give me the power to bend the fabric of the universe." Jadeanu analyzes. Ravah places both of his swords in two separate abyss portals. They reappear out of two huge abyss portals to Jadeanu and Rahricu's sides.

Both blades are huge, and they thrust toward the two with great force and speed. Rahricu evades and launches a light crescent at Ravah. Jadeanu does a backflip then jumps off of one of the swords, then bolts himself toward Ravah, who dodges Rahricu's attack and throws a punch causing a huge fist to appear and punch Jadeanu too.

Jadeanu blocks it with his sword but still falls back to the ground. Ravah shoots off his long nails at his foes. They dodge them, and Rahricu turns to light to move beside Ravah and attacks. They clash swords for a while before Ravah's superior strength knocks Rahricu to the floor. Jadeanu sends a crescent of Blessing energy toward Ravah, who dodges and lifts his hand up to create a giant abyss hand to crush Rahricu, who is still falling. Rahricu turns to light and gets away.

Ravah makes multiple hand motions such as: smashing, side punches, uppercuts, and claps. Huge abyss arms perform those tasks to his enemies. Jadeanu and Rahricu dodge them. Rahricu without flaw. But Jadeanu trips over one of the hands but catches himself and performs a front flip to escape the situation.

When the uppercut comes, he sways back, barely dodging the attack yet maintaining full balance. It would seem as if his "flaws" only make him better in this form. Jadeanu powers up his sword and throws another crescent of Blessing energy. Ravah tries to stop it with an abyss hand, but the attack cuts through, causing him to evacuate.

Rahricu dashes underneath Ravah and charges up energy for three seconds. Ravah quickly moves out of the way, and even Jadeanu steps back. Rahricu unleashes a powerful pillar of intense light energy, much bigger than the ones he used on Jadeanu and Ren. "That condensed energy. If I had been hit with that, I would have certainly lost this fight," Ravah analyzes. "And it's still that big with him condensing it. It would have undoubtedly demolished all neighboring cities if he hadn't controlled it."

Suddenly light bullets proceed toward Ravah from his left and right. He opens two abyss portals to absorb them. The bullets are coming from Rahricu's moving swords. They are shooting on their own without Rahricu holding them. The swords also proceed into the portals. Ravah closes the portals, and now Rahricu's swords are sealed away. Then something comes toward him, thus catching his eye. It's both of Rahricu's swords proceeding directly at his face. "What!?" Ravah shouts as he blocks the incoming projectiles with his swords.

Jadeanu suddenly appears behind Ravah and swings his blade. Ravah looks back in shock. His sharp feathered wings block the attack. He fires a few feathers, which Jadeanu instinctively avoids while still pushing against Ravah's wings. He overpowers Ravah by using wind to push himself while in the air using the Nature Blessing. Rahricu flashes to Ravah's side and kicks him full force in the head, which does some evident damage.

Rahricu reclaims his swords and falls to his feet. Jadeanu falls to his feet, and Ravah levitates down. "He's an angel made of godly energy, so he undoubtedly has more stamina than both of us," Jadeanu strategizes. "We'll have to take him down before we run out of energy." "That can be done," Rahricu claims as his body shifts to a dark purple. "Haaah!" he screams as his body shifts to its dark form.

He casts dancing lightning on Ravah. Ravah dodges the initial strike. But then the lightning spins around and almost hits Ravah. "What an interesting display," Ravah compliments. Jadeanu moves in and swings his blade. Ravah blocks with his swords. Rahricu appears behind Ravah and swings his swords. Ravah turns to the side and blocks Rahricu's attack and is sent more into Jadeanu's attack. Jadeanu's blade cuts into Ravah's face. "That one's strength will be troublesome."

Ravah stomps his foot into an abyss portal which creates a giant foot above the three. Jadeanu and Rahricu jump back as the foot comes down toward the ground. Ravah retracts his foot from the portal, which gets rid of the giant foot. Jadeanu shoots a Knowledge beam from his forehead immediately. Ravah dodges it and rips off one of his cloak scythes to throw at Jadeanu, who dodges it.

Ravah laughs as he places his hand into an abyss portal. His hand comes from under Jadeanu and snatches him into the abyss. In about one second, he emerges out of the abyss, completely bound by hands and abyss liquid. Ravah is preparing to make his abyss burial attack that he once did to kill Jadeanu's brother. The miniature abyss portals surround Jadeanu's helpless body.

Rahricu throws a purple fireball from his sword. Ravah halts his abyss burial attack to block the fireball with his swords. The impact pushes Ravah back slightly. Rahricu quickly moves behind Ravah and shoots another one directly into Ravah's back. The fireball explodes all over Ravah's body, which sends him tumbling onto the ground in smoke.

Jadeanu is freed from Ravah's bondage. Rahricu looks at Jadeanu and smiles. He swings his blade at Jadeanu, who blocks with his blade yet is sent back several inches by the force. Rahricu goes for another attack but restrains himself with his other arm. He turns back to Ravah.

Ravah makes his cloak scythes rotate around him vertically. He spins around with supreme speed and dashes toward Rahricu like a fast-moving sharp wheel of death. Rahricu dodges, and a giant hand comes from Rahricu and Jadeanu's sides, respectively. The hands have sharp claws that swipe at their assigned enemy. Jadeanu and Rahricu block the unexpected attack. Ravah stops spinning and throws his cloak scythes and boomerang crown at them. They actively block the attacks.

Ravah closes in on Jadeanu with a swift axe kick with the spike on his boot ready to skewer. Jadeanu jumps back. Ravah performs a rising kick from the back of his leg, forcing himself into a proceeding backflip. Jadeanu dodges and counters but Ravah blocks with his elbow spike while still in the air. He lands and pushes his blades against Jadeanu's.

He and Jadeanu clash swords several times. Jadeanu kicks at Ravah's thigh, who blocks with his leg, then counters with a kick. Jadeanu evades and counters. They continue for a while then Ravah does a front flip with a downward slash. Jadeanu blocks but is knocked to the floor yet he immediately catches himself. Ravah makes an abyss hand with sharp claws emerge from under Jadeanu as he springs to his feet. The nails slightly scrape him; then he uses the Nature Blessing to restrain Ravah with vines.

Rahricu proceeds toward Ravah's heart. Ravah finds just enough wiggle room to create an abyss portal that spawns a huge sword to block Rahricu's initial attack. Rahricu jets his other sword past the defense and stabs Ravah in the chest. Ravah makes his abyss sword spin at incredible speed to make Rahricu move back, as well as cutting the vines that bind him. Ravah deletes his huge sword and proceeds to Rahricu as his chest wound heals itself. Rahricu swings one of his blades, and Ravah blocks it. Rahricu swings his other, and Ravah blocks that as well.

They both then go for a flurry of attacks. Rahricu and Ravah smile in utter bloodlust from the enjoyment of the fight. They move so fast that it becomes very difficult to see, and all there is to notice is movement and the loud noise of metal slamming into metal as they both attack and deflect each other's weapons. Jadeanu comes in from behind and attacks Ravah with a flurry of slashes. Ravah turns to his side and uses one hand and sword to fend off Rahricu and the other for Jadeanu.

He has trouble keeping up with both of them and ends up receiving a few deep cuts across his body. *'I need to withdraw,'* Ravah thinks. He quickly creates an abyss portal underneath himself and falls in. Jadeanu and Rahricu both nearly kill each other due to Ravah's sudden disappearance. They stop their swords inches away from their throats.

'So I see. Rahricu is learning how to control his dark form now,' Jadeanu analyzes. Ravah's wounds start healing. "You...can stop... his healing with...the Death Blessing," Rahricu says, struggling to control his dark form. Jadeanu taps into the Death Blessing, and Ravah's wounds suddenly stop healing. *'So that's how he stopped Ren's arm from regenerating.'* "Hmm. Perceptive," Ravah congratulates.

Ravah stabs both of his swords through abyss portals which extend them in plus size at Jadeanu and Rahricu. Rahricu dodges the attack and launches one of his swords coated in light at Ravah. Ravah dodges it as Jadeanu closes in on Ravah with a sword slash from above. Right behind Jadeanu was Rahricu's another blade, aimed right at Ravah. Jadeanu dodges it at the last minute by jumping over it while still striking Ravah.

Now Ravah has little time to avoid both attacks. Ravah excellently blocks Rahricu's blade and stops Jadeanu's slash all in one smooth motion. Ravah notices that Rahricu has his arms crossed in Lazarus sign as he levitates upward. The atmosphere dims. Ravah quickly throws his now unoccupied sword at Rahricu's chest. The sword hits Rahricu through his arm and into his chest, stopping short of his heart. Rahricu falls to his knees, and the atmosphere returns to normal.

Rahricu pulls the weapon out of his chest, tosses it to the side, and recalls his swords. *'Lucky him, his arm stopped him from dying,'* Ravah hypothesizes. He and Jadeanu fight on equal terms for a while, then Ravah manages to dig his sharp nails into Jadeanu's flesh. Ravah rips through Jadeanu's gut, and Ravah's pink abyss liquid covers Jadeanu's body into a sphere. Ravah makes an abyss portal under his other sword that stabbed Rahricu and one over his head. The sword falls through the portal and continues through the other for Ravah to catch. With both swords in hand, Ravah crafts several portals above the abyss sphere as he lifts his swords up. "Welcome to the realm with no light."

Rahricu rushes over and blocks Ravah's swords with one of his own. He then strategically shields the sphere with his body, blocking any vital attacks with his other sword. Several huge swords emerge from the abyss portals and attack. Rahricu is pierced in several places. "That should halt him," Ravah concludes.

Rahricu smiles widely and cuts the abyss sphere open with a swift spin maneuver. Then he immediately crosses his arms in Lazarus sign. "What!' Ravah exclaims. Ravah and Jadeanu, who is now free, both move back. Rahricu unleashes a thin pillar of light, followed by many all emerging from the ground.

Ravah moves around calmly but frantically. "If one of these catches me, I'm done for." Jadeanu's whole body suddenly glows in many colors, and all of the Blessings light up. "Being inside that orb gave me the time to think and understand." Jadeanu starts. "I know how to add the power of the Blessings to my blade for a single strike but I just needed to take it a bit further." He pursues Ravah throwing a Blessing crescent that Ravah dodges, then teleports behind Ravah and swings his blade. Ravah turns to him to block. Ravah's swords are sent flying out of his hands. Ravah punches Jadeanu in the face, which does little damage then he is pierced from behind. Rahricu is responsible. Then Rahricu puts purple energy from his blade into Ravah, thus paralyzing him.

Jadeanu wastes no time and cuts him in half vertically. Ravah's false body splits open, revealing a bit of Ravah's actual angelic form with pale white skin and still silky red hair. Jadeanu points the Blessings at the downed Ravah, preparing to kill him for good. "Go on and do it, for I have failed. It is only natural that you take my life as vengeance for your brother," Ravah persuades.

Jadeanu's body returns to his regular body with red eyes and shorter hair. His body stops glowing, and Rahricu returns to his normal form as well. "How about no," Jadeanu responds. "You're no longer a threat. I don't care for revenge; after all, I've learned a lot from my loss. Even a monster like you deserves a chance like me. Our lives are equal, and I see no reason to kill you. Instead, I think I'll just leave you to your own. Maybe that'll teach you even more than death will."

Chapter 18:

The Beauty of Death

"You two truly are magnificent. To best me," Ravah congratulates. "You are different from other humans. Hmhmhmhm. Farewell Jadeanu. Rahricu." Ravah sits there, stalemated. Jadeanu and Rahricu walk away. "You sure you want to leave him there?" Rahricu questions. "Yes. If he wanted to kill us now, he probably would at least make some move to do so," Jadeanu reassures. "But he isn't. So he isn't our problem anymore. Plus, thanks to him I have what I came for."

"And what's that?" "I was slowly learning how to use the power of the Blessings during that fight. All the knowledge I gained in that form stayed with me. I now have the ability to fill my body with the power of the Blessings. That means I have the power to fight a god. I...I'm no longer afraid of Death now."

Jadeanu and Rahricu continue their way back to Life now obtaining all the Blessings. "You have them. Well done," Life compliments. "Now you may proceed to Death. However, I must inform you that only a single soul, the one who holds the Blessings, is able to be transported to Heaven while still alive. The other will have to stay here. I'll allow you to choose who will proceed to the Heavens."

Jadeanu looks at Rahricu. "You're stronger than me. I think we'd have a better chance if you went. After all, you were able to overpower Ravah all on your own," Jadeanu considers. "Perhaps, but Ravah was an angel; this is a god. I'll have to use the Blessings, and you can use them better than I can," Rahricu rebuttals.

"But you are a genius. You've had experience with two of the Blessings; you can master the rest fairly quickly." "That's a big risk though. But think about it Jadeanu. This is your mission. You've wanted to do this for all this time. This is your will, your fight. You've lost people on the way here; the least you can do is fight for them.

After all, if I go up there and die, you regret the choice and live with endless guilt. But if you go, whether you live or die, you'll be happy you get to finish what you started. There is no regret there. I don't know much about people, but I think that's probably for the best. I will admit that I'm scared. The universe likes to take important things from me. I'm r-r-really worried tt-that the world will t-take you away too. Yet still, I can take care of things down here, even if I'm afraid."

"You're right. This is my mission and I should be the one to see it through. Life, I will go and fight Death." "Very well." Life stabs his sword into thin air, which creates a pocket of light within the space. He cuts down the path creating a rip that opens up into a portal of light. "Whoa!" the boys say.

"I should warn you. That this path to the Heavens is dangerous," Life starts. "That is why you'll need the Blessings, even though their direct powers will be nullified. Once you enter the realm, all power will be negated, and the pressure of the space will slowly tear your naked spirit asunder. You'll have to move quickly so as not to die.

And also, the realm shall judge your sins and create obstacles that symbolize them to divert you. The more sins, the more obstacles to halt you. The greater the sin, the bigger or more dangerous an obstacle. This quick path to Heaven is not easy. Not just anyone can make it through.

The only reason you're even able to go through it, is because your spirit has been greatly enhanced. But the sinful will be judged and may not make it through. In contrast, the pure and sinless will have no obstacles and an easy path through. If you can make it to the end, all injuries will immediately heal. And you will be in the gateway of the Heavens. Do you believe you can make it?" "I must." "Then enter." "Please don't die on me," Rahricu adds. "I don't know what to do if you do."

Jadeanu looks into the portal and then dashes inside. Immediately, Jadeanu's sword and gauntlets disappear as his red eyes return to brown. Two angels from outside the realm both come and fly by Life's side. The three of them and Rahricu all watch. Jadeanu sprints full speed ahead on a path of white light.

The path starts to shift. Steps appear, and the path moves upward. As Jadeanu is in there, parts of his body, starting at his face, start to peel off, and underneath the skin, is light. His body is slowly withering away, but it is not painful. He ignores it and keeps going. The angels next to Life sing in their beautiful angelic voices, filling the atmosphere with a sense of divinity.

A piece of the path falls, creating a space between platforms. Jadeanu runs and jumps clean over the hole. Giant silver metal axes appear swinging side to side from the invisible roof. Jadeanu times and avoids the axes then keeps going. The withering of his body continues to spread rapidly as he hurries. A huge step appears, followed by a small wall. Jadeanu hops on the step and then leaps to the top of the wall and jumps down the other side.

The following path shatters into large separate platforms. He jumps from platform to platform, trying not to fall. At the last platform, there is another split with a spike ball swinging back and forth. Jadeanu jumps and bravely palms the spike ball and uses it to swing to the next surface. Jadeanu looks at his hand, which now has a huge hole in it full of light. He ignores it and goes into a jog due to exhaustion.

There is a block in the path. Jadeanu vaults over it and notices an arrow coming his way. He narrowly dodges it and is scraped across the face. Jadeanu looks forward and can see the end of the path. There is a portal not too far from him. Now, the right side of his face is nearly gone, including his eye, yet somehow he can still see out of it. His right arm is nearly gone as well, but he can still touch it.

His chest is also diminishing. He picks up his speed as the sight of the end of the path fills him with determination. A wave of water suddenly fills in the path. Jadeanu approaches the wall of water, and three concealed blades emerge from it. Jadeanu does a spin maneuver around the weapons, barely managing through. He goes through the water and runs for the portal. He looks back at the water with a sympathetic stare, then goes and runs through the portal.

His body completely heals, and his sword, gauntlets, and red eyes reappear. He puts his hands on his knees and pants out of exhaustion. "Stand up straight," an Australian voice commands. Jadeanu does as he's told and notices Life standing there. "I see," Jadeanu whispers. Life closes the portal behind Jadeanu and then touches Jadeanu's throat.

Jadeanu's energy is suddenly replenished. He looks at the beautiful place with amazement. The scenery of Heaven is made of white luxurious celestial stone decorating the pathways in a ravishing manner and has clouds all around. "So this is Heaven?" "It is the Heaven that houses my kingdom. The dead do not gather here but only in the other Heavens, for there are others as there are other hells. Now come with me."

Jadeanu follows Life through a path guided by white celestial stone that leads to a huge temple. "Stop," Life suddenly commands. He knocks on what seems like nothing, but a purple force field stops him from advancing. "Death made it to keep me out," Life elaborates. "Concentrate into the force of all the Blessings at once and create an energy field around yourself."

Jadeanu does as he's told and creates a multicolored barrier around himself. Life adds his energy to the field and lifts it up. Life jumps up and turns his right side into its chaotic side. He palms the orb and shoots it into the forcefield like a cannonball. It travels straight through the field and into the open area that the barrier once guarded. Life walks through the place. Jadeanu's barrier breaks as soon as it hits the ground. He gets back up unhurt.

In front of them stands the temple entrance and an angel with a purple aura standing next to it. "Death is in the sixth Heaven. The one of cloud. He's waiting for you Jadeanu," the angel informs. The angel then flies away. Life leads Jadeanu into the temple. It is Life's throne room. In front of the entrance is a path of stairs leading up to Life's beautiful throne, still colored purple from Death's aura.

Most of the flowers in the fields at the side of the stairway have died, but there are still many alive. There are waterfalls around the vast dazzling garden full of different types of flowers and greenery. Yet the place is entirely abandoned. "This place is beautiful!" Jadeanu blurts. "This place...it is my kingdom," Life explains. "All here has a direct link to Earth. Each flower represents a human life, such as the stars. As you can see, many are dead, and many are alive. And some are sickly and dying."

Life points to a beautiful red rose that is big and healthy. It gravitates its lean toward Life. "That rose is you, Jadeanu. If I were to pick it, you would die here and now. But I shall not. For your Life is good and strong." Life gestures to another flower near Jadeanu's. The flower is a huge purple verbena flower, but one of its leaves is diseased. The flower is much bigger than Jadeanu's and has a strong lean toward Life and towards Jadeanu's.

"That one is Rahricu. He is strong and gravitates a little toward you. That means he is strongly invested in you," Life elaborates. "All nearby flowers to one another are friends or family. You are surrounded by many dead flowers. But Rahricu had none until you. All flowers are arranged in such a vast complex system. Ordered in ways that signify who you can meet and whom you have the possibility to acquaint with. A connection to us all."

Life walks to his throne and touches something behind it. A path of clouds appears next to Life's tainted throne leading to a place far from the current area. "If you follow this path, you will reach the sixth Heaven where Death awaits. Go when you are ready." Life walks away from the path. "You're not coming with me?" Jadeanu asks. "As Rahricu hast said, this is your will and your mission," Life answers. "I care not for Death's defeat. I have other things to do. We will meet again." Life flies out of his kingdom and to space unknown.

Jadeanu walks through the path filled with a sense of unease as he walks on his lonesome, and approaches a huge colosseum door. He takes a deep breath and opens the door. Once the door is ajar, he enters a huge room made of fluffy white clouds. The door behind him closes and seals, making it look like the rest of the room. On the other side of the room, Death is there, sitting down with his eyes sealed shut.

He opens them and gazes at Jadeanu with his stunning purple eyes. Death is absolutely handsome, with long black hair down his back, decorating his contrasting pale skin. "Congratulations Jadeanu. I'm pleased with you for making it this far," Death compliments as he stands up. "Fighting your way up here on your will alone is commendable. You need not fear death, for I have no intention of killing you."

Death makes his double scythe appear in his hand. "However, we shall fight. Show me everything you have to offer. Let us see if you can stalemate me." "Do we have to fight?" "That's up to me. You see, I created this Death Spiral with my will. You aim to end it with your will. Fighting is the balance that decides whose desires will survive. So we will fight."

Jadeanu draws his sword and charges Death. He swings his blade, and Death easily blocks it with his scythe. Death taps Jadeanu on the forehead with his finger. Blood rushes from Jadeanu's nose, and he bolts back to the entry wall of the clouded room from the force. He wipes his nose and runs at Death again.

He launches a crescent of Blessing energy at Death, who dodges it. Jadeanu closes in and swings his blade again. Death blocks and slowly raises his other hand up to Jadeanu's head. He lightly touches Jadeanu's head, which makes him spring face-first into the ground. *'At least the ground is compacted softness,'* Jadeanu analyzes from nose deep in the clouds.

Meanwhile, back on Earth. Ravah stands in his fake purple-skinned body, surrounded by a bunch of people with disappointed faces. "You're no god!" "You lost your fight!" "I can't believe you lied to us, you fraud!" many people yell at Ravah. "You ingrates! I've never lied to you!" Ravah yells back. "Do you not understand that I have asked nothing of any of you?! You all followed me on your own will and believed what you wanted! I don't need to live up to your beliefs."

"You're just a weak excuse for a savior!" someone says, and Ravah gets angry. "Do you people only listen to victory? Do you not realize that I can kill everyone here with ease?" The people start to leave Ravah in their own disappointment. "Suffering from the consequences of failure. I know that feeling all too well. One of the unfortunate advantages of ignorant humans. Always placing the blame of their mistakes on someone else that they chose to follow. That poor soul." Rahricu says to himself.

There is a guy who flies to Ravah's side with a golden glow covering his right arm along with a yellow hue in his red eyes. "My lord, unlike these idiots, I still believe in your power and divinity; but you have failed us, and so I can no longer serve you." The man then flies away. "Do you disagree with my demands Aire? If not, where is your loyalty?" Ravah tells him before he is completely gone. "I just wanted to serve a new god," Aire says before he continues on.

Life approaches Ravah, who is now completely abandoned. "You've lost all your followers. And now thou must face thine punishment," Life says to Ravah as he draws his sword. "Well I shall not go down without a fight," Ravah states as he draws his two swords. "This won't be much of a fight," Life claims. He and Ravah charge at each other, preparing to battle it out.

Back in Heaven, Jadeanu stands back up. All seven Blessings glow, and so do his body and sword. He swings his sword again, and Death blocks. "There we go. That's much better," Death praises. He and Jadeanu clash weapons multiple times until Death closes in and palms Jadeanu in the liver. Jadeanu is sent back several yards and coughs up blood. Jadeanu starts to heal his body.

Death spins his double scythe and tosses a fast-moving crescent of energy at Jadeanu, who dodges and tosses a crescent of Blessing energy at Death. Death evades and stabs one of his scythe blades into the ground. A huge scythe blade emerges from the ground and attacks Jadeanu, who avoids the attack. Jadeanu throws fireballs at Death that he creates to circle around and attack him from all angles. Then accelerates at Death using wind created from the Nature Blessing.

Death destroys all the fireballs by swinging his scythe into them. Once Jadeanu gets close, he distorts gravity to make himself do a multi-spin front flip, then tosses a crescent of Blessing energy at Death. Death is unaffected by the gravity shift, and he blocks the large crescent with the long handle of the scythe. He doesn't even flinch.

'I guess I'm not used to seeing someone actually take the full force of all seven Blessings,' Jadeanu thinks. "You're doing well Jadeanu," Death compliments. Death destroys the crescent and swings his scythe at Jadeanu, who returns gravity to normal to fall down and avoid the attack quickly.

Death and Jadeanu clash weapons a few times. Death dominates in the offensive and leaves Jadeanu on the defense. He trips Jadeanu with the back of one of his scythe blades and swings the other scythe's blade at Jadeanu in the same motion.

Jadeanu blocks and is sent back first into the wall. Death swings his scythe forward, and six little white spirits fly out towards Jadeanu who avoids the attack and brings down electricity from the sky at Death. Death cancels it with an energy swing of his scythe. He then swings his scythe in Jadeanu's direction. An intense wind stops Jadeanu from moving. The clouds are even wavering at the intensity of the wind.

"As you can see. I chose this place because it cannot be destroyed by force," Death explains. "We can fight as hard as we want without harming anything other than ourselves." Death closes in and throws his knee at Jadeanu's face. Jadeanu barely rolls out of the way. Death traps Jadeanu by placing his foot on the other side of him, stopping his rolling momentum. He hits Jadeanu twice, then grabs him by his arm and tosses him on the floor. Death stabs Jadeanu in the right shoulder.

Jadeanu grunts then aims both of his gauntlets at Death and unleashes a huge blast at him. Death quickly withdraws his scythe and spins it vigorously to guard against the blast. Death holds back the attack for a while, but then it continues through Death's defenses, blasting his entire body with a brew of colored energy.

After the blast clears, Death's body is smoking and bruised. Yet he remains standing. "You've actually damaged me," Death announces in satisfaction. Death brings down his scythe towards Jadeanu, who evades. Death's scythe goes into the clouds, and a bunch of huge scythes come from the ground and attack Jadeanu from multiple directions. He dodges them, and Death brings up sharp bones from under Jadeanu. Jadeanu jumps up, and Death makes the bones home on him.

Jadeanu bends the space around him with the Universe Blessing to avoid the attacks with precision as he flips and twists in midair.

"Come on! I have to win. It's what we've all been fighting for all this time. I have to win! For Luke! Ren! Ricardio! Stougma! Kinra! Seinaru! Rahricu! And most importantly, for me and the good of the world that we all share!"

As Jadeanu says that, he makes an attack for each name he says. He throws a blue gas energy ball at Death, then moves his shadow to attack him. He summons a bow and shoots three arrows made of pure power at Death. He generates an explosion in Death's direction and then teleports to him.

Death separates his scythes, blocks most of the attacks, and dodges the rest. Jadeanu swings his blade at Death, who blocks with his scythes. Jadeanu releases his grip on his sword with one of his hands and shoots a blast at Death. Death dodges it and uses his force to knock Jadeanu back. Jadeanu unleashes a huge pillar of light from his body using the Life Blessing. Death avoids it.

Jadeanu proceeds to Death and swings his blade again. Death blocks it with one mini scythe and slices Jadeanu's side with the other. Death puts both of his smaller scythes together again into his double scythe and swings it at Jadeanu. Jadeanu creates a multicolored force field around himself. This move, he learned from Life. Death's slice is halted for a moment, then cuts straight through the barrier and lightly slashes Jadeanu across the chest.

Death and a determined Jadeanu go sword to scythe in combat. Death cuts through Jadeanu's ribs and punches him in his other rack of ribs, thus breaking them. Jadeanu nearly falls but catches himself on his sword. "I can't lose this!" Jadeanu comments as he stands up straight. He and Death run at each other and attack with unseeable speed as they pass by each other like samurais in action films. Filling the air with suspense of what could have transpired.

Blood spurts from Jadeanu's shoulder, and he falls down to the clouded surface. "We're done here," Death tells. "But I can still fight!" Jadeanu expresses as he stands up. "Exactly. Even with your injuries, you can still stand and fight," Death reasons. "You've truly done well. This was never a matter of if you could beat me. Your strength displays that the path of your journey has nourished and ripened your surviving resolve. I have no reason to deny the will you have worked so hard to see through. You win. I will allow the Death Spiral to be undone."

"Really?" "Indeed. For thou hast proven himself. This battle wasn't to see if you could beat me. Life loses its edge if you can beat death. Being aware of an enclosing net of certain doom is what allows a soul to move forward and take on the challenges life throws your way. It ripens your life and gives you an appreciation for what you have and can do. Here you've proven that even in an unknown scenario, you still had the motivation to carry on and bring the hopes and dreams of your fallen comrades to light.

You couldn't beat me but you were going to persevere no matter what. Think about what you've just done! You just fought the god of Death and went at it fearlessly like a warrior till the end! I am proud of that and your allies are as well. Be aware that they all saw the whole thing. I made sure of that. They all saw you giving your all in remembrance of them. They couldn't be more proud of you! Neither could I. I may be Death, but I am also a friend who helps motivate you through your life and frees people from their suffering."

Death gives Jadeanu a warm hug. "Even with all the trials you've been through, you've held on with so much strength. You truly are a remarkable man." Death lets go of Jadeanu. "You were under the impression that me and Life were enemies. But in truth, me and him have always been best friends.

Now heal your wounds and come with me. We shall wait in Life's kingdom." "Wait for what?" "Life's return." "But can't we undo the Death Spiral on our own?" "Potentially, yes. But your abilities with the Blessings are limited. Death Convergence is a complex system; your chances of repairing the world properly are not guaranteed. So we will wait for Life's return."

Jadeanu heals his wounds and follows Death back to Life's throne room. As they enter the throne room, Life approaches the entrance of the room. Jadeanu rushes over to Life, who walks with all the other gods behind him. "Hello Lord Life." "Greetings Jadeanu." "You brought all the other gods." "Indeed. I informed you that I had important matters to attend to. Gathering all the gods was one of them. Death single-handedly created the Death Spiral by causing a disturbance in the order of our systems. To replenish those systems, we will need to bend them all. Hence all essentials."

Life proceeds past Jadeanu and goes up to the front step of his throne next to Death where they greet one another with pure friendliness. The next god approaches Jadeanu. "Lord Spirit." "Hi Jadeanu." Spirit follows behind Life. "Hey Lord Nature." "It's good to see you again, Jadeanu." Nature follows behind Spirit. Next comes Willpower, who looks much less buff than he did before yet is still muscularly defined.

"How's it going Lord Willpower?!" "Well with me and blessed with you Jadeanu. I am pleased with your work," Will responds without any accent in his voice. None of the gods have one anymore. He follows behind Nature. "Pleased to meet you again, Knowledge." "It is always good to see a well-traveled man. Hello Jadeanu." Knowledge follows behind Willpower.

The last god comes up. He is astonishingly beautiful and has light brown glistening skin. He wears a black one-piece with an interesting glow of white on it. His gorgeous straight black hair is the longest of the gods, going down to about his calf muscles in length. "It's a pleasure to acquaint with your spiritual form Universe." "Welcome Jadeanu. To our divinity."

Universe follows Knowledge up to the front of Life's throne.

All seven gods align in a specific pattern, with Life in the center. All of them talk at once. "We have come together to do away with the Death Convergence. Jadeanu, you and your allies have done well to compromise a truce within the era. You all shall have our blessings and favor. Jadeanu, you must hide behind the kingdom wall if you are to survive our power. Do not look at our truest form, for our might will overwhelm your spirit."

Jadeanu runs behind the kingdom entrance wall and closes his eyes to make sure he doesn't accidentally see anything. All the gods fly to a specific area in the sky, all in vertical alignment, then they unleash their power. A new giant being is formed. Even outside of the throne room, Jadeanu can feel the immeasurable power.

Rahricu from Earth witnesses the purple sky return to blue, and the black clouds become white and gray once again. He loses his powers along with everyone else. Everyone's eyes return to their native color. Rahricu looks under his sleeve and notices that even his Death Disease is no more. "He did it," Rahricu comments with glee.

The horrid smell of the dead disappears, but the bodies stay as a remnant of this event that shall live on in history. Some of the angels stay on Earth, but many leave, no longer having a reason to tend to the world. The sword on Jadeanu's back becomes heavier due to him no longer having super strength. The Ancients on Earth remain on Earth, and some angels continue to fight them.

Soon the gods separate back into their seven parts. Life's throne turns back blue and white. The world is rebalanced. The seven Blessings in Jadeanu's gauntlets all fly up and disappear into the atmosphere. "You may face us now," Life calls. Jadeanu runs back into the throne room to see all the seven gods standing side by side in front of Life's throne.

"Now you may return to Earth; you may keep your blade and gauntlets as souvenirs," Life permits as he creates a one-way portal back to Earth. "But I must say that the world you know has been crippled greatly," Life continues. "People are lost and will ravage the planet. They will need guidance from one or two of their own. Two who have proved their righteousness. Two who have helped save the world and want the best for it. You and Rahricu shall inherit the Earth and tend to it well. Lead your people how you've led your life. Lead them to understand the value of the world around them and faith for the world beyond."

"Thank you, Lord Life," Jadeanu appreciates as he walks through the portal. "Thank you all." Jadeanu rejoins Rahricu. "You're back! And it's all over!" Rahricu says with a smile on his face. Tears of joy stream down his cheeks. Jadeanu hugs Rahricu. "It sure is. And we get to make whatever we want out of this world. Let's make sure to make it beautiful again."

A sudden voice, the voice of Life, speaks through their ears despite him being nowhere in sight. "No king is complete without a queen. This world will need repopulation, and seed can't spread without a woman. Your final reward. I permit you to remarry Jadeanu."

Jadeanu and Rahricu look and see two women walking in their direction. "Is that..." Jadeanu starts. "Huana!" Rahricu runs to one of the women and she happily hugs him. "Hey Rahricu! It's good to see you again," Huana expresses. "She and I met each other after I was told to come here by an angel. Apparently she was too. We were promised a great reward. And it turns out we have a lot in common. We both like making things easier for others and reading."

The other woman looks at Jadeanu with her brown eyes, and her light brown cheeks turn red with a blush from apparent nervousness. Jadeanu does the same once he gazes at her astonishing beauty. "Hi I'm Jadeanu." "I'm June." "Uh, I think I'm supposed to marry you." "Hehehe. What?!" "Why don't you come with us and enjoy the rest of our day? We can get to know each other more." "Sounds good to me." "So do you have a plan as to where we should go?" Rahricu asks. "Yeah," Jadeanu answers.

"First, back to your hometown. There's a guy there named Spirit that I want to visit again. Plus if you ever want to visit what's left of your mom, just for reassurance of her passing." "That's kind of messed up," Rahricu mentions. "But I would like to see her again though." "Good! Then, we should continue to the place ruled by King Elcero. I don't know if you've heard of him through your mom, but I want you to meet him and this guy named Stellar."

The four of them all walk away in the bright yellow warm sun. Rahricu starts to imagine his inner mental castle, which was once filled with darkness. Now it is glowing with light, and the beautiful place is revealed to him. Jadeanu, June, and Huana are all in there with him. All of them have pleased smiles on their faces. *It feels so good to have people that are truly there for me. My heart is finally... warm. It's beautiful!'* Rahricu thinks.

Far away back in Texas. Ricardio sits next to his precious Annabelle, cuddling her in his bed as they engage in conversation. An angel opens the door to their bedroom without knocking. Ricardio and his wife look at the angel in fear. "Ricardio. You have sacrificed glory and turned your back on the world for a deceased woman's resurrection. This shameful waste of talent will not go unpunished," the angel explains.

"You need not worry now; I will not take your wife from you. But your punishment may happen to you or skip you for your good deeds but later curse your generation. An abandonment for an abandonment. All I have to show you are many possible outcomes that may have happened if you stayed with Jadeanu."

The angel shows a cloud of images in Ricardio's room. First, showing Ricardio a summary of what happened, then showing different scenarios of what could have happened. One image shows Luke surviving the encounter with Ravah. Another shows Ava killing King Elcero and taking over Elko. Another shows Ricardio dying but Ren surviving the combat with Rahricu. While one shows Rahricu killing them all but never having internal peace.

"Your decisions have weight to them Ricardio," the angel leaves with just that. Ricardio continues to hold onto Annabelle, who doesn't know what is wrong with his choice. Ricardio looks her in the eyes in conflict with himself, then he shrugs.

Now back to what happened between Ravah and Life. Life easily defeats Ravah and stalemates him. "For spreading knowledge of things only to cast evil in the world, you shall be punished," Life tells. "The abyss that was once yours will be your torment. For Jadeanu wills you mercy. That is the only reason I am not going to kill you. Instead, I will send you into the abyss and ensure you can no longer leave it. You will stay there until you can repent. All other angels who have helped you accomplish what you have, will join you as well eventually. And because you have disgraced yourself with the look of a monster, I shall bind it to your spirit, and it shall be your permanent design. You will become the very first demon."

Life does as he says and sends Ravah into the eternal darkness that is the abyss from which he can no longer escape. The hands of the abyss grab Ravah and pull him down into the dark realm as the portal closes, locking him inside. "You forsaken humans. I was fascinated with you, and I loved you, but I see the issue with that now. I'm well past it. I absolutely hate each and every one of you outside of Jadeanu and Rahricu. They are the only exceptions to you weak, disgusting, stupid human filth! None of you others are worth any good. I swear if I ever see a human again, I will torture their soul to oblivion! Each of you should be down here with me! I will curse all your souls with intense sin until you all join me down here! That is my will!" Ravah promises.

And thus ends the dawn of the Death Spiral.

-The End-